MW00425312

THE BEASTS OF SUCCESS

A Novel

Jasun Ether

This is a work of fiction. Names, characters, places, and incidents are products of the author's imagination or are used fictitiously and are not to be construed as real. Any resemblance to actual events, locales, organizations, or persons, living or dead, is entirely coincidental. However, the Dark Forces, the Alliance, Eckhart Tolle, David Wilcock, Corey Goode, Cobra, Ken Rohla, and Ben & Rob from the Edge of Wonder are all very real, and the latter eight should be honored for their work in raising the global consciousness.

First Edition: April 11, 2020

Library of Congress Cataloging-in-Publication Data

Names: Ether, Jasun, author
Title: The Beasts of Success
Identifiers: LCCN 2020905842
ISBN 978-1-7348334-0-9 (hardback)
ISBN 978-1-7348334-1-6 (paperback)
ISBN 978-1-7348334-2-3 (ebook)
Subjects: Dark Humor | Satire | Literary Fiction |
Contemporary Fiction | Humor |
Surrealism | Truth in Comedy

ET/DW/CG/JFK/Q/DJT 4 1 1

Prologue

They decided to bend the line of morality to obtain what was rightfully theirs. For it had become apparent that possessing a strong work ethic wasn't necessarily rewarding, and might not even be recognized. No matter how hardworking and persevering an employee was, advancement was often obtained by those that captured the spotlight through office politics, a charismatic personality, connections, or downright deception rather than job skills or merit. Nice guys really did finish last. Instead of being continually passed over, they thought it best to follow a different set of rules. Rules that created a game's outcome and didn't leave the player as a pawn blowing in the wind, at the whim of another player's actions. Like a player participating in a board game, they began to observe and study the game board from an overlooking vantage point with its entirety mapped before them instead of residing on the two-dimensional board where only a glimpse of the next move was available in front of the naked eye. They threw away the given rules of the board game and implemented their own rules that would ensure victory over those they deemed less deserving.

Life was nothing more than a board game, and only those that realized they were the overlooking players instead of the pieces on the board, truly succeeded in life and achieved what they desired. In understanding the nature and the bigger picture of the game from an omniscient viewpoint, a player could manifest his own destiny infinitely more effectively than any two-dimensional-thinking dimwit on the street who repeatedly walked straight into brick walls, thinking a different outcome would magically materialize through persistence alone. Why do you think certain people effortlessly rise to the top of the heap and acquire worldly fortune and power while most scrape their boots along the pavement day in and day out, sustaining a life of serfdom? What the downtrodden failed to grasp was: it's not persistence and fortitude but knowledge and awareness that paves the way to accomplishment. But it's not exclusively their fault for having such an outlook because society doesn't teach this doctrine, and the few that ascertain it lock it away in a vault, acknowledging it for the most precious commodity it is. Besides, if the masses were privy to such knowledge, it would be readily used and arduous for each individual to manifest their own specific demands upon the universe.

Having applied these newly discovered rules to the worksite, they flourished through the ranks in each of their respected fields. Their diligence finally gave way to advancement and left their colleagues scratching their heads in their wake as they sailed past them with ease, climbing the corporate ladder to the top.

In short, they decided to become the biggest fuckers in the room.

Chapter 1

It was at their biweekly lunch get-together at the Garden Oasis Caffè where Dale first pitched the idea to Jeremy and Tim. The idea that would irrevocably change their paths in life.

The Garden Oasis was a café with Italian-style coffee, cakes, pastries, and light meals. Once they had found out it wasn't a typical American coffee shop that served coffee drowned in milk, they became regulars. It also helped that the outdoor seating area was large and teeming with foliage—large pots on the ground that contained various plants spilling out onto the concrete, as well as trestles covered with ivy—which provided a kind of privacy that most coffee shops lacked. Some areas even held trestlelike canopies dense with plants and vines that acted as protection against the sun on hot days. There weren't an abundance of hot days in the Seattle area, so its presence was more for décor and aesthetics, as well as a shield from drizzling days, weather the city was notorious for.

Jeremy and Tim sipped coffee and slowly savored rich chocolate cake while waiting for Dale to arrive. It was presently a quarter past their usual meeting time at noon. Dale wasn't the type of person to call or message to convey tardiness, he'd just show up whenever he felt like it. Since they were comfortably situated in the outside seating area of the café where they could enjoy the nice spring day, they didn't mind waiting for Dale on this occasion. The chill of an early spring day was offset by a cloudless sky, which provided a warm and sun-washed setting. The rigid winter had not long ago given way to the season of rejuvenation, which birthed the possibility of new beginnings and new ideas.

They talked about trivial matters that had transpired over the last two weeks. The topic of Tim being passed over for a promotion dominated the conversation. It's hard for a person to focus on anything else when a certain situation has imbedded itself in their emotions and mind, nagging at the individual in a vicious circle, which is what Tim was currently experiencing.

Jeremy Blunt, Dale Dickerson, and Tim Lindeman had met during their college days at the University of Washington. Jeremy first befriended Tim in a sociology class during their freshman year. They encountered Dale later during their sophomore year in one of UW's dining halls when Dale had accidently dropped a piece of ham from his sandwich onto Tim's face. Jeremy and Tim would never forget that moment: Tim slowly peeling the ham slice that was covered in mayonnaise from his face and politely trying to return it to Dale, a stranger at the time. Dale refused the returned item, stating that Tim's face was too grimy for him to possibly reinsert the slice to his now ham-less sandwich, and also conveyed that he was miffed about the loss of mayonnaise, which left his sandwich quite spartan. Tim assured Dale that his face was clean. Dale adamantly disagreed and told him his face might as well have the whole sandwich at that point and dropped the rest of it on Tim's face while saying, "Enjoy your *pork parfait*. Oh yeah, there's plenty more where that came from!" Then he abruptly turned and headed toward a vending machine containing sandwiches. From his statement, Jeremy thought for sure that Dale was going to deposit coins in the machine and come back with more sandwiches to apply to Tim's already mayo-sopping face, but instead, Dale exited the dining hall by a door adjacent to the vending machine. Dale left them flabbergasted with their mouths ajar at what had just transpired, mayo still dripping from Tim's sodden face.

Later on that same day, they coincidently crossed paths again and Dale apologized, saying he had been in a horrible mood due to lack of sleep and getting a subpar grade on an important exam. He insisted on treating them to dinner and drinks to make up for the transgression that had occurred earlier that day. Being the generous and amicable person that Tim was, he didn't hold a grudge and apprehensively accepted the offer since it was delivered sincerely.

To this day, it's the only time that Jeremy and Tim could recall hearing Dale apologize for anything, and he'd done many unpleasant things since then. Jeremy and Tim would never know that Dale's dinner plans had fallen through and he just wanted to drink with someone and shoot the shit in order to take his mind off his exam score. The apology had been a ruse, and one he had delivered well, having applied the skills he learned from an introductory drama class.

They hit it off that night and quickly became friends. The amount of alcohol consumed lubricated their spirits, placated any leftover emotional tension, and assisted in building a bridge between two people—Tim and Dale—who were almost opposites in regard to character. But if Jeremy, whose disposition settled somewhere between the two, hadn't acted as a kind of middleman between two people of such difference, it would be highly doubtful they'd all still be friends to this day.

Jeremy and Tim had nearly finished their first cups of coffee when Dale arrived at the Garden Oasis Caffè. Gracing them with his presence, he settled down in a seat. "Good afternoon, gentlemen." He gazed at them with his hawkish eyes that viewed the world in a disdainful manner.

After quickly exchanging greetings Dale rose from his seat and strode into the café to make his order.

Tim reverted back to complaining about the promotion he hadn't received after adjusting his rimless glasses. "There is no logical reason why Judy should've gotten the promotion. I work harder than anyone else in that office, and my work is always superior to Judy's for sure."

Tim had graduated with a Bachelors in Software Engineering. After several months of job hunting he was fortunate enough to land a job at Massysoft, one of the largest software companies in the world. But instead of acquiring a software engineering position, he had only landed a computer programming position. Despite his academic achievements, he had failed to procure a software engineering position due to his lack of boldness and out-of-the-box thinking.

Tim continued complaining and gave numerous reasons as to why being passed over for the promotion was unfair, backing each reason up with logical arguments. Jeremy was only slightly interested from the onset and quickly became rather bored with the topic, but he figured it was a friend's duty to listen to a close friend's struggles and give advice, or to merely let them vent when there was no advice to be given.

Dale, on the other hand, didn't adhere to these guidelines. When he returned to the table he interrupted and diverted the conversation after two minutes of listening to Tim whine. "You can complain all day about your 'unjust treatment,' but it isn't going to solve anything. You're just going to end up more bitter at the end of the day, allowing Judy to have bested you twice."

"The point is about merit, not one-upmanship," Tim replied. "It's not like Judy was deliberately trying to get the better of me, nor was she being calculating and manipulative in order to secure the position. The point is—Judy or no Judy—I deserved that position. I *earned* that promotion through my dedication to the company."

Tim had stopped drinking his coffee and eating his cake and was now frowning at Dale. It was obvious that Tim was agitated because his display of opposition was out of character and differed from his normal cordial nature.

Noticing this, Dale attempted to smooth out the vibe at the table. Normally he would've reveled in conflict, but he was actually trying to bestow assistance, or at least was leading up to doing so through his typical pompous temperament. "Look, Tim," Dale said with the most amiable tone he could muster, "what I'm getting at is that you need to take command of your life or you're not going to go anywhere. I don't know all the details regarding the promotion you didn't receive, but—"

"That's because you weren't listening," Tim interrupted, still agitated.

Dale ignored Tim's outburst and continued, "As I was saying, I don't have all the facts, nor do I want to, but I do know that Judy took enough command of her life to achieve a goal that she set out for herself." Then after a pause, he added, "By the way, is this Judy hot?"

"This is obviously something I'm very displeased with, *Dale*, and I'm not going to satisfy your misplaced horniness with an answer to that immature question," Tim snapped and adjusted his lanky frame in his seat, getting angrier by the second instead of being soothed by Dale's words.

Dale couldn't help but laugh, and then explained himself. "It's not an irrelevant question. I'm saying maybe she got the promotion solely based on her looks, her hotness."

Tim noticeably calmed down. "Not particularly, but our manager is quite fond of her, so it's possible that he finds her attractive."

Dale threw up a hand in the air as a gesture that said: *There you go*. Then he said, "Therefore, Judy used what she had available in her arsenal to solidify her advancement while you were busting your butt, code after code, going about it the wrong way."

"Well, our manager isn't gay, so it's not like I could've enticed him in the same way to give me the position. Besides, my exceptional work should've trumped all physical considerations."

"Ahh, but it didn't, did it? 'Should've' is the key word here," Dale pointed out. "You need to do everything in your power to get what you want, use everything at your disposal. Other people—like your manager—have their own agendas and couldn't care less about what's right, honorable, moral, et cetera."

"Dale does make a valid point," Jeremy said, finally chiming into the conversation, relieved that the discussion was being directed away from Tim whining. He was beginning to think this particular biweekly meeting was going to be exclusively a Tim-whining session.

Tim was processing Dale's words and thinking of a fitting response. "So you're saying I should throw all my principles out the window and start working-over people left and right in order to get what I want, ignoring any possible repercussions, moral or otherwise? Or basically, become like you?" He gestured toward Dale, trusting that his ethicalness would outplay Dale's unscrupulous statement. But who was he kidding, Dale was essentially the embodiment of a shameless man who was incapable of feeling remorse. Tim only spent time with Dale when Jeremy was also present. You could say they were friends of a friend, but being that they assembled every other week, it suggested they were actually friends.

"Listen ..." Dale said, adjusting in his seat, insinuating that he was about to give a long speech. "You believe that your labor was better than your colleagues, so you deserved the promotion. Am I right?"

"Yes," Tim quickly replied. "I definitely deserved it."

"Then would you say that it would be unethical to perform some extracurricular activities in order to obtain what is rightfully yours?" Dale asked, slowly working up to justifying his stance on the matter and enlightening his straitlaced friend.

"It depends on what you mean by extracurricular activities. I'm not going to hire a hit man to whack Judy."

Dale displayed a facial gesture that inferred Tim's suggestion wasn't a bad idea, and appeared to be mentally writing it down—a yellow Post-it note placed on the wall in his brain for possible future actions—but instead he said, "Come on, I'm not talking about murder." He rolled his eyes theatrically. "I'm talking about investing some time in well-placed methodical actions—that are justified—to ensure that other people's agendas don't rob you of your legitimate claims for progression. Working hard isn't enough by itself to move your career forward. Other people will steal your chances of success time and time again because they'll invest time where it counts to get what they want. It's the ones that do what's necessary to succeed that prosper."

Dale paused to take a sip of his coffee, and then continued. "You already have the first step down, Tim: producing great work at your job. This means you may not have to perform that many actions outside the normal scope of your daily duties to make progress."

"Quit being so cryptic and ambiguous with your explanation," Tim said, showing signs of impatience. "What are these *actions* that you speak of?"

Dale knew that if he came directly out with examples of mischievous actions, goody-two-shoes Tim would immediately shut down and reject anything further he had to say. He needed to spend more time validating the necessary actions that Tim wanted examples of, and somehow convince, or even trick Tim into thinking that such misdeeds were prudent and not immoral. Dale thought this way because he believed the end justified the means.

Knowing Tim was a sucker for logical deduction and facts, he would pursue that avenue to entice Tim to step into the realm of blurred ethical lines where right and wrong weren't as apparent and defined, or didn't even matter. Dale also knew that if he could convince Tim before he alighted at the subway's terminus of his argument, Jeremy would assimilate to his ideology somewhere along the journey without any direct effort on his part. Because Jeremy lived in a world where philosophical ideas were paramount and the big picture always trumped the dabbling details, he tended to be less rigid about social ideas of right and wrong. He knew that Jeremy had a moral compass akin to Tim's, but he wasn't as law-abiding and virtuous when the big picture permitted him to skirt manmade, illusory lines drawn in the sand.

Dale wondered why he was wasting time trying to convince them, because using the tools of success for himself was all that mattered. He guessed he was doing it, and enjoying it, because it was an interesting project, and maybe he was more philanthropic than he realized by departing such knowledge. One thing was for sure, it was exceedingly more interesting than listening to Tim moan all afternoon.

"Let me first convey the nature of the situation," Dale ventured. "There are some very important concepts that need to be addressed before getting to specific examples of actions one can take. Besides, the examples are pointless without the reasons to back up why they're done."

A frown appeared on Tim's face, clearly expressing his impatience and irritability due to Dale not getting to what he thought was the point of the conversation. But with a renewed wave of tolerance, he decided to sit back in his chair, relax, and see where Dale was going with this. "Fine. You have the floor," Tim resigned. "Do your worst."

"Oh, I intend to," Dale quipped with a shit-eating grin plastered on his face. "So you invest heaps of time and money in your education to acquire the skills and a degree needed to comfortably place yourself in a career that will not only financially sustain yourself and pay off your college debt, but also provide for your family—in Tim's case, being that he's the only one with a family out of the three of us."

Dale took another sip of coffee and bit into his croissant while Tim and Jeremy anxiously waited for him to get back to his dialog. "It used to solely be a man's job to bring home the bacon, but in today's day and age where the sexes are equal, a woman is just as likely to bring her share of the bacon home for her family, or herself. Take your wife for example, Tim. She's undoubtedly the breadwinner in your family."

A noticeable nerve struck Tim's constitution, and then a perceptible wash of shame poured over his face, but he stayed quiet to see where Dale was taking the point.

Dale continued, "As an attorney, your wife represents some pretty shady companies and individuals, which is the function of a lawyer. Does she sit around whimpering about ideologies and moralities? No. She's employed by clients and does what's necessary to win each case to provide for her family: you and her son, Ricky—"

"His name is Raymond," Tim interrupted.

"Ricky, Raymond, Rudolph, Rapist, whatever—doesn't matter; not the point. Don't interrupt me." Dale paused to glare at Tim, nonverbally threatening him into a state of passivity before continuing with his speech. "Why should any other vocation be different than a lawyer's? Everyone should use their full capacity to win that case, to get that promotion, to advance in life and luxuriate in attained wealth, possessions, vacations ..."

Then Dale shifted gears to prey on Tim's shame. "Even though females are now equals in the workforce, don't you want to make your family proud by adding your equal contribution to the family coffer?"

"Yes, of course I do, but so far it isn't in my power to do so," Tim pleaded. "I *can't* promote myself."

"That's where you're wrong," Dale said, pointing an index finger upward to add emphasis to the point he was about to make. "You *are* the only person that can promote yourself. It's not your fault the person who's in charge of deciding which employee receives the promotion doesn't possess the facts to make a fair choice. Or worse yet, this hypothetical person knows you're the best candidate but appoints someone else due to their preference or their agenda."

To finish off his point Dale switched back to the lawyer analogy, which seemed to be working quite nicely, he deduced from having observed Tim's demeanor. "Like a lawyer winning a case, you need to apply all your abilities and skills in order to seize a promotion by taking action outside of your typical assigned tasks. These actions taken are similar to telling a white lie: it's harmless and the results are almost assured to fall in your favor, providing you're a good liar."

Jeremy jumped into the conversation. "It's apparent that the Great Recession of 2008 America—and the rest of the world—had to deal with isn't going to be completely alleviated in a particular amount of years. Don't believe for a second the fabricated data they keep pitching that declares we've taken a turn for the better and are now thriving. Companies may be thriving again, but individuals are definitely not. This is the new norm. It's what the worldly system has morphed into, for better or for worse."

They both sat their staring at Jeremy, blinking, wondering whether he'd just decided to change the subject of the conversation with no warning or if his statement was somehow relevant to the topic.

Tim raised his palms in confusion. "I'm not sure I agree with that statement, but anyway, this is relevant because …"

"It's relevant because this change creates fewer job positions, less frequent promotions, and so people have adapted to being more vicious in order to advance, or even to keep their current positions," Jeremy explained. "The old phrase it's a dog-eat-dog world has never been more appropriate than it is today. People are scared they won't be able to provide for their families, or even themselves, which provokes them to do unscrupulous deeds they normally wouldn't have stooped to if the world actually had returned to economic growth, or even stability, for the individual, not just for companies."

"But the data does show that we've turned the corner and are now fiscally stable," Tim debated, trying to win at least one argument for the day.

Dale quickly disputed Tim's flimsy rebuttal. "Look around," he said while whirling the last bite of his croissant in his hand, "people are working more hours than they ever have before and earning less money than ever. The two are related of course. There's a record number of people in debt or floating by paycheck to paycheck, saving nothing for the future, or even for that next minor monetary setback: vehicle repairs, dental treatment, hospital bills … Do you call that turning the corner?"

Feeling defeated, Tim sulked and slumped back in his chair, depleted of any opposing arguments. Then he decided to take the high ground to make them feel guilty. "No matter the situation," Tim said with a righteous expression on his face, "one should never lower themselves to unethical behavior in order to succeed in any endeavor." He thought this statement would end the discussion, allowing him to return the conversation to the promotion that was stolen from him, which was still weighing heavily on his mind.

Dale eyeballed Tim. "Haven't you been listening to anything I've been saying? The lawyer analogy that I so eloquently presented in front of your dumbass?" Dale spouted, expressing irritation for having to repeat himself. He was known for having a short fuse and often gave people derogatory handles.

Then Dale recomposed himself, if only for the sake of being able to better persuade Tim to participate in nefarious deeds that Dale felt were justified being that society at large had been bastardized, and fighting fire with fire was the only method for victory. So Dale continued, but this time with a reserved demeanor. "It's only unethical if you use a scheme to acquire a promotion that you didn't deserve. Okay?" He continued before Tim could answer, leaving Tim's mouth ajar in pre-rebuttal. "If you truly deserve a promotion and get passed over for it, someone has acted unethically toward you. And let me tell you, most people won't think twice about doing it. Also, I'm not saying you should stop working hard at your job, but rather, I'm saying you need to apply some effective tactics alongside your strong work ethic in order to be fruitful in the grand scheme of things. For example, gossip, whether it's true or not, could be spread throughout the workplace about a certain colleague that could jeopardize your chances of grasping that coming promotion—mind you, and this is important—a colleague who doesn't *deserve* to get that promotion. Therefore, the gossip that would normally appear villainous would in fact be justified."

Perceiving that he was getting through to Tim on some level, Dale quickly continued, as to not lose pace. Like a boxer witnessing his opponent stumbling around the ring after receiving a damaging punch and rushing to deliver that one tactical, powerful blow to end it all. "In other words, if you let the terminology of ethics repeatedly hinder your actions for survival," he paused shortly and then slowly enunciated four words with emphasis, "*you will go extinct.*" Then he followed it up in a mockingly high-pitched tone while waving his hand, "Bye-bye little Timothy, *bye-bye.*" Then he returned to his normal tone, "It's basic Darwinian shit."

Realizing he was having a little too much fun at Tim's expense and that ridiculing him was counterproductive toward his efforts, Dale articulated in a serious and concerning tone, "No, but seriously. All your hard work will have been for nothing if it's not recognized and rewarded, and I'm sure your work ethic is exceptional, Tim. I don't doubt for a second that you deserved that promotion you speak of. I'm just trying to dispense some wisdom in order to see you succeed at your job."

If anyone else had uttered these words, they would've fallen flat on the floor, stinking of flattery. Dale knew this, but since it was absolutely out of character for him, he presumed Tim might bite.

Tim didn't fully take the bait, but Dale's nice words, which rarely flowed out of his mouth, had at least erased the ridiculing remarks he had just made. It also appeased to Tim's nature of wanting to be accepted and admired. "Hypothetically speaking," Tim said, "let's say that I do apply a tactic and it backfires, getting me fired."

Dale was pleased that Tim was even hypothetically considering playing his game. "That's precisely why you would methodically plan out your strategy and only use it if you were certain it couldn't backfire. If you've put enough thought and intelligence into the scheme—and it goes without saying that we're all highly intelligent people at this table—it should be successful, or at least have no reverse results. Instead of worrying about unforeseeable circumstances, you would confidently construct a scheme down to the minutest detail for your particular work environment and situation," Dale reassured Tim.

Still not being sold, Tim sighed, "I just don't know if I have it in me … and I'm still not certain that it would even produce effective results."

"Well, I put it to the test already," Dale confided with a mischievous sparkle in his eyes, "and it's working for me."

Dale sported a shit-eating grin as Jeremy and Tim stared wide-eyed across the table at him. They were completely intrigued with what he was going to say next, what scheme he had already employed, and what it had done for him.

"You dirty rat," Jeremy laughed. "You were holding out on us this whole time. You've already done the deed. Well, knowing you, I shouldn't be surprised."

"*Hey*, I'm offended by that comment," Dale joked, still sporting his grin, not being the least bit offended. Actually, he was gratified by the remark because it implied that he was a man who knew how to get things done. A man of action, a go-getter. Not someone like Tim, who couldn't get his ass off the toilet to save his life, sitting around all day creating excrement instead of progress.

Dale slowly reached into his inside suit pocket and produced a piece of paper. All the while never taking his eyes off Jeremy and Tim, glancing back and forth at each of them while smiling broadly like a Cheshire cat. He unfolded the piece of paper and held it in his hands, but instead of explaining anything further, he kept staring at them, not looking down at the paper. He wanted to soak in their impatient anxiousness.

"Quit stalling!" shouted Jeremy. He could see that Dale was going to milk the suspense for all it was worth before revealing what the paper was or contained. "I'm going to go inside and get another cappuccino instead of staring at your silent, grinning face." Jeremy feigned getting out of his seat by putting both hands on the armrests of his chair and lifting up slightly.

"Okay, okay," blurted Dale. "Sit down. Let me explain the powerful piece of paper that I'm holding in front of your stupefied faces. This isn't the piece of paper that got the job done. This is just a copy I made so I could share it with you gents."

"But what is it?" Jeremy demanded. "Get on with it. I'm going to hurl the remnants of my chocolate cake onto your nicely pressed suit if you don't spill the beans."

Dale was a stockbroker at Stryker & Marshall, one of the biggest brokerage firms in America. He always wore a suit when he went out in public, even when he wasn't working, because there was always that odd chance he might cross paths with a client, or a possible future client. But regardless of clients, it assisted in reinforcing his pompous mentality that he was superior to others. He flaunted his suits and wore them like they were a piece of himself, an outer shell that created a buffer zone between his vainglorious identity and the peasants that made up most of the population. So naturally he flinched when he heard Jeremy threatening the cleanliness of his suit, his image.

"It's a love letter," Dale revealed, which immediately caused Jeremy and Tim to bust up laughing, Jeremy almost falling on the ground. Dale was the furthest thing from a romantic. He was perpetually single—not by choice—and his dating endeavors, when they occasionally occurred, were fleeting.

"Settle down, you clowns," barked Dale. Not appreciating being the brunt of a joke, he decided to make haste at explaining the letter, but would first cut them down to size. "Have some decency. I'm in a suit for god's sake! Tim, you're sporting clothing items one would find in a J.C. Penney's catalog, and Jeremy … well, you're not wearing a suit." Before they could counter on the irrelevance of articles of clothing they were wearing, Dale jumped into explaining the letter. "Masquerading as a colleague of mine, I wrote this affectionate letter to the wife of one of my colleagues' clients."

Jeremy chuckled. "Leave it to you to use romance as a weapon instead of an act of endearment. That's rich. How did you think of the idea?"

"The idea was preordained to reach me in order to rectify the Edward situation. Edward is the colleague I'm speaking about. He's a dipshit who blindly stumbled into his position through connections. About seven months ago there was a lot of chatter at the firm that I'd be the one moving up to handle medium- to large-sized investors, but Edward received the position purely based on the fact that he's the brother-in-law of a senior executive vice president at Stryker & Marshall. He didn't get the job by means of a proficient or savvy skillset. The man's as dense as a fuckin' flapjack!"

"But how did you deliver the letter to the client's wife?" Tim asked, trying to comprehend how Dale had pulled off this deceptive plan. "And if you sent it via normal postal service, how did you make sure the husband got to it first and was enticed and bold enough to open his wife's mail?"

Dale smiled. "That's a good question, Tim. Let me tell you how I made sure it went down successfully without a hitch. Let it be your introductory lesson in your new class of Scheming 101. I tailed the client out of the building and followed him home so I'd know where to deliver the letter personally."

"Couldn't you just have found out the client's address by snooping in your coworker's office, or something easier?" Jeremy interrupted with his curiosity.

"I thought of that. There was a chance I could've been caught by Edward, or someone else on the floor might've noticed and reported it promptly or after the scheme had finished working its magic. Following Edward's client home was definitely more time consuming, but it was without a doubt the safest way to go about it. Remember what I said earlier? Plan the scheme so there's no possible way of it backfiring on you. Following him home also ended up giving me the frosting on the cake toward making the love letter really sizzle, as I found out that his wife is a big Jane Austen fan."

"What? Did you talk to her?" Jeremy asked, twisting his facial expression, thinking how unintelligent that move would've been.

"Of course not!" Dale rebuked. "That would've been moronic. While concealed within my car, I used my high-grade binoculars to look through a large window. I noticed a hardcover collection of Jane Austen novels: *Pride and Prejudice*, *Sense and Sensibility*, *Mansfield Park*, the lot. This was the spice for the letter that I was lacking. I'd sprinkle in some of that feminine Austen romanticism for her to get wet over. Well, she most likely wouldn't get a chance to read it, so more for her husband to steam with hatred over when he opened her mail. Then, on an early Saturday visit—my second visit to spy upon their house to see if I could glean anything else useful—I noticed the client returning to his house after a morning jog. He collected the mail and scanned the letters in the front yard before he strolled into the house. You know how religious these suburbanites are with their jogging routines. I figured he must have done this exact same routine every Saturday morning. I'd be able to stealthily place the letter in their mailbox before he returned from his jog."

"I see, but how did you know that he would open his wife's mail upon seeing a letter addressed to her?" Tim asked for the second time.

"I did two things to ensure that he'd open it: I used a red pen to write her name on the envelope with big, looping, old-fashioned cursive, and I didn't seal the envelope. I folded it inside instead."

"Nice," Jeremy said with reverence for Dale. "That way he'd know he wouldn't be caught for opening her mail. A quick peek inside and no one would be the wiser if the letter didn't show she was having an affair."

"Read us the copy of the letter," Jeremy pleaded, giddy as a school girl. "Are you going to frame it and hang it on your wall at home or something?"

"No, I'll dispose of it properly. Can't leave any trace of evidence that could lead back to me. I only made a copy so I could share it with you fine lads on this most auspicious day. Here it goes," Dale cleared his throat for dramatic effect and read the letter with his best British accent:

Dear Caroline,

I hope this letter finds you, and finds you well. I revel in the attraction that has lifted us to a higher tone of beauty. Before our courtship transpired, I thought of myself as a man who had nothing to give the world but labour and indifference. But now I stand on the eternal precipice of longing for your desires and quick witted nature. Recalling our first night of ecstasy, after my long walk home, I required a long application of solitude and reflection to realize the nature of our engagement and how it had eloquently pointed out the loss of spice and flavour in my life.

I dream of whisking you secretly away from your needle-nosed husband of great girth who lathers all his affections towards the pursuit of acquiring endless money and pampering his dreadful basset hound. I long for the next encounter of bestowing my attention upon your perfumed, supple bosoms. That of which I attest I will never tire. I will endeavour to subdue my commonplace business affairs and toils for the happiness you deserve. The want of graciousness and warmth will lead me repeatedly towards our hidden cottage in which providence has placed us. There by the warmth of the fire burning in the hearth, we will remain in high spirits and good humour.

May your foolish husband, with his ridiculous moustache, wither away from our favourable idea of procuring everlasting happiness. For he is a tremendous twat that I shall honourably chew up and spit upon the dirty streets for you, my love. Then, for good measure, we'll prance in delight upon his remains until his basset hound swallows every last bit of his bits.

Affectionately yours,
Edward

"Whoa, somebody put in some hours at the library sifting through Jane Austen novels," Jeremy said with a chuckle. "But that last part isn't very Austeny, is it?"

"I broke from style to hit it home. I had to make the husband as furious as possible to ensure he'd hold back nothing when it came time to not only dropping his broker, but also disseminating the offense to his friends, many of whom are also medium- to large-sized investors with Stryker & Marshall. This would ensure those investors to shift over to working through me, the broker they should've been working with in the first place."

"How can you be so positive?" Tim interjected. "What if those investors decided to leave Stryker & Marshall for a different brokerage firm all together?"

"Because the offense was a private matter, and these investors have been profiting from our firm's direction for decades. When it comes to finances, you don't switch horses due to a private matter. You simply rectify the private matter by canning the jockey and staying with the same horse, provided that horse keeps winning of course."

They all took a sip from their coffee mugs.

Dale placed his mug down and continued his story. "On the day I placed the envelope containing the letter in their mailbox, I left a little gift for the client to ensure he'd be aggravated even before reading the letter. By means of observation, I knew the client's weekly jogging route around his neighborhood. So I placed a rather large pile of feces directly around a blind corner the client races around. I was expecting him to merely step in it, but when I saw him returning to his house early, it was apparent it had worked out better than I anticipated. From my parked car's vantage point, I saw him approaching his house with a good portion of his pants and shirt covered in excrement, feces trailing off his running shoes on every stride."

Jeremy interrupted in order to gain more information. "That sounds like a considerable amount of excrement.

Did you spend a whole day driving around collecting dog poo or something?"

"Collecting dog droppings was my initial idea, but then I quickly realized that task would be far too arduous and time consuming. So instead, I shat in a large garbage bag for two weeks."

In unison, Jeremy and Tim recoiled with grimaces.

"I know, tell me about it. It was disgusting. I had to keep that garbage bag in my house for two weeks. But I didn't know how much of it would stick to the inside of the bag and not come out onto the street when I dumped it, so I wanted to make sure the amount was adequate."

Tim shook his head. "No, I'm reacting to the thought of that poor jogger rolling around in your fecal matter. Then having to sport it all the way home until being able to clean it off."

With wide eyes, Jeremy said, "He must've been pretty well caked with excrement after falling into two weeks' worth."

Dale shrugged his shoulders like the matter was insignificant. "Yeah, well, you do what you gotta do. And yes, he most certainly was well-caked and angrily stewing in my dumpings when he arrived back at his house and reached into his mailbox to go through his mail."

Jeremy was surprised. "The guy didn't bother to clean himself before going through his mail?"

Dale sported an oh-well expression. "Urbanites, they stick to their routines, even when well-caked in excrement apparently. I was surprised too. I thought I'd have to wait in my car till he got all cleaned up and came out to collect his mail, but luckily his hands being free of excrement was good enough for him. So while seething, he reaches into his mailbox, collects his mail, and sifts through it until he reaches The Letter. From behind my binoculars, I could see by the curious look on his face that he had momentarily forgotten about the feces dripping from his jogging attire. He stared at my beautifully written cursive for a whole five seconds before turning the envelope over to notice it wasn't sealed. He slid the letter out of the envelope and began reading. His face started to contort, incrementally building with hatred the further along he got down the letter. When he finished the letter it looked like he was about to explode. Even though my car was parked at a safe distance, I found myself slouching down in my seat, not wanting to be caught at the end of his vile gaze if he happened to look around the neighborhood. Then he widened the envelope and shook it upside down. I imagine he was wondering if something like glitter in the form of hearts would come falling out." Dale laughed. "After nothing fell, he threw the rest of the mail on the ground and stormed into the house with The Letter in hand. Worrying about dragging my shit around his house appeared to not be an issue in his mind after reading The Letter. I got a good chuckle when I noticed the first thing he did after entering the house: he marched over to his wife's Jane Austen novels, scooped a handful of my dung off his person, and amply slathered it across the tops of those leather-bound novels. Imagine it, he was so enraged that the repulsiveness of handling my excrement was outweighed by his hatred over The Letter. I'd say I did my job well in constructing that letter. As I slowly drove past his house with my window rolled down and a smile on my face, I heard shouts emanating from his house. Enraged yelling billowed from their loving home as I drove by on that delightful Saturday morning."

Tim shook his head and muttered under his breath, "You're one sick individual."

"So how did it go down? Did Edward get fired or what?" Jeremy asked, not knowing exactly how long ago it was that Dale had orchestrated this scheme he was now telling them.

"After a period of time passed, it all fell into place as I assumed it would. There was no possible way the firm could retain Edward as a broker due to the heat the client and the client's friends directed at Stryker & Marshall's CEO. Naturally, he got fired and those clients are now working with me."

"Wait!" Tim shouted. "All of this has already transpired? I'm a bit confused about the timetable of events. You didn't say anything about this scheme two weeks ago at our last luncheon."

"First, this isn't a luncheon since we're just friends getting together for a casual meal. A luncheon is a formal meal as part of a business meeting or entertaining a guest. It's what I have with clients, not with you," Dale corrected Tim, looking him up and down, insinuating that he'd never have a luncheon with someone who wasn't wearing a suit, or at least some type of attire that conveyed professionalism and respect. "Secondly, this all transpired a while ago. I didn't want to speak about it till it was all done and had gone my way."

"In other words, till you could gloat about it," Jeremy said with a smile, in half admiration. "So you brought a copy of that letter to our lunch to unveil it in a premeditated fashion when the timing was right: sometime after your planned spiel about creating your own success by pulling off schemes at the office."

Dale gave Jeremy a slight nod of his head with squinted eyes to subtlety confirm Jeremy's assumption, but not to fully admit it, which he believed would belittle his actions. Then he slipped a hand into a pocket of his suit pants and produced a lighter. Holding up the copy of the letter, he lit a corner on fire, and then fully extended his arm to avoid tarnishing his suit with fire or smoke. When the paper was three-fourths burned he released it, letting it fall to the ground, eyeing it to make sure every last bit of it burned to eradicate any evidence of his crime.

An old lady dining with her husband at a nearby table scowled at Dale. "Excuse me, *sir*," she snapped. "This is a public place of dining, not your backyard. You can't just burn things here."

Her husband followed in agreement, protecting his role as the male in the relationship. "Yes, have some respect."

Dale flashed a scornful glare at the old-timer. "Look here, pops. I get the job done outside the office as well as inside the office," Dale cautioned the old man, making sure his fist was above the table and visible. "Now snap your trap or I'll make your face the main ingredient in that soup of yours."

In defeat, the old man lowered his gaze down at his soup and muttered something unintelligible while his wife shook her head and grumbled, "Today's youth … no respect."

Tim was slightly ashamed for sitting at the same table with Dale and tried to present the appearance to the surrounding café patrons looking their way that he wasn't endorsing Dale's actions and words, only condoning them. Luckily the surrounding patrons quickly dismissed the commotion and went back to their conversations.

Unfazed, Dale returned to administering the final touches to his argument. "The point is … who knows how long it would've taken me to reach my current level at Stryker & Marshall if I had remained passive, letting other undeserving colleagues scrape their way past me."

"A man of action is a man who gets things done," Jeremy said. "Considering Edward unjustly moved into your position, your actions seem arguably justified to me. On the surface your actions would appear malicious, but after possessing all the details about the matter, your actions are debatably warranted. Well, maybe not the bit about the pile of shit." Jeremy slid his chair back and stood up. "Okay, I'm going to order another cappuccino now. When I return, I think we should enlighten Tim on the concept of justification and socially programmed ethics."

As Jeremy was walking away, Tim said, "Hypothetically, I could relate to Dale's actions, but yeah, I'm having trouble with the ethics of the matter."

It was clear to Dale that much headway had been accomplished in making them see things his way. Tim needed more work, but if he didn't come around during this lunch, Dale wasn't going to waste any more time trying to convince him. Tim could rot in his current work situation for all he cared. But the lunch wasn't over yet, and he was in a good mood, so he took advantage of the progress he'd made and proceeded to gently reiterate the weighty and influential points, as well as draw on new factors and elements those points brought up along the way.

When Jeremy returned, he joined Dale in tenderly coaxing Tim through his undeviating stance on ethics that had shaped his reasoning, a classic case of nurture's contribution. Their conversation went on for another two hours, delving into all correlating concepts, philosophies, viewpoints, and arguments, causing their lunch gathering to stretch longer than usual.

Chapter 2

Throughout the next two weeks Tim couldn't stop thinking about the conversation at the Garden Oasis Caffè. His lingering anger for having been passed over for the promotion was the main reason he kept replaying the café conversation in his mind. He wanted to adapt an outlook akin to Jeremy's and Dale's—well, maybe not Dale's, he's an asshole—but he couldn't get past the wall of ethics he had built in his mind throughout his upbringing. Normally he wouldn't even bother questioning his ideology, but if in fact there were exceptions to the rules of ethics—irregularities he had never uncovered because the road of life never took him down that path before—then maybe he could skirt some undefined rules and bypass the wall that kept him from progressing in his career. He was currently twenty-five years old and didn't want to be languishing in the same circumstances five years down the road.

It was times like these where he appreciated the distraction a family outing afforded. His family dined at the Lucky Joy Chinese Restaurant once a month for dinner. At a square table, his wife, Amber, sat across from him. His step-son, Raymond, sat to the left of him.

Amber had already downed a glass of cabernet sauvignon and was working on her second. She was prone to babbling endlessly after consuming enough alcohol, and she had reached that state. She was rattling on about her current case like she was reading the stenographer's transcript for the day's testimonies. The client she was representing seemed to be part of the Italian Mafia—or what was left of it in America—that had made their way into the brave new world of the West Coast.

"… so before the proceedings, Frank turns to me and says, 'Who should I whack in this courtroom to make me innocent? I'll whack that fuckin' judge if that's what it takes. Just advise me and I'll rub-out whoever. A little rubbin' goes a long way, or, apply a little righteous rubbin' and a person becomes rubbish is what my British friend used to say,' " Amber said before snickering over her glass of wine.

Tim slowly ate while listening to his wife. Amber was six years his senior. She wasn't strikingly beautiful, but her face was still easy on the eyes, and her long blond hair and slender athletic body—obtained from a dedicated workout routine—definitely were attractive to the average person. Exercising, she would say, was her way of transmuting the chaotic energy she brought home from the courtroom, but Tim figured she was the one creating most of the chaotic energy in the courtroom, since she reveled in the art of debate.

Tim and Amber were a bit of an odd match if you solely took into account the duties of her job and the feelings she expressed when explaining her cases. But once her job was put aside, her outlook on life wasn't too much different from Tim's, at least that was Tim's assumption. When she was on the job she was a whole different person, virtue went out the window. She believed that her attorney license granted her immunity from morality. She was just doing her job, and she did it very well.

Raymond wasn't listening to his mother. He was in a world of his own, face buried in his phone, completely immersed in one of his videogames. Raymond was a short and fat fifteen-year-old kid with emotionless eyes on a big, round head. A party and too much beer was the reason he existed. Amber birthed him when she was sixteen, never knowing for sure who the father was, and never caring. Raymond spent more time being raised by his grandmother than by Amber. She wasn't going to let one drunken slip-up detour her from her dreams of becoming a renowned lawyer, so she applied her full attention on her studies and the bar exam, shoving Raymond into the recesses of her mind. She never pondered the consequences of her son receiving a lack of attention and love from his mom.

Tim had tried to be a father figure to Raymond from the beginning of his relationship with Amber, but he stopped trying when he received zero feedback from Raymond throughout the course of dating Amber. At the wedding, two years ago, Tim acknowledged that Raymond was simply baggage—heavy, round baggage—that came along with his lovely wife.

After pausing from her ramble to take another gulp of wine, Amber looked over at Raymond. "Pay attention to your mother's story. You might learn something in life other than what type of gun is the most effective at blowing someone's head off in your videogames." She playfully slapped the back of his head, whacking him harder than she had intended due to her intoxication, causing him to head-butt his phone, knocking it out of his hands and into his plate of chow mein and sweet and sour chicken.

Raymond didn't blink an eye. He just picked up the phone and continued playing as if nothing happened, even ignoring the bit of sauce that was now on his phone.

"It's like we don't exist," Amber told Tim. "He might as well sew that damn phone to his face." Then she abruptly returned to blathering on about her current case, continuing to disregard confidentiality, which she only did with her husband. "Anyway, while on the stand, Frank got so delighted about recalling eating a muffuletta sandwich in New Orleans that he almost casually recounted rubbing-out a snitch while he was partaking of the sandwich at the same time. This is what Frank said," she mimicked his thick Italian-American Brooklyn accent, " 'I was doin' two of my favorite things: eating a muffuletta and rubbin' out a sni—I mean, uh … rubbin' the delicious olive salad from my lips. Central Grocery & Deli—the *best.* Big Tony would go there all the time. It's what made Big Tony big.' " Amber got a kick out of her impersonation and held back a laugh.

Amber swirled her wine a bit, took another sip, and returned to talking about the case. An abundance of wine was her only unhealthy dietary practice. Tim wasn't too fond of listening to his wife talk about her cases, but he abided, knowing that she enjoyed it immensely while drinking.

While paying attention to his wife's story, Tim glanced over at Raymond. He was still lifelessly mashing buttons on his phone, impervious to the outside world. Tim was growing more concerned about Raymond every day. His concern started a year ago when Raymond was involved in an unsettling event: the death of a classmate. It had been regarded as an accident, but lately Tim couldn't help entertaining the idea that malice might have been involved, given Raymond's deteriorating attitude. He was never an affable boy, but he had become more distant, emotionless, and violent at school after the event had taken place.

Raymond had been biking through a park on his way to the grocery store, a regular Sunday routine of his. He encountered a classmate, Howard, at the park. Howard had been known to bully Raymond. Something transpired on that tree-hidden path in the park that remains uncertain to this day. If it weren't for a jogger crossing their path, it's possible that no one would've ever known that Raymond was even at the scene when the incident occurred. The jogger came upon them after the tragedy occurred and witnessed Raymond preparing to take off on his bike while Howard lay facedown on the ground with a metal spike through his head.

When the cops arrived at the scene and questioned Raymond, he told them, "I don't know … he like fell on it, or something. I was just riding my bike to the grocery store when I passed him on the trail. He was walking on the path while I was biking by. He saw me and said hello and then he fell face-first on a spike. I was like, 'Dude, does that hurt?' but he didn't reply or move." When the cops asked him why he was trying to flee the scene, he said, "I was going to get help on my bike. Maybe doctors could, like, unspike his head or something, like, I don't know."

Even though it was a highly irregular incident to have happened naturally, there was no hard evidence to suggest foul play, but that didn't stop Howard's parents from threatening to take it to court. So Amber had a private meeting with them. Either she intimidated them or their own lawyer convinced them there wasn't enough evidence, because they didn't follow through and never took it to court. The cops' ruling as an accident had stood.

At the time, Tim never suspected Raymond could've murdered someone, but recently he feared it wasn't entirely implausible. Raymond's growing lack of empathy and violent behavior at school were compounding in the last year since the event, which gradually made Tim feel like foul play wasn't out of the question. Now, he could imagine Raymond putting a spike through a boy's head and nonchalantly going back to blowing off people's heads in the violent videogames he played all day. Games with titles like: *Killing Spree*, *Headshot Hero*, *Kill Parade*, *Random Killings: The Ultimate Hobby*, *Just another Killing on a Friday Night*. "Kill" was a reoccurring word in the titles of his games. Had Raymond fallen prey to videogame desensitization? Tim had enough to worry about at work without having to entertain the idea that his step-son was a possible psychopath in the making and might one day drag his oversized head into Tim's bedroom at midnight and slaughter him while he slept.

"You're listening to me, right, Tim?" Amber paused from her courtroom stories to question her husband.

"Yes, of course, dear." Tim smiled and nodded his head.

"… so he says," Amber continued in the same Brooklyn accent, "'I'm not surprised Big Tony ended up in that well, but I'm surprised his big body made it down to the water below without getting stuck and lodged in the walls of the well. They don't call him Big Tony for nothin', ya know. Once he did make it to the water in that well, I'm sure he sunk to the bottom like a goddamn stone. They didn't call him Big Tony for nothin' …' "

Tim prodded his sweet and sour chicken with a fork, trying to get a piece of chicken and bell pepper together with a good amount of sauce. He continued to half-listen to his wife rattle on.

"… while a witness—that Frank later had whacked by one of his goons—was testifying, Frank pulled what looked like a business card out of his suit pants and said, 'If we win this case—and you always do—I'll give you one of these coupons as a bonus.' The coupon read GOOD FOR ONE FREE RUB-OUT. Isn't that something, Tim? How nice of him, right?" Amber said jokingly.

"If you know that Frank had someone whacked, how can you possibly represent him?" Tim asked, concerned about his wife's decisions.

"I don't know any of the particulars about it. Maybe the guy had it coming. It's not my business, really. I mean, *it is* technically my business, but it's not a direct issue for the current case, which I need to solely focus on."

"But if he had someone killed, that proves he's a murderer. Isn't he on trial for murder?"

"Yeah, sure, but it's for a different murder," she said, switching to her serious courtroom poker-face. "As his lawyer, I need to direct my attention at the matter at hand. The matter, and only the matter, that I was professionally retained to execute."

"Execute is a fitting word for the scenario," Tim said. "Sounds like what should be done to this Frank guy." Then he quickly added, "If that witness had it coming, maybe someone will off Frank, because it sounds like he has it coming, probably had it coming for a long time now."

"Maybe, but no one better off him before my case is finished," Amber said, reaching for the wine bottle and emptying the remaining contents into her glass. "I'm set to win this case and bring my tally to seven rulings in my favor and zero against."

Tim already knew she had never lost a case, but she loved mentioning it. She put everything she had into winning cases.

It was a game to her and she was very competitive about games, also at winning arguments. She wanted to be the next Ruth Bader Ginsburg and go down in history as one of the best female lawyers of all time.

After another gulp of wine, Amber continued, "If someone offed Frank Panicucci, the case would be dismissed. All my hard work would've been for nothing. Post-mortem trials are very rare, so the case wouldn't live past his death. Frank isn't enough of a major player to warrant providing justice for society in a posthumous trial."

Tim took pride in his wife's success and her courtroom capabilities, even if he didn't fully believe in her rules of conduct regarding her profession. In fact, her courtroom prowess and power rather turned him on. He wasn't the type of husband that dwelled in bitterness and jealousy for having a wife that financially bested him. Rather, he worried that she might begin to resent him for not living up to his potential and not being an equal talent in the business world.

"Looks like we're about finished. Should we get the bill?" Tim asked Amber.

She silently nodded her head in agreement while reaching for her wine glass.

Tim looked over at Raymond and saw him still virtually killing people, eyes transfixed and glazed over. "You finished, sport?" No reply was given. Using a subject that might interest his step-son, he tried again, "How many headshots did you administer during the meal?" Not even the slightest awareness was shown on Raymond's face that someone was trying to communicate with him. Tim rolled his eyes and raised a hand to signal for the bill.

Their Chinese waitress walked over and absently placed their bill on the table and walked away. Tim scanned the bill to check its accuracy. After seeing kung pao chicken on the bill, he realized they never received that particular dish. They got the sweet and sour chicken and the General Tso's chicken, but not the kung pao. He signaled to the waitress again.

When she returned Tim told her, "We never got the kung pao chicken, but you billed us for it."

The Chinese waitress said, "Oh, we make it now. No problem."

Tim politely shook his head. "That's okay, we're full enough and are ready to leave. You can just take it off the bill."

The waitress's eyes went wide like she had just been told the world was going to end. "Let me look at bill." She rudely snatched the bill out of his hands without warning, put it right in front of her intense face, and thoroughly studied it as if her life depended on it.

Thirty seconds had passed and she was still aggressively eyeing the bill. Tim was getting agitated. *It isn't rocket science, lady, just take it off the bill*, he thought, but said nothing aloud in order to be polite.

Finally she spoke, "I did bring kung pao chicken. You ate it. You forgot."

Tim realized by the look in the lady's eyes that taking that dish off the bill meant she wasn't getting the money for it, and if she wasn't getting the money for it, it would ruin the rest of her day. She seemed to think it was already her money if it was written down on a piece of paper, as if the bill was an important business contract.

He thought about paying the incorrect bill in order to avoid having to deal with the matter, but he decided he shouldn't have to pay for something he hadn't received. Even if he had to deal with some penny-pinching Chinese lady, he wasn't going to succumb based on principle. "I'm positive we didn't receive the kung pao chicken," Tim said politely but with a serious look on his face.

"You order many chicken dish. You must have forget. You should order more vegetable dish. It healthier. Better for brain. Help you remember what chicken you order. You Americans eat too much chicken," the waitress said in her broken English.

Tim's agitation had now stepped up to anger. "Eating healthier isn't the point here. The point is *we* didn't receive the kung pao. *We* got the sweet and sour chicken and *we* got the General Tso's chicken, but I know for a fact we didn't get the kung pao."

"You order so much chicken, you don't know what chicken you eat. A lot of chicken on table—you confused. You got chicken on the brain," the waitress uttered, and feigned a laugh at her own joke, a laugh filled with contempt instead of for humor's sake.

Tim looked over at his family for help, but they were oblivious to the situation: Raymond still transfixed on his videogame, and Amber fully concentrated on her phone as well, almost passed out from the amount of wine she had drunk. *No problem, I'll deal with this bitch myself.* "Look, *lady*, we didn't get the kung pao, so we're not paying for the kung pao," Tim said slowly in a belittling tone, as if he was speaking to an infant.

"Kung pao there, that the dish. You got it." She quickly jabbed a wavering finger at the empty plates on the table, making a quick circular motion out of it, obviously pointing at no specific plate.

"Do you realize you just pointed at virtually every dish on the table? How am I supposed to know what dish you're talking about?"

She leaned closer to the table and this time pointed in an area between two dishes that had leftover chili peppers. "That dish kung pao. You eat. You pay me."

Tim realized he was getting nowhere. This lady was as stubborn as a mule, so he decided to try a different angle. "We've been coming here for years, every month. Do you really want to lose our business over one plate of kung pao chicken?" He added, "Kung pao chicken that we didn't receive."

The concept of repeat business meant nothing to her, so she ignored his comment. "You drink many wine. It make your brain turn off. You forget kung pao you eat. It in your stomach, so it not here on table for me to point at. Later you poo and you see chicken and know I'm right. You feel very bad then."

"Are you really going to lose our repeat business over a ten-dollar plate?" Tim asked, trying to get the concept through her thick head. The concept of repeat business clearly seemed to be an idea that didn't exist in her world. Obviously she didn't understand the fundamentals of Business 101. As for her poo comment, he wasn't even going to attempt enlightening the lady as to how the digestion system worked and how it was impossible to discern certain foods from each other by staring at one's fecal matter in the toilet bowl, especially different chicken dishes where sauce was practically the only deviation. Then he added, "I only drank a little wine. My wife drank most of the bottle. My mind is clear, I assure you."

The waitress quickly countered, "No, you drink wine bottle. Husbands always the drinker. Wives watch husbands become dumb from drink. Think dumb things, say dumb things, pee in pants while sleeping ... forget about chicken they eat."

Tim recognized that adding in that last comment about the wine was a bad idea because the lady had completely focused on it and ignored his question about repeat business, which was far more important. He didn't see the point in asking it again because she would merely ignore it or counter with some idiotic statement. An idiotic statement that would seem very intelligent in her pea-sized brain, Tim was sure.

Before Tim could reply with anything, the lady continued, "Your son big boy. Maybe he eat all kung pao when you not look at him." The Chinese waitress scowled at Tim, as if the shame of his son being fat would trump any valid points he had made up to this point.

All the while, Raymond was still in another world, practically drooling over his game as he made his fifty-seventh headshot of the evening. His phone blurting out, "Killing spree! Proceed to kill for extra points or just for pleasure!"

Realizing, again, that he wasn't getting anywhere with this lady, Tim asked to speak to the manager. The waitress, red-faced and steaming mad like a boiling teapot angrily whistling to be removed from the burner, agreed and promptly stormed off in the direction of the door that led to the restaurant's kitchen.

Tim could hear some kind of Chinese language being shouted back and forth behind the closed kitchen doors between two people—the waitress and some male. Tim looked around at the other tables in the restaurant to see if other diners were taking heed to the commotion. A few non-Chinese customers were glancing at his table, but none of the Chinese customers seemed to care or notice at all. Half of the clientele in the restaurant were Chinese. Tim thought maybe this was an everyday occurrence for them, something routine that warranted no attention.

Finally, the waitress and a robust Chinese man strode over to their table. Instead of talking to Tim when they arrived at his table, they turned to each other and continued barking back and forth in Cantonese for a good five minutes as if Tim and his family didn't exist.

From the way they were interacting with each other, Tim gathered they were husband and wife. They must be the owners of the restaurant. It appeared she was filling her husband with every detail that had transpired at the table. Who knows exactly what she was saying, but her husband looked pretty upset as he listened.

Then the man's grimace disappeared as quickly as a light being switched off. He looked at Tim. "My wife told me about the kung pao chicken problem. Clearly your son is obese and has piled all chicken in his mouth before you noticed or had time to eat any yourself."

Tim quickly assessed that the husband's mind had already been poisoned by his wife's views, and it would probably be hard, or impossible, to change it at this point. However, the man's English was much better than his wife's, so maybe he was somewhat of a learned man Tim could reason with. Even though the man had started out by accusing his overweight step-son of downing all the chicken without him noticing, he thought coming across politely and logically would alleviate any confusion or lie his wife might have told him.

"First, let me just say that my family has been enjoying your wonderful food for years."

The Chinese man quickly replied, "Yes, you like the chicken a lot, I'm told. You also like wine a lot."

Ignoring the man's words, that were clearly more poison his wife had fed him, Tim continued to talk politely and sincerely. "We always order and enjoy the kung pao chicken on our visits to your fine establishment, so I would know if we had received it or not on this particular visit. My wife drank most of the wine, and my son hasn't eaten much due to being consumed by his videogames."

"I believe you about your wife," the man said while gesturing to Amber. Her head was sagging down toward her phone that must have been lying on her lap. She looked very drowsy. She possibly had even passed out, but Tim wasn't sure because he couldn't see her eyes.

The man continued, "But I don't see how it's possible that this extremely fat boy could eat so little. I'm sure he took many breaks from being consumed by his videogame to consume a lot of food. Fat boys love chicken." The man turned to his wife and quickly rattled off something in Cantonese, to which they both smiled and abruptly laughed at. Then the man continued without giving Tim a chance to talk. "We have a story in China. It's hard to translate into English, but it goes something like this: One day an obese boy ate much chicken and became big and round like balloon. Then he take flight over many hills and mountains. The pandas watch plump boy float away, but the father spend too much time and attention in the rice fields to notice balloon-boy float away, or the loss of chicken that the boy had floated away with in his gluttonous flight. This flight continued for many moons, but balloon-boy still round and not come down. Father notices the loss of chicken, but takes long time to realize missing son."

The Chinese man had apparently finished and was staring at Tim in a way that seemed to convey that these wise words made it very clear he was right and Tim was wrong about the current kung pao disagreement. But Tim didn't see how this story, which sounded awfully fabricated, had anything to do with the missing kung pao chicken that was still displayed on Tim's bill. Tim's mind reeled. *What the hell is he talking about? Have I slipped into the Twilight Zone or something? And how the hell does this man know English vocabulary like gluttonous?* Tim stared back at the Chinese man, speechless, his anger having temporarily taken a backseat to astonishment.

The Chinese man and his wife both displayed beaming smiles, happy with Tim's dumfounded expression, which they mistakenly thought meant he had seen the light and his error regarding the kung pao chicken issue. The kung pao chicken that Tim would have nightmares about that night. Nightmares that would include his balloon-shaped step-son floating over endless misty mountains while stuffing his fat face full of greasy chicken during his gluttonous flight.

Tim recomposed himself and instinctually turned to his wife for help, but she was still incapacitated due to the large quantity of wine she had partaken of. *Damn! If Amber was conscious, she'd destroy these halfwits with her usual courtroom-battling mentality.*

Before Tim could gather up his wits enough to respond, the man explained the Chinese story to make sure Tim understood its wisdom. "So as you can see, in this story, you are the father who didn't pay enough attention to his son, and the result is chicken that you thought you never had, you did have but is now stuffed in your son's stomach. Now, as you can see, your son is more obese than *ever before*. That is his punishment for his selfish gluttony and causing us to argue. You need to pay more attention to your son, and your son needs to quit stuffing his face with chicken or he will float away like a hot air balloon." The Chinese man wore a self-righteous smile on his face.

Tim was still astonished by this man's lunacy, especially since the man was robust himself. He was done with this absurd nonsense. "Oh my god, screw this," he said after reaching his breaking point, waving both arms in the air. "Listening to your lunacy isn't worth recouping ten dollars.

I will pay the bill, including the ten-dollar kung pao chicken dish we never received, and my family will never return to your establishment *again.* I hope you enjoy the ten dollars because you'll not be getting any more of my hard-earned money. No repeat business for you. You'd better invest that ten dollars well in order to make up for all the lost future money you could've received from my family had you not been complete imbeciles tonight." Tim crossed his arms over his chest. "Yeah, *fuck this*. I'm outta here."

Tim's words didn't seem to faze or matter to the man and his wife. The man's wife said, "Fuck this, fuck that. You Americans always fucking. Fucking will not fix chicken problem."

"Lady, don't talk to me anymore. You're insane," Tim rebuked. He put down the money for the bill and waited for them to give him his change, as he wasn't going to leave a cent for a tip. He gathered up all his fortitude to wait for his change and restrain himself from going ballistic and smashing everything in the restaurant.

Once he got the change he woke his wife, who had indeed passed out, and his family made their way out the door to their car. Raymond walked the entire length of the distance, from the restaurant seat to the car seat, never taking his face and fingers away from his videogame. Tim knew that Raymond was somewhat aware of what had occurred because he left his seat without needing direction from Tim, but he mentally seemed miles away, completely apathetic toward the jabs made at his obesity. Amber on the other hand, after waking from her wine-induced coma, needed a little physical assistance from Tim to reach their vehicle.

The Chinese patrons in the restaurant gave no care to the quarrel that had ensued, but were very quick to laugh and judge with pointing fingers when observing Tim's drunk wife stumbling out of the restaurant.

The Chinese man and his wife strolled back into the kitchen.

"That man doesn't understand the concept of repeat business," muttered the wife in Cantonese. "He's very dumb. If I don't collect the ten dollars, as well as any other amount of money other customers might try to not give me, we won't have enough money to own and operate our business. Then there wouldn't be any business to make repeat business. You can only repeat business if you handle your business correctly the first time you had business. He was just trying to steal ten dollars from us."

Her husband aggressively nodded his head in agreement without saying anything, as if nothing needed to be said about Tim's preposterous idea of repeat business.

His wife continued to vent, "I overheard them talking. The wife is a big-time lawyer. She's very rich. The man is a cheap lowlife, making an argument over ten dollars' worth of chicken. He should've just paid instead of trying to make us lose face in front of our customers."

Her husband kept nodding his head. He wasn't listening anymore and was simply nodding to appease her.

The wife continued raving in Cantonese. "He's just mad for now, but they'll come back. They're hooked on our MSG. We hook all foreigners on MSG and they have no choice but to return. Chinese are used to MSG. It's like salt to us so we don't get hooked, but foreigners get hooked big time. Foreigners go crazy for MSG. If they ask, we say, 'Oh, we don't use MSG. MSG is bad.' They don't know it's in the food and they get hooked like drug addicts—fish on hooks. They always wander back to our restaurant, drooling, wanting their next MSG fix. Our beloved CCP would be proud that we're still serving the people even though we're not in China. We proudly stay true to the core principle of the Chinese Communist Party by serving the people. … Serving them MSG." She produced a loud cackling laugh. "Stupid foreigners."

The woman didn't seem to realize that she was the foreigner in America, but to her, it didn't matter where she was in the world; China had the biggest population, which made them the people of the earth. Everyone else was a foreigner, even in their own country.

On the drive home, when Amber had awakened from her stupor, completely unaware of the argument that had transpired at the restaurant, she said to Tim, "I'm always satisfied after eating at the Lucky Joy. It's my favorite Chinese restaurant. I can't wait to eat there again next month. Next month again, right Tim?"

Tim gripped the steering wheel hard and gritted his teeth, but he loved his wife too much to deny her culinary cravings, so he said with a tense face while staring at the road before him, "Yes, dear."

Chapter 3

Two weeks after Dale's Scheming 101 class, it was time to regather at the Garden Oasis Caffè. This time around only Jeremy and Tim showed up. Dale phoned Jeremy and told him he wouldn't be joining them. He didn't give a reason why and Jeremy didn't ask:

"Hey, Jeremy, I won't be able to join you guys this time."

"Okay. Well, see you in two weeks then, yeah?"

"Yeah, sure. You can count on—"

Jeremy heard a crashing sound over the phone and Dale barking at someone, "You almost spilled that coffee on me! Do you have any idea how much this suit costs?" Then Jeremy heard a sniffling teen in the background. "I'm sorry, sir." Then he heard Dale shouting again, "This suit costs more than your face, kid! How much do you think your face costs, boy? How much? Give me a figure and we'll work with it." Then Jeremy heard the stammering teen reply, "I'm sorry, sir. My face costs nothing, sir. It costs nothing." Then Dale again, shouting, "That's right, *bucko*, your face is worthless and this suit is worth *much*. Your worthless face shouldn't even be able to gaze upon a suit like this. Avert your eyes! Avert them now!" and Dale's phone disconnected.

Shrugging his shoulders in reaction to what he'd overheard, Jeremy slipped his phone back into his pocket. He couldn't imagine Dale becoming any more commanding and abrasive after having climbed the corporate ladder, as the guy already acted like a scion.

Jeremy threw on a charcoal-gray twill overcoat and a scarf, grabbed his keys and wallet, and made for the door to meet Tim at the café.

It was one of those early spring days where the winter had fought its way back in a relentless pursuit to stay in the limelight, even though it knew its days were numbered. But it wasn't cold enough to stop them from dining alfresco, their preferred dining area in order to relish the fresh air, foliage, and quiet atmosphere. It was known to get quite loud in the indoor seating area due to a surplus of chatter that reverberated off the café walls.

They had dressed warmly, jackets firmly buttoned over layers of clothing, knowing the day's slight chill would have more sway upon their bodies once they became immobile for a period of time while ensconced in their chairs.

Tim didn't mind the reprieve from Dale's presence, but Jeremy was disappointed because he had been looking forward to unveiling the scheme he had performed at work, which he had done according to Dale's instructions. He could've briefly told Dale over the phone, but he felt a face-to-face revealing of the narrative was more appropriate. After all, Dale had surprised them in the same way. Dale would have to wait to hear about it on their next biweekly gathering. Informing Tim would have to do for today, but Jeremy wasn't sure how Tim would receive it. Would Tim be happy for him due to the success of his scheme, or would Tim be judgmental and get all righteous on him?

He decided to put it off until gauging Tim's mood, and perhaps it wouldn't be a suitable time at all to disclose the scheme. Given all the details of the situation, he felt he hadn't done anything amoral. Consequently, he was feeling good about the whole thing and didn't want anyone dampening his high-spirited mood.

"Have you been thinking about what Dale talked about last time?" Jeremy asked Tim while clenching two hands around the mug that held his cappuccino, attempting to absorb all the heat it was giving off.

Tim had been slightly detached that afternoon, dwelling in an introspective mood. He looked up from a lemon tart dessert he'd been playfully nudging with a fork. "Actually, the topic we discussed has been something I haven't been able to expel from my thoughts … unfortunately. I don't advocate Dale's ideology, but he did make enough valid points for me to ponder their fairness, or lack of."

Jeremy slowly nodded his head with an expression of agreement and understanding. "I'm sure we both agree that Dale could care less about moral virtue, but that doesn't mean everything he said was groundless. For example … is it wrong to defend yourself from an attack, whether it be direct or indirect, and not only parrying blows from your opponent to ward off harm, but also counterstriking to ensure that no possible future attempts could be directed at you? Don't you have the right to stop anyone from derailing you for their own personal gain?"

Jeremy paused to take a sip of his cappuccino while holding up an index finger in the air to indicate he wasn't done talking yet. "There are many ruthless people in the world that will stab you in the back if you let them. Many aren't bothered by acting a little unethical if it serves them, especially in today's dog-eat-dog world. And what if their actions aren't considered ruthless from a collective standpoint, or even just in their own minds. What's considered unethical to one person may seem benign to another, and so they'd believe there'd be no consequences for their actions."

Tim gazed off into space, pondering Jeremy's words. "I understand what you're saying, but I've always thought of ethics as static ideas, not something that wavered due to variables involved in each possible circumstance and different people's outlooks."

After a sip from his cappuccino Jeremy took a different approach along the same line of thought. "Those who hold to rigid beliefs quickly become outdated. For example, look at religious dogmas. Religion is slowly dying because it's not adapting with the times, and when it does adapt to the current era, it's a blatant confession of its perpetual lies—but that's an entirely different conversation altogether. We all need to adapt to the current times as humanity evolves. Would you have opposed Copernicus or Galileo's ideas in order to stick with the status quo? I'm not saying we should throw ethics out the window; I firmly believe in a set of ethics like you do. Where we differ on the matter is the 'variables involved,' as you say. Take my analogy of an attacker trying to kill you. I think we can both agree that not only do you have the right to defend yourself, but to also kill the attacker if they won't stop till you're dead, a you-or-them-type scenario. This falls within the legal lines of killing in the name of self-defense—"

"Sure," Tim interjected, "but we're not talking about someone trying to kill another person."

"Yes, of course," Jeremy agreed, "but I'm saying there are actions that are legal and considered ethical that would normally be quite the opposite. It all depends on the variables involved in the circumstance. It's extremely unethical to kill someone if you weren't defending yourself, but ethical if you were. Now apply less severe cases to this same equation and you'll find that certain actions taken at the workplace, or wherever, could be considered not unethical due to the circumstances involved. That's the point I'm trying to make."

"Okay, I see where you're coming from. That sounds logical to me."

In the back of his mind, Jeremy felt a growing sense of anxiousness for withholding from Tim the scheme he'd carried out at work, but he continued to hold his tongue on the matter until it felt right. He could always wait two weeks and tell both Tim and Dale at the same time.

"Supposing your equation deemed a certain scheme ethical, or at least not unethical"—Tim scratched his head in thought—"I don't think there's any action I could perform at work that would be effective enough to ensure my advancement anyway. So if there's nothing I could do, there's no reason in even contemplating whether I'd do something or not."

"I thought the same thing at first. But you'd be amazed at what schemes form in your mind after applying some thought. Sometimes even a little reflection is all it takes to get the creative juices flowing. And sometimes all you need to do is tentatively cast a want out into the ether for it to mentally or physically materialize by a seemingly magical set of circumstances."

"Hmm ... right." Tim nodded his head. "I think I've experienced that before. But even if that's true, it doesn't mean that ideas arise invariably. Sometimes, no matter how intelligent and creative one is, an ever-present brick wall resides in certain scenarios due to a lack of available maneuvers."

"Sure, but I would imagine a workplace where people heavily rely on computers would be rife with maneuvers if one was savvy enough," Jeremy said, hoping the statement would spark some imagination in Tim's mind.

Tim contemplated for a moment and then replied, "I remember a prank I pulled in a network connectivity class at UW. When a classmate we—my two friends and I—despised was away from his computer, leaving it unprotected and unlocked, I inserted a USB stick in his computer, quickly installed a simple remote access application, and made sure the volume on his speakers was set to a loud level. One of my classmates that was in on the trick created a diversion that kept the targeted classmate engaged in conversation with his back to his computer while I did those things."

Tim paused to take a sip of coffee before continuing, "Later that day during a lecture the professor was giving, I accessed the student's computer via the remote access application and opened a porn site we had previously made sure would include humiliating audio on its homepage. We sat in the very back row, so no one could witness us accessing his computer on my computer screen. Luckily the targeted classmate sat in the front row, which made it easy for several people to see what was on his computer. While the classroom was quiet, except for the professor's voice, a lusty female's voice billowed out from the student's computer speakers. 'Hello. You have entered the erotic sex zone.' The professor, as well as most of the students in the class, immediately turned toward the student. The classroom fell deafly silent while the shocked student frantically reached for his mouse to close the browser that contained the porn site. Several students had seen the porn on his screen and were snickering, but he was able to close the browser before the professor singled him out in front of everyone. The professor briefly eyed the student in silence, and then returned to his lecture. The student was sweating and slightly shaking, completely dumbfounded as to why the Web site had popped up on his computer.

"After about fifteen minutes, when the student had settled down and the professor was still lecturing, we did it again. But this time when the student tried closing the browser, I battled for control over his mouse cursor movements with my own mouse in order to allow the lusty woman's voice to spew out more dialog. 'Oh, so you're my new boy toy. You're going to eat out my pussy until I tell you to assume the position on the floor so I can take a ride on your stick. Your stick is legally mine now. It's my toy from now on.'—or something like that, I don't remember the exact dialog. After about fifteen seconds we let the student have full control over his mouse cursor so he could close the browser. At that point it was too late for him; the whole classroom was rolling in laughter and the professor was seething, veins in his forehead swelled as his blood rapidly boiled up to his head. Then the professor chastised him in front of everyone. I remember verbatim what he said because we joked about it for the rest of the course. 'Brice, get a hold of your raging-teenage hormones. This is a university classroom! The hallowed halls of learning! Not your sweaty dorm room where god knows what perverse deeds transpire on a regular basis. Pull yourself together or I'll be forced to expunge you from this class.' The student was swimming in humiliation, completely red-faced. Instead of trying to explain the situation to the professor, he sagged his head in shame. We guessed he was too distressed and embarrassed to draw further attention to himself by trying to explain his innocence, which probably would've been futile and enraged the professor even more."

Jeremy enjoyed Tim's story and had chuckled during its recounting. "Wow, I wish I had been in that class. I didn't know you had it in you."

"Hey, I'm not as square as you and Dale think. Don't you recall that time in high school we snuck into Spanish class during lunch break to adjust our grades, nudging up some of our points in different areas on the teacher's Excel spreadsheet?"

"Yeah, I do remember that," Jeremy recalled. "You came up with that ploy because you had to secure your straight-A grades. I didn't even care about upping my grade. I just went along with your cunning plan because it was exciting, and you were dead set on pulling it off and needed a second person as a lookout."

"Yeah, thanks for that," Tim said. "I don't know if I would've had the nerve to do it by myself. I remember we had been given a C on a Spanish video assignment because Mrs. Brown had other students grade their peers instead of her doing it. We made a joke about one of the other students at the end of our video because we thought it would help our chances in getting a better grade through humor, but it backfired when that student and some of his friends gave us Fs out of spite. But I rectified their spite with my crafty plan of changing our grades on the teacher's computer."

Jeremy realized that Tim had just unknowingly pointed out a direct correlative point to what he was trying to convey earlier. "What happened and how you reacted in your story is exactly the point I was trying to make with the killer analogy. Normally it would be unethical to cheat and change your grade, but in this scenario it was warranted because of the unfair set of circumstances. You justified sneaking onto the teacher's computer to change your grade because it wasn't fair that she left the grading in the hands of our moronic, biased classmates."

"Oh," Tim said with surprise. "I guess you're right. I completely didn't see that correlation … but now it's completely obvious."

Holding back from telling Tim about his recent scheme at work was increasingly weighing on Jeremy's mind. He was aching to tell someone about it. He didn't want to keep the success story all to himself for another two weeks.

Jeremy worked as an ORA (operations research analyst) at one of the largest management analyst companies: Cohesive Analytics. He was tasked with handling the operations of three small businesses. For the past two years he'd been trying to pick up more businesses under his belt, which was essential before being able to handle medium-sized companies, but he'd had no luck in doing so.

It looked like Tim had come around from being distant and was now in a genial mood, so Jeremy decided to spill the beans about his scheme, but he wasn't sure how to bring it up. "So … Tim. I got to tell you something," he said with a mischievous smile as he reached for his cappuccino.

The phrase "I got to tell you something" is usually followed by something intriguing or unsettling, thought Tim. So naturally the phrase piqued his interest, and even more so being that Jeremy was displaying a naughty smile, which conveyed that his something to tell would be intriguing and not upsetting.

Tim smiled in return, eager to hear what was about to come out of Jeremy's mouth. "Okay, what is it?"

"It's not like I planned it. It just kind of fell into place. It presented itself and was just too good to pass up."

Tim leaned forward on the edge of his seat. "What is *it* that you speak of?"

"I took Dale's advice to heart and pulled off a scheme at work."

Tim abruptly shifted to the back of his seat in concern and surprise, his eyes widened. "It was only two weeks ago that Dale gave that speech. How could you possibly have put it into effect already?"

"Like I said, I didn't plan it. It just perfectly presented itself. I will say, though, I wouldn't have acted on the opportunity if Dale hadn't seeded my mind with the idea."

Tim beckoned Jeremy to tell the tale, not knowing how he would feel about what Jeremy was about to divulge. "Okay, I'm all ears. Let's hear it."

Jeremy took a gulp of his cappuccino before diving into the story. "I'll start with the justification of the scheme so you'll understand the scenario and hopefully not judge me."

Tim casually nodded and tried not to take a preemptive stance against Jeremy until he had at least heard his reasoning.

"There's this guy, Chad, at work that everybody hates because he has made a habit out of relaying incriminating backroom dialog and secrets to our boss in a brown-nosing way in order to get in the boss's favor. He's responsible for getting one employee fired by doing this, and it's also the reason why he handles the most small businesses at our company. He didn't acquire those businesses because he's better at his job than his colleagues; I'd say his skills are average."

"Your justification sounds pretty convincing," Tim said. "I know someone kind of similar at my work: Brad. Man, I hate that guy."

Jeremy began to recount the scheme. "Chad was having issues with a newly updated section in the software we use to help manage a certain aspect of a company's time-allocation allotment. Don't worry, I won't bore you with the technical details. On one of these occasions Chad blew up and yelled at his computer, 'If this new update continues to ignore me and not save my allocation changes, I'm going to beat the hell out of this computer with a red aluminum baseball bat!' Many people in the office heard him since he was yelling. He's known for having a temper, and a short fuse to boot."

Jeremy took a sip of his cappuccino then continued, "At first I didn't think anything of it, but later that day while passing the sporting goods section in a supermarket, where I was picking up motor oil for my car and some household items, a rack of aluminum bats caught my eye. Chad's rant immediately popped up in my mind and I was seized with the weirdest feeling: it seemed like the bats were begging me to purchase them. None of the bats were colored, but the idea of spray painting one red to frame Chad popped up in my mind. But I shook the silly idea out of my head and went about my shopping. However, I returned to that supermarket the very next day because I had forgotten to purchase some of the items that I needed. I crossed paths with the aluminum bats again and this time my reaction was automatic: I walked up to the bats and grabbed one. Then I grabbed a bottle of red spray paint, which oddly enough was in eyeshot of the bats.

"When I got home I spray painted the bat and left it lying on some newspapers to dry. That bat stayed on those newspapers for days. Every time I walked by it I felt stupid for having bought it. But three days ago, on Thursday, I ended up using the bat when it happened again: Chad went ballistic over the same software update issue. His previous outburst paled in comparison to this eruption. He jumped on his desk like an ape, pointed an accusing finger at his computer, and started shouting all kinds of obscenities at it: 'Acknowledge my system changes, you piece of shit' and 'You outdated technological freak of nature' and then 'The red aluminum bat is coming for you, you digital piece of fuckery!' His last threat to the computer held the same comment about a red aluminum bat from his first flare-up. When I heard him say it, I could almost hear my red spray-painted bat at home telepathically telling me it was time to use it to close the deal. It was fortunate that he repeated that last threat because my colleagues, who were enjoying his tantrum like it was a show, might have forgotten that red-bat comment from his first outburst since it had happened ten days prior.

"After he was done yelling at his computer like a rabid dog, he stormed out of the office, leaving early for the day. At that point I knew if I returned afterhours to an empty office to destroy his computer with my aluminum bat, everyone would assume that he followed through with his sporting-goods threat."

"Did you really do it—use the red bat on his computer?" Tim asked, stunned by the imagery in his head of Jeremy ravaging some worker's computer with a bat.

"I certainly did, and I didn't feel the least bit of remorse for having done it because the douchebag completely deserved it." Jeremy took another sip of his cappuccino and continued the story. "I wasn't very productive for the rest of the working day because I kept going over in my mind what I was going to do. The more I thought about it, the more excitement and anxiety built up inside me. By the time I left work I was brimming with anticipation. There was an internal part of myself that tried reasoning with me while I waited at home for it to get late enough to return to the empty office with the bat: *We're not the type of person to bring a bat into an office and annihilate a computer. That's not our M.O. Especially not an aluminum bat; it'll probably make a horrendous pinging noise upon impact.* But I dismissed those thoughts because the whole affair had lined up so perfectly that it seemed like some force had manufactured the opportunity from the beginning. Why had I been so drawn to purchase the bat? Why had I forgotten to buy some items at the supermarket that required my return? Why had the red spray paint been in direct line of sight with the bat? Why did Chad use the same red-aluminum-bat threat at his computer for a second time? It all seemed preordained. I had sent my invocation out into the ethers and it was returning to the physical plane of existence to manifest. I would've been a fool not to follow through with what I had set into motion.

"I tried making myself busy at home doing chores while I waited for it to get late enough to return to the office, but I couldn't focus on even the simplest task because my mind was locked in an endless loop of performing the deed and making sure all its details were meticulously conducted to avoid any possible evidence leading back to me."

"There's something I'm wondering, though," Tim said. "Wouldn't your electronic badge show that you entered the building at a peculiarly late hour and be evidence against you?"

"I forgot to mention that part. I left a small piece of cardboard blocking the lock on a backdoor exit that nobody uses. It kept the door ajar a few centimeters so no one would notice if they happened to walk by it. On my return, I would be able to slip into the building undetected."

"Doesn't your office have security cameras?" Tim asked.

"Nope. Our company doesn't have the need for such security, not like your company does. But just in case I was wrong and missed a hidden camera somewhere, I wore plain, black clothes with a black baseball cap to hide my features."

"You thought of everything, didn't you?" Tim said while raising his eyebrows.

"Remember what Dale said? Something about covering all your ends and making sure there's no evidence or possibility of your actions coming back to haunt you. I took that advice to heart, so the worst thing that could happen would be that my actions didn't fulfill my wishes: Chad getting fired. No trail would lead back to me whether he got fired or not."

Jeremy continued after drinking some coffee. "So I snuck into Cohesive Analytics like a ninja, brandishing my red spray-painted aluminum bat. I stealthily tiptoed through the office and finally made my way to the target's computer. I stood before it, sizing up the monitor and tower for a bit, calculating what angled swings would do the most damage with the fewest amount of blows. I knew it was going to be noisy so I wanted to get it done and leave as fast as I could in case there was that unlikely someone lurking about, like a janitor, who might hear the noise and come to identify me. But once I started going to town on the computer, it was so therapeutic that I lost track of time and delivered far more blows than what was necessary. I beat the hell out of those 'digital pieces of fuckery,' as Chad had called them. The whole time I was mashing away, I imagined Chad's stupid face and all the exploits he had pulled at work. Each strike of my bat, with its high-pitched pinging clank, lowered both ends of Chad's grin until he was wearing a sad frown in my mind. A sad frown fit for a clown.

"Then I snapped back to reality and felt a wave of fear because I realized I had put myself in unnecessary danger of being caught—if in fact there was someone in earshot's distance. I hauled ass for the backdoor exit, this time choosing to leave like an Olympic sprinter instead of a ninja. I caught a glimpse of myself in a mirror on the way to the exit. I looked pretty badass with my black clothes, black baseball cap, and red bat, which wasn't as red anymore because there were many streaks on the bat where the red paint had stripped off onto the white computer tower and monitor. Even though I had an ounce of fear pumping through my body, there was an even greater sense of power and confidence that was palpable, and the image of myself in the mirror really hit those feelings home. It was me, a more sinister side of me, but me. It also felt like I was looking at a mirror image of a character in a movie. A character playing a role where right and wrong didn't apply, only the storyline mattered, and what was written in the script was to be followed without question.

"On the drive home I stopped my car in a remote location, used a rag to wipe off the prints on the bat, and tossed it into some thick bushes."

" 'Wipe off the prints,' " Tim laughed. "It's not like your prints are in the police's database."

"I know, but once you get into covering all traces, it just happens naturally. Or maybe I've just watched too many movies."

Jeremy was pleased that Tim wasn't judging him for his actions, at least that was his perception. "I was giddy to arrive at work the next day like a kid for Christmas morning. I couldn't wait to see everyone's reactions to what was sure to be an unprecedented spectacle. When I arrived at the office the next day, there was already a group of people huddled around Chad's computer, or what was left of it. It looked like a brilliantly constructed work of art. My coworkers were staring at it incredulously, scratching their beards or heads, trying hard to grasp the meaning of it. Like a group of visitors staring at an abstract painting in a museum, they were each putting in their two cents about what it meant, how it made them feel, how it had come to exist. I thought it best to be a passive spectator while standing among them, doing my best to duplicate their gawking expressions, but all the while internally admiring the piece of artwork I had so lovely crafted out of Chad's computer. I'm sure my artwork was more purposeful than anything Chad would've done on that computer.

"It didn't take long for one of my colleagues to bring up the fact that Chad had cursed at his computer and stormed out of the office early the day before. One of them commented on the numerous red marks and streaks on the scattered pieces that were once a computer. They agreed that something had forcibly dismantled the piece of equipment, but weren't agreeing on the instrument that had been used. Obviously they had forgotten Chad's red-aluminum-bat threat, so I murmured into the assembled crowd, 'Maybe it was a bat,' hoping it would jog someone's memory. At first it seemed like the hint was lost on them, but then one of them woke up from their trance and spoke up, recounting Chad's red-bat threat. Then another worker vocalized that they recalled Chad shouting a red-bat threat on two different occasions. They all fell into lockstep and began to surmise that Chad had perpetrated the computer-killing, and used a red aluminum bat to do it. It was all coming together as I had foreseen.

"The head of our office, an old British man named Thomas Bell, strolled over to the scene to see what all the commotion was about. Thomas is an old-school Brit who believes in an unbending assumption that all things should be good and proper, often to the point of being easily persuaded by others that uphold, or appear to uphold, the same principles. Therefore, it took no time at all for the numerous workers to completely convince Thomas that Chad was guilty of destroying company equipment.

"Thomas said, 'This disturbed man must be sacked. Very well can't have lunatics running about the office brandishing baseball bats—aluminum or otherwise—mashing to bits the company's equipment. Next thing you know he'll be mashing people. I won't have it! This sick man will be sacked and escorted out of the building immediately upon his arrival. Assuming he has the gall to even show up today.' "

"That worked out perfectly," said Tim, "but I guess their unanimous assumptions made sense. Who else would possibly do it?"

"Exactly. If you jump on opportunities that present themselves and make a detailed exploitative plan, it's not hard to create your desired outcome."

"So did Chad show up for work?" asked Tim.

"He sure did," Jeremy said with a smile. "This is where it gets good. Let me finish up the story. I'm almost done. Upon making it to his desk, Chad was met by the company's human resources representative, Linda, and two beefy male employees that volunteered to act as security guards, as our company doesn't employ actual security since there's never been a need for it till then. Words are exchanged back and forth. Linda informs him of his severance package and lets him know that he should be grateful he's getting one at all and that the company won't be pressing charges."

Tim interrupted, "Isn't it common practice for HR to do that in the private confines of their office, away from the workforce?"

"Yeah, but Linda was too afraid that Chad would break out a bat and start beating her to death after she informed him of his termination."

Tim and Jeremy laughed, and then Jeremy continued, "Chad continually denied doing the deed and got more furious each time his appeals were dismissed and interrupted by Linda. He got so enraged that he started shouting at Linda, 'I didn't smash the computer! I don't even own a baseball bat!' Linda calmly specified in a businesslike tone that it was a red aluminum baseball bat, to which Chad replied, 'If I don't own a baseball bat, I can't very well own a fuckin' red aluminum baseball bat, you dumb bitch. *Hello.*' Chad repeatedly tapped a finger to his head while saying, 'Anyone home up there, McBitch?!'

"When the situation heated up, Linda made a signaling glance at the beefy employees filling in as security guards. They each grabbed one of Chad's arms and forcibly ushered him toward the exit. On his way out he was twisting his head around to get as many verbal attacks in at the HR lady as possible before being ejected from the building. 'I'll tell you this, if I had a red aluminum baseball bat, I'd smash your dumbass face in with it! I'd hit you so hard you'd fucking disintegrate, bitch-face! I'd play baseball with your sad excuse for a face! Your bitch-face would sail out of the park. Homerun! Fans would be screaming as I set a new bitch-face-distance record ...' and out the door he was escorted.

"The entire office was deadly silent for a few seconds, and then applause simultaneously erupted throughout the office. It was obvious that everyone was elated to see Chad ejected from the building. He was finally reaping what he sowed. All his backstabbing actions had come full circle. Instead of feeling any kind of remorse for my actions, I felt like an unsung hero, taking pride in having the will and dedication to carry out the secret plot. Everyone in the office would've been patting me on the back and jubilantly shouting my name if they had known I was the one who got Chad fired."

Before Tim could say anything, Jeremy added, "So before you label my actions, Tim, keep in mind that he got his comeuppance. And my colleagues distinctly demonstrated their agreement."

"Given what the guy did," Tim said, "no, I don't think it was wrong. Damaging company property is the only thing I can find disagreeable, but I guess from a bigger picture perspective sometimes eggs have to be broken to make an omelet, and in this case the eggs were merely some replaceable electronics and not a person. Chad wasn't an innocent bystander, so he doesn't count as being represented as an egg in this scenario. He wasn't a casualty of war, rather, he started the war, it sounds like." Tim added, "It appears that the greater good was served by your actions."

Jeremy was pleased that Tim had stopped simply labeling things as good or bad at face value without taking into account all the variables involved. It had taken a while to persuade Tim to shift his rigid mindset to something more analytically comprehensive and reasoned, but it was worth the effort. "I'm glad you see it my way." Jeremy finished off the last of his cappuccino and started working on his half-eaten *mille-feuille*.

"Seems like it was a victory for your office as a whole, but did you directly benefit from it?" Tim asked.

"I thought for sure that I'd be able to pick up at least one of the companies he was managing after his departure, but I ended up taking on more, replacing Chad's role as being the employee who manages the most small companies."

Jeremy swallowed another piece of his French pastry. "It's important to note that schemes aren't the only deciding factor in one's advancement. If I hadn't possessed skills in my field and shown my dedication to the company through hard work, I wouldn't have been given the extra companies to manage. Schemes can be very advantageous, but could fall short if not backed up by good old-fashioned hard work to ensure you fill the void after a scheme has transpired. I didn't find out till yesterday that I had acquired so many of Chad's companies. We don't normally work on weekends, but they called me up to put in some overtime to get up to speed on some of the companies Chad had managed. It was annoying working on a Saturday, but it was a one-off irritation, and representing the most small companies makes me a shoo-in for advancing on to dealing with medium-sized companies when the position becomes available."

"Wow. That really couldn't have worked out any better for you. Quite effective. I guess there really is something to be said about applying a little extra work beyond one's regular duties."

"Yeah," Jeremy agreed. "I'm not sure how long it would've taken me to get where I am now if I had kept going about things the conventional way."

This made Tim wonder how long he'd be stuck in his current position at work if he didn't change up his routine. He wasn't mentally equipped to destroy something with a baseball bat, but perhaps there was something minor he could put into effect to gain advancement, something that wasn't arduous or risky, and was justified of course.

"Mmm, this *mille-feuille* is excellent," Jeremy said. "I usually get one of their chocolate cakes since they go well with coffee, but I'm glad I deviated from my usual choice today. I shouldn't get the same thing every time. Deviation leads to new experiences and possibilities."

Indeed, deviation does lead to new possibilities, thought Tim. Maybe it was time for him to deviate a little in life to experience something different, something better.

They sat for a minute in silence, enjoying the crisp, chilly air as they ate their pastries. They were the only patrons in the alfresco area. People must have thought it was too cold to sit outside. The lack of patrons and the absence of Dale made their biweekly meeting calmer and more serene than usual.

Chapter 4

It had been one of those fights where trying to recall what ignited it left Tim confused and wishing he hadn't done or said whatever the offense was that had made Amber so heated. He presumed she was on her period, and it was solely the reason why she was emotionally and verbally lashing out at him. But he had learned to never attempt to diffuse any argument by indicating this to her because it always made the situation worse.

This particular quarrel had become more substantial than their previous squabbles when Amber brought up the stall in his career plans as a belittling tactic to subdue him and win the argument. Tim wasn't sure if she was merely using the point to cripple him, because people often use whatever is at their disposal to hurt another in a heated argument, regardless of their true feelings on the matter. Or was it truly something she was greatly displeased about? Tim wasn't sure, but it was a matter he had dreaded would surface at some point due to the lengthy amount of time his career had been stalled. Now here it was, finally arising as a formidable issue in their marriage. Maybe Amber's competitiveness went beyond her own career aspirations and encompassed his as well. Maybe she desired a showcase marriage that included two high-profile professionals.

One thing was certain. He'd do whatever it took to keep their marriage afloat. Amber may not have been perfect, but neither was he, and he had invested too much time in their relationship for it to fail.

The fight had concluded with Amber stomping out of the kitchen, where they had both been preparing dinner, leaving Tim to carry on making supper by himself. At least that's what he decided to do to help calm Amber's mood.

Just as Amber was tramping past the front door on her way to the bathroom, the doorbell rang. "Who the hell could that be?" she roared, still fuming from the fight.

Whoever it was, they were about to face the wrath of Amber, Tim thought, as he continued chopping ingredients.

Without hesitation, Amber turned the door handle and swung the door open, revealing two clean-cut boys wearing white dress shirts, black slacks, narrow black ties, and holding books in their hands.

The boys were initially taken aback when Amber thrust her disgruntled face over the threshold of the doorway to examine the offenders that had rung her doorbell, but they promptly recovered in order to serve the greater good of the Lord.

"Excuse me, ma'am, do you have a moment to talk about our Lord and Savior, Jesus Christ?" said one of the boys.

"Really?" Amber snapped, tightening her forehead. Then she eased her expression. "You know what, this is perfect. This is exactly what I need right now. Come right in and take a seat in the living room. Let's talk about the Savior," she said while opening the door and directing them with a gesture of her arm toward the living-room couch.

The boys weren't sure if she was being sarcastic or authentic. Her tone of voice surely sounded sarcastic. They were no strangers to encountering sarcasm on their mission to spread the Good Word, but they had never been invited inside while it was being displayed. They were apprehensive about entering the house, but they overcame their fear by replacing it with a paramount duty to serve the Lord. And it wasn't often they were invited inside to disseminate the information people needed to save their souls from eternal damnation.

The skinny boys gingerly stepped inside and followed Amber into the living room while the older boy introduced himself and his missionary partner. "My name is Braxton, and this is Kyler."

Without introducing herself, Amber gestured toward the long end of the L-shaped couch. "Go ahead, take a seat.

This is the first time this residence has ever had the privilege to communicate with Mormons."

In the kitchen, which was located next to but out of eyesight from the living room, Tim was eavesdropping on the conversation as he prepared the dinner. Those unfortunate boys were carelessly wading into quicksand, he thought. God help them. But he knew it would be entertaining to listen to, and more importantly, it'll quench Amber's current bloodlust and possibly mitigate adversity directed at him for the rest of the evening. God bless those defenseless boys.

"Actually, ma'am, we prefer to be called members of the Church of Jesus Christ of Latter-day Saints instead of Mormons," Braxton politely corrected Amber.

"That's quite a long handle, isn't it?" she said with a fake smile. "Do you mind if I just call you what everybody else calls you: Mormons? It's a lot shorter."

Kyler mumbled, "LDS will work."

Amber's eyebrows raised and her head slightly shifted back in surprise. "This household doesn't contain LSD, and it's hardly something a visitor would request from a host in substitute of addressing said visitor by their preferred lengthy handle. Anyway, I thought being a Mormon meant you didn't do illegal drugs, and how will acid work instead of having to address you by that long handle?" All of this Amber rattled off before either of the boys could get a word in edgewise. Her brain was working overtime from the triple-shot latte she had partaken of an hour ago, and the recent argument with her husband also assisted her current adrenaline boost.

Both the boys chuckled lightheartedly, and Braxton, the more experienced of the two in missionary work and well-versed regarding their gospel, straightened out the misunderstanding. "He said LDS, which is short for Latter-day Saints. It's a shorter reference you can use to address us by if you like. And I assure you, ma'am, the only place we drop acid is in the garbage, along with all the other mind-altering chemicals that cloud the brain from revering the Lord and following His word. His word on high rather than us being high."

"Oh, I see," Amber replied. "Well, before we get started, can I interest you in a cup of coffee?" Her mind was prime and sharp from the caffeine running through her blood and she wanted them to have the opportunity to start on a level playing field, without a handicap, before she began destroying their religion in her living room, a courtroom-style scuffle. She labeled this newly appointed case in her head: Amber versus Mormonism. She didn't know much about Mormonism, but if it was anything similar to Christianity—and if she recalled correctly, Mormons considered themselves Christians—she would have plenty of ammunition to effortlessly sink their pious ship. Or would it more correctly be pious shit? Amber equally despised all religions. She had logically abandoned religions in favor of hard, factual science. Every time she saw a religious book, she imagined herself quickly flipping through the book while using a big red stamp to mark every page with a big fat BULLSHIT.

This battle, and her subsequent victory, would be the best medicine for the undesirable state her husband had put her in. Or maybe it was the fault of her menstrual-cycle hormones. *No!* It was definitely her husband's fault. These feeble Mormons didn't realize they had wandered into a serious court case. First, she would feign interest and affability until she ascertained the groundwork of their religion and beliefs. Then, she would use basic logic to debunk their religion. Given a basic background, she knew any religion could be discredited. Only religions based on a way of life rather than built on some almighty, holier-than-thou, redeeming "God" could survive the shells of logic's artillery.

Braxton replied to Amber's offer, "Thank you, but LDS members don't partake of caffeine or alcohol, being that they're poisons for the body."

"Okay, suit yourselves." Amber took a mental note as if she was in a courtroom: *Let the record show that the defendants have been offered an elixir to arm their wits and have refused.* Then she said,

"You may proceed by informing me what holy book or books you follow."

"Sure. The Church of LDS mainly follows the King James Version of the Holy Bible, but we also adhere to the Book of Mormon, as well as some other forms of scripture."

That was all Amber needed to hear. Since they followed the Bible, they also followed the same mistranslations and alterations in it that many other religions did. The knowledge she had acquired at the age of seventeen to debunk her parents' religion, Christianity, would also work in discrediting Mormonism. But she was sure there must be more doctrines and goodies packed within the Book of Mormon she could use as fuel to the fire in burning down their religion. She'd coerce them to disclose information about the Book of Mormon before unveiling her cannonry, which she would meticulously prime before firing and blowing them to smithereens. Then, safely upon her battlements, she would dump hot oil upon them to guarantee the job was complete, making sure they'd never return to her door again.

Instead of sitting on the couch next to the boys, Amber was slowly pacing back and forth between the 75-inch TV and the couch. In her mind, the TV was the judge and an imaginary jury sat on the side, lingering on every word.

"Can you tell the court—I mean, me—the main difference between Christianity and the Church of LDS?" Amber said in a cold, professional manner.

The boys became slightly uncomfortable by the change in her manner, but they trudged forward regardless, eager to serve the Lord and all His glory. Braxton started playing a hymn in his mind to give him strength. *Glory to God on high! Let heaven and earth reply. Praise ye his name. His love and grace adore* … With renewed fervor, he replied, "The Church of LDS is the original Christian Church started by Jesus Christ; it was restored by Joseph Smith in 1830 when the Book of Mormon was finished being translated."

Still pacing in front of the TV, Amber said, "Can you tell us more about this book you speak of, the Book of Mormon? And how it came into existence."

Braxton wasn't sure why she was using the word "us" instead of "me," but he was glad she was showing so much interest. "Yes, of course. The Book of Mormon is an account of the prophets that lived in North America from 600 B.C. to A.D. 400."

"Hence the name Latter-day Saints," Amber offered.

"Yes, that's right." Braxton was happy she had picked up on that without being told. "Joseph Smith was guided to golden plates that resided in a hill on his parents' farm near Palmyra, New York, with angel Moroni's help. Angel Moroni forbid Joseph to show the plates to anyone. Their wisdom could be read only after being translated to English, which became the Book of Mormon."

"And may I ask where these golden plates now reside, and has their authenticity been validated?" Amber asked.

"After the translation of the golden plates from ancient Egyptian to English was complete, Joseph returned the plates to the angel Moroni, so they could never be examined."

Amber thought that was a convenient way to evade the testing of their authenticity. And she had never heard of ancient Egyptian hieroglyphs being discovered in North America, but she decided to let that unbelievable piece of information go undebated since this wasn't a real court case. The lack of authenticity of the golden plates was more than enough for her to scrutinize.

Amber paused from her pacing. "So the plates can't be accepted into evidence. That is a shame. And the account of Joseph and his holy plates being unearthed from a hill on a farm in New York could be marked down as hearsay since there were no witnesses. Isn't that correct? Would you like to say anything on Joseph's behalf before we proceed?"

Braxton shifted forward and perched on the edge of the sofa, aching to reply and defend the Church. "Actually, Joseph later obtained testimonies from eleven men that witnessed the existence of the golden plates."

"But I thought this Moron angel forbid Joseph to show the plates to anyone?" Amber countered, slowly picking up her pace toward a full-on attack. "Do you recall making this statement?"

"Angel Moroni," Kyler anxiously corrected Amber.

Amber dismissed his correction. "Please answer the question. Remember, you are under oath."

"Under oath … what are you talking about?" Braxton stammered.

"And is it true, Mr. Member of the LSD Church, that your congregation practices polygamy, a practice that is illegal in the United States of America?" Amber fired at Braxton.

"The Church of LDS stopped practicing polygamy in 1890 when the Lord inspired Church President Wilford Woodruff to make the decree," Braxton said in defense.

In the kitchen, Tim had halted preparing dinner to more clearly eavesdrop on the carnage and search the Internet on his phone for damning information about Mormons. He was indifferent to Mormonism, but he might be able to win points with his wife by making an appearance in the living room to assist her with facts, if timing served right. So, upon hearing the last remark about polygamy, he seized his opportunity and popped into the living room. Tim addressed his wife, "I have something here regarding Mormons and polygamy and ask to approach the bench, if I may."

Amber flashed a quick smile at Tim, the first smile she had given him all day. She turned to the two boys on the couch and said, "Let me direct your attention to an expert on the matter of Internet searches, Dr. Lindeman."

The boys were bewildered by the man that seemingly popped out of nowhere, and the general fact that they appeared to have teleported into some kind of courtroom predicament.

Tim looked down at his phone and read, "Mormons only—"

"LDS!" Kyler shouted.

Tim looked up from his phone and spoke to the boy, "Uh, no thanks. I don't do acid. As I was saying," he looked back down at his phone, "Mormons only ceased practicing polygamy in 1890 from government pressure. The United States refused to give Utah statehood unless polygamy was abolished and monogamy was adopted by the Mormon people. There is no record of the Lord inspiring anyone to move to a stance of monogamy." Then he addressed his wife, "May I step down?"

"Yes, you may. Thank you for taking time out of your busy schedule to make an appearance." Amber directed her attention toward a cabinet to the left of the couch where she imagined the jury would be seated, and said, "Let it be known that Dr. Lindeman is a renowned expert on Internet searches regarding Mormonism and the overall nature of the polygamy issue as it pertains to statehood in America. He holds doctorates in Internet searches from Bring 'Em Young & Sodomise 'Em Universities."

Tim gave a half bow and quickly disappeared into the kitchen. He went back to preparing dinner, proudly glowing for being well-received by his wife. He felt a little bad for the Mormon boys, but their door-to-door antics were obtrusive and annoying, so they kind of deserved it.

Kyler, who had remained mostly quiet, piped up at last, "Who the hell was that? There's no Internet search experts, lady."

Braxton quietly chastised Kyler for his choice of diction.

Amber turned around and addressed the TV, "Your Honor, may the jury be instructed to disregard the defendant's last remark?" She paused for a second and then said, "Thank you, your Honor. At this time I would like to call into question the validity of the Book of Mormon." Amber turned to Braxton, "May you give the court a brief summary of the information contained in the book in question?"

Kyler stood up. "This is bullshit. This lady's crazy. She's talking to her TV. Let's get out of here."

Braxton told Kyler, "Lost sheep need our guidance, especially those not right in their mind. Please sit down." Kyler did so, reluctantly.

"I'll rephrase the question. May you tell us very briefly what's contained in the Book of Mormon?" Amber asked again.

"I'll do my best," said Braxton. "According to the Book of Mormon, some Jews came to America around 600 B.C. to avoid persecution in Jerusalem. They divided into two groups, the Nephites and the Lamanites, and fought each other. After His crucifixion and resurrection, Jesus Christ appeared in America to preach to the Nephites, the righteous group of Jews. In A.D. 428, the righteous Nephites were defeated. For this, and their rejection of Christ's teachings, God cursed the Lamanites with dark skin and a degraded existence. God decreed that the Lamanites would not reclaim white skin and a civilized way of life until they accepted Christ's teachings."

"Would it be fair to say that your god prefers white-skinned people, and thinks dark skin is unholy? Is your god a member of the Ku Klux Klan, a group commonly known as the KKK?"

Kyler shouted, "How dare you call our God a KKK member!"

Meanwhile, on the second floor of the house, Raymond was glued to his laptop, completely oblivious to the proceedings taking place under his bedroom. He was playing *Random Killings: The Ultimate Hobby.* The pool of saliva on the carpet under Raymond's drooling, gaping mouth grew wetter and wider as his laptop blurted out praise and instructions, "Triple kill! You have become more proficient at the hobby of killing. Practice your hobby further and gain more experience points to reach round ten. Make sure it's random; don't think too much about it and use random items as weapons to butcher people with. It's a hobby other people are just dying to watch you excel at. Keep up the good work."

Back in the living room, the courtroom drama continued, unabated.

In response to Kyler's outburst Amber said, "I'll rephrase the question. Is your god racist?"

Before either of the boys could answer, Tim popped back into the living room with his phone. "May I address the court?"

"Let me direct your attention to Dr. Lindeman, the expert Internet searcher regarding Mormonism." Amber motioned for Tim to take the floor. "You may proceed, Dr. Lindeman."

"Thank you." Tim looked down at his phone. "The Lamanites the defendant spoke of—the Lamanites depicted in the Book of Mormon—are the present-day Native Americans. Native American activist groups have expressed their dismay against Mormonism for depicting Native Americans as cursed, living a degraded existence, and possessing an inferior skin color. Some LDS Church leaders even stated that Native Americans' skin would turn lighter if they grew closer to God and assimilated to white LDS members' way of life. Regarding these matters, Native Americans have sued the Mormon Church."

Being completely surprised and shocked by this information, Amber temporarily fell out of character. "Really? The Native Americans—is that true, Tim?" She caught herself and snapped back into character. "I mean, thank you, Dr. Lindeman. You may step down from the bench."

Tim hustled back into the kitchen.

Kyler sharply turned to Braxton. "Is that information about the Native Americans true?" he asked with an astonished look on his face. Kyler was fond of the Native Americans and their connection to the Earth. He even had a poster on his bedroom wall of a quote and image of Chief Sealth, the Native American chief the city of Seattle was named after.

Braxton looked down at the floor, almost in shame. "Yes, that's true."

Amber resumed pacing back and forth in front of the couch. "The exhibit our expert witness has given will be accepted into evidence." The information regarding the Native Americans in Mormonism was equivalent to a jury hearing several eyewitnesses stating that they saw the murderer doing the killing in a murder trial. She didn't even need to dip into her arsenal of religious facts to put this case in the bag. She crossed her arms and got ready to finish the case. The thrill of winning had alleviated her foul mood. And Tim's appearances as an expert witness had been crucial to her case, she noted. She'd make sure he was rewarded for helping out.

In order to make sure she wasn't alienating any fans of Jesus in the imaginary jury box, she decided to express some positive information about Jesus. Not that she cared one way or the other about Jesus or any religion he might be associated with, but purely for getting in good favor with the jurors that might be religious. "At this time I would like to make it clear to the living room—I mean court—that the person being indirectly brought up often here in this case, Jesus, shouldn't be directly associated with the creation and failure of Mormonism or any other religion. Jesus isn't on trial here. In fact, I encourage the jury and the attendees in this courtroom today to pursue his teachings through an unadulterated source, like that of the Essenes who wrote the Dead Sea Scrolls. Jesus was a wise, enlightened individual. If he wasn't, his teachings wouldn't have stood the test of time."

On that last note, Braxton's devout composure started to show signs of deterioration. "The Bible is *the* Holy Scripture. Its validity should never be questioned."

Once again, Tim suddenly appeared in the living room with his phone. "May I approach the bench to address more evidence I have expertly acquired during one of my professional browsing sessions?"

"We're going to be wrapping it up for a recess soon, Dr. Lindeman, so please make it brief." Then Amber winked at Tim. "The court is in your debt for all the valuable expert evidence you've brought forward today."

Before Tim was able to dictate the material on his phone, Kyler yelled, "Who the hell is this guy?! Quit popping your dumbass head into this room, holding that phone like its crucial evidence."

"Order in the living room!" Amber commanded. "Show some restraint, defendant! Don't turn this living room into a circus."

"Are you serious?!" Kyler replied. "It was a circus the moment you opened your trap and started talking to TVs and addressing random furniture throughout the room."

"I won't hesitate to hold you in contempt, sir." Amber snapped. "Show some respect to this living room and to our expert witness." Amber turned to Tim. "Dr. Lindeman, you have the floor."

Tim looked down at his phone and read, "Historical fact dictates that in A.D. 325 a council was convened by order of Roman Emperor Constantine the Great. The Council of Nicaea's purpose was to unite the cult *Sol Invictus* (Invincible Sun)—which Constantine was a leader in—with Christianity in order to form the Universal Church of Rome. Many changes to the religion of Christianity took place at that council. The two biggest being: A massive revision by changing verses and important words in the Bible, and eliminating certain verses and whole books from the Bible. The two notable teachings from Jesus that were altered at the Council of Nicaea were: heaven and hell were created and every reference to reincarnation was omitted. This created huge ramifications that degraded some of the fundamental ideas of what Jesus taught. Political reasons and civil control were at the heart of these adaptations and reorganization."

Then Tim added, "This next part is not considered historical fact, but mystical groups that claim to hold the unadulterated teachings of enlightened beings like Jesus,

Buddha, Muhammad, Krishna, et al., say it's paramount to convey that the most important fundamental idea that Jesus taught was altered by the Christian Church even before the Council of Nicaea. Jesus said people would be able to do everything he could do and greater, which signified that anyone devoted and unwavering enough could become as enlightened as Jesus was. Maybe not in one incarnation, but attainable at some point. When the Church made Jesus God's only son—and part of the Holy Trinity—they consequently took away the power of the people and made them forever grovel before a doctrine, never being worthy of attaining transcendence themselves. It was a huge slap in the face of Jesus's teachings. It directly went against what Jesus had taught his disciples. In doing this, the Church deified Jesus. In fact, it was common practice for the elites to hijack religions in order to scramble, twist, omit, and completely flip ascended masters' teachings in order to keep the populace controlled."

Kyler yelled, "I hate this guy and his phone! I'm going to grab his fucking phone and beat him with it, beat the teachings of the Lord our Savoir into his thick skull and make him prostrate before the Lord."

Braxton didn't restrain or chastise Kyler since he was also angered by what Tim had said about Jesus. He ignored his partner's rant and directed his own shaming words at Tim. "How dare you call Jesus a mere mortal!"

"These mystical groups say how dare you for incorrectly interpreting Jesus's teachings," Tim calmly replied, as he had no personal opinion on the matter and was simply assisting his wife for brownie points.

Kyler sprang from the couch and yelled at Tim again, "I'm going to force that phone down your throat, Dr. Dickhead!"

"That's it!" Amber yelled in a theatrical manner as opposed to expressing real anger. "This living room finds you in contempt!" Amber turned to a random piece of furniture in the living room she hadn't addressed yet. "Bailiff, restrain the defendants and escort them out of the living room immediately."

Kyler strode over to the piece of furniture that Amber had addressed as the bailiff—a small end table—and started pummeling it with his fists while shouting, "You will not restrain a missionary of the Lord!" After the boy had pummeled the end table into pieces, fists bloody, he began stomping on the remains while yelling, "The Lord's work is never finished!"

Tim said, "I'm sure the *Lord* wouldn't approve of you obliterating our end table."

"The Lord works in mysterious ways," said Kyler while continuing to jump on the remains of the end table.

Amber turned toward the cabinet that represented the jury. "The evidence is overwhelming. Not only have you heard many pieces of information discrediting the defendants' views and beliefs, but they have murdered a bailiff right before your very eyes. As jurors you're not to be swayed by sympathy, but you should know that the bailiff leaves behind a loving wife and two—"

Kyler interrupted Amber while still jumping on the remnants of the end table. "Members of the jury, you're instructed to disregard this nutcase lady and her phone-toting husband, or whoever this dickhead who pops in from another room is."

Instead of finishing her interrupted sentence, Amber said, "Do you wish to say anything before sentence is imposed?"

Kyler fully immersed himself into the courtroom scenario that Amber had created. In Amber's courtroom jargon, he replied, "I would like to direct the court's attention to the end table that I have obliterated in the name of the Lord. I'm an instrument of the Lord and I do His bidding. Furthermore, I move to strike this nutcase lady." The boy advanced toward Amber with a massive scowl on his face, fists clenched, ready to physically strike rather than merely striking verbiage from a court's transcript.

Amber took on a defensive stance as the boy came at her. She remained tranquil and said, "No objection, your Honor. Let the defendant proceed."

Tim's first response was to protect his wife against physical assault, but she appeared to be relishing the fact that the missionary boy had given into violence rather than saintly behavior. Also, she had taken many self-defense classes and was quite fit due to her regular workout routine; she was more muscular than the boy. He also predicted that she might hold it against him if he intervened, chastising him about equality of the sexes and the females' ability to protect themselves instead of always needing a male figure to safeguard them. He didn't want all his newly acquired brownie points to be erased in one fell swoop, so he took a step back and waited for Amber to hopefully throw the boy to the floor. Tim clenched his teeth and watched the distance between Amber and the young boy become shorter and shorter.

Braxton extended an arm, gesturing for Kyler to stop. He was angry at Amber as well but knew that violence wasn't the correct way to solve anything. Also, the Church would unequivocally frown upon them walloping someone. But he wasn't close enough to reach his partner, and Kyler was moving too fast to be stopped.

While scowling, the ends of Kyler's mouth undulated. The minuscule amount of muscle the boy possessed quivered in rage. His legs and arms pumped back and forth as he closed the gap between himself and Amber.

Right before the moment of collision, Tim saw that the boy chose to bum-rush Amber instead of going for a punch. Just when Tim thought Amber might not be trained for bum-rushing, she got down on one knee, pivoted slightly to one side, and used all her thigh, torso, and arm strength, as well as the boy's own velocity, to catapult him over her shoulder and into the wall behind her.

Kyler's raging face instantly turned into a frantic, wide-eyed expression as he sailed over Amber's shoulder and through the air upside-down with both arms flailing, hopelessly seeking to regain equilibrium.

The boy hit the wall flush against his back, producing a loud *thud*, and a split second afterward his head followed suit and also struck the wall.

A feeling of relief washed over Tim. He exhaled deeply and wiped his forehead. *Thank God that boy got his ass handed to him.*

After hitting the wall the boy crashed to the floor, the top of his head taking the brunt of the fall, and then his stomach taking a pounding as his body flopped onto the floor.

Lying on the floor like a stunned insect, the boy found it hard to breathe after having the wind knocked out of him. He began dry heaving as his stomach voiced its displeasure. Then the heaving was no longer dry; a thick stream of vomit ejected from his mouth onto the carpet. The vomitus consisted entirely of pieces of McDonald's Chicken McNuggets and sweet 'n sour dipping sauce.

The Mormon boys had a McNugget eating contest before embarking on their door-to-door missionary work for the day. Today was their ninth eating contest and Kyler had finally won. He had scarfed down 166 McNuggets and walked away the champion, moaning and staggering. Braxton had been distraught about losing for the first time, and for a moment was elated when Kyler almost threw up in McDonald's after quickly lifting his arms in a celebratory fashion.

It had been agreed that anyone who threw up automatically lost. Kyler had lost on their second challenge after vomiting: While stumbling toward the McDonald's exit after downing 174 McNuggets for the win, he had hurled all over a family's meal before making it to the exit. Directly after the family had sat down to enjoy their Big Mac meals, smiles on their faces turned into shock, and then steaming anger. Nothing tops a fast-food connoisseur's anger when they're thwarted from enjoying their heavily processed, addicting meal.

The hurling had turned the victory over to Braxton and he pranced around doing a little victory dance as Kyler was getting barked at by the family with vomitus on their food and hands. As vomitus dripped from his lips, Kyler repeated, "May the Lord forgive me for ruining your Big Macs," several times in his food-coma state.

Tim and Amber were completely confused when Braxton started victory dancing in their living room while his partner was upchucking all over the carpet.

"You know what that means?" said Braxton with glee as he two-stepped back and forth. "I've won nine times in a row. Boom!"

They may have been missionaries, passionate about going door to door to spread the Word, but they were still young boys steeped in the joys of adolescence.

Kyler, half-conscious, started pleading to the chewed-up McNuggets that were now vomitus on the carpet. "No, please don't leave me. We finally were victorious. Please come back." In a confused daze, Kyler began scooping the vomitus up with his hands and putting it back into his mouth to regain his victory.

Braxton pointed at him. "No, you can't do that. Once it's out, it's out. You lost. You can't regain your victory by eating vomit. The contest is about eating McNuggets, not vomit that used to be McNuggets."

Kyler begged, "It's not vomit. It's just chewed up McNuggets that wanted to rest on a fluffy carpet for a while before returning to my stomach. I'm still the winner."

"Nope. That's not how it works. You lost. Just accept it. You ate more than you could stomach. My dream of ten wins in a row is still alive."

"No, no, no!" Kyler stopped scooping up his vomitus, stood up quite quickly, and wobbled over to Braxton. "There needs to be a clause added to the rules about psycho ladies. If a psycho lady throws the winner against a wall, causing him to spew up his McNuggets, he should retain the victory.

It's not the winner's fault that there are psycho ladies out there just waiting to throw winners against walls."

Astounded, Tim and Amber glanced at each other to validate that what they were witnessing wasn't an illusion, and then quickly turned back to the intriguing theatrical production in their living room. The boys were so wrapped up in their argument that they had temporarily forgotten about Tim and Amber and their missionary work.

"Shall I make some popcorn for the Mormon show?" Tim asked his wife.

"You might miss the climax of the show while you're away," she replied. "Best to enjoy it while it lasts."

"But if it continues for too long, we'll have to kick them out because dinner is waiting in the kitchen. I finished it while you were tearing apart their religion."

"Right," Amber agreed, never taking her attention off the boys.

Kyler's nausea suddenly returned. He gripped his stomach. He had stood up too quickly and was now starting to feel the effects. While standing directly in front of Braxton, engaged in debate, his mouth bulged with vomit, but he tried his hardest to contain it, to stop it from exiting his body. He stared at Braxton with protruding eyes, attempting to convey a warning about the McNuggets that would soon make their exodus.

Like a greedy king, Kyler tried to hold them back, but the McNuggets had found their Moses and were demanding an exodus of their kind from his wretched stomach. And it didn't help that they had to mingle and exist in an enclosed space—Kyler's stomach—with Sweet 'n Sour, their archrival. Now, if the boy had chosen Spicy Buffalo, Hot Mustard, or Tangy BBQ dipping sauce, they might have been able to negotiate a deal, a compromise: perhaps diarrhea or a stomachache so he could remain the champion. But as it stood, the Moses McNugget would offer no olive branch to the boy for his greedy actions of devouring so many of his McNugget people—the chosen people—and forcing them to dwell with the two-faced beast known as Sweet 'n Sour. The Moses

McNugget would wait no longer. He refused to endure the slavery and the torturous exposure to gastric acid the villainous boy-king had subjected his people to. The time for evacuation was now at hand. Led by the Moses McNugget, staff held high and waving back and forth like he was parting the Red Sea.

Unable to repress the chunky flow, Kyler's mouth was forced open and a thick stream of acidic mush made its sudden trajectory toward Braxton, who was still directly in front of Kyler, having failed to understand Kyler's silent warning.

Braxton's eyes widened in shock and instantly took the first brunt of the spraying attack from the escaping McNuggets, which stung and blinded him. He instinctively turned from the attack and attempted to flee, but ended up blindly running headfirst into the wall directly behind him. *Whack!*

After the nasty impact, Braxton fell backward onto the floor, lying unconscious as the stream of vomit from Kyler's mouth continued to drench his body. Kyler was too distraught to even turn in a different direction to save his partner from being immersed in soupy chunks.

Transfixed, Tim and Amber gawked at the sensational spectacle that would be imprinted in their minds for the rest of their lives.

The stream didn't subside until the fearless McNugget leader had shown the way out of the wicked kingdom. This exodus seemed to last a good five to ten seconds. The pursuing Sweet 'n Sour sauce made its way up the esophagus in anger, trying to catch up and regain ownership of the McNuggets. But it was too late. The flailing Sweet 'n Sour sauce was sucked back down the esophagus when Kyler closed his mouth.

In the aftermath, Braxton was utterly saturated in glistening vomitus. It shimmered and danced upon his passed-out body while the chosen McNuggets rested, relaxed, and kicked-back in a land flowing with pasteurized, homogenized milk and sugar-syrup honey (i.e., Braxton's face). An adulterated land promised by a wrathful god from the Old

Testament, or more like a wrathful extraterrestrial from the Old Testament.

After Kyler had recovered from hurling, it dawned on him that his partner would drown in vomitus if it wasn't cleared from his breathing orifices. So he expeditiously kneeled down and removed the abhorrent-smelling slime from his partner's nose and mouth while pleading to God, "Please Lord, save him from my McNugget vomit. I'll gladly relinquish my victory if you let him live."

Braxton showed no signs of life as he simmered in his partner's vomitus.

Kyler's emotions turned to total vexation. He repeatedly slapped his partner's face while shouting, "The Lord commands you to rise and finish your missionary work. There are too many heathens in need of converting to lay motionless in a pool of McNugget discharge. In the name of our Lord and Savior, rise and become productive again!"

Tim cringed as each slap flung bits of vomitus about the living room. "This is going to take a lot of effort to clean up, and it'll probably take forever to expel this repugnant stench."

The Mormon visit had somehow turned into something that resembled an exorcism: one boy lying unconscious while the other slapped him and shouted biblical phrases. After one of the slaps Braxton came to and started coughing up the vomitus that had ran down his facial orifices.

Kyler lifted his arms in the air. "Praise the Lord. You have returned to do His good works! In your resurrection maybe the Lord has bequeathed you with supernatural abilities that will allow you to scatter the heathens from the face of the Earth!"

"Are we in Disneyland?" Braxton mumbled.

"What? … No, we're in some heathen's living room trying to spread the Good Word of our Savior," Kyler explained. Then he turned his head and stared at Amber while still talking to Braxton, "But the Word has failed to have an effect this time around, and we're having trouble with a physically fit, menstruating woman from hell who's trying to use her abnormally hard living-room walls to destroy us. To top it off, this same hellish woman has conversed with random furniture throughout her demonic house, as well as a phone-toting underling that randomly pops into rooms in an ungodly plot to renounce our religion."

Amber rolled her eyes.

Still senseless, Braxton unintelligibly mumbled something about pirates and fairies and proceeded to sing the lyrics to "It's a Small World After All."

"Thank god he's all right," Amber said with minimal amount of emotion. "You may leave now. And don't forget to bring your heavily altered and fabricated biblical-brainwashing books with you."

Kyler hissed at Amber, "Don't you dare utter the name of God from your filthy lips! The *Lord* will judge you on His second coming when He descends to Jackson County, Missouri."

"And why is Jackson County, Missouri, going to be the first destination on Jesus's itinerary?" Amber asked, apathetic toward the answer yet still minutely curious what answer the boy would spit out.

"If you were privy to the contents of the Book of Mormon, you'd know that Jackson County, Missouri, is the location of the Garden of Eden."

"You better get your facts straight, boy," Amber replied. "The Garden of Eden was located in modern-day Turkey, Iraq, or somewhere in Persia. Maybe even Australia. Archaeologists aren't certain on its exact whereabouts, but they're goddamn certain that it wasn't in America."

"Don't take the Lord's name in vain, you succubus! The Lord shall judge you. Yahweh proclaims your banishment from all the heavenly realms!" Kyler shrieked.

"No-weh," Amber comically replied. "Now off with you, shrieking boy, before I have my unusually hard living-room walls attack you again. We have supper to eat."

"Have you no decency. We've got a man down," Kyler said, gesturing toward his partner who was still incoherently murmuring Disneyland-ride lyrics.

"Like I said, we got supper to eat. Either your partner walks out of here of his own volition or you drag him out." Then she added, "You're lucky I won't be pursuing a civil suit against your vomiting vandalism."

Kyler quickly placed the Bible and the Book of Mormon back in his backpack and began dragging his partner by the backside of his collar through the front door that Tim was holding open for them.

Tim kept the door open and watched Kyler drag Braxton down the stoop and along the path through the front yard. They only made it halfway to the hinged gate where their Huffy bikes lay before the neighbor's naughty kids started pelting them with cherry tomatoes and yelling obscenities, "Paint those morons red!" "Tag those fags!" "Liquidate their monkey-suit-wearing asses ..."

The fence that surrounded the Lindemans' front yard was only about three feet tall. It was more like a property marker than a means of privacy, so it wasn't a barrier that hindered the kids next door from harassing the Mormon boys. They were completely exposed to enemy fire and had already been badly wounded before unknowingly stepping into a front yard that was now a battlefield.

Hearing the commotion, Amber moseyed on over to the front door where Tim stood watching the Mormons attempting to escape their yard. "Looks like their god has abandoned them," Amber jested. "They're now bait for those bastard GMO kids."

Amber and Tim called the Riley kids next door the GMO kids because their diet consisted mostly of GMO foods due to their mother's lack of finances. When they weren't eating GMOs, they were eating other cheap, highly processed food.

They stood in their doorway and enjoyed the new show that had developed in their front yard. The neighbor's annoying kids were doing something useful for a change: giving them a second act of entertainment to savor, an act they weren't a part of this time and could enjoy more leisurely.

"Dinner can wait a bit. Let's enjoy this show," Amber told Tim.

Kyler's pace had slowed considerably due to the latest obstacle of thrown cherry tomatoes. Braxton continued to be a deadweight-burden. His eyes were half-open, but he was still mentally in Disneyland.

"This calls for evasive action," Kyler told his dazed partner. He grabbed his Mormon-issued walkie-talkie out of his Mormon-issued backpack to radio for help. "Mormon Command, Mormon Command, this is Lunchbox 3! Over!"

A crackly voice replied over the walkie-talkie, "Lunchbox 3, this is Mormon Command. What's your situation? Over."

"We have contact. We're currently in tactical retrograde and need airstrike and medevac! Contact report over!"

"Roger, Lunchbox 3. Send over."

"Contact from enemy forces grid: 436 852. I repeat: 436 852. Over!"

"Roger. What's your 20? Over."

"Enemies 3, direction north of my grid at 50 meters!"

"Roger. Over."

"Small arms fire & IDF requesting airstrike! Over!"

"Roger. Secure your location and wait out."

Kyler tried his best to shield the incoming rapid fire of GMO cherry tomatoes as he lugged his partner to a nearby bush for cover. Both boys had been hit several times but none of their primary organs had been jeopardized.

"Hang in there, partner. The Lord will see us through this. Don't you give up on me. Don't give up on me, *you hear me*?" Kyler pleaded to his unresponsive partner. He painstakingly trudged the short distance to the bush, dragging Braxton with the little amount of strength he had left after their previous battle in the cursed living room. He laid his partner behind the bush and ducked down for cover, concealing as much of his body as possible while panting hard.

Tim and Amber were still at their front door, thoroughly enjoying the unfolding drama.

"This could get really interesting," Amber said.

"Yeah," agreed Tim, "and when action involves the GMO kids, you never know what ridiculously amusing events might occur. Remember that time they got in a fist fight with the mailman because their plastic superhero rings weren't delivered on the day they were expecting them? They ended up arriving the next day, after the mailman had already been pummeled and had to wear a few facial shiners for a week. I don't think a superhero is supposed to beat the shit out of their mailman. Seems like a super-dick move to me."

Amber added an event that she recalled. "Or that time they caught squirrels with homemade traps and cooked them over a campfire because their mother ran out of food for a couple of days."

They fell silent and continued eyeballing the show with *Mona Lisa*-like half smiles.

The three GMO kids had reloaded and returned to full-firing capacity. GMO tomato after GMO tomato peppered the battlefield. They shouted phrases and sentences at each other to keep their unit's morale high. "Cherry their asses." "Get some." "I ate their god for breakfast." "Turn those morons into minced meat …"

The GMO kids maneuvered to a different angle where Braxton's head was exposed, barely poking out beyond the bush. The kids excitedly jostled for the best position, trying to secure the spot behind the fence that would provide the clearest and truest angle to the newly exposed Mormon's head.

Kyler tried soothing his fallen partner with encouraging words. "That airstrike is coming any moment. Mormon Command will send down lightning bolts from God to decimate those savages. Hang in there, partner. This ain't over. I'm gonna get you outta here alive."

All of a sudden Braxton's head started getting peppered with countless GMO tomatoes. *Pitter-patter, whack, pitter-patter.* The GMO tomatoes hitting their mark, one after another, could be heard across the front-yard battlefield.

"Oh yeah!" Bobby yelled with glee. "We're lighting up his goddamn face." At fifteen, Bobby was the oldest of the GMO kids. Despite being quite plump, he was unusually strong for a fifteen year old, and he had the meatiest fists in the neighborhood.

"Pepper his goddamn face till it opens up real nice like," shouted Nash, the second oldest GMO kid at the age of thirteen.

Kyler's training kicked in. He instinctively tugged his fallen partner clear of the deadly territory, making sure Braxton's now red-stained head was safe behind the bush.

The GMO kids triumphantly jumped in the air and heckled the Mormons. "Suck on that, moron." "God says eat your vegetables instead of wearing them, you dumbfuck."

Tim hollered at Bobby, "Tomatoes are fruit, not vegetables, Bobby. Make your taunts correct so they're more effective!"

"Shut your trap, Mr. Linderloser, or we'll direct our forces at your dumbass and have our way with that whore you call a wife."

Tim opened his mouth in preparation to verbally defend his wife's honor, but was silenced before uttering a word when Amber gripped his forearm and whispered to him, "It'll be best to not make this a third-party altercation. Let those little bastards keep their focus on the wounded Mormons."

Kyler's Mormon-issued walkie-talkie began crackling, "Lunchbox 3, Lunchbox 3, this is Mormon Command. Over."

"Mormon Command, this is Lunchbox 3. Still waiting out. Over."

"Uhhh … Airstrike is not a go due to weather conditions. I repeat, airstrike is not a go. Can you avoid contact and make it to the LZ? Over."

"Whiskey, Tango, Foxtrot!"

"Hey, Lunchbox 3, keep it clean. You're a member of the LDS Church for God's sake. Over."

"Sorry, Mormon Command. Can't avoid contact. Requesting ground units for assisted extraction! I say again, requesting extraction!"

"Extraction is a go. Four ground units will rendezvous at your location, neutralize threat, and extract you to the LZ. Hold tight, Lunchbox 3. Over."

"Roger that. Over and out!"

The GMO kids continued maneuvering around their yard behind the short fence, trying to make each shot count, thoroughly enjoying Mormon target practice until they ran out of ammo.

"Oh, man. No more tomatoes," said Bobby. "Let's go inside and play videogames."

"Screw that. I'm gonna kick their heads," growled Nash as he sprang over the short fence, clawing his way up and over it like a feral dog chasing a cat.

Bobby looked at Mash, the youngest brother, and shrugged his shoulders. "Sounds good to me. Let's get 'em."

They both followed suit over the fence and sprinted toward the wounded Mormons. Scaling a short fence and running for a mere two seconds had already tired the GMO kids. Their daily routine of eating poisonous food and mashing buttons on their videogame controllers made it clear that only their fingers were fit, while the rest of their bodies screamed in agony at the sudden exertion. They huffed and puffed their way to the wounded Mormons, worn out, but a gleaming excitement could still be seen in their eager eyes in the anticipation of a good ass-whooping.

Kyler cautiously peeped over the bush to spot the cause of the ruckus. The first thing he saw was Bobby's fat face, followed by Bobby's meaty arms that grabbed ahold of his neck, causing them both to tumble to the ground and struggle for the upper hand.

Braxton was still lying on the ground dazed, but was slowly coming to his senses from the commotion. In his peripheral vision he noticed two kids quickly approaching. "Excuse me kids, do you have a moment to talk about our Lord and Savior, Jesus Christ?" he muttered like a broken automaton.

"Fuck him up double team style," Nash instructed Mash and began repeatedly kicking Braxton's head while Mash kicked the side of his ribcage. "Do you have a moment to get the shit kicked out of you?" jested Nash as he continued to boot the Mormon's head.

Kyler, who was now in a headlock applied by Bobby, thought all hope was lost as he slipped closer and closer to unconsciousness from the loss of oxygen. As he faded, he looked over and saw his partner being persistently kicked like a rag doll by two crazed, excited kids.

A flickering glint of sunlight blinded Nash and abruptly caused him to stop kicking Braxton's head. Mash also stopped kicking the Mormon's ribcage to look in the direction of the flashing light to see what had temporarily blinded his brother.

It was the sun reflecting off several silver Huffy bikes racing toward them in a V-shaped formation. There were eight bikes in total, which meant four Mormon ground units (two Mormons comprised one unit). As they advanced toward the battle the GMO kids could hear their war cries, or rather, war song. "Oh come all ye faithful, joyful and triumphant. Oh come let us adore Him, oh come let us adore Him in Christ the Lord."

"Incoming morons!" yelled Nash, warning his brothers.

Bobby released Kyler from his headlock and threw him to the ground. While scowling at the incoming Mormons he rolled up his sleeves in preparation to face a tussle that just got real. No more easy pickings. Now his legendary meaty fists could show their true worth. "How dare they roll up on our turf, singing moronic songs no less. These two morons have been bested. Direct your attention to the fresh-moron meat, my brothers. Leave no moron standing. And no matter what happens, don't let them slip into our house to jabber their religious nonsense to Oversized Marge or she'll eat us alive for sure."

Oversized Marge, Large Marge, Hefty Marge, or something of the sort, were titles they had lovingly bestowed upon their obese mother who continuously ate fried chicken in front of the TV and never missed an opportunity to abuse her kids. Her abuse was almost always verbal since her substantial chunkiness didn't afford her the opportunity to ever lay a hand on her kids. Their father, who had never married their mother, took off years ago, abandoning them in a slowly deteriorating house, a small house that was considered the black sheep of the neighborhood because it was the only residence that wasn't appraised at a value of at least three-quarters of a million dollars. Nobody in the neighborhood had a clue as to how a dump of a house could've weaseled its way into their upper-middleclass community, or how its owners were able to pay their property tax alone.

Once, a friendly couple new to the neighborhood had brought an organic apple pie to Oversized Marge's door as a peace offering and had tried to explain the concept of depreciating house values in their neighborhood due to her house's dilapidation and her yard's abandonment. Oversized Marge had responded by snatching the pie from their hands and threatened to eat them instead of the dessert if they didn't shut up, mind their own business, and beat it. The affable couple naturally fled and never returned. The pie, however, was well received because most of Oversized Marge's income went to property tax and the utilities bill. Only a small amount would remain to pay for cheap, highly processed food or GMO food that filled their family's stomachs and was hastily lowering their IQs and deteriorating their bodies and its organs' abilities to function properly. They'd soon be additional customers the pharmaceutical company would gladly take under its wing and help unburden the State from paying out Social Security, as they'd surely expire before making it to the age to collect.

Scientists could look upon the Riley kids as the perfect experiment to demonstrate what becomes of a kid growing up on a mostly GMO diet.

Amber had represented the largest GMO-making company in one of her cases, so she had become knowledgeable about GMOs and their effects upon the human body. She knew that bad parenting was only a small part in why the GMO kids had turned out so vicious and edgy. She'd be surprised if they even made it past thirty years of age before succumbing to cancer and the myriad other ailments and diseases that would assist cancer in finishing them off.

The arriving Mormons tossed their bikes on the ground and quickly made their way through the Lindemans' gate. Neatly pressed white dress shirts and slim black ties worn by boys that fought on the side of the Lord filed into the yard. They took off their backpacks and wielded them as weapons, crazily swinging them at the GMO kids.

Bobby's meaty fist made contact with the face of the first approaching Mormon, laying him flat on his back and putting him temporarily out of commission, stars twirling around his head.

Nash screamed at Bobby while dodging swinging backpacks. "Call in the dogs! We're outnumbered!"

Bobby reached into his jeans pocket and produced a whistle. He puffed up his chest and blew as hard as he could into it. A high-pitched sound sailed through the air.

Two bulldogs immediately crashed through the Lindemans' fence, flinging wood shrapnel into the face of one of the Mormons, leaving another one out of commission. "My eyes. Good Lord, my eyes!" Each bulldog chose a Mormon and viciously gnawed on their legs, which took two additional Mormons out of the fight.

"They've unleashed the hounds of hell. God help us," mumbled Kyler as he lay on the ground still recovering from Bobby's brutal headlock.

The four remaining Mormons pooled their efforts to succeed in the extraction process: two of them wielded their backpacks at Nash and Mash, the biggest one took on Bobby, and the last one helped the wounded Mormons that weren't being chewed upon by the dogs back to their bikes.

Desperately trying to regain the upper hand, Bobby threw a volley of punches at his Mormon opponent. One of them landed with force: a Mike Tyson-like uppercut shot to the chin that temporarily dazed and sent his opponent staggering backward, but not falling to the ground. Bobby knew he was up against a formidable opponent this time because his opponents would normally collapse to the ground after receiving such a substantial blow.

The Mormon quickly reclaimed his footing and wits. "You've left me no choice, heathen. Now you'll feel the wrath of the Saints, the Latter-day Saints, not the decrepit relics from ancient times depicted in the Bible." He unzipped his backpack and produced the Book of Mormon, a special limited-edition silver-bound copy. A shaft of sunlight broke through the overcast sky and illuminated the holy item. It gleamed in the sunlight as the Mormon brandished it, swinging it left and right in a warming-up manner while chanting, "I invoke the wrath of God. Let me be the cleansing rod. To the bottom of the ocean, he'll swim with cod. Hellfire upon him, he'll be reduced to clod."

For the first time in all of his numerous tussles, Bobby felt fear. He tried his hardest to cover up this fear by expressing an even bigger scowl and vocalizing taunts. "The only place your moronic book of bullshit is going to end up … in your ass. I'm confident it'll fit up there because you've been sodomized by your church's elders throughout your boyhood days of gaydom."

"The work of the Lord steamrolls effortlessly over immature taunts," the approaching Mormon stated. "I'll give you one last chance to repent, heathen. Prostrate before the Lord, beg for forgiveness, and be on your way, or be banished by the Sacred Book that shineth in your hedonistic face."

"Your bullshit book won't shineth when it's up your ass covered in your own fucking feces. I'll give *you* one last chance to revoke your false god, ride away on your little fuckin' Huffy bike, and pawn off your bullshit book for some big bucks so your mom can stop whoring herself out to random sailors and traveling carnies. The ball's in your court, moron."

The Mormon flashed a devious smile and gingerly made his way closer to the heathen that kept barking taunts at him. "Some people will never heed the Word. In these cases the only action that remains is beating the Word into them by force, a holy brandishing, if you will."

"I will not!" shouted Bobby.

The Mormon took a sudden step forward, shifted his weight, and swiftly brought the Sacred Book up to Bobby's face like a baseball-player powerhouse smashing a ball—Bobby's head being the awestruck ball. Bobby was instantly rendered unconscious and slumped to the ground like a sack of potatoes, meaty fists and all, creating a loud thudding noise that carried throughout the battlefield and alerted his brothers and the hounds from hell.

Discovering that the whistle-bearer had succumbed, the hounds of hell opened their jaws to release their captives and retreated back to their dilapidated dog houses on the other side of the fence. Nash and Mash lost their morale and took several backpack swings to the face before cowering on the ground to escape further blows.

Presuming the Lord's work was done, the Mormons finalized the extraction process they had been summoned to perform: helping every last Mormon back to their bikes so they might live to spread the Word another day. Two of the Mormons hadn't adequately recovered to operate their bikes, so they held on to the backs of their brethren, leaving two of their bikes behind.

Before they pedaled away from the battle scene, the Mormon who had brandished the Sacred Book lifted his arms in the air and declared, "We leave these grounds victorious but with sad hearts for those who failed to convert and bask in our Lord's light. But if we are summoned once more to your quarters, it won't be for conversion, but to cleanse the earth of your hedonistic filth. When that wrath is directed toward you, only then will you know the *true Lord* when vengeance is exacted upon you!"

The Mormons raced down the street on their bikes, eager to continue the Lord's work, some wounded, some covered with vomitus. Their silhouettes rapidly faded as they darted toward the sunset like Greek chariots leaving a battlefield of strewn out Persian soldiers in their wake.

Nash and Mash hobbled over to their fallen big brother. They poked and prodded him with sticks in an attempt to wake him, but Bobby's body didn't respond.

Mash scratched his head. "Do you think he's dead?"

Nash took his gaze off of Bobby and turned to Mash. "There's no way someone can get killed by a book. Especially a moronic religious book."

"Should we check his pulse or something to make sure he's alive?" asked Mash.

Nash noticed the Huffy bikes the Mormons had left behind and completely ignored his brother's question. "Hey, those morons left some bikes. Maybe we can walk away from this battle with some spoils of war after all." Taken over with excitement, Nash disregarded his backpack-beatings and raced out of the yard toward the bikes. Mash trailed after him.

"Sweet!" shouted Nash. "They left two Huffy bikes. They're basically in mint condition. We've got wheels now, bro! Now we can ride around town and screw with everybody. We'll exact so much havoc on this town that those morons' god will label this area a wasteland and never send his monkey-suit-wearing dumbasses to bother us again."

Nash fondled his new bike while he dreamed of gallivanting around town causing mischief and mayhem. With their new getaway transportation they could steal candy and beer at countless convenience shops and grocery stores. They'd snatch phones out of pedestrians' hands and resell them. Mailbox baseball would have to wait till they acquired four wheels, but for now they had been upgraded to a level-two status of hellions on wheels, which they would milk for all it's worth.

Mash had been quietly staring at Nash, watching his brother's mind reel in thought, practically drooling in delight with a psychotic smile plastered to his face. "What's up, Nash?"

Hearing his brother's question, Nash woke from his reverie. "I'll show you what's up. It all begins now. Come with me, little brother. It's time to put our newfound wheels in motion and start much commotion, no more lonely nights in our bedroom with lotion."

"Whoa. I didn't know you were a poet."

"With these new Huffy bikes anything is possible. We can be anything we want from now on. Let's show 'em who we are." Nash took off, pedaling down the street furiously. With Mash following swiftly behind him they slowly disappeared over the horizon.

"Well, that just happened," Amber stated, still standing by her husband's side, having observed the whole incident from their doorway.

"Did you see that shaft of light come down on that Mormon's book?" Tim asked his wife.

"It was just a temporary break in the clouds. That's all."

"So … what's to be done about the potential dead boy on our lawn?" Tim anxiously asked his wife who knew all the best actions to pursue regarding the law and its possible repercussions.

Amber stared at the motionless boy on their lawn. "He's probably only knocked unconscious and will at some point awaken to stumble off on his own accord. If he's dead, I doubt Large Marge will bother dragging her obese body over here to scrape her dead son off our lawn. I don't even know if she's capable of walking that far before succumbing to gravity. Due to the indifference she holds for her sons, a significant amount of time will most likely pass before she notices his absence. So if he is dead and starts rotting on our lawn, we'll have to take some kind of action to get rid of the carcass to avoid being held liable for having him expire on our property. I doubt Large Marge is intelligent enough to know about such legal matters, but better to be safe than sorry. But I'm sure that brat will regain consciousness any minute now and stumble back to his decaying house. Anyway, dinner is waiting. Let's go."

The Lindemans' front door closed.

Chapter 5

While plugging away creating code at work, Tim couldn't stop thinking about how the inevitable had happened. His wife had finally vocalized her dismay about his stalled career. Since he had always feared it would surface at some point, it didn't come as a surprise, but that didn't mean it wasn't shocking when it had emerged. His fear had become a reality, giving sway to a negative timeline that included a divorce, followed by a lonely existence in a smelly bachelor pad that entailed nightly TV binges while consuming takeaway Chinese food and pizza. In order to secure the positive timeline he still resided in, he would have to unclog the obstacle hindering his career advancement.

Losing his wife was something he couldn't accept. He'd do whatever it took to sustain a coexistence with Amber. She was his everything, his family, his better half.

Action needed to be taken to secure the love of his life by gaining advancement in his career. If he kept being passive, his life had a high probability of heading toward a dead end. If he stayed within justifiable boundaries, he could both solve the problem at hand and not be held karmically liable for participating in any amoral actions. The actions he would take would fall in a gray area. He wouldn't turn to the dark side for ill-gotten gain. No, he would keep his morals intact while simultaneously thriving against the cruel adversities in the world.

As luck would have it, one of the software engineers was due to relocate abroad to one of the company's joined efforts for a startup venture. It was no secret that the vacancy would be filled by an in-house computer programmer with engineering skills. Rumors had been circulating that Brad Taylor was going to be the employee promoted.

Brad was a good-looking, corn-fed American that almost went pro after his college quarterback days, but ended up falling back on his computer degree after he failed to get drafted by a football team. He was a hack that floated by with passable work, but he played the game of office politics well, schmoozing with anyone in the office for personal gain. He especially schmoozed Rob Murphy, the person that would decide who'd fill the opening position. The same person that had chosen Judy for a promotion over Tim. The last thing he was going to allow was Rob to rob him of his advancement again.

On top of the pile of valid reasons why taking stealthy action against Brad was fair was the fact that Brad hadn't worked for the company as long as Tim, and Brad tended to periodically bully Tim for amusement while passing time at work. There was a part of Brad that was still stuck in high school. Tim's passive, slightly nerdy demeanor must have reminded Brad of his good old days when he was king of the hill and his existence seemed to matter greatly in life. Instead of his current role of being just another pawn working for that next paycheck, getting by in a humdrum existence without a full stadium rooting for him.

Tim looked up from his computer and saw Brad buttering up Rob by the water dispenser. Tim's blood began to boil to the unjust situation mentally mocking him: he was diligently working at his cubicle churning out code, as he normally was, while Brad did nothing but drink water and spout out trivial bullshitlike banter in order to butter his way to the top. That guy would smear butter all over his ass if it meant winning the ass-sledding competition held every January, if such a competition existed that is.

You buttering bullshit bastard. Tim was steaming in hatred behind his flimsy cubicle walls. Walls that didn't even reach higher than his neck, leaving him with no privacy, exposing him to the harsh elements—his colleagues—that were constantly taking advantage of him, and possibly out to get him.

Calm down. Don't venture into a disdainful world of paranoia, Tim counseled himself. *Hatred and paranoia heavily reduce one's IQ, and I'll need to muster all my wits to sink Brad's buttery ship that's constantly transporting canned bullshit across the Atlantic.*

Tim took several deep breaths to calm down and let his IQ raise back to its normal level. An IQ level that far surpassed the sum of every dumbass Brad existing throughout all conceivable alternate realities. The IQ of even the smartest Brad from all possible realities was equal to his expired goldfish's IQ.

The goldfish had been his college pet that had died in his dorm room when a drunk student had defecated and urinated in its bowl as a prank one night when the door had failed to be locked by his roommate. Tim would flush Brad down the toilet like he had that goldfish. There, at the bottom of the septic tank, Brad would simmer with likeminded pieces of shit, fighting for every scrap of feces that came floating by, their only means of sustenance. Meanwhile, on the surface of the Earth, dust and leaves would collect on Brad's throne of buttery banter after several months of his abdication had set in.

Tim took a break from coding and dropped into a meditative state for pondering possible actions that could be taken. He quickly sifted through several dead-end ideas that might leave him exposed or wouldn't be adequate enough to banish Brad. Brad, or as Tim liked to call him, Buttery Bullshit Brad, or TB, which stood for both Triple B and tuberculosis. To Tim, Brad was akin to a bacteria that focused on attacking a person's vital organs while he spewed his bullshit stories in their face. It was almost a daily occurrence for Tim to notice TB running amok by the water cooler, animatedly enacting one of his bullshit tales to colleagues, trying his hardest to relive his high school and college glory days by seeking admiration in the eyes of his colleagues.

Instead of pouring his focus into creating code, which didn't seem to be advancing his career no matter how well he did it, Tim continued to think of the best possible scheme.

Tim suddenly jerked in his chair with excitement when the perfect plan had been mentally procured. He looked up and saw Brad laughing with Rob and another colleague over some joke Brad had finished spewing in their faces.

Laugh it up, Brad. Pretty soon I'll be the last one laughing when you're caught in a porn storm that will bring about your demise.

Tim returned to coding but kept partial attention on Brad's whereabouts. When Brad wandered toward the bathroom, Tim sprang into action. He grabbed a miniature wireless camera that had been gifted to him from a relative who was obsessed with ordering the latest electronic gadgets. He casually strolled over to Brad's desk while glancing around to make sure no one was paying attention to him. This was the one time he could recall where his normal state of being ignored by his coworkers came in handy. Without anyone noticing, he was easily able to slip the tiny camera among the knickknacks that cluttered a shelf that overlooked Brad's keyboard. He moseyed on back to his cubicle, brimming with delight.

Eventually Brad returned to his cubicle and logged back onto his computer.

Boom! Gotcha! Tim couldn't believe how easy that had been.

He waited for Brad to leave his desk again, which didn't take long given his lackadaisical work ethic. On his way to the office kitchen, Tim paused at Brad's empty desk to collect the camera, casually slipping it into his pocket.

Back at his desk, Tim plugged the camera into his desktop computer and transferred the video from the camera to his computer. Then he played back the video clip in slow motion to ascertain the password. He was completely shocked after deciphering the one-word sentence that was Brad's password: Imgaybuttheydontknow69%Yeah!.

The password was quite long, and rather revealing. It appeared Brad was one of those closeted gays that was hiding behind a macho facade instead of embracing his true nature. This newfound knowledge would assist Tim in bombarding Brad's computer with the correct type of porn. Any porn would do but why not be factual in this endeavor. And who knows, maybe using porn that Brad was actually interested in would help the deed play out more smoothly.

For the next step, Tim searched for and downloaded a remote access program he could install into Brad's computer via a USB stick. It was an advanced program that would initiate during bootstrapping and allow him to utilize it before a user was logged on. This was essential because he'd be accessing Brad's computer while it wasn't logged into. Luckily Brad, and most of the staff in the cubicle section of the office, never turned off their computers. They simply logged out at the end of the day.

Tim installed the program onto his computer and timed how long the process took: twenty seconds. It was now time for the hardest part of the operation: logging onto and installing the program on Brad's computer while Brad was away from his computer, and without anyone noticing.

The office camera would capture him doing the deed, but it wouldn't matter because there wouldn't be any reason for someone to rewind and playback the camera footage to spot him. If he did it smoothly, it would appear as a clear-cut case of porn activity at the workplace according to Occam's razor. Even if Brad tried to convince his superiors that it was a complex ploy to get him fired, any rational person would surmise that Brad merely couldn't wait till returning to his residence to gleefully stroke his snake. They'd chalk it up to a porn addiction and that would be the end of it, cut and dried.

Tim decided that lunchtime would be the best time to carry out the deed, when Brad, and most of the cubicle staff, made their way to the tenth floor of the building to dine at the company's in-house cafeteria.

He checked the time: lunchtime was only an hour away.

All the company's large buildings possessed a dedicated floor for sustenance, allowing their workers to down some food without having to leave the building. Their company was brimming with funds and offered perks to their employees that most companies wouldn't dream of giving. Of course it wasn't purely an altruistic move by the company to install such cafeterias. The company got a percentage of the profits from the food providers and hoped the saved commute time would transfer into more productive work time from their employees.

As the time approached, one-by-one the office workers began departing for the tenth floor to chow on some grub, gossip about employees, and talk about upcoming software programs. Tim normally brought a homemade lunch and ate it at his desk, therefore, it wouldn't appear the least bit odd or raise any questions that he stayed in the office to eat his lunch.

Luckily it ended up being one of the largest turnouts for tenth-floor diners that day, leaving only a few employees lingering at their computers, plugging away at code in order to make that deadline, or like himself, antisocially partaking of lunch in their own cubicles. All the cubicles near Brad's were empty, and the few remaining employees seemed entirely engrossed in their tasks, which meant they most likely wouldn't notice him temporarily parking his butt on Brad's chair.

He thought it best to stroll to the bathroom first and visit Brad's cubicle on his way back to his desk. He needed to use the restroom facilities anyway.

While in the restroom doing his business, he could feel his heartbeat picking up its pace, reacting to the anxiety his mind was creating.

Deep breaths. You're not doing anything devious, just doing your business in the bathroom and making a pit stop along the way back to your desk. Just another day at the office. Besides, no one would expect goody-two-shoes Tim to do anything sinister. They all expect me to continue to take it up the ass for the team, never being rewarded for all the hard work I've put in day after day.

Right now TB is probably stuffing his hellacious cakehole with an array of pork products. When the processed pork products are introduced into his body and take up alliance with free radicals, they'll team up to encourage cancer growths throughout his entire body in order to cut his lifespan short—doing the world a favor. Meanwhile, I'll be sliding into his chair and introducing tactical software onto his computer that will eventually seal his doom, severing his connection with this company. How Brad deals with his future cancer from his continual intake of pork products is his own business. Why am I thinking about Brad's diet and cancer? That doesn't matter. Focus on the task at hand, Tim, come on. Jeez.

Tim walked over to the sink to wash his hands. While washing his hands with soap he noticed they were shaking in anticipation of the deed he'd soon perform. Even though there was little chance of him getting caught, there always existed a possibility that something could go awry and lead to severe repercussions, possibly termination if damage control wasn't enacted precisely.

Having entertained thoughts of negative outcomes, his hands began to shake more predominantly.

He nervously yanked his head up and gazed at his reflection in the mirror. For a second he thought he saw a vein protruding on his forehead from the surge of tension, but chalked it up to a hallucinatory moment after he leaned forward to get a closer look in the mirror, examining the contours of his face to find nothing out of place. Then he noticed a rivulet of sweat trickle down the side of his temple.

Who am I kidding, I can't do this. It's not worth the risk. If I get caught, I'll be fired. I've never been good at lying or making up excuses to get out of things. No, it's not worth the risk. Instead, I'll request a meeting with Rob and assertively make my case as to why I'm the best candidate for the promotion. After stating my case, he'll easily recognize that I'm the right person for the position. There's no way he'd be dense enough to give the position to Brad.

He felt a renewed calm wash over his body and mental state. He widened his eyes and took in a deep breath to clear the remaining pockets of tension in his body. Then he bent down to the sink and splashed some cold water in his face a couple times to invigorate his mind and cleanse it of any thoughts of wrongdoing.

Feeling more at ease, he opened the bathroom door and stepped out into the hallway. While making his way down the hall he gave himself a mental pat on the back for deciding to do the right thing. He reasserted to himself that virtue was paramount and stooping down to the level of scheming to achieve one's goals would always come at a cost, no matter how much the scheme may seem warranted.

He popped into the office kitchen and retrieved his sack lunch from one of the refrigerators before returning to the hall. When he reached the end of the hall and stepped into the cubicle area, he noticed that the room was virtually vacant. While he was in the bathroom, the few workers that had remained in the office had inexplicably vanished.

While strolling back to his cubicle he squinted his eyes and thoroughly scanned the entire room. He spotted only a single worker in a far-rear corner who was completely absorbed in his work. Besides the solitary worker, the rest of the office was deserted to the point that a few tumbleweeds might soon make their appearance. Tim couldn't remember the last time he had seen the room so vacant.

Perplexed, he paused in mid-stride and gave his brain precedence to determine the reason for this unforeseen circumstance. His mind managed to procure a piece of information he'd forgotten. A new bakery had been scheduled to open today on the tenth floor and had disseminated the offer of an opening-day promotion for free pastries. It was clear by looking at the office that the bakery's marketing strategy had been tremendously successful. His greedy colleagues would get hooked on a sugar addiction that would solidify repeat business for the bakery.

Now that the mystery was solved, Tim resumed ambling toward his cubicle, still baffled that such an occasion would fall directly on a day that would've benefited his scheme. He thought it must be Satan's ploy to sink his hooks in him with the old bait-and-switch maneuver: dangle the desirable treats in front of his face until they were taken, and then abscond with his soul down to hell, cackling triumphantly while Tim realized the treats had been replaced with dirt by some sleight of hand in the interim. *Well, I'm going to stay on the path of righteousness, thank you very much*, Tim demurred the Devil.

He couldn't help but eyeball Brad's cubicle on his way back to his seat. Brad's utterly vacant cubicle. He had abandoned the planned deed but part of him couldn't ignore Brad's empty cubicle. This insistent part of him was forcing his mind to focus on the previously targeted area, knowing this opportunity was too golden to pass up, and it would be damned if the weak part of Tim that was now running the show was going to squander such a perfect opportunity.

As he passed Brad's cubicle a force akin to a powerful magnet tried its hardest to take control of his body, coercing him to sit down in the enemy's chair and reinstate the mission, but he managed to thwart the malicious pull and somehow awkwardly blundered back to his cubicle like a fish exerting all its energy to swim upstream. If there had been workers in the office to witness his stumbling maneuvers, they might've questioned his sobriety.

He sat in his chair and plopped the sack lunch on his desk, took out his sandwich, and began to eat. He stared at Brad's empty cubicle in a trancelike manner while munching away on his tuna sandwich. Out of curiosity he looked around the office to see if its occupancy had changed. Nope, there was still only that one person.

Welp, doesn't matter how many people are present. I could be the only person left in the office and I still wouldn't fall prey to the tempting scheme.

Directly after this thought, the diligent worker stopped typing, sprang out of his seat, and speedily made for the elevator. There was no denying the heavy pull free pastries produced.

Tim stopped in mid-chomp, leaving food sitting in his mouth as he took in the reality of being the sole survivor of the free-pastry offer. With tuna fish still stuck to his palate he aggressively swiveled his chair all the way around to make certain he was the only person in the office. His scanning eyes completed their 360-degree turn and ascertained that he indeed was completely alone in the office.

"Oh, fuck it," he said to himself, loudly plopping his sandwich on his desk and fumbling in his pocket for the USB stick that contained the remote access application. He left his chair and strode over to Brad's cubicle.

He typed the rather long password into the computer but got an incorrect password notification when he attempted to log in. Had he failed to get the correct password? No, he had double-checked the video clip in slow motion to allow zero room for error. After keying in the password on his second attempt, he received another incorrect password notification. He looked down at his hands, the possible reason for his failure, and sure enough they were shaking like they had just moments ago in the restroom.

He sat for a moment and took in a deep breath, hoping it would help calm his nerves and allow his fingers to be precise enough to get the job done. This was crucial because a third unsuccessful log-in attempt would result in a lockout for a duration of time. He didn't know what the duration of time was because he had never locked himself out of his computer. If it was long enough to still be in effect when Brad returned, the cameras might be checked if Brad raised enough stink about it, which would lead to irrevocable consequences for Tim.

After Tim managed to pacify his shaking hands, he carefully pressed each key in the password, allowing no room for error. He held his breath and pressed ENTER.

Bingo! He was in.

While reaching for the USB stick he'd placed on the desk, a shadow fell upon it. He jerked his head back in a panic to find out whose shadow it was. Upon spotting the shadow's source—a person Tim didn't recognize—he jolted back in the chair and almost toppled over onto the floor.

"Hey, what are you doing?" the man asked with a deadpan countenance that pierced Tim's irises, tore through his body, and gripped his very soul.

The jig was up. Horrible images flashed through Tim's brain: Brad reprimanding him in front of everyone; Rob calling him into his office; Rob delivering a cold, professional spiel about ethics before terminating him; Tim placing his belongings in that proverbial hey-look-I've-just-been-fired box while everyone in the office disdainfully gawked at his every movement and expression; Tim awkwardly heading toward the exit while colleagues shook their heads, yelled in his ears, and spat in his face; Tim stepping outside the building where the very air rebuked him and repeatedly whispered in his ear that he was a loser; his wife clearly stating her wishes for a divorce while throwing random kitchen appliances at his face with unmatched precision; Tim wallowing in a tiny apartment full of unpacked boxes with low-quality frozen pizza lying before his many-days-unshaved beard as merciless flies kamikazed his many-days-unshowered head while advising him to commit suicide so they could nibble on the rest of the pizza and finally move on to his decomposing body for their sustenance.

All the while, the man was gazing at Tim's glazed-over, terrified face, waiting for a reply. Having not received one yet, the man asked a different question. "Are you okay?"

The man's second question snapped Tim back to reality. "Uh ... yeah, I'm fine. I think there was something wrong with my lunch. ... Expired ingredients or something."

Tim's right hand was nervously fiddling with the USB stick severely enough to grab the man's attention. The man kept his focus on the USB stick for an uncomfortable amount of time before speaking again, "I'll say. Something is very fishy here."

Tim dropped the USB stick on the floor and stammered, "What do you mean? I'm not doing anything." Daunting images started flooding Tim's mind again. This time the kamikaze flies were vultures picking his bones clean right in front of an emotionless Raymond who was transfixed on his latest videogame, delivering endless headshots while drooling on the floor.

"I mean it smells like you ate some kind of fish. Maybe you left it in the danger-zone temperature for too long. Seafood can be unforgiving if not fresh." The man stood silently for a couple of seconds. "Well, if you're not doing anything important, can you show me how to submit my code to the backup server? No one has shown me how to do it in the week I've been here."

A huge wave of relief washed over Tim, erasing all the negative images running through his mind. The reason he didn't recognize this guy was because he was a new hire. This guy had no idea he was sitting at Brad's desk. He didn't even seem to know Tim's name.

"Sure, I can help you with that," Tim happily replied. "Just give me a second and I'll be right over."

"Thanks. Much appreciated," the man said while he made his way to his cubicle.

The man must have been in the other kitchen down the hall, or perhaps he was first in line to collect a free pastry and came directly back to the office instead of having lunch in the cafeteria. Whatever, it didn't matter. He was safe.

Tim collected the USB stick from the floor and shoved it into a port in Brad's computer. In about twenty seconds the application was installed in some random system folder where it wouldn't be noticed, and during the custom installation process he unchecked the boxes that would've created a desktop icon and a start menu shortcut. Then he put the USB stick back in his pocket, logged out of Brad's computer, and went to help out the new guy.

Later that night Tim began the daily process he named "porn pasting." He'd use a twice-removed remote access entry into Brad's computer by using his home personal computer—equipped with a virtual private network to mask his IP address—to remotely access his work computer and then remotely access Brad's work computer. Then he'd visit as many pornography Web sites—gay pornography sites to suit his enemy's particular sexual preference—in the hope that enough cookies, malware, and hopefully viruses would infect the targeted computer. He'd also download photos and videos from shady sites and save them in various folders throughout Brad's computer.

The goal was to not only leave a trail of breadcrumbs for any technician that might be called upon for assistance when computer irregularities encumbered Brad, but also to catch the attention of passersby with sexual pop-ups due to malware or viruses, and even leave a ridiculous amount of evidence to incriminate Brad if a manager became suspicious enough to inspect his computer. Tim was pretty sure a few individuals, or even one blather-mouth, would witness the sexual content on Brad's computer and create enough gossip throughout the office to catch the ear of Rob, or one or more of these witnesses might possibly report the activity directly to Rob.

No matter how it went down he was confident that it was only a matter of time before the news found its way to Rob and Brad would be terminated. Not because of his sexual preferences—Seattle was one of the most progressive cities in America—but simply because the company held a very stern policy about pornography being accessed on company devices and during working hours.

Tim believed everyone had the right to their own sexual orientation—love is love. He wasn't using gay porn to mock Brad and assure his termination, but if Rob was homophobic, then it would help the cause.

Despite day after day of "porn pasting," Tim didn't notice anything highly unusual at work in regards to Brad's behavior. Brad had seemed more reserved than usual, and perhaps a bit tense, but that could've been solely due to what most employees were currently dealing with at the office: the release date for a software program the company was currently working on was rapidly approaching and tensions were rising due to employees having to put in extra hours. The timing was rather perfect for Brad to be caught red-handed, as it would distinctly express his failure at a time when the company required all its workers to demonstrate their commitment and diligence for the company's illustrious image and reputation to stay intact by meeting the deadline. But Brad wasn't playing ball.

Numerous questions were running around in Tim's head. *Is Brad even aware of the pornographic images amassing on his hard drive? Did he notice any unusual URL history in his browser? Is he getting raunchy pop-ups? Is there any malware or viruses hindering his work?*

The effectiveness of his scheme was put into question. He'd allocated too much time and preparation for his toil to be fruitless. Just like the company's approaching deadline, Tim had his own looming deadline: the promotion of a programmer was coming due in two weeks and one day. Tim was counting the days, and was now fretting over their completion.

Frustrated, eyes red from night after night hidden away from Amber, staring at a computer screen while "porn pasting," losing valuable sleep, Tim lurched out of his chair and headed to the office kitchen for the energetic aid of black coffee. Passing Brad's cubicle on the way to the kitchen, Tim detected nothing awry other than the fact that Brad was actually hard at work.

Tim staggered into the kitchen. Vexed and fatigued, he sluggishly stumbled toward the coffee machine while mentally cursing Brad. *Dammit! Every night I'm forced to watch sucking and fucking as far as the eye can see and Brad's dumbass appears oblivious to my lusty offerings.*

Utterly exhausted, Tim almost passed out while pouring the coffee in his cup and inadvertently seared his left hand with the scorching liquid. "Shit." He frantically waved his hand back and forth to remove the hot liquid and rushed over to the sink. While holding his hand under the faucet, immersing it in a torrent of cold water, thoughts of porn and Brad came rushing back. *Well, I'll simply have to keep dipping his computer into porn night after night, boner pic after boner pic; the dipping shall continue. But what if it has no impact? What if—*

The perfect solution burst into Tim's head: he'd do it live! He'd remotely access Brad's computer while at work during opportune times when a coworker was conversing with Brad or lingering by his cubicle. Brad would have to be focused somewhere other than his screen so he wouldn't notice that someone was controlling his mouse cursor.

But then Tim realized that people might see the porn displayed on his computer too, as Brad's remotely accessed computer screen would be shown on Tim's monitor while he was doing the deed.

He quickly thought of a solution to remedy that issue: he'd install a privacy screen on his monitor. With a privacy screen attached his screen would be opaquely hidden from any wandering eye. Some of his colleagues were already using them so no suspicion would arise if he started using one as well.

The next morning, carrying a privacy screen he purchased the day before, Tim arrived at work clearheaded and chipper due to skipping a night of "porn pasting."

He attached the privacy screen to his monitor and walked around his cubicle to ensure every viewing angle, other than directly in front of the screen, showed an uncompromising dark screen. Then he made a trip to the office kitchen to retrieve a cup of coffee, walked back to his cubicle, placed the coffee on his desk, and, with a smile brimming from ear to ear, attempted to crack his knuckles in order to finalize a series of completed tasks before jumping into some diligent coding to set the tone of the day.

But being that he wasn't a regular, experienced knuckle-cracker, he almost dislocated a couple of his fingers instead of getting any popping-action relief. "Ow!" He winced and swiftly pulled back his arms to cradle his hands and nurse them with a light massage.

Laughter broke out beside Tim. It came from Brad, who happened to see the embarrassing moment on his way to his desk.

"Nice one, retard. Only real men can pop joints. You best save your fingers for fondling your geeky keyboard and pencil during your special late-night sessions." Brad continued to scoff all the way to his cubicle like an alpha-male ape vocalizing dominance.

Brad returned to his cubicle and began joking with a coworker, glancing back at Tim and mimicking Tim's failed knuckle-cracking. They busted up with laughter at Tim's expense.

Tim mumbled under his breath, "Laugh it up, TB. Soon your ship will be capsized in a sea of persistent pornage."

Tim scowled at Brad and held his stare while mechanically lifting his cup of coffee to take a sip. Having forgotten to check the temperature, he scalded his puckered lips with the hot contents in the mug.

"Aah!" He quickly spat out the small amount of piping-hot coffee that had entered his mouth.

With renewed vigor, Brad, having witnessed this new folly, doubled over in his chair while clutching his stomach in laughter. Then he straightened up and started mimicking Tim's new failed action to his neighboring coworker. In full mockery, the sounds they produced were akin to two hyenas high on cannabis.

If there had been any ounce of doubt or guilt about what Tim was about to do to Brad, it had vanished in that second. This, after all, was a place where adults conducted business, not a fraternity house where the most testosterone-pumped ape ruled like a king.

Sadly, deep down inside most adults harbored a place that wasn't immune to immature coolness. Tim suspected this because most of his coworkers admired Brad. Brad, the guy that never produced any exemplary work, or even good work as far as Tim was concerned. How did someone like Brad even acquire a job at one of the most prestigious software companies in the world? By removing Brad from the equation, Tim knew he'd be saving his colleagues from that weak aspect of themselves that Brad was continually exploiting, whether they were conscious of it or not, and he'd irrefutably be doing a favor for the company. Any company that included Brad in its workforce ran the risk of demise by way of cancer; Brad being the cancerous tumor that would spread throughout an establishment, resulting in countless Brads running amok throughout a corporation's framework, infecting colleague after colleague with charismatic tales contrived of buttery bullshit, which would eventually cause a systemic breakdown and the ceasing of a company's heartbeat. Consequently, Brad's purge from the company would be more of a humanitarian act than a selfish act.

The day slowly slipped by, code after code had been inputted by Tim. While he carried out his daily work he tried his hardest to be patient for the opportunity to remotely control Brad's computer. With everyone diligently working Tim began to think it was going to be a fruitless day until he noticed Leggy Laura walking toward Brad's cubicle. Tim's heartbeat abruptly picked up its pace twofold: one being the prospect of sabotaging Brad, the other being the view of Laura's voluptuous legs, which she never missed a chance to flaunt.

Laura Davis was one of two females working in the cubicle area that was slightly attractive. Her face was on the plain side, but a little makeup and a copious amount of confidence went a long way to make her attractive by most male's standards, especially geeky male programmers' standards.

Patricia Miller was the other somewhat pretty programmer that Laura Davis was quite chatty with, being that they shared a common bond.

Leggy Laura elegantly placed her right hand on the top of Brad's cubicle wall and made sure her lovely legs were in Brad's view instead of being blocked by his cubicle walls. She gracefully brushed her hair behind her left ear and initiated some small talk.

Not knowing how long this opportunity would last, Tim pounced into action. He had already executed the background-running remote access program to control Brad's computer on his own desktop the moment he knew Laura was headed

Brad's way—well, after he enjoyed the movement of Laura's legs for a bit.

You're barking up the wrong tree, Leggy Laura. TB plays for the other team. But don't worry, I'm about to enlighten you to that fact. Already having a particularly revealing Web site's URL copied, and while Brad's face was turned toward Laura instead of his screen, Tim took control of Brad's cursor and hastily moved it to the URL field, pasted the copied link, and smashing ENTER.

A Web site opened up on Brad's computer that revealed a very graphic homepage illustration: a video of a man sucking another man's penis. To Tim's dismay, Brad didn't have his speakers turned on, which would've easily and quickly alerted everyone's attention around him.

Even though Laura stood at a viewable angle of Brad's screen, she was solely focused on Brad and appeared to be thoroughly entertained by one of his many buttery-bullshit remarks.

Dammit, Laura! Look at his screen! There's a dude sucking another dude's dick for Christ's sake. Well, I don't know if he's actually doing it for the sake of Christ; I don't know the backstory to this particular video. But I'm sure Christ appreciates all forms of love. You, however, Laura, not being as diverse and hip as Christ, will surely be utterly appalled. Look at the screen!

The silent video continued to play in the background of Brad and Laura's conversation, showing no signs of detection by them or anyone else around them. Laura flipped her hair in flirtatious fashion and produced a fake giggle to one of Brad's jokes.

Hello! Look at the screen. Tim looked down at his screen to confirm the remote access program was working properly. Yup, everything seemed in order. A segment of the video showed the entire penis of the man being pleasured as the pleasurer temporarily drew back and started coughing. It shocked and completely transfixed Tim. *What the hell! He's got that thing souped-up or something. It's ginormous! That guy looks easily under six-feet tall, so there's no way it would naturally be that long.*

It's definitely a custom job. He's going to rip a hole in the back of that guy's head if he's not careful.

Tim released his gaze from the fascinating video to check on the targeted area: Brad and Laura were jabbering on, still unaware of the souped-up man and his pleasurer going at it. Tim shook his head. *You're missing some good stuff, Brad. This titillating piece of art would surely wet—*

Finally having noticed something moving rapidly on Brad's screen, Laura turned toward the screen and bent down a bit to get a closer look, squinting in disbelief. Brad, witnessing Laura's strange expression, also turned his head toward his screen to see what was amiss or captivating. Brad's eyes instantly bulged in shock as he wondered for a second if he himself had opened the Web site, since it was material he immensely enjoyed watching regularly at home behind closed curtains and locked doors.

Laura shifted her gaze back on Brad and saw within his eyes something more than astonishment: she noticed a sense of arousal. She instinctively looked down at Brad's pants to gather more evidence and spotted the beginnings of a tentlike structure being erected. Her whole body violently shuttered. Then she shook her head repeatedly back and forth in incredulity as she slowly backpedaled away from his cubicle.

Brad quickly closed the Web site and looked around to see if anyone besides Laura had seen what was on his screen. It appeared nobody had, nor did anyone seem to notice Laura slinking away from him in utter distress. He was lucky everyone was focused on their work to meet the deadline.

Then Brad focused back on Laura in an attempt to salvage his dignity. He held up two palms toward her and opened his mouth to vocalize an excuse, but nothing came out. He sat in his chair looking like a mime that had forgotten the next part of his routine. Then some half-audible words fell out of his mouth. "Must be a virus or something."

Still slowly backing away, Laura pointed at Brad's crotch as if to say, *But I saw evidence that supports the notion that you were enjoying the so-called virus: the erecting of a sturdy wigwam any Native American would be proud of.*

Brad replied to her pointing gesture by shaking his head back and forth and mumbling like a weak person on their deathbed. "No erection. No. … Just natural folds in pants. These are loose-fitting pants. Folds are produced easily and can be substantial. No erection. Please Laura …"

But Laura, unconvinced, turned her back on him before he finished explaining and headed straight to Patricia Miller's cubicle to tell her closest colleague the disturbing news.

Tim pretended to be hard at work while he took in what was unfolding. Trying his hardest not to bust up laughing, he covered his mouth with a hand to suppress the outburst that was striving to escape. *You want to relive your college days, Brad? Well, here's a play straight out of my college playbook. It's called intellect over brawn … or how about intellect over Brad. A good old dose of porn pasting never hurt no one*, Tim thought, using the double negative on purpose.

Leggy Laura whispered the disturbing news to Patricia. While she did so, Patricia's face displayed revulsion with her mouth ajar. Both ladies stared at Brad as words were passed back and forth, first as whispers then gradually picking up volume. They saw Brad staring back at them, looking like a depressed mime with two hands up on an imaginary wall. His mouth was moving, apparently saying something, but they couldn't hear a word of his mumbling from their location across the room.

Brad looked like a college quarterback reacting to a game-losing interception. He continually slurred excuses and objections like an invalid. "No erection … Please don't … I'm the cool guy—it's me Brad. Please … no erection … Loose-fitting pants make folds … Big folds."

After Laura finished recounting the short tale, Patricia went back to focusing on her work and Laura returned to her desk to do the same, both shaking off the unbelievable incident.

Brad saw Laura and Patricia going back to work and ignoring him. To his surprise, no one else in the room seemed to notice what just occurred, nor even took note of his half-audible groveling, so he sucked up his pride and returned to his work.

Irritably perplexed, Tim stopped coding to contemplate the current situation. It looked like Brad's house of cards were assuredly and rapidly crumbling before his eyes, but Laura and Patricia kept it to themselves and didn't appear to be taking any additional steps against Brad. And everyone else in the room wasn't privy of what had just transpired, despite Brad's reproduction of a mentally handicapped mime posing naked in Times Square before a live audience.

Tim almost slammed his fists on his desk in a spout of frustration. He was positive it was checkmate, but now he was back to square one. Tim's exasperation created an image in his mind of a robust dildo crashing through the ceiling above Brad's desk and falling to whack him square on the head, creating a squishy sound as it made contact. Then the ceiling tile above him completely giving way to produce a torrent of oily dildos, each walloping, smacking, and slapping Brad till he was wriggling and squirming around his dildo-filled cubicle, encumbered by so many dicks that he began to confess his gayness and love for the glorious cock.

As Tim shook the image from his mind, he noticed Matt—a coworker that sat closest to Patricia—making his way down the far aisle that bordered Rob's office. Maybe Matt overheard Laura and Patricia's conversation, Tim thought. Maybe he was going to Rob's office to squeal on Brad.

Tim was pleased to see Matt knock on Rob's door and enter the office after he was given the okay. Rob's blinds weren't closed so Tim could see through the glass wall of Rob's office. The two men started conversing.

Tim contemplated the situation. By no means did Matt appear to dislike Brad, but perhaps Matt thought he had a shot at the coming promotion if Brad was taken out of the running. In today's dog-eat-dog world there was plenty of backstabbing going around; it had become the new norm in the career world. Or maybe their conversation was entirely about work matters. No, their conversation looked a bit too intense to merely be about a coding issue. Tim continued to stare through the glass at the two men's mannerisms and facial expressions, desperately trying to solve the mystery as he watched their silent conversation. He wished he could read lips.

"I distinctly heard them whispering about it, and their tones clearly expressed how appalled they were," Matt explained to Rob.

Matt had heard the ladies' entire conversation and had been trying to convince Rob to take some kind of action, but Rob had expressed to Matt that he wouldn't act upon trivial gossip and stated that even if it was true, a virus or invasive malware could be the culprit, which would be removed by IT if and when Brad reported the issue. Rob also said that Brad wasn't behind in his workload and showed no signs of breaking such a serious office offense.

In the end, Rob appeased Matt by promising to monitor Brad's screen for the remainder of the day. As the manager of the cubicle section, Rob had the right to monitor any of his employees' computer screens using the preinstalled company software that resided on the programmers' computers. Rob never used the monitoring software before because he felt it was too intrusive, nor was he planning on keeping his promise to Matt to watch Brad's screen. The white lie pacified Matt and was sufficient to end the discussion and put Matt's attention back where it belonged: completing his pertinent workload in order to meet their deadline. This particular deadline was probably one of the most important in all of Rob's seven years with the company, so he needed all his employees thoroughly engaged in their tasks instead of occupying their time with cheap gossip.

From Tim's viewpoint Matt looked slightly satisfied when he exited Rob's office and headed toward the kitchen area, but Rob didn't appear to be taking any action, nor did he show any signs of concern. Perhaps their conversation had nothing to do with Brad after all.

Matt soon reappeared from the hallway and made his way into the cubicle area holding a mug. From Tim's vantage point it appeared that Matt was scrutinizing Brad from afar, and possibly taking the long way back to his desk in order to walk past Brad's cubicle. Tim could see Brad bent down close to the floor, searching for something in his desk drawer. If Matt actually passed Brad's desk and took a quick gander at his screen …

Tim executed the remote access program, copied the same URL he used before, and waited for Matt to get closer while repeating in his head: *Stay down Brad, stay down.*

When Matt reached Brad's cubicle, he saw Brad bent down and fidgeting in his lowest desk drawer, looking for something. Then Matt pivoted his head to take a glimpse at Brad's screen. Even though Matt had heard the entire whispered conversation between Laura and Patricia, what he saw on Brad's computer still shocked him: a graphic video of a man holding another man's head down to suck him off, controlling the man's head up and down in rhythmic fashion, working the man's head as if it were merely a toy that could be purchased at a local sex-toy shop. Matt assumed Brad was searching for his hidden special lotion in order to discretely lube-up right there in the office.

Tim saw Matt inaudibly, but distinctly, mouth the words, *What the fuck*, and change his walking direction so abruptly that he spilled some liquid from his mug onto the floor. After Matt turned and marched away, Tim closed the browser window so Brad wouldn't know porn had been on his computer.

Matt wore a huge grimace and strode toward Rob's office. Matt could clearly see that Rob hadn't kept his promise to monitor Brad's computer because Rob's face wasn't contorted in astonishment from viewing what he had just seen.

Matt burst into Rob's office without knocking, closed the door behind him, and proceeded to verbally lay into Rob. "Obviously you didn't keep your promise," he snarled at Rob.

"I just saw a suckfest on Brad's screen as he was searching in his desk drawer for lotion to lube-up with."

"Suckfest—what are you talking about?" Rob responded, highly annoyed that one of his employees had barged into his office without knocking and was now barking at him like a rabid dog.

Matt noticed Rob's irritability and quickly brought his temper down a notch. "I just happened to be walking by Brad's cubicle and saw a pornographic video of a man giving oral pleasure to another man in a very gaylike manner. And he was searching for lotion to lube-up with."

Rob furrowed his eyebrows in disbelief and confusion. "Gay guys were lubing-up on Brad's computer? What?"

Annoyed that Rob wasn't comprehending this serious matter, Matt slowly enunciated the dire issue. "I clearly saw, without a doubt, porn on Brad's computer just now."

Rob stared and blinked at Matt, and then said, "Did you see him actively engaged with this porn you speak of? Viewing it with delight, clicking on links that brought up more pornographic windows, licking his chops, something that would irrefutably make him guilty of whipping up porn in the workplace under his own volition?"

Matt stood there anxiously racking his brain, slightly shaking, but not producing any words for a reply. Since he hadn't seen Brad looking at the porn on his screen, Matt couldn't say Brad was definitely engaged.

"Do you see what I'm getting at, Matt? If you didn't see Brad enjoying porn on his workplace computer, by default we have to assume that it's a virus or malware—like I said earlier."

Matt scrunched up his face and started twisting his body around like a child having a hissy fit because his mom wouldn't buy him a candy bar at the supermarket. "But Rob, that's twice porn has been seen on his screen today and witnessed by a total of three different people."

Rob kept his cool. Any other boss wouldn't have tolerated this from an employee, but Rob was an affable manager that tried to be as lenient as possible. He liked portraying the boss that was your friend and only laid down the law when duty called for no other action. Rob placed both his palms down on his huge desk as if the desk had spiritual powers to calm him, and then spoke softly, "Laura and Patricia haven't vocalized anything to me about this issue, and even if they had, we'd be having this same discussion. You know how viruses and malware work: they propagate intermittently and repeatedly to the user's discontent and affliction."

There was a long pause while Rob reflected further on the issue. Then, like a versed negotiator, Rob added, "Look … I'll tell you what I'll do. I'll keep a small box of Brad's monitor on the corner of my—"

"But you said that last time."

"This time I'll actually do it, okay. And if I see him actively engaged and enjoying porn on his computer, I'll lay the law down on him without leniency. And if I don't see him actively engaged, licking his chops and whatnot, tomorrow I'll ask him if he needs IT's help to eradicate any possible viruses."

Matt whined, "I think that it would be best if—"

Rob raised a hand to silence him. "That will be all, Matt. Thank you. Please return to work now."

It had been a trying day and Rob wasn't his usual friendly self. He really didn't feel like running a children's daycare and had more work to complete than usual, which meant he'd probably be putting in a little overtime before heading home. The last thing he needed was to be held captive in his office by a whining baby instead of completing his work and getting home at a decent hour.

Internal curse words reverberated around Tim's head when he saw Matt exiting the office, grumpy and defeated-looking, and Rob diving back to work, seemingly not taking any action regarding the situation—again—and appearing annoyed about being harassed by Matt rather than irate at Brad.

The hours passed and employees began to leave for the day, Matt being one of them. He slammed a desk drawer shut before departing, unmistakably infuriated that Rob hadn't reprimanded Brad in any way, and believing Rob hadn't committed to his promise to monitor Brad's screen for the second time. The office had been reduced to thirty-percent capacity. The remaining workforce included Brad, Rob, Tim, and various other people desperately trying to avoid falling behind in their work with such an important deadline looming.

Negativity grew in strength within Tim as the day passed without another opportunity surfacing to sabotage Brad. More opportunities would undoubtedly present themselves in the coming days, but Tim was more discouraged about Rob coming through. He'd been given the information twice and had done nothing. If Rob hadn't taken any action today, who's to say he'd take any action in the future. The situation appeared bleak.

Having put in enough overtime, and feeling trounced, Tim decided to call it a day. Before leaving he decided to mess with Brad one more time. He initiated the remote access program and observed Brad working on some code. For five minutes Tim periodically pressed random keys to ruin Brad's code. Brad noticed most of the time and deleted the extra keystrokes, most likely thinking he had mistyped due to exhaustion.

Aggravated with all his typos, Brad put his palms in his face and rubbed them around, striving to ward off fatigue. Then he grabbed his mug and downed some cold coffee.

In the interim, Tim hijacked his cursor and opened up a Web site that promised to possess the best gay-porn images on the Internet: QUIT WASTING YOUR TIME GOING ELSEWHERE WHEN YOU CAN CUM AT THE BEST PLACE. WE'VE GOT THE BEST MALE GAY PORN ON THE INTERNET, HANDS DOWN ... ON YOUR PENIS. HAVE A BALL ... OR TWO. WE PROMISE YOU'LL CUM TO US AGAIN AND AGAIN FOR THE PENIS AND BALL SHOW, THE BEST SHOW ON EARTH!

Brad put down his coffee mug, stared at the screen, and read the Web site's promise. Instead of automatically closing the browser as he'd done before, he glanced left, right, and back. He took into account that Laura and Patricia were gone for the day, the cubicles around him were empty, and the few people remaining at the office were fully concentrated on their tasks.

That excellent blowjob video had gotten him quite horny. He'd been incapable of expunging it from his mind all day. He thought he'd briefly checkout this site for a few minutes and see if they actually possessed the best gay porn on the Internet, which was a heavy claim. If it was as grandiose as it reputed, he'd message himself the Web site's URL to thoroughly tackle it at home. Tomorrow, he'd contact IT to resolve this virus issue on his computer.

Tim was expecting Brad to quickly close the browser and get back to coding, but he was checking out the site. *Oh, shit. I hooked him with pleasurable material. Too bad it doesn't matter, because no one is around to catch him. … Great, I've just become Brad's personal porn-finding agent. This is what my life has been reduced to.*

Brad browsed around a bit and was absolutely impressed with the site. Being aware that no one was near him, and being so excited by the content, he mumbled to himself, "Wow, they have a plethora of free videos and images. The camera work in the videos is professional, not amateur league—nice lighting, great angles, outstanding themes. They got blowjob videos in all kinds of settings—even in public toilets. Wait, how is that possible? Must be an in-house set. The attention to detail is mesmerizing. They've got face sitting—nice! What's this? I've not seen this before. The Human Toilet." Brad swiftly glanced around the office again, double-checking for absolute certainty and saw he was completely safe and could checkout this one video before calling it a day.

Brad clicked on the video labeled THE HUMAN TOILET. A skinny man wearing a shirt that read THE ELITE: THE TOP .001% was reading the newspaper while sitting on a muscular guy's face. Without looking down the skinny man nonchalantly began defecating into the submissive man's mouth. The muscular man made excited gurgling noises while masticating and swallowing the excrement as fast as he could to make room in his mouth for the next load.

Bug-eyed and captivated, Brad stared at the screen and mumbled to himself, "I've never seen that before. I'm not sure I can get into that. Maybe if I'm really horny … No, it would probably just gross me out. But if they did it more elegantly, it might be good. But that's probably hard to do elegantly. … That muscular guy sure has a nice body, though, and a rather large unit. He's really enjoying being a toilet." Brad absently began moving his tongue around, fully moistening his upper and lower lips.

Tim was horrorstruck by the video on his screen. He was quite sure he'd never look at his monitor in the same way again, it would be forever tainted.

Rob was about to pack it in and call it quits for the day. He had completely ignored the tiny box in the bottom right-hand corner of his monitor that displayed Brad's screen. The box had started out larger, but had been quickly shrunk and ignored.

Before closing all the windows on his screen, Rob noticed some weird movements in the tiny box in the corner of his screen. He scrunched his face in confusion and dragged his mouse cursor down to the box to enlarge it to solve the mystery. With the box now taking up his full screen, Rob's mouth instantly fell ajar in disbelief and horror. "What the hell! He's eating that man's shit! Looks like he's really liking it too."

In his shock, Rob temporarily forgot that the tiny box he had enlarged and was now completely revolted with was coming from Brad's computer. Rob thought for sure it had to be a virus because no one would willingly view such a video, but Rob turned his head in the direction of Brad just to make sure. Staring through his glass office wall with squinting eyes to heighten his distance of sight, he clearly saw Brad captivated by the video on his screen: Brad's mouth was agape and his tongue was slowly licking his lips.

Rob was utterly disgusted. "What the hell! He's licking his chops to this shit show."

Then it dawned on Rob that it wasn't just a sick video, it was porn, and it wasn't straight-man's porn, it was gay-man's porn. "Brad is gay?"

Being a Seventh-day Adventist Christian, Rob was as homophobic as a person could be. Like the separation of

Church and State, Rob kept his religious affiliation veiled from the workplace, so nobody knew about his religious background.

In his head he relived all the now repulsive moments he had shared with Brad: Brad resting his hand on Rob's shoulder as they heartily laughed at the punch line of one of Brad's jokes; Brad, with a smile on his face, squeezing between Rob and some other colleague in the kitchen on his way to the coffee machine; Brad patting Rob's stomach at a barbecue event, joking about pregnancy after Rob ate three hot dogs; Brad licking ketchup off a hot dog after accidently squirting too much out of the ketchup bottle; Brad shooting Rob a smile during an elevator ride. The images went on and on in Rob's mind. He pressed his hands to his temples. "Oh, Lord, make the images stop. For the love of God, this can't be happening."

Then his mind went back to the video. "Oh, God. Brad wants me to shit in his mouth—or maybe Brad wants to shit in *my* mouth. That sonuvabitch! He will not shit in my mouth! Not today, sir! Not any damn day!"

With his body shaking he snatched up the phone and called the receptionist. He told her to send up as many security guards as possible to escort a terminated, and possibly dangerous, employee off the premises. After he returned the phone to its cradle he slumped down in his chair and eagerly waited for the guards to arrive and deal with the problem. Trying his hardest to keep the venomous memories of Brad out of his head, he counted the seconds till the guards arrived.

Everyone remaining in the office was startled when seven obese security guards barged into the cubicle area from the hallway. They were panting after having rushed to the scene as urgently as they were instructed to. They gave everyone in the room the once-over, frantically trying to deduce who was the individual that posed the threat.

Brad lowered his gaze from the guards back to his computer screen where The Human Toilet was still playing. At the same time he stopped the video by closing the browser,

Rob yanked his office door open and aggressively pointed at Brad, arm shaking, finger wavering. "That's the one! Get him!"

Brad's pea-sized brain took a moment to process the situation and finally came to the conclusion that Rob somehow knew about his porn perusing, and wasn't too happy about it. In fact, he appeared to be quite irate about the concept of the video, and its very existence, especially since toilets had been invented long ago and were being sold to straight people as well as gay people.

As the security guards made for their target, Brad entered the fight-or-flight response, and chose the latter. Being that Brad played quarterback in college and all the security guards resembled linemen—but were composed mostly of fat rather than muscle—his decision to take flight was instinctive. In his mind, he mapped out a running route around the cubicles that would draw the security guards away from the hallway entrance, his escape path.

The leftover office workers were clueless and stunned, and some were invigorated that something more entertaining than coding was taking place during their overtime. But no one was more entertained by the extravaganza than Tim, who was equally stunned but far from clueless. He was aware of the monitoring software on all the cubicle computers and quickly assumed that Rob must have started utilizing the software to monitor Brad after Matt's repeated squealing. In celebratory fashion, and with a grin that extended to Maine, Tim grabbed a bag of caramel popcorn out of his desk and began to munch away while enjoying the overtime show.

Running amok around the office—jumping on desks, leaping over cubicle walls—Brad's initial planned-out route failed and gave way to a circus performance, like a quarterback awkwardly and frantically changing directions to avoid an onslaught of arm-snatching linemen. The obese security guards, who were already worn out when they entered the office, were sweating profusely from all the maneuvering. Brad took advantage of their perspiration by slipping out of the grip of the first security guard that made contact with him, and also by slipping through two bulging stomachs that tried enclosing on him, like a soap bar in the shower.

Rob stayed near his office door, keeping his distance from Brad's perverted hands. He jumped up and down and shouted like a crazed sports fan in the bleachers. "Go that way! … Block him! … Don't touch him too much, he'll enjoy it. … Watch out, he might try to shit in your mouth—his signature move in college, I bet. … Show some hustle—why are all of our security guards so fat?"

A clear, straight path to the hallway opened up before Brad. He wasted no time and sprinted toward it. When a security guard jumped into his path, Brad used his patented stiff-arm to knock the security guard to the floor and continued his sprint toward the hallway.

After witnessing the stiff-arm and Brad's clear path to the hallway, Rob exploded into an emotional tantrum. "Get him!" he whined like a rabid sports fan vocalizing their disdain while watching their hometown football team lose from an opposing team's long run down the field toward the end zone.

Two female programmers, who didn't know why Brad was being chased, jabbered away in conversation, gushing over the physicality and athleticism that Brad was displaying. "He's so dreamy," one of them said as Brad galloped past their cubicles.

Brad raced toward the end zone with a pre-celebratory raised arm that held an imaginary football. While closing the gap between himself and the end zone, he turned his head to smile and gloat at Rob and the exhausted linemen. But before Brad entered the end zone, he was suddenly halted by the huge belly of a late-arriving security guard that had just stepped into the office from the hallway.

This giant security guard's monumental obesity had postponed his arrival to the scene, but as he stepped into the cubicle section dripping with sweat from having taken the stairs—since his poundage exceeded the elevator's weight capacity—he instantaneously became the MVP that saved the day.

Upon impact, Brad's face was momentarily lost in a vast sea of flab before he bounced back and met the floor. Dazed, he looked up with blinking eyes at the impediment that had appeared out of nowhere. He was infinitely astonished by the impediment's sheer size. It took him a moment to realize this monstrosity was a man.

The quarterback, being temporarily stunned and stupefied, allowed enough time for the linemen to draw near. So when Brad gathered his wits and made an attempt at rising off the floor to evade capture, all the security guards were close enough to dive through the air and land in a heaping pile on top of Brad, jostling and squirming around as if Brad was a fumbled ball they were all trying to recover. Grunts and growls emanated from the tightly knitted ball of men as arms grabbed and mouths slobbered.

Under the mass of so much blubber, Brad opened his mouth to vocalize excuses to Rob as a last-ditch effort, but before his mouth could produce words it was expeditiously filled with blubber because he lacked a helmet with a facemask for protection. Due to asphyxiation and being at the bottom of a huge pile of crushing lard, a blubber-induced blackout followed.

Chapter 6

Dale Dickerson opened the door and stepped into Awakening Soul Soother Café, where he was supposed to meet up for lunch with his online date, Valerie. The café was even worse than Dale had imagined when he read its name in a texted message from Valerie, who had chosen the location. The title of the café suggested its New Age influence, but he had no idea the place would be littered with spiritual knickknacks and completely brimming with wishy-washy clientele that sported tie-dye shirts and earthy-colored, grungy pants.

Dale gritted his teeth and painfully examined the place, taking in all its awfulness. The atmosphere alone felt like it was soiling his impeccable suit. He took a few steps forward and scanned the crowded café for someone that resembled the female on his phone. While doing so he accidently kicked a chair leg that contained a bitter hippie, who was seated with his fellow discontented hippies.

"Hey man, watch the chair," the hippie said as he turned around to see who had offended his seating area. The hippie gave Dale a once-over from bottom to top: polished black leather shoes, dark-gray tweed pants and suit, starched white dress shirt.

"Whoa, man, the IRS finally found out I haven't been paying my taxes for the past ten years and is here to collect," the hippie joked to his friends while looking at Dale. Laughter escaped his friends' mouths.

In Dale's peripheral view he noticed a hand raised in the air waving back and forth. The hand belonged to a female that looked similar to the female on his phone. Before walking in her direction, Dale turned back to slander the bitter hippie who was wearing a tie-dye shirt with colorful text that read ACID BATH. "Looks like someone forgot to take their micro-dose of acid today, or maybe you mistakenly consumed too much gluten for breakfast. Or perhaps you're resentful for having woken up today realizing the world revolves around money instead of love and sexually transmitted diseases."

An eccentric expression crept onto the hippie's face while he half-lifted his arms in surrender. "Hey man, crimson and clover, over and over."

Dale hadn't the slightest idea what the man was talking about, but he was pretty sure he wasn't talking about colors and flowers. Or was clover a weed? Well, if he spotted these hippies in his backyard, he'd definitely remove them like weeds, even if their tie-dye shirts were colorful enough to deceitfully pass as flowers. Getting up close to them to smell their pungent odor—instead of a flower's fragrance—would most surely be enough evidence to classify them as weeds. Stubborn weeds that attempted to buck the system by creeping up between logically placed cemented sidewalks that paved the way to buildings of high finance. He had crushed many of their kind under his polished shoes as he made his way toward the office. They were the dying remnants of a generation that thought pervasive love could spark a peaceful revolution. What they weren't aware of was that love wasn't more powerful than fucking. The honorable elite factions that hold the reins of an ordered society continually raped the hippie's love movement until it was nothing more than acid flashbacks and bad hygiene, which conveyed the power of fucking over love.

Seeing no reason to reply to the hippie's cryptic statement, Dale walked away from the disgruntled weeds toward the arm-waving female. As he got closer to Valerie he was reminded of the issue about photos used on dating apps: females only uploaded photos that looked at least twenty percent better than their actual everyday appearance. Taking this law into account, Valerie was in the ballpark of what he'd expected: moderately good-looking face, but just as nicely dressed as in her online photos. She had long blond hair that spilled over a white blouse that matched a pale-yellow pleated short skirt and white tennis shoes. She didn't fit into the dress code the other diners adhered to, which pleased Dale greatly.

However, the female seated next to her, who must have been Valerie's friend, was adhering to the café's unspoken dress code: she wore a brown long-sleeved shirt with a phrase in bubbly font that read KARMA PATROL. She also sported a nose ring and light-brown hair tied back with a brown scrunchie. Her face was prettier than Valerie's, but he found her attire and style went a long way to negate her beauty.

Valerie was flashing a bright smile while she directed him to the vacant seat across from her and her friend. Valerie appeared affable and chipper, perhaps a bit ditsy, while her friend sat in stark contrast: a brooding expression with undertones that conveyed a judgment had already been passed in the whole two seconds she had rested her eyes on Dale; a judgment that had found Dale guilty of being just another asshole in a suit.

Valerie courteously stood up from her chair to greet Dale. "Hi, Dale. It was easy to spot you because you're wearing immaculate suits in all your online photos—and here you are now in an equally as immaculate suit. Come, have a seat and take a look at the menu."

"I could use a good cup of coffee," Dale said.

"Oh, you have to order and pay for the coffee separately up front with the barista. Their menu only has food," Valerie said, gesturing to the barista and then to the menu on the table.

"All right. I'll get a coffee and be right back."

She nodded while Dale departed for the barista.

After ordering a latte, the barista directed Dale to use the electronic point-of-sale pad to make his payment via credit card. After agreeing to the coffee price and sales tax on the pad, a tipping screen popped up displaying tipping-percentage options in different boxes with the NO TIP option being half the size as the other boxes and outlined in red instead of black. He stared at the tipping screen with his finger frozen in the air above the pad. In his peripheral vision he could see the barista beginning the process of making his drink while wearing a huge fabricated smile. She wore a T-shirt with images of crystals and text that read FUELED BY CRYSTALS & COFFEE.

Dale subtly shook his head. *This is ridiculous. Am I supposed to tip this person because she's putting on a fake smile for me? I don't pay for fake smiles, or real smiles—I don't give a fuck about smiles. Why do they want a tip for something that involves no service? I had to walk here to get it, and they aren't going to walk it to my table when it's done. Not that such a simple task of walking a very short distance would constitute a tip anyway. Have Americans become that obese and lazy? And now I have to wait here till it's done. They should be paying me for having to stand here and wait, wasting my time. I'm going to press the no-tip box and let them label me an asshole, it's better than being labeled a complete sucker.*

Dale was tempted to rip the electronic pad from its stand and shove it up the barista's ass while shouting, "Here's your goddamn tip, you inflated asshat. You're no different than a bum on the street holding out a cup." Instead, he merely pressed the NO TIP box and collected the receipt that spat out of the machine. He knew that once the barista was privy to his selection she would hand him his drink with eyes drenched in disdain as if she just found out he was the Unabomber or something. And sure enough, that's exactly what happened. Dale was happy his drink had been made prior to her knowing he hadn't tipped because there's no telling how shoddily she could've made his drink. Hell, the drink would probably taste bad regardless, he imagined, given the type of café it was.

While walking back to Valerie he took one hand off the saucer and touched the side of the mug to check its temperature: it was scalding hot. He'd have to wait at least fifteen minutes before he could even sip it, and being too hot usually conveyed that the barista didn't know what they were doing and the coffee would taste bad. He wasn't surprised.

Valerie cut her conversation with her friend short to welcome his return. "Dale, I hope you don't mind that I brought a friend. I find it makes a first date more relaxing. This is my friend, Aioli."

"Are you kidding? The more pretty girls at the table the merrier," he said while picking up the menu. His statement had drawn an even bigger smile from Valerie, but produced a glare of death from Aioli. "Aioli … like the sauce?" Dale asked.

A frown fell upon Aioli's face. "Yeah, like the damn sauce."

"Please forgive Aioli. She gets the sauce comment almost every time when meeting someone new," Valerie said after an anxious laugh that was aimed at keeping things light and playful at the table.

"Hey, I love aioli sauce," Dale said. "The name isn't so bad. I once knew a girl named Barbecue because her mother thought Barb was too short and simple."

"Really?" Valerie asked, amused and surprised.

"No, just kidding."

Aioli, still hidden behind her menu, sarcastically laughed and said, "We got a real comedian here."

Silence covered the table as they browsed their menus.

Dale ended up ordering the Moist Chicken Sandwich and their Signature Cheesecake. Valerie ordered the Macedonian Salad and the Tiramisu. Aioli ordered the Acai Bowl and the Lemon Tart. Dale thought it was fitting how Aioli would order some kind of bullshit meal like an acai bowl and a dessert that was as sour as her personality.

In response to Dale's confused face when the waitress set their desserts down on the table before the meal, the waitress said, "Don't you know our motto? Life is uncertain, eat dessert first."

"Whatever floats your boat," Dale responded and dug into his dessert, or rather tried to but failed because the cheesecake was a frozen brick that rebuffed his fork. As Valerie and Aioli enjoyed their desserts, Dale attempted to whittle at his glacierlike cheesecake.

After giving the cheesecake much scrutiny, Dale realized it was the furthest thing from being "their Signature Cheesecake" because it was the exact cheesecake sold at Costco, and they hadn't even bothered to hide the fact by drizzling chocolate or fruit sauce on it. It was an item his parents used to purchase regularly at Costco so he was very familiar with it. This café had simply bought a box of cheesecake at Costco and was reselling each slice for about four times the price, and freezing the hell out of it in the process.

"Mmm … try this lemon tart, Valerie."

Dale followed with his own invitation. "And then try a bite of this twice-bought cheesecake."

Valerie extended her fork toward Aioli's dessert. "Twice-bought, what do you mean?"

"They bought this at Costco and are reselling it with a hefty markup."

"I'm sure it just looks similar. They wouldn't do that," she said before inserting a piece of Aioli's tart in her mouth. "*Oh*, that is good."

Annoyed, Dale muttered, "No, it's definitely secondhand cheesecake." He reached for his latte but retracted when the hot mug seared his hand. "Great. I got a frozen dessert and a scalding coffee, both unfit for consumption." Before either female replied to his bitter remark, he continued complaining, "And can you believe they try to force a tip from you at the barista stand for simply making a coffee. On top of that, they'll assuredly hand us a bill with a tip line on it after we're done with our food, despite the fact that you have to get and refill your own water at the counter over there. The only thing the waitresses do is put your food on your table and walk away. That's not service and doesn't deserve a tip. I don't believe in the concept of tipping regardless, but this racket they got going here is asinine."

Aioli halted a fork load of tart heading toward her mouth in order to chastise Dale. "Says the stockbroker in an immaculate suit that would cost any waitress in here a month's salary."

The statement was obviously supposed to damage Dale's character, but he was only dejected by her statement because it insulted his suit. While pinching his suit's lapel he countered, "This tweed suit consists of the finest Italian blended wool and is infused with premium French linen. I assure you, it would cost more than a month's wages from anyone of these classy ladies in this joint to afford such a luxurious garment. So please … retract that statement. Furthermore, the amount of money I possess or don't possess is irrelevant to the fact that the concept of tipping is a scheme for suckers and fuckers alike."

"Well, I'm assuming you're the fucker in this scenario," Aioli replied, and quickly added with indignation, "Waiters and waitresses don't even make minimum wage and rely on tips in order to make a living. Only an asshole would take their service and stiff them after a meal. All their hard work given away for free like slaves."

Dale shook his head while mock clapping. "The classic brainwashed response to the tipping scheme. Wow, I didn't see that reply coming."

Aioli's blood began to boil. She responded with attitude, "Well, why don't you enlighten us feeble-minded girls, Mr. Immaculate-suit man."

"Okay, I'll enlighten you, but first lay off the suit," Dale sternly said, and then proceeded in an unruffled tone. "First of all, tip stands for 'to insure promptitude,' which means paying someone extra to do a job that they should've done correctly at their prior agreed-upon pay. Do you see other vocations stooping to the same methods? Do you give a cashier a tip in order to make sure they promptly scan your groceries? No, that's their job and they're paid by their employers. Do you give a nurse a tip to ensure better care and decrease the chances of dying in a hospital? No, that's their job and they're paid by their employers. Do you tip governors to ensure they do their jobs properly? No, giving politicians money beyond their base pay is called a bribe, which is illegal. So essentially, waiters are preemptively working for that bribe."

Aioli was about to rebuttal, but Dale swiftly continued, "And I haven't even explained the biggest hoax yet: how restaurant owners hoodwinked their customers. The most influential restaurant chain owners bribed congress in order to pass a bill in the 1960s to allow restaurant owners to pay their workers substantially less than minimum wage if tipping was practiced in their restaurants. In this way, they'd legally be able to pay their workers peanuts and force their customers to pay for their workers, along with the food and drinks they purchased. When you, as a customer, step into a restaurant that revolves around tipping, you're instantly getting raped up the ass when you cross the threshold of an establishment. Even before you've partaken of your acai bowl—or whatever bullshit meal you've selected—the staff have already envisioned several times how much money they're going to rape out of you before you escape through their front door."

Aioli finally had a chance to rebuttal. "You speak as if restaurant owners are raking in the cash through this *ploy* that you speak of, but yet, most restaurants find it hard to stay in business let alone make a decent profit. And even when they do, most restaurant owners don't get wealthy from all their hard work."

"That's a good point, I'll give you that," Dale said. "It's much better than your first classically regurgitated statement. Yes, not all restaurant owners are getting wealthy from this scheme, but that doesn't mean it's not a scheme, and doesn't rationalize why their workers are allowed to be treated like slaves. Restaurant owners shouldn't deceive their clientele into paying their workers. Instead, they should pay their workers decent wages and price their food higher. Let the customer decide if they want to buy their food or drinks for the price that's listed on the menu instead of paying a lower-marked price for their food, temporarily believing that's all they have to spend, and then later be reminded they also need to pay the restaurant owner's workers in the form of a tip … or be labeled an asshole if they don't—it's blackmail. And the pathetic thing about this scheme is that the waiters—the slaves—perpetually enforce this scheme upon the clientele, so the battle is always between the customer and the waiter, while the restaurant owners—the real assholes, not the customers that don't tip—count the money in the backroom that their slaves have generated for them. Restaurant owners have effortlessly created the social stigma that labels a customer an asshole if they don't pay their workers' wages. What the fuck is that? How did that become acceptable?"

Aioli still considered Dale an asshole, but he was making some logical points. She wasn't going to go as far as saying he was right, but his opinions held weight and sound deduction. "Interesting viewpoint, Mr. Suit, but you sound pretty righteous for a stockbroker. It's highly hypocritical to speak about how money should be moving around from person to person when your kind on Wall Street get filthy rich by moving money around for the sole purpose of tricking other people out of their hard earned dollars. And at the end of the day, after all this money has been moved around and all the shouted 'buys' and 'sells,' your kind creates nothing useful in the world, no tangible items or valued services benefiting the world." Then she brought up a hand and tapped a finger a few times on the text written on her shirt: KARMA PATROL. "Watch out," she cautioned while doing the tapping.

Valerie was leaning back in her seat like a cute rabbit hiding in its burrow. She was sad about where this date had headed. She realized it was a mistake to have brought Aioli with her. She was supposed to be the stern friend that helped protect her from possible losers, not the stern friend that scared away her future rich husband. Dale Dickerson really was dapper and handsome in his immaculate suits. Fashion and style—and money—really meant a lot to her in a spouse.

After the long debate about tipping concluded, Dale's latte had gone from scalding to lukewarm. "Great." He pushed the latte and the cheesecake away and crossed his arms like a stubborn child, signaling his displeasure and a refusal to consume them. Then he directed his attention back to Aioli. "That's where you're wrong, Aioli. I have acquired many services"—he glanced at Valerie—"and quality items from moving money around in the stock market. The most impressive being my lavish collection of majestic suits. They're sure to entice without having to roll the dice."

"You missed my point—" Aioli began, but was cut off by their waitress's arrival. "Oh, never mind."

The waitress announced their meal orders while placing them on the table in front of them. She wore a long-sleeved black T-shirt with an image of Mercury and text underneath that said something about Mercury retrograde.

Dale gestured toward his cheesecake and latte that lay in the middle of the table and told the waitress, "I'm very much finished with these items and can't stand the sight of them any longer. Please remove them from my presence at once." He held up a stiff hand like he was about to forcefully backhand someone.

The waitress gave Dale the stink eye while collecting his discarded food and drink. While she performed the removal Dale read the text on her shirt: I'VE MASTERED MY SHIT, SO IF WE'RE ARGUING DURING MERCURY RETROGRADE, YOU'RE THE ONE BEING A BITCH, NOT ME. I'M ENLIGHTENED, ASSHOLE.

Valerie enjoyed her Macedonian salad, Aioli ate her acai bowl without emotion—as if she was forced to order such a menu item in order to adhere to some kind of hippie/New Age code—and Dale was dismayed with his moist chicken sandwich because it was awfully dry, which completely contradicted the first word in the food's title on the menu.

It was the last straw that broke the camel's back. Dale thrust his chair backward and swiftly manhandled the plate that held the dry sandwich up to the front counter.

As he was marching away Valerie said, "He sure is intense, isn't he?"

After a spoonful of acai Aioli replied, "In a negative way, yes. He's also a whole lot of other stuff. He's probably one of those onion-type people where different layers are revealed one by one over time, but I'm guessing every one of his onion layers will expose something disturbing and defiling."

Dale found the Mercury-retrograde waitress standing behind the front counter and vigorously spat out his displeasure. "*Hey lady*, I specifically ordered the *Moist* Chicken

Sandwich because I had a desire for something moist and wet. Despite this dish's title, the chicken is absurdly dry."

After being momentarily taken aback from being shouted out, and thinking Dale's 'moist and wet' comment was perverted and a bit rapey, she replied, "Oh no, let me take this back in the kitchen and have the cooks fix it at once. Like, this is so awkward." Although her courteous words were textbook for dealing with disgruntled customers, they were delivered with an austere countenance. She was already imagining exactly what she'd do to his sandwich the moment she was hidden beyond the kitchen door: fiercely spit a copious amount of saliva all over his chicken and thoroughly rub it around with her thumb to soften his meat and return it to his table with a huge grin on her face. Then she'd glance at him every once in a while to take pleasure in the fact that the rapey asshole was eating her spit.

Dale heard the words that offered a solution, but her stark expression and unsympathetic tone were saying something else entirely. They articulated something that he would do if he was in her shoes. "Yeah right, I know what you'll do back there." Dale pointed toward the kitchen door. "You'll moisten up this chicken really nicely with your spit. And perhaps you'll tell the story to a cook or two and have them include their contributions. Maybe add a little urine or bathroom-tile scum to top it off. Then you'll place it on the table before me with a big grin on your stupid-bitchy face."

He paused to enjoy her dumbfounded expression, and then went on, "No, I think I'll eat the fries and later on mash the sandwich into your car's grill, or shove it into your tailpipe, or simply smear it around your windshield with delight. Which would you prefer?"

The shocked waitress said, "I don't own a car. I take the bus."

"Yeah right, no one takes the bus. Buses don't even exist—they're a *myth*."

"Umm ... They are those long and tall vehicles that—"

"Shut up! They're a *myth* … *folklore*. … Well then, you know what? I'll flush this dry shit down your toilet and hope it plugs it up real nice like."

Dale noticed a good amount of café patrons venomously staring at him as he returned to his table after the verbal altercation. He could care less about other people's judgments, and most of these people weren't even people. They were sub-people with sub-par ideologies, and he was willing to bet half of them didn't even think that spectacle at the counter was reality, being that they were currently frying, stoned, blazed, tripping, or in some other way mentally incapacitated. Cocaine was the only drug Dale honored because it allowed him to retain his focus, didn't cloud the mind with distortions, was expensive, and went hand in hand with any successful Wall Street executive.

Valerie showed her sympathy when he returned to the table. "Well, I hope that matter got resolved."

Dale began nibbling on his fries and replied between bites, "Yup, it's all taken care of."

This lunch had proven to be very entertaining for Aioli. Dale was a bona fide douchebag, but in her current dark mood she was partially enjoying their conversations and his café performances. Misery loves company, and Dale's misery was definitely overshadowing her own.

Valerie put her hands on the table and carefully began to slide her chair back. "Please excuse me. I have to use the ladies' room." Dale and Aioli silently nodded in reply.

Dale's phone began to vibrate with an incoming call. He fished it out of his pants and saw Jeremy's name on the screen. "You mind if I take this?"

Aioli lifting one hand in the air with an outlandish expression. "Whatever, I don't care." Then she went back to doodling in a small artsy sketchbook she'd taken out of her purse when Valerie left for the bathroom.

Dale accepted the call. "Hey, Jeremy."

"You're not going to believe what Tim did at work," Jeremy excitedly spouted over the phone.

"Oh yeah, what's that?"

"He finally followed in our footsteps and pulled a scheme at work."

"You're kidding. What did he do?"

"He used a remote access program to take control of a colleague's computer and got him caught with porn on his screen. Due to his company's strict policy on porn, the guy got fired on the spot. But there's more. When a bunch of security guards attempted to escort him out of the building, he resisted and tried to escape. The guards, who were really fat, had to jump on him to stop him and he ended up at the bottom of a pile of guards. The extreme pressure on his body made him blackout. The fired employee was in a coma for a day."

Dale shifted back in his chair and widened his eyes in amazement. Then his eyes narrowed and a smirk crept up on his face. "Well, well. I didn't think he had it in him. Very nice."

"Yeah, I was equally as surprised when he told me. And it worked out for him: he got promoted instead of the guy that got canned. He said his boss didn't have enough time to ponder who was next in line for the promotion, so he simply went by the numbers: employee's stats regarding amount of code completed and their accuracy. Tim was easily on the top of that list so the promotion went to him. He's now a software engineer."

"Looks like there's some hope for him yet," Dale said. "He's finally growing a backbone."

"I hear a lot of chatter in the background. Where are you?"

"Nowhere. Just some abominable café that's jam-packed with hippies, hipsters, and spaced-out New Age cadets, all itching to get home to read their daily horoscopes." Dale cupped a hand over his phone and leaned toward Aioli, "Not you. You're all right in my book."

Aioli's deadpan face sarcastically replied, "Aww, you're quite the charmer."

After a few more back-and-forths with Jeremy, Dale ended the call and put his phone away. He looked up at the café's TV on the wall, which displayed some weird channel that he was finding hard to believe existed. Some hippie freak in a tie-dye shirt sat on a couch in his living room, which was filled with crystals, miniature pyramids, and other New Age knickknacks. The closed captions on the screen showed that the hippie was jabbering on about karma, Mother Earth, forest sprites, and other delusional topics. He presumed the café must have purchased some kind of expensive TV package in order to receive this rubbish on some high three-digit channel.

"How pathetic," Dale mumbled to himself. He noticed that the remote control for the TV had been left on a colorful New Age-looking cabinet within arm's reach. He extended his arm to snatch it up and flipped through a couple channels, ultimately stopping on *The People's Court.*

The current case being depicted was captivatingly asinine. A redneck man named Bob was accusing a different redneck man, named Alvin, of training his dog to dump on his lawn. Alvin countered by accusing Bob of killing his dog when it went missing for weeks. Then, according to Bob, Alvin took up his lost dog's job and started dumping on Bob's lawn himself in the dead of night when Bob was sleeping. Bob had collected all Alvin's dumps in individual plastic bags and was demanding a lab test be done to match the fecal matter to his neighbor. If the match was found positive, Bob wasn't asking for any financial compensation, but rather, a court issue ordering his neighbor to consume all the dumps he had left on Bob's lawn. More specifically, Bob wanted it done upon a table covered with a white tablecloth situated on his lawn with him seated on the other end of the table, allowed to capture Alvin eating his own business on film so he could upload it for his online followers to enjoy. Bob added that he'd allow Alvin to consume a beverage of his choice—non-alcoholic—to assist in downing his dumpings. And for dessert, he'd have to consume his leftover dog's excrement, which—

A waiter grabbed the remote control out of Dale's hand and turned the channel back to the blathering hippie. "The remote control is not allowed to be used by customers," the snippy waiter told Dale. Before the waiter spritely turning on his heels and walking away with his chin held high in the air, Dale read the text on his T-shirt: I'D RATHER BE MEDITATING THAN HAVING MY VIBRATION LOWERED BY BEING IN YOUR PRESENCE.

"Goddammit! I wanted to know if that guy had to eat that other guy's shit." Dale said to himself.

"Spoiler alert," Aioli said. She had followed Dale's mesmerized stare to the TV and had been equally consumed by the show's entertainment value. "Alvin won't be forced to eat his shit. There's no way a judge would pass such a ruling. I'm surprised they even aired that case on national TV."

"You never know," Dale said. "Judges can be some of the most twisted people on the planet. You never know what ruling will spew out of their freakish mouths." After a pause, he disclosed, "I need to use the restroom."

He stood up and waded his way through hippies and hipsters only to find the men's restroom locked with an out-of-order sign on it. Being that he had a great urge to urinate, this predicament vexed Dale. He'd simply use the women's restroom, but Valerie still occupied it, so he held back his urge and returned to the table to nibble on more fries. He tried his best to restrain himself while he waited for Valerie to vacate the bathroom. While waiting, he overheard a hipster seated behind him talking to his hipster girlfriend:

"You can taste the superior texture and robustness of the bean's flavor that comes from the single-origin coffee sold at this café. Single-origin coffee means it comes from one farm and isn't a mix of different blends of coffee beans …"

Dale wouldn't have cared enough to interject if he wasn't under massive urinary strain, but he was extra irritable by the burden and couldn't hold back. He turned around in his chair and leaned forward so that his mouth was uncomfortably close to the hipster's ear, and he proceeded to bark into that ear with bits of spittle occasionally being flung toward the side of the hipster's face. "The single-origin coffee label alone means the beans came from one region in a country. It doesn't mean the beans came from the same farm or isn't a blend of different beans. Get your facts straight, pretentious dipshit. Besides, the general single-origin coffee label was created to cater to pretentious idiots like yourself so you'd happily shell out more money for a mere label that most likely means nothing. It's like labeling a food organic when that type of food is only grown organically anyway, but they con you into paying more for the same product because you're brain-dead. Don't you know that hipsters are supposed to be hip? Hence the name. You're the exact opposite of hip. You're a phony hipster; a phipster."

Rather than replying or even acknowledging Dale, in fear that they may get their heads bitten off, the two hipsters carefully slinked away to a different table as far away from Dale as possible.

"What did I miss?" Valerie said as she gracefully returned to her seat.

Aioli looked up from her sketchbook. "A little coffee-bean rant and a court case revolving around redneck rivalry focused on excrement."

As Aioli filled her friend in on the details, Dale stood up to use the women's restroom, but before he took a step he noticed a café staff member—the one that took the remote control from him—seemingly guarding the women's restroom with crossed arms, staring directly at Dale. *Shit.* He sat back down in his chair, realizing what was going on: They must have locked the men's restroom because of his threat about clogging their toilet with his dry chicken sandwich. And they were also hell bent on making sure he didn't skirt their efforts by sabotaging the ladies' toilet instead.

If he attempted to use the ladies' restroom, he knew that an altercation would ensue. He knew he'd have no trouble besting the hippie staff member, but also knew he wouldn't be able to contain himself from administering anything less than a comprehensive beating, given his highly irritable mood from all the annoying circumstances this café had thrown at him, and the current pressure on his bladder. Also, a beating could lead to a lawsuit against him, which would be a mental hassle and not worth a couple exhilarating moments of beating the crap out of the hapless hippie.

Dammit, this psychotic New Age café literally has me by the balls. A real possibility of being forced to relieve himself in his pants crept up in his mind. He countered this involuntary thought by assuring himself that he'd happily drop his trousers and do his best impression of a sprinkler, watering the despicable patrons around him rather than soiling his luxurious suit pants. However, this defiant act could also result in a lawsuit, a multiple lawsuit. He didn't want to be the next asinine case on *The People's Court.*

His only option was to leave the café as soon as possible. He lifted a hand to give the bill-signing gesture to their waitress, who already had the bill ready and had been itching to deliver it, wanting Dale to leave as soon as possible. The bill was expediently placed on their table. Dale insisted on paying it in order to speed up its return and his departure from the café. It also ensured that no tip would be given.

Their waitress was more than happy to immediately collect the bill after Dale quickly slapped his credit card down on it. She hurried back to the credit card machine and was back at their table in a flash, carefully placing the bill's plastic tray on their table with her finger situated on Dale's credit card, making sure it didn't slide out of place. Knowing for certain she wasn't going to receive a tip, she decided to deliver a message to Dale before he departed. "Here's your bill. You can tell a lot about a person from their name," she said while giving Dale a fuck-you smile for an extended period of time. She kept the devious smile on her face as she turned away from Dale, and kept displaying it all the way back to the counter, as well as from where she stood idly behind the counter.

"What was that all about?" Valerie jealously snapped, having misread the situation. "She's got a thing for you and is tactlessly making it clear. Right in front of my face. The nerve."

Dale bent down to examine the bill tray, wondering why the waitress had taken great care in placing it on the table in a certain way. He could see she hadn't written anything on the bill, but she had left a hidden message for Dale: rather than his credit card being placed on top of the bill, as usual, it was partially under the bill so part of his last name on the credit card was covered up. Instead of seeing DALE DICKERSON, he only saw DALE DICK.

Dale rolled his eyes and lifted his head to meet the waitress's smiling stare from behind the counter. He held her stare with an unreciprocated glare while simultaneously taking up a pen in his right hand and drawing a big zero over most of the lower half of the bill like a kindergartener using a crayon.

All these New Agers and Hippies are phonies, he thought. They're supposed to exude love and light to all living beings, but instead they hid behind judgmental and holier-than-thou fronts, accosting everyone with their passive aggressive nature and bitterly texted tie-dye shirts.

Valerie smiled at the big zero Dale had scribbled on the bill over the line for the tip. "Yeah, that's what she deserves for her audacity. My god … the nerve of her."

Dale's bladder renewed its threats and forced him to halfway double over in his chair. He clenched his pelvic muscles in an attempt to blockade the flow. "What do you say we get out of here," Dale said while wincing.

Aioli laid her sketchbook on the table and stretched her arms in the air while yawning. Then she said, "I feel like relaxing here a little longer if you two don't mind."

Valerie turned to Aioli. "Good idea. I want to stay here and make that bitch feel uncomfortable."

After hearing their intentions, Dale's bladder intensified its threat, sending him a direct message of protest toward the females' spoken plans. He was looking forward to having sex with Valerie's taut body, but he was now at the point of no return. It didn't matter if they ended up staying only five minutes longer—he couldn't stay a second longer. *Screw it. I've got to go now!*

To Valerie and Aioli's astonishment, Dale ejected from his seat like a fighter pilot and bolted for the exit, practically knocking over every hippie and hipster in his path to the front door. A burned-out hippie called out, "Look, the Man's got him by the leash. Run to your board meeting, you sucker in a suit."

Dale yanked open the door and flung himself out of the café. Then another horror dawned on him: he had no idea where the closest public bathroom was.

"Oh, fuck it." He frantically unbuttoned and unzipped his suit pants, whipped out his unit, and began to urinate all over the large window in front of the café. A sweet sigh of relief escaped his mouth. The pressure had been lifted and the feeling was just capital.

Halfway through his stream, he brought his upward-tilted head down to eye level to survey the café goers' reactions to his public display of indecency. A mix of utterly shocked wide open-mouthed faces and hysterically laughing faces stared back at him. Valerie was one of the wide open-mouthed faces and Aioli was one of the few laughers.

While almost done with his business he was conducting with the window, Dale noticed something interesting about the name of the café that he couldn't believe he hadn't spotted before. Awakening Soul Soother Café, or it's more appropriate acronym name: ASS Café. How fitting, he thought, given their food tastes like it has been dispensed from someone's ass.

Chapter 7

Accepting the invitation to his colleague's house-warming party was a regretful mistake. Dale surreptitiously slipped out of the crowded dining room, leaving the din of chatter behind him as he padded along the long hallway toward the bathroom. He didn't really need to use the bathroom, he simply wanted to escape the dull conversations of his colleagues. He thought it was abundantly clear that Josh Johnson had organized the dinner solely to show off his new home and flaunt his hot wife.

He had desperately wanted to decline the invitation and felt inner torment when he had relinquished and accepted. He had consented purely to meet the social requirements that kept him in good standing with influential people that could ultimately decide his future advancement at Stryker & Marshall.

Lingering in the bathroom sparked a flashback from the day before: his urinary debacle at the ASS Café. He chuckled to himself while staring at his reflection in the mirror. That despicable café had thwarted his lusty plans of steamy sex with Valerie's taut body. What a shame.

The sound of footfalls made their way down the hallway. Dale reached for the doorknob to exit, wanting to avoid an awkward verbal exchange that might proceed after the person on the other side of the door encountered a locked door. But he halted his hand on the doorknob when he heard the footsteps cease and quiet voices conversing in the hallway.

With his ear to the door, he recognized the voices of Josh Johnson and Garret Williams. Josh was quietly cracking a joke about Blaine Covington, a senior vice president. Josh said Blaine always hauled at least three doughnuts out of the break room daily, and expressed that it was only a matter of time before he succumbed to a second heart attack from his predominant diet of sweets and cured meats. Then he went on to speculate that Blaine's wife, Rachel, had been shagging at least two other guys during their three-year marriage. He joked that instead of Rachel getting the three-year itch from her marriage, she'd been a three-year bitch, pounding dick left and right.

Luckily neither of them needed to use the bathroom and they returned to the dining room after Josh showed Garret a picture he'd taken, a picture he seemed rather proud of. Dale had noticed the framed picture on the hallway wall on the way to the bathroom. It was a reflection shot of the building they worked at, taken through a large puddle in the street after a downpour of rain. It was satisfactory at best and definitely didn't warrant the gloating coming out of Josh's mouth.

Dale exited the bathroom after they were gone. He took a couple steps toward the chatter in the dining room before pausing. Instead of directly returning to his colleagues' annoying conversations, he decided to tour the ground floor of the house a little more. He could say he'd been looking for the bathroom if someone came across him.

Near the end of the long hallway, in the opposite direction of the living room, he spotted an abnormally narrow door. Opening the door revealed a sharp decline of stairs that descended to a basement.

Basements had always intrigued Dale. He thought a man could be summed up by what was kept in his basement. He descended the stairs with a mischievous smile, imagining what he'd find. Maybe some dead bodies in a large freezer, or a neighbor decomposing in a bathtub full of lye. He gleefully rubbed his palms together in anticipation as he continued to step down the stairs.

His excitement instantly evaporated when he reached the bottom of the stairs to find the room almost completely empty. It looked like they hadn't gotten around to utilizing the room yet. However, one item in the basement did catch Dale's eye: a French Victorian-style rotary dial telephone. The only other time he'd seen one was at an antique shop he was forced to peruse while waiting for his girlfriend at the time.

Upon closer examination he could tell it was vintage, not a modern knockoff for those that liked old-style commodities. He fondled the receiver and ran his hands across the brass base, admiring the craftsmanship. When he brought the receiver closer to his eyes to inspect it, he heard a dial tone. It was operational and still connected to a phone plan. How odd, yet magical.

There was no way it was Josh's or his wife's. From what he'd seen in their house they had little taste and seemed to prefer sleek modern goods. It must have been forgotten by the previous house's owner. The phone being in an almost empty basement, along with its ornate brass finish, gave it the appearance of a magical device, like a genie lamp.

Thinking of the gossip he'd overheard Josh speaking moments ago, he fantasized using the magical device to secretly disclose Josh's gossip back to its defamed parties. Then he imagined all the victims marching to Josh's house with pitchforks, shouting outside his door for his head, eventually setting the house aflame, then jumping repeatedly in the air with crazed euphoria in celebration after hearing the screams of Josh's family burning alive within.

Dale snapped out of his reverie and almost dropped the receiver when he realized he might be able to bring this fantasy to reality, or at least a modern-day version. He put the receiver back on its hanger, picked it back up, and carefully went through all the tedious swipes on the rotary dial to call his phone number.

His phone started vibrating in his suit pants. It worked. He fished his phone out of his pants and read the display screen: AGATHA MARPLE, along with a number. Dale had an app installed on his phone that revealed the name of the callers that weren't on his contact list. Agatha Marple must have been the house's previous owner. Somehow she had not only forgotten this prized vintage phone, but had also failed to end its landline plan with the phone company. Maybe she had Alzheimer's.

Maybe she had been hit by a bus and her relatives didn't do a proper job finalizing her affairs. Maybe she got murdered in this very house: Colonel Mustard with the candlestick in the library perhaps.

He didn't know how the vintage phone being left behind had come to pass, but he could use it to prank call his colleagues and spout off accusations and jokes infused with details that might allow his coworkers to finger Josh as the culprit.

But if he couldn't access the phone, he wouldn't be able to use it of course. The solution to that problem was already staring Dale in the face: a small sliding window near the basement's ceiling that accessed the backyard. It was big enough for him to shimmy through and could be left unlocked and slightly ajar for easy access.

It appeared the Johnsons never used this room, so they wouldn't notice the small change in the window's state. Even if they did wander on down to the basement, they wouldn't notice the window being opened a smidge, or that the lock was in the unlocked position.

If he made a sufficient amount of pranks with this beauty of a phone, this plan might just work. Concurrently, Dale would have to ensure the opening assistant VP position left in Josh's wake would be seized by no one other than himself. He scratched his chin in thought as he quietly ascended the basement stairs and headed back toward the din of chatter.

While the women remained in the dining room, the men had spilled into the library where their conversations continued over *digestifs* and more comfortable furnishings. Dale walked into the library where twelve suits were twirling snifters and tumblers. Several conversations—mostly about the market and clients—were dispersed among small groups throughout the room.

"There you are, Dickerson," Josh said after a swallow of brandy. "What's your poison?" He moseyed over to a glass bar stand that held an array of decanters.

"Hair of the dog that bit me. Cognac. Neat. Don't be stingy." Dale took up residence on a leather divan close to Andy Singer, the VP that Josh worked under. He turned toward Andy, who was listening to a conversation but not actively engaged. "Heard you were looking for a tennis partner for doubles."

"That's right. I was hoping Johnson could've filled that role, but he doesn't play. Seems he's not a sporting man." The latter statement was directed toward Josh Johnson, who had strolled over to hand Dale a snifter with cognac. Josh shrugged at Andy's comment.

Dale extended his hand to collect the drink from Josh. "Well it just so happens that I played some tennis at university. Not on the team or anything, but with some friends of mine who did."

"Hmm, is that right?" Andy took the last gulp of his whiskey and held up his empty tumbler, shaking it around in the air, beckoning Josh for a refill. "Next Sunday around noon, the Seattle Tennis Club. What say you, Dickerson? You got what it takes to play with the big boys?" A masculine, intoxicated chuckle escaped Andy's mouth as he heartily slapped the thigh of a senior VP, Paul Bryce, seated next to him, presumably one of the aforementioned "big boys," Dale assumed.

"That would be grand. I've been wanting to pick the game back up. I'll break out my dusty racket. I don't possess any balls, but I could pick some up if needed."

Andy cackled and slapped Paul Bryce's thigh again. "The man has no balls! Well, we'll have to rectify that. Don't worry, we have more than enough balls. Just bring your racket and white attire to adhere to the club's dress code. The Pro Shop will restring your jacket, or you can purchase a new one if it's unsalvageable. After tennis we'll visit their massage room, and then we'll have lunch at the Bistro, their on-sight culinary delight that overlooks the tennis courts and the waterfront."

Paul Bryce hadn't drunk as much as Andy Singer—not yet anyway—and looked slightly annoyed about his thigh being repeatedly slapped, but he was more than happy to break away from a conversation to weigh in on the ball jokes. "Not to worry. You'll be swimming in balls before lunchtime, I assure you. Yes. Brimming with balls, as it were."

Dale flashed a light-hearted smile in response. "The Seattle Tennis Club is located in Madison Park, right?"

Andy Singer nodded his head while taking in whiskey. "We'll be arriving via their private beach access in Bryce's yacht, so you'll want to meet us in the outside lounge."

Dale had never had the pleasure of visiting the Seattle Tennis Club. With its panoramic views of Lake Washington and Mount Rainier in the background, it had been the place to play tennis since its 1890 inauguration.

As the evening went on into the night, Dale produced enough counterfeit smiles to last him a lifetime. Each one coming more easily as flowing libations of cognac lubricated all forty-three of his facial muscles.

After fiercely smacking the alarm clock that offended his aching head, Dale rolled out of bed with a slight hangover. Groaning and cracking his upper-back and neck muscles didn't seem to be lessening his pulsating head, so he stumbled into the bathroom in hopes that a warm shower would ease his ailment.

No luck. It remained and reminded him of the minor headaches he'd awoken with in the past that had progressively built as the day dragged on instead of gradually tapering off. It felt like it was going to be one of those bastards, so he pounded down some headache medicine, knowing that he'd most likely have to down two more pills hours later when the bastard hadn't subsided. Best to kill the sonuvabitch as soon as possible instead of waiting for it to slink away on its own accord.

Unlike his past hangovers, this one was well-earned. He had become quite chummy with Andy Singer and some of his future tennis pals, even if solely due to the assuasive effects of alcohol. He was confident about holding his own or even outperforming them in the game of tennis. Perhaps he'd even have to dumb down his game a bit to avoid jealous animosity. He'd have to further win their fondness among sobriety on the tennis court, but he would already be in their good graces due to last night's intoxication.

A week after the Johnsons' house-warming, Dale decided to make the first prank call. Friday and Saturday night escapades would work best, as he'd be able to sleep in late the day after.

In the dead of night, he'd snuck into the Johnsons' yard after parking his car a few houses away. Instead of motion-activated lights, the front yard was littered with solar-powered lights in the shape of small glowing birdhouses on metallic poles that were staked into the ground.

Due to the absence of fences in the front yard and backyard, nothing impeded his route to the small sliding window in the backyard that afforded access to the basement. There were also a few birdhouse lights in the backyard near the house, enough to assist him in finding the sliding window but few enough to allow shadows to veil his presence.

It appeared this part of the scheme was going to be a piece of cake. He smirked at the thought and bent down to the ground to slide the window open. Aware of the fact that he'd be shimmying through a window near the dirt, he wasn't sporting his ubiquitous attire: an immaculate suit. Instead he wore dark sweatpants and a dark long-sleeved T-shirt. His proclivity for opulent attire left him feeling destitute and filthy in the peasant rags he was currently sporting, and he hadn't even wiggled around on the dirt in front of the window yet. He wasn't going to enjoy this, but sometimes you have to get a little dirty to get the job done.

While slowly sliding the window open, he heard a low growl behind him. *Oh, shit. I didn't know they had a dog.*

Dale slowly started turning around, hoping his steady movement wouldn't provoke the mongrel. After making the slow turn he spotted a tiny dog about six feet away. He didn't know what type of dog it was—he hated dogs and never bothered learning the names of different breeds—but he knew it couldn't harm him due to its stature. But if its growl turned into barking, the Johnsons could be alerted, and he'd be screwed.

As if the mutt had read his thoughts, the little shit began barking, or that's merely what those stupid creatures did in response to everything. He stood and pressed his back against the house in response to the dog's provocation. "Good doggy, good doggy. Now shut the fuck up, please." The dog kept barking. "I'll spit on you, you little shit. Cut it out." The dog ignored his threat and continued barking. Dale's negotiating face turned stern. "I'll stomp on you. These sneakers will snuff the life right out of your putrid existence if you don't cease and desist."

He heard a window open on the second floor directly above him.

"What's the matter, Houdini?" Josh called down to the dog. "You cornered a squirrel or something?"

Dale thought about making a beeline out of the yard and back to his car. There's no way Josh would recognize him in his peasant's clothes, and the dimly lit yard wouldn't advertise his face. But he decided to stay put, flush against the house, hoping Josh's viewing angle would stay limited. But if Josh stuck his head out the window, Dale would be spotted.

"What's Houdini barking about?" Josh's wife asked. Her voice was much quieter than Josh's, so she was either in another room or on the far side of the room with the window.

"I don't know because the stupid screen on the window doesn't allow me to stick my head out to get a better view. I told you we should take all the screens off. They're tacky."

They quarreled a bit about the screens and how they prevent mosquitoes from entering the house. Then his wife went back to bed, and Josh spoke to the dog one last time before slamming the window shut. "We're trying to sleep, Houdini. Quit barking at the house. When you get a job you can buy a one-point-seven million-dollar house that's more to your liking. Okay?"

After the window slammed shut Dale aggressively whispered to the dog, "Yeah, shut up, you ungrateful little shit." But the dog kept yipping.

He remembered a hard candy he had earlier felt in the left pocket of the sweatpants. "I got a treat for you, little dipshit." He quickly removed it from its wrapper and tossed it in front of the dog.

Houdini looked at the mysterious item and back at Dale, switching his eye contact several times between the two. He finally ceased yipping and cautiously approached the candy. He sniffed it, licked it several times, and started biting it. Then he darted his eyes back and forth from Dale to the pieces of bitten candy on the ground.

"Good, isn't it?" Dale whispered. The dog didn't agree and started barking again.

He needed to shut the dog up, and keep it quiet or he wouldn't be able to perform his scheme. But besides the one piece of hard candy, he had no tools at his disposal to pacify the dog. He desperately tried thinking of a solution as the pooch continued to bark, but no idea was surfacing.

Due to his hatred for dogs and a well-thought-out plan going down the drain, a sharp flash of anger coursed through his body and brought his blood to a boiling point. In a fit of rage he became aware of a tool he could use to silence the dog and put his plan back on track. His eyes locked on the closest birdhouse light five feet to his right. He ripped it out of the ground, unearthing a metallic spear at the bottom of the birdhouse's pole. Using all his might, he brought the spear down upon the dog and skewered it in one go. The barking was abruptly stopped and turned into quiet whimpering, and then silence.

A confident, in-control smirk returned to Dale's face. "Now that's a legit shish kebab." Problem solved. Now for a quick cleanup. Crudely using dirt, he rubbed the blood from the middle section of the pole and hid the rest underground when he returned the birdhouse light to its original spot.

He eyeballed the dead dog and then lifted his gaze past the backyard to the tree line, which was about twenty yards away. *I can do that*, he assured himself. He picked up the dog and drop-kicked it as hard as he could, aiming to send it over the backyard and into the woods. The dead dog flew a few feet forward, then suddenly and forcefully arced around in the air, circling all the way back to Dale and slamming into his chest, all in a matter of one second.

Gore splattered all over his long-sleeved T-shirt. Blood flecked his face, which was turning away in surprised horror as the dog made full contact, pounding viciously against his upper chest.

After stumbling back a few steps, he turned back toward the dog with fists raised in a boxing stance, ready to pummel the hell out of Houdini, the dog that apparently escaped the clutches of death—living up to his name—and was now after revenge. But instead of jumping for Dale's jugular, the dog lay motionless on the ground, sure as dead.

"What the hell?" Dale perplexingly whispered. He cautiously bent down to examine the hopefully deceased dog, but saw nothing extraordinary, just a dead little dog. The dog's stillness gave him the boldness to bring his face closer for a more in-depth inspection. Then he saw it.

"Oh my god," he murmured to himself. "I thought I was going crazy. Thought the little shit was supernatural or something and had it out for me." The dog had a narrow black leather collar that was connected to a thin black rope, which appeared to be fastened to a stake in the ground. It was the reason why the dog had circled back to him in midflight like a smacked tetherball.

The dog hadn't been much of a Houdini for failing to escape such an amateur prison. Maybe the Johnsons were scared the dog would run away from the new house, not yet accustomed to calling it home. That and the house was fenceless.

He untied the rope from the dog's collar and got back into a punting stance. While holding his breath, he punted the dead dog into the woods. It easily cleared the backyard and sailed between two evergreen trees.

Dale raised his arms in triumph. "And the field goal is good," he whispered. Then he heard the dead pooch splat on something hard when it made contact with the ground, deep enough into the woods to stay hidden from the Johnsons and provide sustenance to rodents, maggots, and whatnot.

"Escape that Houdini, you little dipshit," he whispered into the still night air.

Instead of feeling guilty for having killed a dog, Dale felt victorious and philanthropic. He had singlehandedly accomplished three goals: Scored three points with a field goal, supplied creatures of the woods with nourishment, and liberated a dog from its human captives. Not just because it was tied up, but because centuries ago humans had domesticated wolves and messed with their genes through countless crossbreeding with other domesticated wolves. After centuries of this aversion, the result was a pathetic creature that was needy, smelly, suffered from ADHD, and continually slobbered everywhere. No wonder dogs were always barking; they were mad as hell at what humans had done to them: turning them into pitiful slaves with Stockholm syndrome.

Wolves, on the other hand, still held their dignity and strength, and were probably plotting to rid the world of humans and cleanse the earth of the abominable species—dogs—man had created from their proud genes. This very second, somewhere in the mountains, they were devising their plans for the takeover. Dale respected wolves and sympathized with their plight. He was happy to have helped them out a bit by dispatching one of the many Frankenstein-like laboratory experiments that roamed the earth.

Back to the matter at hand now that the dog was done for. He shimmied through the small sliding window, landed on the floor of the basement as quietly as possible, and slinked to the vintage phone. The magical phone that would allow him to anonymously coax his fellow colleagues into demanding the removal of Josh Johnson's flesh from his body by way of some medieval method.

Harold Allen, a senior VP, would be the first to be prank called. From his sweatpants pocket, Dale took out a slip of paper that held private cellphone numbers, Harold's being on the top. He had written them down prior, thinking it best to leave his phone in his car so it wouldn't get in the way or possibly get damaged while he crawled through the window. He picked up the vintage phone's receiver and carefully dialed in the numbers on the rotary dial.

It rang several times. If Harold didn't pick up, he'd move to the next phone number on the list. Maybe he was a hard sleeper. Maybe he put his phone on silent mode before sleeping. He realized from the beginning that nighttime phone calls wouldn't always connect, but when they did, they'd connect with a less cognitive person due to grogginess, so they'd be easier to mess with.

The whole idea was to leave hints that the prank caller was someone they worked with, and hopefully enough people would utilize enough spoken details to finger Josh in particular. But the vintage phone's number being connected to Josh's household would most likely be how Josh got incriminated. If he got enough people at work furious, they'd be more motivated to dedicate some time for detective work and trace the call to its physical origin.

The phone call was answered after about fifteen rings. "Hello," a groggy Harold Allen spoke into the phone.

Dale rattled off his opener in an infomercial voice, "Do you or someone you know suffer from being a complete fucking moron? Is your stupidity greatly affecting your loved ones and colleagues? If you answered yes to any of these questions, don't worry, we have the miracle solution for you, all in one pill. A pill called Swallow Your Idiocy Away."

"If anyone is an idiot here, it's you for making a phone call in the dead of night while people are trying to sleep," a disoriented Harold snapped. "I'm not an idiot, and I don't need your goddamn pill."

"Excuse me, sir, your wife, Sharon Allen, disagrees," Dale said, still using an infomercial voice. "Let's pull up a quote from her, shall we? 'The idiot can't even use a toilet correctly. I should pay a dog trainer to teach him how to squat down and do his business properly instead of paying a housecleaner to repeatedly wipe up all his misdirected urine.' "

Having heard his wife's name, Harold figured this was more than just an anonymous prank call, and so he became both fearful and angrier. "I don't know who this is, but I'm calling bullshit on your quote. My wife wouldn't say that."

During Josh's house gathering, Dale actually had overheard Harold's wife comment on his toiletry aim after she had drunk much wine with the other wives in the kitchen. Of course, she had commented about it very briefly and without foul language and attitude.

"In honor of our miracle pill, Swallow This, You Fucking Idiot ... I mean ..." Dale had temporarily forgot what he'd originally called the imaginary pill. "Sorry. I meant, in honor of our miracle pill, Swallow Your Idiocy Away, we'll provide you with more damning evidence from your disgruntled better half. Sharon, your wife, uploaded several photos of your urine-peppered toilet on a wives' forum under the thread title THE IDIOT SATURATED THE TOILET AGAIN, and also under the thread title BAD AIM, A SMALL-DICK PREDICAMENT."

Harold was almost certain these allegations were false, but even the slimmest possibility of them being halfway true scared the hell out of him. "You're spouting fabrications. Listen, buddy, I got your phone number ... I can find out where you live." Harold hoped the threat was sufficient enough to convince the prank caller to hang up and not call back.

"Excuse me, *sir.* I know for a fact that you can't track down my address, because you're an idiot who hasn't been swallowing *our miracle pill*: Swallow, Dumbfuck," Dale had again forgotten what he'd initially called the miracle pill, "or... whatever I said it was called. So start doing the right thing today: stop thinking and just swallow our daily pills. It's the pharmaceutical way to instant happiness. A month's supply is only ninety-nine, ninety-nine. That's right, only ninety-nine dollars and ninety-nine cents. So call now, operators are standing by."

Seeing how his threat had no effect, Harold decided to point out the lunacy of the caller's fast delivered prattle. "Why would I call someone? I'm already on the phone with you. You didn't even give me a number to call, moron."

"That's an excellent point, sir. You're showing potential. Maybe you'll only have to be on our miracle pill for six months. After this joyous call with me, call 1-800-858-5555. Again, that's 1-800-85—"

"Shut up, moron!" Harold shouted into the phone before ending the call.

Dale had to cover his mouth with both hands in order to stop himself from laughing loudly. He was positive that Josh and his wife couldn't hear him talking on the phone in the basement while they resided on the second floor. It was too great of a distance, and million-dollar houses tended to have superb soundproofing. But a loud laugh could reverberate off the walls, so he wasn't going to push his luck.

His prank call antics had made him feel like a kid again, but it felt invigorating instead of immature. Besides, many late-night couch potatoes were subjected to infomercials touting asinine products every night, similar to the one he'd just made up. And pharmaceutical companies raked in billions by forcing all kinds of pills down the throats of the ill-informed populace. So in light of these facts, was his prank call really that immature? If it was, it wasn't any more immature than the millions of idiots that were swallowing their prescribed pills every day.

Dale hung up the phone and decided to call back and rattle off the one-eight-hundred number a few more times to utterly piss off Harold, but Harold didn't pick up the phone again. Obviously he had recognized the number and knew better than to invite a lunatic back into his ear.

Dale had originally planned on making one prank call per basement visit, but when he thought longer about it, that logic didn't make much sense for two reasons: each visit increased his chances of getting caught, and the faster the prank calls were delivered, the quicker the rage would build at the office and provoke people to find the prank caller's physical address, which would hopefully lead to Josh's front door and not Agatha Marple's new address. If Agatha—the previous owner of the vintage phone—was even still alive and had a new address.

In this new line of thought, he'd make one more prank call for the night. The next number on his slip of paper was Gerald van Buren, a senior execute VP, top of the heap, not counting the CEO himself, Patrick Babcock.

Gerald van Buren must have been a night owl because he answered the call on the second ring and didn't sound like he had just woken up. "Hello."

Dale put on a Brooklyn accent for this prank call. "Hello, Gerald van Buren. This is Bob. I'm what you might call a go-getter. And, well … I've done it again. I've gone and gotten something big. Well, in your case, something small, very small: enlarged photos of your dick with my professional mega-zoom camera. Believe me, this camera is top of the line. Super-enlarged photos with any other camera would've produced heavily pixelated blocks where your meat Popsicle resides, given the smallness of its stature. So here's the rub. Give me buku bucks or your small dick pics make the rounds on the Internets. Ya know, the usual juicy places: E-mailed to your son, Lucas; your boss, Patrick Babcock; friends; colleagues. As well as other juicy places on the net, like forums and whatnot. I don't need to send it to your wife cause she knows already. So here's what you'll do to avoid all that. You'll throw a duffel bag with said buku bucks under the bridge next Tuesday. Ya hear me, small man?"

After hearing the long-winded threat, Gerald van Buren's first reaction, being a man of details, was to clear up some ambiguity. "What bridge?" He figured that if the prank caller couldn't name a bridge in the Seattle area, it was most definitely a baseless threat made by a prank caller that could've resided anywhere in the country, because information like sons' and bosses' names could easily be found online.

Dale was surprised with Gerald's short reply. He had been anticipating a confrontational reply that would've spanned at least two sentences. He paused for a bit to allow Gerald to say more, but when only silence hung on the line, he shrugged his shoulders and gave an answer to the question. "The bridge that has cast a shadow over you your entire life. It's called I Know You Don't Got Buku Bucks So I'm Gonna Release Your Small Dick Pics Tomorrow Bridge. So, yeah, remember the duffel bag for next Tuesday."

Although annoyed with the phone call, Gerald rested assured that it was merely a baseless prank call. And he didn't buy the Brooklyn accent. "Sure buddy, you don't even know what bridges I live by. Why don't you go back to playing videogames and your half-eaten peanut butter and jelly sandwich, you prepubescent twerp."

Dale remembered a conversation where Gerald van Buren had gloated about living in one of the richest neighborhoods in Seattle on the shores of Lake Washington near the University of Washington. Was the neighborhood Laurelhurst or Madison Park? He couldn't remember, so he named a bridge that was near both. "Montlake Bridge. Duffel bag. Buku bucks. Next Tuesday. You best make the drop, or I'll be dropping the photos on the net."

"There's nothing but water under the Montlake Bridge. The bag would sink under water, moron."

Dale figured his guess had been good enough because Gerald was now flustered. "That's where your life will end up—under water—if you don't make the drop. So, yeah, remember next Tuesday."

"*Listen here, bucko.* I'm not—"

Dale hung up the phone on a shouting Gerald van Buren. He'd forgotten how amusing and humorous childish pranks could be. The end justified the means, he told himself. The deceitful deeds left along the path leading to a clever man's wealth were like a trail of bread crumbs. The crumbs would be quickly consumed by naive birds and vermin, leaving the trail spotless, akin to a man grabbing abandoned, dirty money left on the street.

He'd have to make more prank calls, but he was done for the night. A job well done deserved a good night's rest. He unplugged the vintage phone so his prank-call victims couldn't call back while he was away. Then he shimmied out the window, crept around the house from the backyard to the front yard, and made his way back to his car. He replayed the prank calls in his head and chuckled as he drove home.

When he got home he threw his clothes and sneakers, which were crusted with dried blood, into the bathtub. He'd deal with them tomorrow morning: clean them, burn them, whatever. All he wanted to do now was sleep. He dived into bed, threw the blankets over himself, felt the soft pillow form around his head, and started to doze off like a carefree newborn.

After swiftly falling asleep and heading into dreamland, he dreamed he was the most famous dog punter in the land. Families would pay him large sums of money to see how far he could punt their dogs. Each time was the same: families would joyfully jump and clap as they watched their dogs getting punted and sailing through the air. Then he'd throw up his hands in the air to hail victory as the family ran to his side, patting him on the back and begging for autographs.

After several nights of sneaking into the basement to make prank calls, some disgruntled dialog began popping up in conversations around the office about the calls. Unfortunately his colleagues' resentment didn't produce enough antagonism to instigate a witch hunt for the perpetrator.

Dale was growing impatient. This particular scheme involved too much work, and he wasn't even sure it would generate results. The repeated twenty-minute drive—one way—to the Johnsons' residence was growing tiresome by itself. Maybe he had constructed a dud of a plan this time around.

Thoughts of doubt clouded Dale's mind as he drove on empty streets in the dead of night on his way to the Johnsons' basement for another round of prank calls. In order to incite action as quickly as possible, he'd include a prank call to the CEO himself.

After parking his car and slinking toward the Johnsons' residence in his peasant rags, he noticed a lost dog flier for Houdini posted on a street light pole. "Good luck with that," he whispered to himself while snickering. He imagined Houdini's eviscerated corpse being feasted upon by unrelenting maggots and forest creatures. He was now a gourmet snack and nothing else.

The route from his parked car to the basement window became a cakewalk after he had noted the most shadowy areas along the path, and because there wasn't a yipping dog to meet him in the backyard.

After shimmying through the sliding window and plugging the vintage phone back into the wall socket, he picked up the phone to make his first prank call for the night. Why not start it out with a bang and make the CEO his first mark.

Patrick Babcock picked up on the fourth ring and sounded exhausted. "Hello."

Dale put on a Southern blue-collar accent. "Hello, Mr. Babcock. Just calling to confirm the pickup and crushing of your Aston Martin One-77 for this Monday. Never smashed a car worth more than a million dollars before, but hey, I guess there's a first time for everything. You make the order, we smash—"

"What are you talking about? If you put a finger on my One-77 …"

Dale guessed the man was too fatigued to vocalize a threat. "Don't worry, we're good at what we do. We'll smash it till it resembles a little cube. All evidence of your whoring within the structure of the car will be concealed when it takes the shape of a tight metal box."

"What whoring? I made no such order! You don't have the authority to do anything with my One-77."

"I'm looking at the order form now. Looks like your mistress made the order. She marked on the form that the vehicle was under her name because you're a scumbag that's always hiding your assets from the IRS. Hell of a thing to add in the comment section. So we do have the authority, sir. But I agree with you on the whoring bit; the interior of a One-77 is way too compact to enjoy any whoring. Only a gymnast could do you in a car like that. Maybe your mistress meant the whoring that happened in fancy hotels after the One-77 did its job at luring females inside and then preparing them for a different ride altogether at the hotel, after the exhilarating car ride over had got 'em all moist and ready to go. Hell, I'd get—"

"I'll have your head if you touch—"

"Hey, shut your pie hole. I wasn't done talking. Don't interrupt me, Badcock, you sonuvabitch! I was sayin' I'd get wet ridin' in a One-77 too, so I can relate. But no matter how sexy a One-77 is, I wouldn't fornicate with you at any destination it pulled up to."

"I don't participate in any whoring. I don't care what slander that bitch wrote on that form. Furthermore, you'd have to illegally break into my garage to collect the One-77. Your form's authority is useless, so shove it up your ass."

"Your mistress gave us a remote control to open the garage door, so we don't need to break in to collect it."

"That still doesn't give you the authority to enter my house!"

"Well hell, remote control or no remote control, I'd break into your garage just to lick a One-77. Hell, it'd be the fanciest thing I've ever put my tongue on. Yeehaw! I'm gonna lick it. You can be sure of that, Mr. Badcock. One way or another, I be lickin' it."

"It's Babcock, not Badcock. … How about I give you ten thousand dollars and you shred that order form and never let that bitch in your office again?"

"That's a tempting offer, Badcock, but my tongue is holding out to slather a long saliva path on something worth 1.87 million dollars, not a measly ten large."

"Why do you want to lick it? Why would you want to crush it? It's one of the rarest cars in the world."

"Why do we crush cars? We don't get that question a lot. The most obvious reason: they take up less space. What a stupid question. You don't got enough sense to pour piss out of a boot."

"If she made the order and gave you the authority with a form, why are you calling me instead of her to confirm the order?"

"Well, I'll be. You're absolutely right, Badcock. My apologies. We'll call her. Goodbye."

"Hey, hold on—"

Dale hung up the phone on the CEO.

He didn't know the guy personally, but he had heard of his infidelities and the bit about the car being under a mistress's name, which seemed to be adequate information to piss the CEO off. He didn't know Mr. Babcock personally and didn't derive any particular pleasure in making a fool of him over the phone, but it had been exhilarating to lambaste the CEO of Stryker & Marshall, simply because he had the ability to reach Babcock on his personal line and chastise him, even if only anonymously. He found it utterly electrifying to best a tycoon. It was a pure ego boost.

Roasting the CEO would hopefully galvanize Stryker & Marshall into tracking down the origin of the prank calls, which would conclude his latest scheme and remove the need for the time-consuming trips to the Johnsons'. He also couldn't wait to stop donning peasant clothes. Merely wearing the rags made him feel inferior, weak, like someone who'd never be a multi-millionaire.

He picked up the receiver for the last prank call of the evening. The final prank call period, with luck. The mark: Dorian White, executive senior VP. The phone had rung fifteen times without an answer, so he hung up. He looked for the next person on his list.

The next mark: Blaine Covington, senior VP. Dale made the call and it was answered on the fifth ring. "Hello."

Dale mimicked a teenage voice going through puberty, cracking and breaking constantly. "Hello. Is this Mr. Covington, Blaine Covington?"

"Yes, this is he."

"Hello, Mr. Covington. This is Timmy at Pizza Porkster. Your business card was the lucky winner in our drawing."

"Which entails …?"

"Free pizza every Sunday for six months."

"Okay. Let's get down to brass tacks. How many pizzas every Sunday and are there topping exclusions?" *Sniff.*

Given it was a Friday night and Blaine Covington was talking very quickly and sniffing occasionally, Dale assumed he was on a late-night cocaine binge. "You get two pizzas every Sunday and there's no topping exclusions, but our topping choices are more limited than most pizza joints."

"Hit me. What are they?" *Sniff.* "List them off."

"We've got the usual toppings: pictures of you engaging in various narcotics; quit eating all the doughnuts in the break room or I'll sucker punch you in the gut; your wife, Rachel, is screwing two other dudes besides you and loves to engage in all-night rompathons; your Mercedes isn't the newest model ha-ha; that eBay user is still awaiting your payment for the penis enlargement suction machine; and pepperoni. You know, all the usuals, sir."

Sniff. "Most of those don't entice me. I'll just stick to pepperoni, kid."

Dale was caught off guard by Blaine Covington's response. At least the guy had a sense of humor. But this next part would surely ignite his paranoia and arouse wrath. "All righty. Let me verify your address." Dale rattled off Blaine Covington's address.

"How'd you get my address, you little cocksucker?" *Sniff.*

"With that new phone app called Ha-Ha Now I Got Your Address Bitch, or NIGYAB for short. So yeah, no worries, we got you covered … bitch."

"Hey kid, if you send any of those toppings to my door, besides pepperoni, it'll be the end of you. You hear me?"

"Well, we very well can't deliver the two dudes screwing your wife on a pizza. Physically, that would be a hard task, virtually impossible. Even if we did pull it off somehow, they'd ruin the pizzas for sure—shoe prints, hand marks, dislodged cheese, you name it. Jeez. So we'll probably stick to pepperoni, your Mercedes isn't the newest model ha-ha, and the various narcotic pictures, because just pepperoni would be kind of boring. Sound good, sir?"

Sniff. "You little jackanapes! I'll shove you in a jack-in-the-box. I'll decapitate you and put your head on the coil spring and the whole bit. I'll make your dead mom a pizza topping and feed it to your—"

Dale hung up the phone and unplugged it. That call had started out the most docile of all his prank calls, and then ended up the most vindictive. It was definitely effective, that was for sure. Although, the prank call to the CEO held the most sway. If anyone could snap their fingers and make an employee disappear instantly, it was Patrick Babcock.

During the two months Dale had been enacting his prank-call scheme, he was simultaneously spending time with his new tennis pals, the self-proclaimed Big Boys. A group of colleagues that held high-ranking positions at Stryker & Marshall and had tendrils embedded throughout the financial field.

Before, Dale feigned affability at work and at the few doings he felt obligated to attend outside of the office in order to stay in good standing with his colleagues. Now, he was spending quite a bit of time with the Big Boys. At first he thought the time spent with them would be tiresome and annoying, but it ended up being not as unpleasant as imagined, and sometimes even gratifying. As time passed he was surprised to find himself looking forward to their assemblage.

It first started out as tennis games accompanied by lunch, and then began to include swanky bar excursions and even late-night soirées at lavish estates belonging to the families of the wealthiest of the Big Boys. Being accepted by a group of individuals that possessed major influence at Stryker & Marshall, as well as financial circles outside of their company, would surely help him climb the ladder, along with his self-promoting schemes, of course. After all, Paul Bryce was the nephew of Patrick Babcock, information Dale had become aware of after spending enough time with the Big Boys.

Stryker & Marshall's most illustrious offices resided in Manhattan, where they allocated most of their top brokers. The brokerage firm's resources existed where the money resided. The company's top-performing brokers had been situated in New York, Miami, and Los Angeles, but in the last decade or two, Stryker & Marshall had been positioning some of their top talent in San Francisco and Seattle due to the influx of wealth amassing in the two cities from booming companies.

An investor could reach a broker by phone from across the country, but providing wealthy individuals with in-person meetings with brokers on their own turf was the surest way to regale new capital. This trend had poached some of the savviest brokers—like the Big Boys—away from New York.

Seattle had even enticed the CEO of Stryker & Marshall, Patrick Babcock. He had left his opulent manor in New York to personally ensure a smooth transition into the Seattle market. After growing a liking to the natural beauty in the area, he purchased a mansion and had begun spending more time out of the year in Seattle than he'd initially anticipated.

Out of his several residences, he had been spending the last half of summer and the first half of autumn in his Seattle mansion, usually fleeing the city after three quarters of the leaves had fallen. He might have considered spending more time in the area, but Seattleites didn't rub him the right way. Their politeness was a thin layer covering their I-don't-give-a-fuck-about-you attitude. New Yorkers didn't bother putting on that false layer; they just went straight to the fuck-you part. Babcock, being a New Yorker himself, appreciated that candor, that directness.

In the past, Dale would've had to conduct business in New York to roll with major players, but the times were changing. Although schmoozing with influential colleagues to climb the corporate ladder wasn't a groundbreaking idea, Dale's lone-wolf mentality had never included the method into his advancement plans. He had been relying solely on his schemes because he never conceived his abrasive personality would ever allow him to befriend enough big shots, but it turned out that many big shots' dispositions aligned with his. He now realized why wolves ran in packs: to more easily round up the large population of sheep and devour them. He also acknowledged that he could only climb the corporate ladder so high and so fast by solely using schemes. Joining a fierce and powerful pack was also essential.

The first thing out of the ordinary that Dale noticed when walking into the office on Monday was an Aston Martin One-77 parked in the designated CEO parking spot. Patrick Babcock wasn't always at the office on Mondays, and when he did visit the office he'd roll up in his Porsche or Lotus. Looks like he hadn't taken the prank call lightly and was protecting his most prized ride from annihilation. The thought brought a smile to Dale's face as he strolled to the entrance door, coffee in hand.

The second thing out of the ordinary was the higher flow of foot traffic in the hallways around the office, but this one could've been his imagination. Dale strode through the halls to his small office and placed his Dark Java next to his keyboard.

Dark Java, a premium coffee shop, had recently opened their second location in Seattle. The first location had opened last year in SoHo with much buzz. It had instantly become the most coveted beverage in Seattle.

Dale took a greedy gulp and sent the first dose of caffeine running through his system like a runaway train. His mind would be efficiently firing on all cylinders when the potent twelve-ounce cup was empty. It was akin to a line of cocaine, but completely legal. Assisted by the caffeine, he started his morning ritual of consuming all the financial news before moving onto selective market research, then fine-tuning his personally tailored investment algorithm. A side project that was proving to be effective and lucrative.

"I want his head on a stick!" Patrick Babcock yelled while pounding a fist on his mahogany desk.

The three senior executive VPs Babcock had called into his office flinched from the emphatic sound of the CEO's meaty fist swiftly meeting wood.

Gerald van Buren was the first to reply. "I got a similar prank call on my private line about two months ago."

"Did they threaten to turn your rare sports car into a tiny box of scrap metal too?"

"I don't have a sports car. But the caller delved into personal matters and knew details about me that a stranger wouldn't have known." He was praying that Mr. Babcock wouldn't force him to vocalize the personal matter. Luckily for him, Dorian White jumped into the conversation next without a pause.

"I didn't receive a prank call myself, but right before you called me into this meeting, Blaine Covington and Lucas Hanover were telling me about prank calls they had received. Blaine's happened last Friday night, the same night as yours, Babby."

Then Sterling Breckenridge chimed in, "I also received a prank call on my private line about two weeks ago. The caller also knew personal details about my family and myself. The caller threatened to stuff dead rats in my exhaust tailpipe, and then went on to talk about his extensive collection of peanut butter from around the world, and how he would abduct my family members one by one and drown them in a heaping vat of said peanut butters. He was clearly deranged, but the fact that he knew personal details about my family and me left me feeling uneasy long after the call had ended."

Babcock dispensed with everything Breckenridge had just said except for the one bit that mattered to him. "We've got a madman threatening to vandalize our priceless cars. This prankster clearly works amongst us … in this very office." Babcock's stocky frame widened in his navy-blue suit as he stretched out his arms to indicate the entire building. Beads of sweat could be seen trickling down his thick forehead as he exerted his heavy-set frame and continued steaming with anger.

Babcock reached a finger toward his office phone and put his secretary on speakerphone. "Sandra, tell Blaine Covington and Lucas Hanover to join my current meeting ASAP."

Susan's monotone voice was heard on the speaker. "Okay, Mr. Babcock. By the way, it's Susan."

"What's Susan?" Babcock asked in an annoyed tone.

"My name," Susan replied with her typical emotionless voice.

Babcock ignored her. He sternly glanced at the three executives on the other side of his mahogany desk, idling his gaze on each executive one at a time, hoping they had something pertinent to add to the discussion while they waited for the arrival of the two senior VPs, but no words were spoken. So Babcock rested back in his leather chair and crossed his arms, making himself comfortable while he waited. "Maybe they know something about this prankster that we don't."

It didn't take long for Blaine and Lucas to emerge through the doorway and join the meeting, but they could impart no leads to the CEO, only agree that they too had been threatened by someone that possessed personal details about them.

"The guy was a nutcase," Lucas Hanover stated. "He professed to be a primordial wizard that had only been spoken about in ancient lore and threatened to banish my immediate family members to the nether regions, except for my rotund father-in-law, whom he would cast a spell upon next blue moon to sit on me until I was thinner than an outlet grocery store's slice of deli meat. Then we argued awhile about the existence of deli meat in outlet grocery stores. I told him that deli meat's brief shelf life would render them expired before making it to discount grocery stores. He said if I didn't shut up and retract my deli-meat statement, he'd make me expire in less than a fortnight."

Gerald van Buren leaned in closer. "Did you retract the statement?"

Lucas Hanover frowned in disgust. "No, I hung up on the whack job."

A loud clearing of Babcock's throat silenced their conversation. He had grown annoyed by the time wasted on irrelevant chatter. "Time is money, boys. Let's not get into trivialities regarding the matter. Let's just pinpoint the cocksucker and remove him quickly. We have far more pressing matters to attend to, so let's waste as little time as possible in silencing this prankster and get back to making money."

Lucas Hanover suggested typing the prank caller's phone number into an Internet search to ascertain his address.

They did so and found a telephone directory being the top result. After clicking on the link, the Web site associated an address with the inputted phone number, but no names occupying the residence were listed. A few of them thought the address was oddly familiar, but they couldn't recall how they knew it.

With Lucas Hanover in control of Babcock's keyboard, he backpedaled to the search results and found the same names displayed on the fourth- and fifth-place results. Both results associated the listed names with the prankster's phone number and an address, but none of the listed names looked familiar to them: Hercule Marple, Agatha Marple, and Tommy Marple.

Lucas Hanover offered up the next move. "I was just about to pop out of the office to get a Dark Java matcha latte before you summoned me. While I'm out there I could swing around to this address and check out the place. Maybe uncover why the address looks so familiar to me. Looks like it's not too far away."

"Yeah, do that," Babcock replied. "And bring me back a Dark Java Premium while you're at it. Get it on the way back so it isn't cold." Babcock was feeling better already in anticipation of his Dark Java.

"Okay, I'll get right on it, Mr. Babcock." Lucas fled the office like the building was on fire.

Babcock fidgeted with one of his cufflinks while staring down the remaining brokers in his office. He then delivered something akin to a pep talk in a severe tone. "We must deal with this prankster quickly and move on. The world depends on our services. Services that must not be impeded. We don't break our backs producing things that have no real value: clothes, furniture, filtered water … food. No! We're titans of finance. We move intangible things and ideas around the world on digital platforms. No one else in the world can accumulate as much wealth as we do by simply moving around ones and zeros on computers."

He paused for effect before continuing, "Most people don't understand how we can generate abounding profits from nonphysical objects. Half the time we create profits from a mere idea on the Internet, something that never existed as bills or coinage—a fucking figment of the imagination from the inception. Gentlemen, we might as well be fucking wizards." Babcock tapped a hand on his desk. "Meeting adjourned, boys. Now, go fiddle with those ones and zeros and produce me another mansion in the Hamptons."

Everyone laughed and began filing out the door and back to their offices, enthusiastic about conjuring up their own mansions and Bugatti supercars from thin air.

Forty minutes later, Lucas Hanover returned with two Dark Javas in his hands, sporting a confused countenance.

"Mr. Hanover has returned, sir." Susan's toneless voice reached through the phone.

"Send him right in, Suanne" Babcock replied.

Lucas Hanover drifted into the office and stood before Babcock with a perplexed face.

"What are you waiting for? Bring me that Dark Java Premium ... and take a seat." Babcock wanted Lucas to explain his puzzled face, but first he wanted his coffee.

Lucas did what he was told.

After taking a gulp of coffee and savoring the flavor, Babcock said, "What's with the confused face? Looks like you have something to tell me. Spit it out. I don't have all day."

Lucas Hanover held his matcha latte with both hands like a shy schoolboy. "The moment I arrived at the house, I understood why the address was so familiar. It's Josh Johnson's new residence."

"Who's Josh Johnson?" Babcock didn't know any assistant VP's names, nor VP's names. He wasn't particularly good with names. An employee had to of risen to the ranks of senior VP or executive senior VP to have the privilege of being known on a name basis with Babcock, and only executive senior VPs had the privilege of referring to Mr. Babcock as Babby, but only in the presence of other executive senior VPs. "Josh Johnson. Sounds like a pop singer or a basketball player. Well, who is he?"

"He's an assistant VP that works under Andy Singer."

"And you're positive this prankster's address matches Johnson's residence?" Babcock asked while noting Josh Johnson and Andy Singer's names down on a notepad.

"Positive, one hundred percent," Lucas said. "He invited some colleagues—myself included—over for a dinner and drinks about two months ago. That's why I initially recognized the address."

Babcock furrowed his eyebrows. "So why wasn't his name listed under the address in our online search? The Internet has that address down as the Maple residence, or whatever it was."

"The Marples must have previously owned the house. Johnson recently purchased the house so the Web site hasn't been updated yet, but I assure you, that's Johnson's house and that's his address."

"Okay. Good job, Han …" Babcock had already forgotten the employee's name who sat before him.

"Hanover … Lucas Hanover, sir."

"Right. Well done, Hanover. You may go now." Babcock greedily enjoyed another gulp of his Dark Java while watching Lucas exit his office.

Babcock absently tapped the notepad containing the two names he'd written down, then he reached for the office phone. "Suzana, tell Andy Singer to report to my office."

"Okay, sir. It's Susan, sir."

"Don't start with me again, Suzan. Goddammit! Do you effectively move ones and zeros around on the Internet, Suzie?"

"I'm not sure what you mean, sir." Susan said, emotionlessly.

"*Exactly*. And that's why I don't give a rat's ass what your name is. If I refer to you as Sundae, that's what you'll goddamn go by. Now do your job and send in …"—Babcock glanced down at the notepad—"Andy Singer."

"Yes, sir."

Andy Singer was in Babcock's office in less than three minutes, hoping the entire way that his summons wasn't due to a blunder he may have committed, because it was the first time Babcock had requested his presence. His anxiety only intensified after he sat down and Babcock eyeballed him for a couple seconds while taking a swig of coffee.

"Josh Johansson works under you as an assistant VP, yes?"

"I think you mean Josh Johnson, sir."

Babcock looked down at the notepad. "Right ... Johnson."

Babcock gave Andy Singer the entire rundown of the matter at hand. And then Babcock asked, "Is there a technicality regarding Johnson's work that you can assign to his termination? I'd rather make his exit quiet and fast, as we don't have sufficient evidence to call him out on his midnight-phone lunacy. The guy obviously has some kind of mental problems and needs to be let go today."

"There is a thing or two I could use. Also, I can cook up a few things regarding his clients to ensure he feels he's at major fault about something. He won't speak to his clients again if he's terminated today, so he'll never know I was lying."

Babcock finished off his Dark Java. "I knew I could rely on you, Singer." Then he squinted his eyes at Andy Singer in examination. "Hey, don't you spend time with my nephew, Paul Bryce?"

A smile dawned on Singer's face for having been validated by the big man. "Yes, we spend time together often outside the office. We also play tennis every week or two."

"Yes, tennis. That's where I recognize you from. The Seattle Tennis Club." Babcock chucked his empty coffee cup in the trash can and leaned back in his leather chair. "Tennis is a sport for gentlemen. Us gentlemen have to stick together."

"I couldn't agree more, Mr. Babcock." Singer was feeling more confident by the moment.

"Please, address me as just Babcock. Being a close friend with my nephew gives you some benefits."

Singer was now on cloud nine. "Thank you Mr.—I mean, Babcock. And if I may be so bold, if you're looking to fill Johnson's slot, a fellow tennis gentleman, Dale Dickerson, also a friend of your nephew's, would be ripe for the position. He's been making some intelligent trades and his clients are very happy with his performance."

Babcock strummed his chin. "As you're probably aware, Stryker & Marshall only delegates a fixed number of positions for VPs, senior VPs, and execute senior VPs, so filling a recently abandoned assistant VP position isn't necessary. But, regardless, it sounds like this individual deserves a promotion. You may fill him in on his new honorary title after Johan … phone-lunatic guy leaves the building with his shit in a box."

"I'll get right on it." Singer rose from his seat and made for the door.

Babcock leaned forward in his chair. "There's one more thing you can do for me."

Singer removed his hand from the door handle and turned around. "Of course, Babcock, whatever you want."

"Go pick me up a Dark Java Premium after you dismiss that lunatic."

"Sure thing." Singer left the office.

Babcock pressed his palms together and started rubbing them up and down in delight. "The day just keeps getting better and better."

Chapter 8

Jeremy's next target was Smittie Hardmeat, an advanced ORA. Smittie had suffered a heart-wrenching divorce two years ago and had been depressed ever since. Anyone who observed him for a couple seconds could clearly see how dead inside the guy was. He had become a hollow shell of a human being that loathed his existence.

None of this was Jeremy's business, but when Smittie lifelessly skated by at work, clogging up a position—a position that Jeremy wanted—it had become Jeremy's business.

There were only a finite amount of advanced ORA positions, and most of them were lifers waiting for an opening position down the hall where the lavish offices of the senior ORAs resided. The long hall that separated the ORAs and the advanced ORAs from the senior ORAs was akin to the curtain that separated first class from economy. If a non-senior ORA employee was seen wandering in the first class area, they'd quickly be reprimanded and ushered back to their designated quarters, much like what a stewardess would do on an airplane.

At Cohesive Analytics, the most prestigious resource analytical company in the nation, an ORA made a nice salary, an advanced ORA a great salary, and a senior ORA pulled down a six-figure salary. Jeremy was more fortunate than Tim and Dale when it came to climbing the corporate ladder because he only needed two promotions to move to the top of the heap.

Jeremy's first scheme had given him more small companies to work with, making him a shoo-in for the next available advanced ORA position, provided he kept up his outstanding performance. But no matter how well he performed his job, he could only get promoted if a position became available.

And that's where Smittie Hardmeat's clogging up of the promotional ladder became a thorn in Jeremy's side.

He'd be doing Smittie a favor. The guy was stuck in a rut and needed a change of scenery, a swift kick in the ass to be forcefully moved to greener pastures. When one doesn't read the signs given along the path of life, they'll eventually hit an abrupt wall and be forced toward their correct destination. A rude and painful correction, but a necessary one. Jeremy was going to be Smittie's abrupt wall. He'd perform actions that would appear malicious on the surface, but would actually be charitable in the long run.

These were the thoughts flowing through Jeremy's mind as he eavesdropped on a conversation between Smittie and Thomas in Thomas's office. Thomas was advising Smittie on the necessity of staying up to date by periodically shifting the allocation of resources to better fit a company's changing needs. It was clear Thomas wasn't happy about Smittie's performance, but evidently the situation wasn't severe enough to fire the poor bastard.

Part of their job was to keep track of collected and relayed data in order to adjust resource allocations for optimal flow. Apparently, but not surprisingly, Smittie had been keeping his allocation schematics static instead of making adjustments when they were needed.

Being that Jeremy's cubicle was closest to Thomas's office, and Thomas's door wasn't shut, it wasn't hard for him to listen in on the conversation. All the ORAs—like Jeremy—occupied cubicles in the middle of the large room. The advanced ORAs possessed offices along the periphery of the room. Thomas, who managed the ORAs and the advanced ORAs, had the biggest peripheral office that was located directly behind Jeremy's cubicle. Smittie's office was directly to the left of Jeremy's corner cubicle. He was nicely positioned to conduct a scheme against the burned-out divorcee. A scheme he hadn't devised yet.

After their discussion was over, Jeremy heard Smittie compliment Thomas's taste for having chosen a premium and stylistic mouse. It was bulky and alien-looking, possessing all the bells and whistles. Having bought it less than a week ago, Thomas accepted the praise and declared it was his new pride and joy.

If such an ordinary device was someone's pride and joy, that someone's life must've been quite boring, Jeremy thought. But it did give him an idea. An idea not comprehensive enough to be a scheme, but a single effortless act that could manufacture tension and possibly disdain between the two: he'd swap their mouses.

Being that Thomas always followed a proper schedule that one could set their watch by, Jeremy would arrive at work before Thomas and make the swap. Thomas would assuredly arrive at the office before Smittie and spot his large, bulky mouse through Smittie's interior office window on his usual path to the restroom or break room, where he boiled water for his daily tea. Then he'd most likely recall Smittie's compliment about his mouse.

The next morning arrived and the simple swap was made. The ramifications proved to be more substantial than Jeremy imagined.

Smittie never saw Thomas's mouse in his office, as Thomas switched them prior to Smittie's arrival, all the while cursing under his breath about how improper and unfathomable the situation was.

A bewildered Smittie got a mouthful when arriving to work after Thomas established that Smittie wasn't merely taking the piss about the swap, because he was playing dumb about it. Even though Smittie repeatedly denied it, Thomas continually blamed him for nicking his pride and joy, stating that no one else held a motive to pull such a dodgy move. The five-minute argument finished when Thomas was knackered about the whole affair and trudged back to his office, cursing bloody this and bloody that under his breath. He was properly miffed and considered Smittie the biggest fool on the planet for having thought he wouldn't notice the absence of his pride and joy.

Smittie's typical apathetic and lethargic approach to life worked against the believability of his refutation. When someone was very sure a person did something, that person would naturally have to put up a hysterical defense to avoid being branded for the wrongdoing. Smittie's post-divorce disposition was so glum that he didn't possess the ability to get worked up about anything. He had concluded that life, and everything in it, was a perversion that one best succumb to instead of fighting against the inevitable flow of the tide.

Jeremy didn't account for how effective and weighty Smittie's disposition would be in the result of the swap's aftermath. In fact, the two outcomes—Thomas's vexation and the lifelessness of Smittie—worked so well together that the act could actually prove to be a scheme, not just a solo deed. If he simply kept moving people's possessions into Smittie's office, the whole office would grow irate with him. When a person was in Smittie's depressing presence for too long they'd normally feel the desire to blow their brains out with a shotgun, but Jeremy's scheme would cultivate a new feeling directed at Smittie: pure hatred.

The scheme alone would probably not be adequate to dispatch a longtime employee, but tack on two years of a lackadaisical performance by Smittie and it would be enough to push him over the edge, or rather, push Thomas's temper over the edge and get Smittie fired.

Over the course of a month Jeremy relocated various coworkers' items into Smittie's office in the morning hours when the office was either empty or sparsely occupied. Smittie's uncaring nature had long ago spread to his desk, causing it to be disorganized and littered with all kinds of items, which made it easy for Jeremy to add to it without Smittie noticing.

For his first relocation, he moved Bob Hamill's favorite mug.

When Bob finally found it, he was apprehensive with his choice of words directed at Smittie, being that the mug had text that read WORLD'S BEST HUSBAND, coupled with the fact that Smittie had been a two-year depressed divorcee. Bob wasn't sure if Smittie had casually grabbed it out of the break room, or if he was living out some kind of fantasy where he *was* the world's best husband.

While stumbling over his choice of words in order to discreetly repossess his mug, Thomas, holding a cup of tea, or cuppa as Thomas called it, on his way from the break room, overheard enough of the one-sided bungling conversation and popped in to help Bob out.

"How are you two getting on today?" Thomas politely asked, even though he assumed what was amiss from having heard Bob's stammering.

Bob tilted his head toward Smittie's desk where his mug lay. "I was just telling Smittie that he accidently picked up my mug from the break room."

An unresponsive Smittie slouched in his chair as Thomas took a gander around his messy desk, quickly spotting Bob's mug. It was easily recognizable as Bob's because there was an image of Bob's face plastered on the mug. Thomas lifted up the mug and directed the image of Bob's cheesy, smiling face toward Smittie. "It's got his blooming face plastered on it. For God's sake, what are you daft?"

Smittie stirred in his chair and started showing some liveliness by uttering some denials. "I didn't take that mug. I've never used that mug. I don't know how it got there."

Having dealt with Smittie only yesterday about his mouse, Thomas's miffed state was rekindled. "Your excuses are a damp squib. His bloody face is on it!" While keeping his glare on Smittie he handed the mug to Bob.

Smittie began to get agitated because there was something in life he had to start caring about, even if only temporarily. He also had no idea what "damp squib" meant, which helped spark some emotions of vexation. He sternly enunciated his words, "I did not take Bob's mug. I have my own goddamn mugs." He carelessly shifted one arm over a part of his desk where a few mugs were, knocking over a couple of them with his arcing arm, causing the month-old liquid inside to spill onto the desk and crawl under countless items on the desk.

After Smittie's ill behavior, Bob slinked out of the room, leaving Thomas to deal with the aggression. "No sense in throwing a wobbly. The matter has been dealt with. Just try not to be so careless around the office." While leaving the room Thomas paused at the doorway and turned around. "And clean up this rubbish," he said while pointing a finger at Smittie's trash-laden desk. Thomas was anything but chuffed as he stomped back into his office with his cuppa.

After a matter of minutes, Jeremy swore Smittie had already forgotten about the altercation, as he was seen pressing buttons on his keyboard in a sluggish manner with an impassive countenance like nothing had happened. The guy was clearly on some type of heavy regiment of emotionally suppressing medication prescribed by a psychiatrist. A psychiatrist he'd probably been visiting for the past two years in an attempt to salvage his life after the divorce.

Over the next three weeks, Jeremy pulled several relocation jobs. Each one adding another colleague to the I-hope-Smittie-gets-dysentery team, or the more infuriated I-hope-Smittie-falls-on-several-forks team.

For his latest relocation, he moved Frida Knight's book, placing it on one of Smittie's books that had been lying on his disarrayed desk. The thin how-to book belonging to Smittie had a dark and perplexing title: HOW TO COMMIT SUICIDE EFFECTIVELY EVERY TIME.

When Frida discovered her book was missing, she did what everyone else had been doing around the office when their belongings had suddenly vanished: pay a visit to the office of Smittie Hardmeat, or two nomenclatures he'd recently been given by his vexed colleagues: Smittie Softmeat and Smittie Barely-There-Meat.

Jeremy wasn't sure if "Barely-There-Meat" regarded Smittie's permanently out-to-lunch state due to his meds, or a reference to his phallus. Regardless, Jeremy was pleased that derogatory titles were being dispensed, a clear sign of friction that assured his plan was working.

Frida casted a shadow over Smittie's slouching body and zombified face, which was fixed down on his keyboard and wondering why his office had become slightly darker. When Frida started barking at him he jumped in his seat.

"I've come for the book! Where is it?"

After the shock, Smittie began scanning his desk for a book that wasn't his. He knew the drill. His fingers glided over the book she must've been referring to. The front of the book read KNITTING WITH GRANDMA BAKER, and its cover displayed a grandma passed out in a cozy armchair with a knitting project in her lap.

Smittie lifted it toward Frida while commenting on the cover. "Looks like she expired while knitting that pretty scarf for her nephew."

Frida snatched the book out of his hands, annoyed at his remark. "She's not dead, she's just napping."

She noticed the how-to book on his desk that had been under her book and gasped. Then her face returned to displaying anger. "Don't touch my things, Softmeat."

While she stormed out of his office, he uttered to her back, "Softmeat? What the hell? Take it. I don't want your goddamn grandma book. Who puts a photo of a dead grandma on the cover of a book? Not very smart marketing."

He had been taking more than his prescribed dosage of meds in order to deal with the past weeks' worth of discord and animosity at the office. The heavy doses had been making him both tired and irritable. For the last few days he had either been nodding off behind his computer or squabbling with colleagues, or both at the same time.

Smittie was dozing off again. He almost fell out of his chair but caught himself and jerked back awake. While using the back of his hand to wipe some saliva from the corner of his mouth, he noticed a foreign object among the various trash on his desk: a red stapler. He shook his head to relieve some grogginess and reached for the stapler. There was label-maker tape applied to the top of it that read CHEN, SU-WEI.

He thought it best to return the item before another irate coworker stormed into his office. He especially didn't want Su-wei added to the list of colleagues that hated him, because he thought she was the most alluring female at the office. He got partially aroused just thinking of her. He didn't get the least bit hard, though, because one of the side effects of his medication was lack of performance. It didn't stop him from feeling turned on, but nothing was happening downstairs. That's when he realized he really had become Smittie Softmeat.

Not that it mattered much. He hadn't been anywhere near a sexual encounter since his divorce. His sexy wife was probably banging her boyfriend—whom she'd left Smittie for—every night for the past two years. Maybe she was getting it on with several lucky guys, and maybe also females. Meanwhile, due to his meds, he was having difficulties with the simple act of pleasing himself. During the act, he'd get mad and look down at his underperforming unit and berate it with a slew of nasty words.

Perspective is an interesting thing; he had never considered his wife to be all that sexy until she became his ex-wife. He imagined that she had become sexier in his mind solely because he couldn't have her anymore. No matter how hot one's wife was, they would always lose that hotness in their husband's mind after repetition. It would be like eating the same food every day. You'd get sick of it. Everything in life became pointless when repetition was applied, so what was the point, he thought. You'd have to change everything—lovers, jobs, cities, hobbies, diet—every once in a while to retain the zest of life. But society wasn't set up to cater to that type of liberating lifestyle. It almost seemed like society, no matter what country you lived in, was intentionally constructed to drain people's souls. Well, it had certainly accomplished that task on him.

He shook his head again to wake up from his negative daydreaming. If he kept himself medicated for the rest of his life, he could partially escape the pain of existence. He found this a soothing thought.

He got out of his chair and almost fell flat on his face due to his right foot having fallen asleep. Hoping to assist the direction of blood flow, he tapped on his thigh and waited till the ability of walking had returned to him. Then he donned his Seattle Mariners baseball cap to hide his disheveled hair. In the last year it had basically become a part of his body since he had lost the inclination to wash and style his hair. The dark navy cap with an aqua-colored bill had hid his flaky, shaggy hairdo, saving the precious eyes of anyone he came in close enough contact with. Fashion didn't matter much to him these days. He'd often leave his black trench coat on for the whole work day. He was lucky there was no strict dress code at Cohesive Analytics.

With stapler in hand he exited his office and trudged across the room to Su-wei's office, which was located across the large room. Her office door was open, but Smittie lightly knocked on it anyway to get approval before stepping in. After she briefly lifted her head from her computer to give him an approval to enter with a tilt of the head, he drifted over to a shelf that contained some of her belongings while he waited for her to pause from her work.

He examined the shelf's contents and rested his eyes on a picture frame displaying two seductive women. Picking up the frame to get a closer look, he was able to recognize one of the females as Su-wei, sporting attire that she often wore at work: an elegant blouse and a short skirt that accentuated her shapely legs all the way down to her bow ballet flats. The other woman in the picture, who was equally as attractive, looked slightly younger and wore similar attire, but was wearing heals instead of flats. They were both gorgeous: light makeup applied, styled hair, charming smiles, dressed to impress. The photo was probably taken before a special night out on the town. In the background of the photo he saw a plethora of business signs stretching down the street that contained Chinese characters. Looks like the photo had been taken in Taipei, Su-wei's birth city.

While gazing at the picture, he felt a knot forming in his jaw that needed to be cracked. They had developed ever since he started taking his meds and could be relieved with a simple cracking of the jaw. This one felt larger than normal, so he opened his mouth really wide and adjusted his lower jaw slightly to one side to pop it while habitually widening his eyes in the process.

He had been so focused on popping his jaw that he didn't notice Su-wei pausing from her work and walking over to him. From her vantage point he was basically drooling over the picture: mouth completely agape, eyes ogling. The only aspect that was missing was his tongue hanging out of his mouth. Su-wei made a tongue-clicking sound that people—especially Asians—make when they're expressing disapproval or irritation. Then she snatched the frame out of his hand and placed it back on the shelf before chastising him. "Quit drooling over my daughter, you pervert. 變態."

"Your daughter?" Smittie uttered in surprise.

"Yeah," Su-wei snapped. "She's nineteen. Fourteen in this picture," she stated to add insult and insinuate that he was a pedophile.

Smittie didn't know how to react, what to say. He found it hard to determine the age of Asian females. Besides, she was dressed up like an adult with makeup and everything. The only response he could muster was a baffled shake of the head with his mouth partially open, as if to convey that he wasn't a pedophile. So many rich pedophiles had been exposed in the news in the last few years that every mom was labeling a male a pedophile if they even dared to smile at their children.

What a messed up world it had become when one couldn't even express a common courtesy.

Su-wei noticed her stapler in his hand. "That's where that went. I didn't say you could borrow that. Give me that." She seized it from his hand. "Next time ask before you borrow something. It's a common courtesy. And if I ever see you drooling over my daughter again …" She returned to her seat without finishing her threat and went back to work, completely ignoring his presence.

"Just wanted to return your stapler," he mumbled. "You have a pretty daughter, Su-wei." In his medicated, distorted mind he thought the compliment might smooth things over a bit, but quickly realized that it was perhaps one of the worst things he could've said, given the context of the situation.

After his comment, a larger scowl defined Su-wei's face as she worked, but she continued to ignore him, giving him a clear signal to get the hell out of her office and leave her alone. And that's what he did, with his head hanging low.

Having kept Smittie under close observation, Jeremy, even though his cubicle was pretty far away from Su-wei's office, had caught the gist of what transpired through visuals alone. He also heard snippets of Su-wei's fuming dialog, as did many of his colleagues since she had practically yelled a couple statements at Smittie.

A most insidious plan popped into Jeremy's mind. The proverbial light bulb had illuminated over his head. How wicked and creative the idea was. But was he considered a creative or perverted person for having thought of it? Either way, it would be the topper to seal Smittie's fate. Smittie was already teetering on the edge, so it wouldn't take much to push him off. This last exploit would not only knock him over the cliff, but would catapult his ass far into the canyon.

He'd wait two days and do it on Friday. Friday would benefit him in two ways: people typically showed up a little later to work, which would give him the extra time to set this one up, and management preferred to lay off staff at the end of the work week for psychological reasons and office morale.

The thought that he'd soon be moving into Smittie's office gave him a sense of accomplishment. He dove back into his work with boosted vigor.

When Smittie returned to his office, scanning his filthy desk for other foreign items, he felt a wave of anger rise against the anonymous saboteur. If he was feeling this level of emotion, must be time to pop in some more meds. Glorious meds. His one and only true savior from this hellhole called Earth. But before he placated his mind back into submission, an intelligent thought was able to slip to the surface before the next round of meds kicked in. He'd put a hidden camera in the corner of his office above the door that would catch the saboteur once and for all. Then he'd reveal the camera footage to Thomas and be exonerated for all the past transgressions that had been placed upon his head. He'd buy the wireless camera after work and install it first thing tomorrow in the early morning.

As planned, Smittie showed up early the next morning on Thursday and installed the tiny wireless camera before anyone else arrived at the office. He felt unusually optimistic about something in life for a change. He would be revenged. Given his optimism, he only ended up nodding off in front of his computer once for the entire work day.

Jeremy also held a sense of optimism for the final act that would occur tomorrow. The act that he believed would send Smittie packing. Goodbye cubicle section and hello advanced ORA position, he thought.

Jeremy was the first to arrive to the office on Friday. Before anyone else reached the office, he quickly went about setting up the scene that would provide evidence for Smittie's incrimination.

He grabbed the picture frame in Su-wei's office. He entered Smittie's office, placed the standing picture frame on Smittie's empty shelf located on the wall to the left after walking through the doorway. Then he turned Smittie's extra chair that resided in the corner of the room by the shelf so that it was facing the corner of the room where the picture frame on the shelf rested at eye-level from a seated position in the chair. After simulating jerk-off movements while seated in the chair in front of the picture, he carefully produced a homemade concoction he'd brewed up last night that would resemble a semen stain once applied to the seat. Luckily for Jeremy the extra chair in the corner of Smittie's office had a white fabric seat, which would make the stain more pronounced and easier to spot.

Now that the scene was all set up, he exited Smittie's office, returned to his cubicle to start working for the day, and waited for the shit to hit the fan when his colleagues showed up.

The whole thing was caught on Smittie's hidden camera.

One-by-one, workers arrived and started their typical Friday morning routines. Thomas made his first cuppa for the day and settled into his office. Ben Hutson, an advanced ORA that resided in the office next to Smittie's, strolled in with his everyday Starbucks latte and masculine men's magazine. Many other people showed up and slowly began working, but it wasn't until Su-wei arrived that things got interesting.

Because Su-wei's office was organized to adhere to her slight case of OCD and her minimalistic lifestyle in regard to possessions, she identified the empty spot on her shelf where the picture frame was supposed to reside the moment she stepped into her office. The first thing that flashed through her mind was the image of Smittie gawking at the frame with bulging eyes and a gaping mouth.

"That pervert," she muttered to herself as she marched to Smittie's empty office to reclaim her picture. The first thing she noticed after entering his office was the odd position of his spare chair. Why was it facing the corner of the room? Right after she asked herself this question, she found the answer when she looked in the direction of where the chair was facing. It was facing the only item on Smittie's shelf: her picture frame, which was facing the chair.

She threw up her hands in exasperation and mouthed, "Why?" Then she said, "Whatever," as she approached the frame to seize it. Her hand reached out and clutched the side of the frame, but before she snatched it up, something caught her eye on the white chair below: a big cum stain.

She released her grip on the frame, instantly recoiled her arms, and then slowly backing away as if the whole area was contaminated with life-threatening diseases that could kill her in a matter of minutes. "Oh my god. That sick perverted *freak*."

She was startled again as she backed into Thomas, who had heard the commotion and hustled over to Smittie's office to see what was amiss.

"What's all the kerfuffle, Su?"

With eyes still widened, she said while pointing at the chair, "That freak stole a picture of my daughter and me from my office and jerked off to it in that chair. There's a big cum stain on the chair." After a short pause, she added, "And my daughter, Vivian, is only fourteen years old in that photo."

"Blimey!" Thomas dropped his scrummy caramel biscuit he'd been partaking of with his cuppa. He cautiously walked over to the chair like a frightened girl trying to kill a spider. He saw the wankstain as clear as day. "Manky! That nutter has lost the plot."

Thomas turned around to see Smittie arrive, zonked on meds, slouching in the doorway, wearing his trench coat and adjusting his baseball cap. Su-wei was keeping her distance from Smittie but was staying close enough to see what Thomas would say to him.

Thomas scowled and pointed a stern finger at Smittie. "You're a proper wanker, you are."

"What's all this? What are you talking about?" Smittie's slurred response crawled out of his mouth.

Thomas motioned two arms toward the chair. "Do I need to spell it out for you? Are you dead from the neck up?

We've seen your latest exhibition, tosser. You've done bugger all this morning besides wanking, you lazy sod."

Smittie's heavily medicated mind slowly put the pieces together and realized that his saboteur had struck again. He didn't know what they were all steaming mad about, but this time he wouldn't be blamed for it. A lopsided devious smile crept onto his face.

Thomas reacted to the smile. "You even look the part. You're a full-blown nutter, you are."

Smittie disregarded the comment and kept wearing the creepy smile. "It was the saboteur, not me. I haven't been taking anyone's things, and this time I have the proof," he slurred while pointing up at the small wireless camera above his head.

"What's that? What do you got up there, you nutter?"

"It's a camera that I installed yesterday. I wanted to prove to you that somebody has been setting me up."

"You can't install cameras in the office without my approval."

"It's just the one, and it only records my office."

Thomas calmed down. "I still don't think company policy allows that, but show us the recording."

Smittie nodded his head and wobbled to his leather chair. He went through the motions of logging in and proceeded to fiddle with the camera's software on his computer.

Smittie had accidently taken a double dose of meds in his car to deal with heavy traffic on the way to work. The acute stress of the commute had made him forget he'd already taken a second dose. Along with his straight-out-of-bed dose, he was currently digesting a triple dose of meds, and they had almost reached their peak capacity. It was a miracle he'd made it to work without crashing his car.

Thomas pushed the stained chair all the way into the corner to get it out of the way and called for Su-wei to bring in a chair to view the video. Then he stood behind Smittie, looking at the computer screen.

Su-wei tentatively followed Thomas's instructions, trying her best to keep as much distance as possible from the soiled chair in the corner, but since the office's condition was a far cry from hers, she felt her skin crawl no matter where she resided in Smittie's trashy office. She wanted to leave as soon as possible to avoid catching any number of the countless diseases she believed were lurking within the office's confines. If anyone other than her boss had instructed her to come into this dump of a room and take a seat, she would've told them where to shove it.

Smittie had almost dozed off a couple times before he'd brought the recording to the desired spot. He wasn't sure why he felt extra tired today. But it was okay. All he had to do was keep it together for a bit and show the proof the camera had captured to exonerate his name. He pressed play and mumbled, "Please lean forward to make sure you get a good look at the true culprit."

Both Thomas and Su-wei obliged. The three captivatingly stared at the screen and waited for the culprit to walk through the door.

Smittie felt like he was going to pass out at any moment. It took all his strength to battle the fatiguing toll of his meds.

Then a figure appeared on the screen. They leaned in even closer and strained their eyes. The culprit was wearing a dark coat and hat, but his back was to the camera, preventing identification.

"Wait for it," Smittie said.

The figure set down the picture frame and positioned the chair, his back to the camera the whole time.

"He's going to turn at some point. At the latest, we'll see his face when he walks out the door," Smittie assured them. Then he added, "What's he doing anyway?" Smittie hadn't seen the stained chair, so he didn't know exactly what the saboteur had done.

The figure on the screen sat in the chair and started making jerk-off motions with his left arm, his head titled to the left a bit as he stared at the frame. But they still couldn't see his face, only make out that the hat had a bill that was considerably lighter in color than the rest of the hat. The camera's video quality wasn't the best.

Smittie cringed. "Oh, damn. That guy's masturbating in my office. Whoever he is, you need to fire this guy, Thomas."

"I intend to," said Thomas. "We have a firm policy regarding wanking it at the office."

After the figure had presumably climaxed and lightened his load, he got up and walked toward the door with his head held low. He was walking toward the camera but with his face hidden below the bill of his hat.

Thomas's face was now inches away from the screen, trying to catch the smallest detail. "You should've purchased a better camera, Smittie. The video quality is wretched. Looks like 240p. A far cry from high definition. What did you do, take a time machine back to 1990 to purchase this camera?"

"It was on sale for an incredibly low price. I guess I know why now."

Thomas said, "It was probably slapped together in some Chinese sweatshop."

Just before the figure exited the office, Thomas recognized a familiar symbol on the man's hat, which he could now identify as a baseball cap being that it was now quite close to the camera. "Wait. Rewind it and pause it just before he exits the office." Smittie followed his boss's order.

After staring at the paused image for a couple of seconds, Thomas and Su-wei exchanged glances. From their expressions, they both were able to discern that their thoughts about the paused image were the same: The symbol—the Mariners logo—on the baseball cap was the same symbol on the cap Smittie was presently wearing. Also, the color of the cap and its bill were also the same as Smittie's—it was identical. Smittie would've recognized it himself had he not been completely doped up on drugs.

Then it also dawned on Thomas that the man's dark coat was very similar to the black trench coat Smittie was currently wearing. He felt like a moron for not having caught this earlier.

The realization likely hadn't entered his mind because why would Smittie be so adamant about them watching a video that incriminated himself. Thomas figured that the prescription drugs Smittie had been taking had finally turned him into a complete nutter. Maybe the lunatic had forgotten what he'd done an hour ago in his office and was watching the video's footage without realizing he was the figure on the screen.

Thomas's subdued anger now flared back up to blazing levels. Stepping away from the monitor, he verbally laid into Smittie. "The guy in the video is you! He's wearing the same baseball cap and trench coat that you're wearing right now. Have you gone completely mad? Did you arrive early to the office to have this little wanking session, leave for a coffee, and come back having completely forgotten about it?"

Smittie's mind would've been reeling in perplexity about the current situation, but instead he was having to divert ninety percent of his attention to not passing out right in front of his boss. So instead of replying to Thomas's question, he simply shook his head to indicate no.

Without a verbal response, Thomas continued, "Ever since your divorce you've been gutted and narky! I understood this—the entire office understood this—so we cut you some slack." He motioned an arm to indicate all the workers in the large room, most of whom had started eyeballing the situation when Thomas began shouting. "But it's been two years, and instead of showing progress, you've managed to slip to an even darker place. What you do on your own time at home with dishy girls on your computer screen is none of my business, but you can't be wanking at the office, splattering office chairs with wankstains." He motioned toward the soiled chair in the corner of the room.

Like most of the people in the office, Jeremy had stopped working and was staring at the spectacle. Given his cubicle's location, he had a front row seat.

Yesterday, he might not have seen Smittie installing the wireless camera, but he did see him fidgeting with a remote control pointed at the corner of his office above the door.

Putting two and two together, he surmised that the remote control was being directed at a surveillance camera of some sort. It didn't take a rocket scientist to figure that out. Initially this turn of events had thrown a wrench into the gears of his plan. But before the working day ended, he thought of an adjustment to his plan that would not only make it possible to go ahead with the deed, but could prove to make it even better.

So after work he had purchased the same styled Mariners baseball cap as Smittie's and a basic black trench coat. The coat wasn't exactly like Smittie's, but it was close enough. Good thing Smittie had a bland taste in clothing. He extensively worked in the baseball cap by repeatedly bending the bill and smashing the cap. All he had to do was stay aware of his position in the camera's view, never allowing it to get a shot of his face, which wasn't hard given the coverage the cap afforded. And the trench coat had worked wonders at concealing his homemade concoction to replicate a semen stain, as well as hiding the fact that he wasn't actually jerking off. It all worked out perfectly.

"That's not my cum," Smittie bellowed from his seat, not having enough strength to stand to confront his boss's accusation. "I demand a sample be taken and brought to a lab for testing. I'll provide a sample of my actual semen for irrefutable proof that they're dissimilar."

Thomas's head was about to blow. "Oh, we've seen enough of your cum for a lifetime, sir! There will be no sampling collected at all. We saw you in the video. We damn well know it was you. You are sacked, sir!"

Su-wei, still planted in her seat, was seething. She knew she'd have to spend money to buy a new picture frame because there was no way she was going to use the one Smittie had fondled, or whatever he'd done with it off camera. She'd have to ask for assistance from someone in the office to remove the picture from the frame because she wasn't going to touch it. Then, after her OCD fully kicked in, she didn't see how she could even keep the picture, her favorite picture. The scumbag's fluids and diseases could've somehow penetrated the frame's glass and latched itself onto the photo within, impregnating the picture. She was pretty sure she didn't have a digital backup copy of the photo.

Having enough of this nonsense, Smittie launched out of his chair. He wasn't going to take this abuse sitting down. But he stood so quickly that he became instantly lightheaded and started to wobble around. This, coupled with the fact that his triple dose of meds had reached their full working capacity, finally caused Smittie to lose consciousness. He crumbled to the floor right in front of Su-wei, who was still seated. His baseball cap flung off his head when its bill hit the floor. Smittie lay asleep on his back, eyes closed, mouth slightly ajar.

Su-wei was of course delighted that Smittie got fired and was lying passed out on the floor due to his drug addiction, but in that instant, it wasn't enough to extinguish her rage. She wanted him to be completely humiliated for what he'd done to her favorite photo that now needed to be discarded in the trash.

So she raised both of her shapely legs above Smittie face for a moment, swiveling her feet at the ankles like she was exercising her leg muscles. Then she slowly brought her feet down on Smittie face, aggressively pressing the bottom of her cute ballet flats into Smittie's passed out face. Then she began sliding them around his face, rubbing the dirt on the bottom of her shoes around his face. Crumbs of dirt trickled into his mouth, grime mixed and stuck to his wet lips. Finally, she put the left heel of her ballet flat into his mouth and worked it around to widen his ajar mouth. When her heel had opened his mouth thoroughly, she rested the heel deep in his mouth, cushioned on either side by Smittie's lips. Then she casually placed her other foot on top the other, crossed at the ankles, wiggling her feet back and forth. Her feet were propped on him like his face was a stool. A huge satisfied smile shined on her face.

Thomas reckoned he should stop her, but he thought the dishy girl had a right to seek a little revenge, so he stood by and chuckled instead. Besides, he was equally as furious at Smittie.

A dozen people deserted their workstations and ran to the scene in order to take pictures and get short video clips, laughing all the while. None of them had ever seen this happen before and knew it would garner much praise and commenting on their social media outlets.

"The only thing he's good for is being a foot stool and cleaning the dirt off the bottom of my flats," Su-wei said with a vengeful smile on her face, addressing a colleague's phone that was taking a video clip.

Chapter 9

Dale exited the taxicab, unwittingly stepping directly into a large puddle that immersed his left leather shoe and waterlogged his sock.

"Goddammit! Thanks for stopping right in front of a massive puddle, you asshat," he barked at the taxi driver as he shook the water from his shoe.

The driver casually shrugged his shoulders. "You wanted me to stop in front of the bookstore, so I did. I don't create the weather, pal. It rains all the time in Seattle. You need to learn to be more careful, lest you get wet."

Dale repeated the greasy, robust man in the taxi as he attempted to exit the taxi for the second time. " 'Be more careful, lest you get wet.' What are you, a fucking fortune cookie on wheels?"

"Hey, I call it as I see it, hot shot." The taxi driver sped off before Dale closed the door, letting inertia do the job instead.

"Impatient sonuvabitch," Dale grumbled as he stabbed through the rain on Pine Street and headed toward the double front doors of the two-story Barnes & Noble. Once inside, a sigh of relief escaped his mouth as he took refuge from the weather.

Seattle could be one of the nicest places on the planet during summer, but for the rest of the year it tended to be dismal: overcast, rainy, cold. Of course it was all a matter of perspective and comparison. He figured people from the Northeast and around the Great Lakes would never think of Seattle as too cold. Residents from the Northeast of the country might only complain about the numerous overcast days, and the lack of quality delicatessens, and also the non-existent subway system.

In fact, Seattle is held on record for having the most overcast days of the year out of any other metropolitan city in America. A factoid he'd come across months ago. It's the reason Seattle, and the Northwest in general, possessed some of the lushest foliage in America. But Dale wasn't a nature lover, so he didn't reap that benefit. He was a city dweller through and through.

The constant overcast city made a person feel like they were living in a simulated reality where the designers were too lazy to create a variable of sky palettes:

"And we're all done. Our simulated city, Seattle, has been coded."

"Shouldn't we give them a variation of sky colors instead of the constant generic gray preset the city simulator is loaded with?"

"No. We've already spent countless hours of coding to give them some of the biggest companies in the world; abounding greenery; beautiful views of mountains and sea; no hurricanes; no subfreezing temperatures—well, very rarely; no heat waves; and the false assumption that they produce the best coffee in the world. Great coding on that last one by the way. If they end up wanting more after the simulation goes live, that's just plain greedy."

"Yeah, I guess you're right. Let's go binge on low-quality TV shows instead."

"Yeah! Now you're talking. I'll pop up some popcorn for us."

Dale couldn't remember the last time he'd visited a bookstore. Reading wasn't one of his hobbies. In fact, he couldn't think of any hobbies he partook of. He wasn't sure if his nightly movie watching counted as a hobby. Anyway, he didn't have the need for hobbies. Hobbies were bullshit. Making money is what he concentrated his time and effort on. When he wasn't at the office, a large amount of his time was spent tinkering and improving his investment algorithm in his home office.

Bookstores were more of Jeremy's thing. That guy read up a storm. He imagined Jeremy slowly examining the entire fiction section in Barnes & Noble, losing touch with reality for hours before emerging back in the real world through the store's double doors. Unlike Jeremy, Dale planned on being in and out within five minutes. He was here solely to buy a finance book Babcock had written so he could place it on his shelf at work, never being read, hoping one day Babcock might catch a glimpse of it and like Dale a little more for possessing it. There was nothing in the book that would further Dale's knowledge about the market. Actually, he'd probably become dumber if he read it. Babcock hadn't even written the book anyway. Ninety percent of it was ghostwritten. Why would anyone ghostwrite anything? Dale didn't have a clue and didn't care enough to spend time finding out.

Dale was having a hard time locating the book in the finance section. And the longer his search took, the madder he got, being forced to listen to some dipshit author talking about his how-to-adopt-a-child book in an area that had been partitioned off for the book reading, which just happened to be located next to the finance and classical literature sections. About twenty numbskulls sat in chairs in front of the regurgitating author.

How depressing, he thought. This guy had wasted countless hours constructing a book about how to acquire little shits, and now he was wasting more time, and other people's time, as he talked about it. Couldn't they have gone online to easily learn about adoption and why having kids was a bad idea in general? The only thing kids were good at was siphoning an adult's cash flow with endless expenses and clogging up countless hours the adult could've dedicated to producing more capital. Basically, they were parasites. Next thing you knew, you'd be living out of a cardboard box after having to pay their college tuition. And just when you thought your investment had come to fruition after they acquired a lucrative job, you'd be shut out. They were so sick of being around you for most of their lives that they wanted next to nothing to do with you. Having kids was an extremely brainless business move. He had no idea why so many people had fallen for that scheme—the child scheme. Even he wasn't cruel enough to derail a person with that abominable scheme. Killing someone in a scheme would be a lighter sentence than a scheme that would force kids into one's life. Better to be out of your misery than tormented for the rest of your life with kids.

He was highly annoyed about having to listen to this guy spout off sentence after sentence from his how-to book on inviting little parasites into your life. *Dammit, I wish this dipshit would shut his trap. I got to find Babcock's book and get the hell out of here.*

It seemed there were how-to books about everything nowadays. Why did they sell? Do people not understand how to use the Internet? He guessed it was a growing trend because people wanted everything spoon-fed to them so they wouldn't need to use any brainpower.

Dale had woken up on the wrong side of the bed and had been growing extensively more crotchety as the day went by. Adding to his displeasure was a headache he'd woken up with that he hadn't been able to shake no matter how many headache pills he dumped into his system. All the added artificial caffeine in the pills used to offset grogginess had made him anxious and ill-tempered.

The more time he spent out of the office and in the public, the more he had to deal with asshats and dipshits. Dale wished the general public would take up hobbies that would benefit him: like walking off cliffs, pressing themselves into meat grinders, diving into wood chippers, or anything that kept them at home so he wouldn't have to deal with them. But right now he'd settle for just this dipshit, this singular dipshit, and his how-to book to be silenced. *How-to … I'll show you how to shut the fuck up by stuffing that book down your throat.*

Maybe Babcock's book wasn't here. Maybe Barnes & Noble had deemed the book not worthy of their finite shelf space. Well, it would be a wise decision, Dale thought. But maybe it was here somewhere hidden behind some other books. He'd made the effort to get here, so he might as well take the time to do a thorough check.

After having scanned most of the books in the finance section, Dale thought he could do readers and Barnes & Noble a favor by tossing the whole finance section to make room for other books. Other books that didn't contain useless prattle. No one was going to get rich by listening to all these hacks who only wrote books on how to make money in the market because they couldn't make money for themselves in the market and chose to make money writing a bullshit how-to book instead. Didn't people understand that and see through all the numerous hollow pages in this section? *What a waste of trees, and I don't even care about trees. And that adoption author is definitely a tree killer. God, I wish he'd shut the fuck up! I wish trees would sprout legs and come barging through the front doors and seek revenge for their obliterated brethren by ramming themselves down his goddamn throat.*

"… and this is where you take time to hold and cuddle your new son or daughter. Your new bundle of joy that's the gift that keeps on giving …" rambled the adoption author.

This last line read from the author's book, coupled with not being able to find Babcock's book, combined with having a waterlogged shoe and sock, combined with an acute headache, as well as a number of other mishaps that had reared their moronic heads throughout the day, shorted a fuse in Dale's brain at that moment.

"That's it!" he shouted, which caused the adoption author to pause his reading for a moment and look in Dale's direction with an anxious face before returning to his jabbering.

Dale quickly shuffled over to the classical literature section to arm himself. It's time for war, he thought, as he used a finger to scrape a path along the shelved books, seeking a thick novel to wield at his foe. His finger ran across *War and Peace* and stopped. *Perfect! Do your worst, Bonaparte.* He yanked the book off the shelf, marched toward the reading author—invading his peaceful partitioned space—and whacked him upside the back of his head with the hefty novel.

Completely taken off guard, the author was silenced midsentence, glasses flinging across the room, body toppling to the floor.

Dale shouted in a deep announcer's voice, "K.O. Winner!" while thrusting his hand that held *War and Peace* into the air triumphantly.

The audience gasped in shock, and then quickly became furious about the violent act. A lady in the front row was particularly infuriated—the author's wife or a loyal fan, Dale thought. She leaped out of her chair like a poisonous frog. Before Dale understood what she was doing, she had selected her own weighty novel from the classics section and was running toward Dale. She obviously sought revenge for his transgression.

She paced toward Dale, stammering, "You … You … Dumbass! *The Count of Monte Cristo* will lay you out cold."

"It's Dumas," Dale corrected her.

She swung the book toward Dale's midsection, but he parried her blow with *War and Peace* and countered with his own offensive move. A back and forth exchange of thrusts and parries ensued, a literal literary battle.

After Dale started to gain the upper ground with a few connected blows to the woman's hideous face, another audience member grabbed a book and entered the fray to assist the weary woman. The short man screeched at Dale, "Miserable people like you don't appreciate the joy of family." His weapon of choice, *Les Misérables*, the unabridged version, naturally.

With two against one, Dale's performance tremendously declined, but he took blow after blow without falling and began to connect some of his own thrusts once the two had gotten cocky.

A gothic teenager, who wasn't part of the audience but wanted in on the action, strode over to the classical literature section and crazily started firing volume after volume of *The Decline and Fall of the Roman Empire* at Dale until all six volumes had been discharged in machinegun fashion.

After the barbarian onslaught, Dale had tumbled to the ground and took on a fetal position under the Roman volumes in an attempt to lessen his misery from the revengeful blows still raining down upon him. The poisonous-frog woman and the short man started getting really into it now that Dale wasn't fighting back, their mouths frothing with glee as they continued to lay their books into Dale's squirming body.

Chapter 10

Waiting for Dale, as usual, Jeremy and Tim had taken up residence at a table in the outside area of the Garden Oasis Caffè under a trestlelike canopy that was dense with ivy and climbing hydrangea. The rain had subsided for the day and left a thin layer of shine on the ground, but the leafy canopy had left the table and chairs under it mostly dry.

They talked about trivial matters while savoring their first cups of coffee for the day.

It had been a year since Jeremy became an advanced ORA by getting Smittie humiliated and fired. Jeremy and Tim had both pulled off schemes in the past month, Tim's second scheme and Jeremy's third, but they were waiting for Dale's arrival before diving into story time. Tim didn't have much of an imagination for planning schemes, so he had stuck with his tried-and-true porn method for his second scheme.

Neither of them were aware of Dale enacting a scheme since his prank calls with the antique phone in the basement. But Dale had been spending more time with his colleagues and skipping many of their café gatherings, so it was possible he had pulled off another scheme without informing them. They had been seeing Dale about once every two months for the past year. It seemed Dale was slowly slipping away from their friendship. To this, Tim was indifferent. Jeremy missed him sometimes, but understood that these transitions in life were normal, and this reminded him of Greek philosophy. Quoted by Plato, the Greek philosopher Heraclitus said it best: "There is nothing permanent except change. All is flux, nothing stays still. One cannot step twice in the same river."

Offering up some trivial conversation, Jeremy asked Tim, "How's the family doing?"

Tim shrugged his shoulders. "Pretty much the same as always. Nothing new on the frontier interesting enough to talk about. What about you? Are you still sticking to the idea of staying single?"

"A simple yes or no answer to that question won't adequately express how I feel, but the short answer is 'yes.' Let me elaborate a little. Many people solely look to relationships to ensure their happiness because that's what their social conditioning has taught them. They feel they can't be truly happy as long as they haven't found that 'special someone.' Those people will never be content if they continue on that path because only they can make themselves content. Another person will only divert their unhappiness for a period of time. They seek to be entertained and find joy in others because they can't successfully entertain themselves and find joy from within. This is why love relationships are so sought after; they provide almost constant entertainment from someone else. Most people feel bored in solitude, so they seek the company of another person in order to be relieved from their thoughts or boredom. They don't understand that contentment, purpose, and love come from within, not in the form of someone or something outside of themselves. They already possess what they seek, they just aren't aware of it."

Tim scrunched up his face in disagreement. "So you're saying no one should bother being in a relationship? And marriage is a sham?"

"No, I'm saying that people won't derive contentment from outside themselves. Marriages and relationships can be great experiences and can help a person grow and give them a chance to better themselves, whether they last or not. Not counting my fleeting sexual experiences and short-term relationships, all five of my substantial relationships were beneficial and very enjoyable at times. I'm glad and appreciative I had those experiences and wouldn't change a thing about them. They weren't failures or a waste of time just because they ended, like most people tend to think. Would you consider a close relationship with a friend for several years a failure when they moved to another country and you never saw them again?"

"No, of course not," replied Tim.

"Exactly, of course not. You'd be glad for the meaningful time you'd spent together and naturally gravitate toward a different close friend, or something of the sort. It isn't any different than a love relationship ending. In fact, it would've been a failure if any of my past relationships had transitioned to marriage, since marriage isn't the best lifestyle for me, given how marriage is approached in our world. However, marriage can be great for most people, given they don't think it's their savior for a content life. Undoubtedly, over the course of marriage, all those people who think it's their savior will realize marriage is capable of as much joy as it is pain, affording them the opportunity to notice the big billboard in front of their faces that tells them to look inside themselves for true contentment. Unfortunately people's social conditioning will hide that fact from them their whole lives. It's interesting how such a huge billboard could be kept invisible through the misconceptions of social conditioning.

"I'm one of those rare people that loves solitude and gets tired of living in the same place and being in the same relationship for too long. Since I'll only end up hurting a person who's seeking a relationship that's everlasting, the honorable thing to do is to abstain from getting into a relationship with those type of people, which is most people. Given enough time, my relationships with those type of people turned into an unstable up-and-down rollercoaster ride: exhilaratingly lifting my hands one moment and vomiting my guts out the next. They were seeking their happiness through me instead of themselves, and got mad at me during the periods they weren't happy. I've rode the ride several times and enjoyed it, for the most part. The ride has definitely helped me grow and better myself, and I know that I've helped loved ones do the same, whether they realize it or not. Now I'd rather enjoy my personal cultivated garden where I might not experience as many highs, but my average state of contentment consistently resides on a higher level than when in relationships, and without all the fluctuations. My years of experience have helped me come to the conclusion that I express love differently from how it's expressed in our current worldly paradigm. For example, I'd be able to enjoy a love relationship on a different planet where it was given freely, not contract-binding, not needy, not prone to jealousy, not stifling, not exclusive, and allowed me to have adequate alone time and contemplation. I believe that's what love will eventually evolve to on Earth, but I won't see it happen in this lifetime."

Tim wasn't in the mood for one of Jeremy's philosophical rants, but his cordial nature hindered him from stopping his friend. On most days Tim was enthusiastic about delving into philosophical conversations with Jeremy. But unlike Jeremy, he wasn't able to enjoy it every day. And when the philosophical conversation's subject was about love and relationships, Tim didn't relate to his friend's beliefs and mindset, which impeded their usual back-and-forth repartee. Given enough time, Tim knew Jeremy would move on to a topic more stimulating, something on which their viewpoints would satisfactorily overlap. He didn't hold it against Jeremy because, after all, he was the one who had brought up the topic by asking Jeremy about being single. He made a mental note to not do that again.

"There is some truth to what you're saying, but don't you get lonely?" After asking the question, Tim realized he had just ignored his mental note.

"There's a much greater chance of me feeling lonely around other people than when I'm by myself," Jeremy said. "I recall Henry David Thoreau stating the same thing in *Walden*. I related and agreed with everything Thoreau said in *Walden*."

"Well, just don't hole yourself up in a cabin in the woods and blow your head off with a double-barreled shotgun."

"You're mixing up writers. Thoreau didn't kill himself, he died of tuberculosis. It was Hemingway that shot himself, and not in a cabin in the woods by a lake, but in Idaho."

Tim thought of a quip. "I'd contemplate suicide too if I found myself in Idaho for too long."

Jeremy wanted to get back on topic. "Anyway, the fact that you asked if I get lonely after everything I just said, tells me you haven't grasped the fundamentals of what I just spoke about at length. A person who's complete by themself doesn't get bored or lonely. Loneliness and boredom are symptoms of not having put in the work to become complete with oneself. Any state of needing something outside yourself is a correlation to the lack of being connected to wholeness, which allows contentment."

Jeremy felt that Tim wasn't any closer to understanding him on this topic despite the longwinded dialog he'd just dispensed, and it wasn't the first time they had spoken about this topic. Tim's lack of comprehension didn't surprise him, though, because he had been faced with the same misunderstanding from an innumerable amount of people regarding the topic. He had reached the conclusion that only rare people—himself and Thoreau—could fathom the complexities of the matter. But nowadays, in the youngest generation, a growing amount of people were coming to the same realization in some way or another, which is why Jeremy believed that love relationships would be redeemed and set free at some point in humanity's evolution.

Tim was sure it was a temporary phase Jeremy was going through, because people were meant to derive happiness from others, and being in a long-term relationship with a loved one was the most essential aspect of living a meaningful, gratifying life. He didn't know what he'd do if he ever lost Amber. The thought was too atrocious for him to even contemplate. He understood relationships weren't easy and required a lot of work, but they were worth the work because life would be pointless without a close bond with someone else who'd always be by your side no matter what life dealt you.

Before this thought tapered off in Tim's mind, Dale had arrived, slamming a tower of books down on their table. Jeremy and Tim looked up at him and took in a sight they'd never seen before: Dale with a rumpled suit rather than an immaculate suit. There were also small cuts and abrasions on his hands and face.

Jeremy set his coffee mug down. "What the hell happened to you? And when did you take up an appreciation for the classics?"

Dale slumped into a chair, exhausted. "I got into a book battle at Barnes & Noble with a bunch of asshats. Some dipshit was giving a reading of his how-to book and I couldn't stand listening to him a second longer, so I beat some classical literature into his head and knocked him out. His occult followers started wielding their own classical literature. They only bested me at my own game because they fought dishonorably by teaming up on me instead of taking me on one at a time."

Jeremy laughed. "A book battle. This would only happen to you, Dale." Jeremy took a sip of his cappuccino while glancing over the titles of the books, and then said after swallowing, "That explains why you're all beat up, but why the classical literature? And this adoption book? Oh, and Eckhart Tolle. Nice to see that you're trying to better yourself and obtain enlightenment."

"Sonuvabitch," Dale mumbled while staring at the tower of books, cursing at the situation instead of Jeremy. He explained, "The author I knocked out woke up to see me lying on the floor, getting pummeled by his rabid followers. He stopped his followers and didn't threaten to press charges, stating that I had already received my punishment from the vicious pummeling. I swear, those disturbed followers started sporting wide grins and laughing hysterically while smacking me with books after it became apparent that I wasn't able to fight back anymore.

"Anyway, the dipshit author may have let me off, but the bookstore manager said he'd call the cops unless I bought all the books that were mangled in the skirmish. That's what the book-reading weasel called it, a goddamn skirmish. So I had to purchase the classics that took part in the 'skirmish.' That's my blood on *The Count of Monte Cristo*," he used a finger to indicate the spot, "but don't you worry, I shed some of their blood too. That bitch's blood is here on *War and Peace*," Dale pointed it out while bearing a smile, the first smile he'd displayed all day. "I had to buy the author's how-to book because it got slightly damaged from hitting the floor after I whacked the author unconscious. Then the store's staff added *The Power of Now* to my forced purchase, stating that my brazen character was in dire need of it. Instead of arguing, I readily paid the extra fifteen dollars so I could get the hell out of there.

"I went into the store to get my boss's stupid finance book, which they didn't have, and I ended up with all this instead." He used two agitated arms to present the tower of books. "I'll just buy Babcock's book online. Should've done that from the start. I never buy books and forgot you could get them online."

Dale stood from his chair and headed toward the patio door. "I'm going to get some coffee. Feel free to take any of these books. You know I don't read books." He stopped short and turned around to add, "But not the how-to book. I'm going to burn it tonight in a ritualistic sacrifice." Then he disappeared inside.

Jeremy took *The Power of Now* from the top of the stack. "Have you read this, Tim?"

"No, what's it about?"

"It's life-changing material, non-fiction. You should read it," he said while handing it to Tim.

Tim looked it over. "Looks like all the other ridiculous self-help books."

Jeremy smiled. "That's what I initially thought when I first came across it, but it's so much more than that. It deserves to be in its own category. It's much more effective than other self-help books because it gets to the root of the issues. The root and issues you and the other self-help books don't even know exist. You can't fix something if you don't know it's broken. This book is so mystical that it belongs in the metaphysical section instead of the self-help section."

Tim tilted his head and shrugged. "Okay, I'll give it a go. If you speak so highly about it, it must be something special."

Jeremy took the six-volume series of *The Decline and Fall of the Roman Empire* for himself. He shared the same sentiments as Alexander III of Macedon (Alexander the Great): an innumerable amount of present-day issues and situations can be solved or dealt with correctly by looking to the written works of the greats who faced the same or similar circumstances in their day. Jeremy always considered himself a resourceful person that could intelligently deal with a certain matter after applying some dedicated thought, but only a fool thought the wisdom from the Greats of the past wasn't relevant in today's modern world. Why reinvent the wheel when the blueprints for its construction have already been written down and recorded for future generations?

Dale returned to the table with a latte. He sat down, placed his mug on the table, and slapped his palms together and rubbed them up and down mischievously. "So boys … done any scheming lately?"

Tim went first, recounting his second-time-around porn scheme to its climax.

"… so while our team lead was in Arash's office, a video of an Indian man raping a fair-skinned Caucasian female pops up on his computer with audio blaring, 'Oh, yeah, rape me hard, brown sugar. You're in control. Oh, oh yes! Rape me in the …'

"Arash quickly turned around and wheeled his chair toward his computer, shouting at it with his thick Indian accent, 'Stop it! Shut up lusty woman. Go away porn-based activity.' When he was accused of viewing rapey porn at work, he adamantly declared in his defense, 'I'm not doing the raping. I don't even enjoy the raping, so why would I watch the raping. I'm not even a rapey individual. I'm a good man with wife,' his English increasingly deteriorating the more flustered he got. After his computer was confiscated and searched, they found thousands of rape-porn images in a folder I hid deep within some system folder that I named I'M DOING THE RAPING. They easily pulled it up after performing a basic program and file search, using the word 'raping.'

"Since Arash knew he didn't create the folder, and he couldn't conceive why anyone would hack into his computer to put it there, he … this is hilarious …" Tim paused, unable to stop his laughter. "He hypothesized that it must have been added in the latest security update in order to assist Massysoft Security Protector in detecting and flagging viruses, spyware, and malicious software under the disguise of innocuous porn." Tim guffawed and repeated the statement in summary, "He tried to convince our team lead that the rapey-porn images were a basic part of our operating system."

All three of them busted up in intense laughter, doubling over in their seats. Jeremy almost came to tears from laughing so hard.

After they settled down, Tim said, "But yeah, like I told Jeremy already, I still didn't get the promotion. They gave it to Asif instead. He deserved the position just as much as I did, so that's fine … but I did that whole scheme for nothing."

"You didn't do it for nothing," Dale said. "Next time a lead software engineer position becomes available, Arash won't be in your way and you'll be the top pick. Because your company is ridiculously huge, it shouldn't take too long for another lead position to open up in one of Massysoft's numerous buildings."

"Yeah, I guess that's true," Tim acknowledged.

Then Dale added, "And I must say, hearing the narration of your story was reason enough for enacting the scheme. Rapey-porn images being part of Massysoft's operating system … that's rich. Looks like you got this porn scheme down pat," Dale told Tim. "So who'll be your next target to perish from propagated porn?"

"I won't use porn in a scheme again. It would be too suspicious: everyone just happening to be porning it up at work, you know."

Jeremy nodded his head in agreement. "Good thinking. Looks like you'll have to get creative again to pull something new out of your hat for the next one."

Dale leaned slightly toward Tim and addressed him. "You've been a software engineer for over a year now, pulling in the big bucks. Doesn't it feel good to be adding your fair share to the family coffers? Aren't you glad you came around to my way of thinking?"

"It does feel good. Amber appears to respect me more, but she might have always respected me the same amount and the change in her attitude toward me could only be in my head. I have a habit of overthinking things sometimes."

"Oh, I'm sure she respects you more." Dale smiled and nodded his head, agreeing to his own words. "Amber is a terrific woman. You could learn a lot from her. You're lucky to have her." The only thing that Dale envied about Tim's life was that Amber was in it. Strong, intelligent, attractive women like that were hard to find in their current male-dominated society that was still aiming to breed subservient females. He had no idea how Tim was able to snag her.

"Yeah, she is," agreed Tim. "She's my world. I'm lucky to have her in my life, for sure."

Dale held up his latte in the air as if to second the thought. "Yeah, you're *damn right* you're lucky."

Tim's appreciation for Amber quickly turned to minor annoyance toward Dale, as Tim felt Dale's remark was insinuating that Tim didn't deserve a woman like Amber. Well, maybe he didn't, but he didn't want to hear it from Dale's rude mouth.

Jeremy went next for storytelling time. Since Tim's first porn scheme had worked so well, he took Tim's advice and used the method under his tutelage. He decided to make it a double attack and use porn that was both gay and rapey. Being that Thomas was an old-fashioned bloke, homophobic at the least, he figured it would be an open and shut case. It was sad that so many people were unprogressive in the area of sexual orientation, but it was fortunate that one of them was his boss.

Dale and Tim relaxed in their chairs and soaked up the story till its finale.

"… and right when Thomas entered Ben's office, I took control of his computer and opened up the porn Web site page that displayed a video of a gay guy raping a straight guy, complete with a repeating uplifting singsong sound bite over the video clip that sounded like a theme song for a 1970s TV show: 'Gay guy raping the straight guy. Oh yeah. There's gonna be some raping … during the dating … we're not talking 'bout mating … there's gonna be a lotta gyrating … enough to help your 'bating …' "

Dale interjected, "That's catchy. I like it."

Jeremy continued, "Ben's face flushed out of embarrassment and anger, and he snapped at his computer, 'Goddammit! Again with the gay-rapey porn on my computer. I'm not gay, computer, so shut up.' He told Thomas, 'My computer's been trying to push gay-rapey porn on me for weeks now.'

"Finally, Thomas exploded about the issue and let Ben have it. 'If you're not gay, then why are these aggressive gay acts being performed on your desktop, *sir*? In fact, your aggressive gayness is oozing all about your office like some wretched fog. You're like Jack the Ripper prowling the London streets at night, but a poofter version. You can't disguise it with your masculine magazines. I know it's just a facade. For repeatedly breaking one of our strictest policies—pornography at the workplace—you're sacked, sir!'

"While Ben was being hauled out of the office against his will, shouting refutations and curses, Thomas wouldn't hear it and yelled back, 'I don't want to hear another poofter word out of your rapist mouth, sir! You've already been sacked, I say!' "

After taking a drink of his cappuccino, Jeremy said, "Another one bites the dust due to the power of porn and all its social stigmas."

"Nice. I told you it would work," Tim said. Then, after a pause, he looked at Dale. "What about you, Dale? Done any schemes since your prank-call scheme?"

"I've been working on phase two of my advancement plan: building close ties with a pack of powerful wolves at Stryker & Marshall. I've been doing it for a year and am now as thick as thieves with this pack. I didn't consider it an extracurricular activity like scheming, though, because I found that I highly enjoy the company of other wolves. Phase two was the reason I was able to acquire the role of assistant VP so quickly."

He took a gulp of his latte and added, "Actually … I did pull off a successful scheme about six months ago. I almost forgot about it."

"*Six months ago*, and you didn't tell us?" Jeremy was stunned.

"Well, I wasn't planning on being an assistant VP for that long, so it didn't seem like a big thing. Plus, I didn't see you guys till about two months after I did it, so I kind of forgot to mention it."

"Well, let's finish off the round of storytelling with you, Dale," Tim said. "What do you say?"

"Sure." He took a greedy gulp of his latte before starting. "I hired boys to dress up like 1910 street vendors selling newspapers. They were called newsies in their day. I bought vintage newsboy caps for them and the whole bit so they looked authentic.

"You're dressing up little boys now are ya?" Jeremy jested.

"Hey, you're the one who thought of it that way, so that's all on you, m'man. Now, where was I? Oh right, so I found out where the targeted VP's four top clients worked and had the newsies stand across the street from their offices doing the customary shouting to hawk their papers. I had them shout headlines like, 'Extra, extra! Read all about it! Lousy Larry embezzles millions.' 'Larry Leno's perpetual pyramid scheme dwarfs Bernie Madoff's.' 'Larry the Louse Leno steals clients' money for his drug and hooker addiction. Read all about it!'—you know, stuff like that.

"I instructed them to run away if anyone tried buying their newspapers since they weren't selling papers that held the actual damning stories the boys were shouting headlines for. I could've gone the extra mile and had fake stories printed on fake newspapers, but I didn't feel that was worth the effort or necessary. Besides, newspapers are already full of fake news to begin with.

"I told these newsboys that Larry Leno was a Wall Street scumbag and gave them counterfeit stories to smear his name and galvanize the boys into delivering a performance full of pomp and zest. I specifically told them that they must hawk their newspapers with *pomp* and *zest* or they wouldn't get paid.

Jeremy interrupted, "That silly plan actually worked?"

"Hey, you'd be amazed what an investor is willing to believe when large amounts of his capital is tied up in investments by one person. Even if they twenty-percent believed it, it could still be enough to take cautionary action. And it worked: three out of four of his top clients ended up dropping Larry Leno as their broker within a month's time. Stryker & Marshall took note of this and acted accordingly, transferring the VP to our only office branch in the Midwest. A locale where he'll be smelling fresh horse and cow dung daily, I reckon."

Jeremy recognized that Dale's omission of the telling of the scheme when he first completed it to be another example that conveyed how Dale was slowly drifting out of his life.

They talked mostly about frivolous matters regarding their work and home lives for the rest of their gathering. Jeremy tried recommending *The Power of Now* to Dale, but was unsurprisingly met with complete refusal. When it was time to leave, they took their selected books from the tower home with them and left the rest on the café table for someone else to scoop up.

Just as he stated he would, Dale brought the adoption book home with him and drank a snifter of cognac while watching it burn in his backyard. The amount of kerosene he squirted on the book caused it to incinerate in a towering inferno. In the evening's waning light, the flames illuminated his face and accentuated his satanic smile, portraying an image comparable to the devil himself. The only aspects that were missing were horns and maniacal laughter.

Chapter 11

Tim pushed the shopping cart while Amber threw this and that into it. Raymond sluggishly followed them from behind. Raymond accompanying them to the supermarket, or anywhere outside of his videogame den of a bedroom, was a rare occasion. On this instance Amber had practically forced him, claiming it would be good for him to get out in the real world every now and then.

"I've got to get some things from the international aisle," said Amber. "Why don't you wait for me here?" Amber headed off without waiting for a response from Tim.

Tim parked the cart near the end of an aisle that was full of Little Debbie snacks. After a long day at work he was feeling quite tired, so he stood by the cart and zoned out with a fixed gaze that focused on nothing in particular.

Raymond waddled over to the array of Little Debbie snacks, mumbling as if under a spell, "Little Debbie snacks. Gotta eat 'em all." He grabbed a package of Fudge Brownies, Devil Squares, and Swiss Rolls and plopped down cross-legged on the shiny waxed floor. Each package was forcefully ripped open, and he began carelessly inhaling the snacks right then and there. The delightful goods vanished one after the other into a mysterious black hole that was his mouth, a black void of space that NASA scientists were still flabbergasted about and had assigned think tanks with the task of cracking the enigma. Chocolate and cake fell to the floor after being mashed up against the sides of his mouth, cheeks, and nose as he went at the snacks like an animal that hadn't eaten in days.

Tim was so out of it that he didn't notice what Raymond was doing until he was half done with each packages' contents. "Hey buddy, maybe we should pay for those before you eat them."

Raymond paid him no mind and continued gobbling down snack item after snack item.

"Maybe you should watch your weight a bit," Tim advised with a polite tone, not wanting to sound like he was pointing out the fact that Raymond was a chubby boy that had been expanding further every year.

Raymond uncommonly replied to Tim while between bites of Devil Squares. "It doesn't matter how fat I get, my online avatars are unchanging." Then he polished off one of the packages and turned to reach back and grab a package of Honey Buns, Salted Caramel Cookie Bars, Glazed Mini Donuts, and Chocolate Marshmallow Pies while mumbling, "Must have variety." He started laying into the new snacks as if they were his first.

With raised eyebrows Tim blinked his eyes in disbelief and shook his head. "Whatever." He figured he'd pick up the empty wrappers and put them in the cart and pay for them at checkout. He didn't have the energy to deal with this absurdity right now.

It wasn't long before Raymond was reaching back for new packages to gorge on: Chocolate Cupcakes, Peanut Butter Creme Pies, and Nutty Buddy Wafer Bars. "More variety, more pleasure," he mumbled to himself. "Go big or go home. The more the better."

Tim listened to the boy's mumblings and wondered if those phrases were slogans the boy had been brainwashed with. Maybe some secret government agency had been abducting him from his bed every night and had been strapping him to a chair in a hidden facility while they MK-Ultra-ed him.

An elderly female cashier returning from a break happened to cross their path. She stopped dead in her tracks and incredulously stared at the obese boy with a gaping mouth. "*Excuse me, sir*," she addressed Tim in a harsh tone. "You have to pay for those before consuming them."

In Tim's fatigued state, he thought, why is it that "sir," a word that was created to show formal respect, was almost always used disdainfully instead of respectfully? "Sir" was how a police officer addressed you before filling your body full of lead. He figured that nowadays "sir" meant the same thing as "hey, shithead."

The elderly lady walked up closer to Tim, getting right up in his face. "Hello?! Anybody home up there?" she said while staring at his forehead, tempted to knock a few times on his head to see if indeed the residence was empty.

Tim was so dead tired that he had forgotten to reply to the lady and had gotten lost in thought about the word "sir" instead. He stepped back a bit to reclaim a comfortable distance from the aggravated lady and replied, "Sorry, ma'am. I'll bring the empty packages to the checkout area and make sure they're paid for."

"That's beside the point. He's getting chocolate cake, fudge, and what appears to be ample amounts of his own slobber all over the floor. It's a safety hazard as well as horrible marketing for the fine people that produce Little Debbie products."

"Of course it's his own slobber. Who else's would it be?" Tim uncharacteristically replied due to exhaustion. "And what do you mean by horrible marketing?"

The bitter lady was growing highly irritated with Tim's display of apathy toward the situation. "It means, *sir*, if anyone gets an eyeful of your little porker of a son downing Little Debbie snacks, they're definitely going to think twice about purchasing Little Debbie snacks on their visit, as well as on any of their future visits, afraid that they'll end up like your overtly round son. The gluttonous speed at which he's consuming those snacks is cause for alarm, and certainly puts your parenting skills in question. If I had a ruler, I could hold it up to his obese body and demonstrate how his girth is expanding at this very moment."

Raymond completely ignored the lady and continued mashing snacks into his cake hole while producing loud slobbering noises akin to a dozen pigs at a feeding trough. The only sound absent was an occasional squeal. It wasn't that Raymond didn't hear the lady calling him a porker; his apathy toward the lady's words was due to his mastering the art of desensitization in regards to people's opinions, violence, and pretty much everything in life.

Tim had no energy to invest in calming the lady. He shrugged and nonchalantly stated, "Truth be told, he's not actually my son. He's my wife's son."

"What does that mean? If he's your wife's son, then he's your son. You families today are all messed up. What happened to the good old days when it was simple and uncomplicated? Back then we didn't go around collecting sex experiences and labeling relationships as "It's complicated" on the social media Internets. We hunkered down and collected each moment of love with that special someone. My God, if Al Gore knew what the Internets would've amounted to for younger generations, he would've thought twice about taking the initiative to whip it up in his spare time. He should've never invented the Internets."

Tim became nauseated by the putrid energy spewing forward from the elderly woman who was steeped in bitterness and anger. It was pointless in responding to her. She was set in her ways and nothing would free her from her deranged mental state that would surely envelope the rest of her living days in a toxic mist till she went out with a bitter scowl on her face and permanently clenched claws for fingers. He really was tired. These were dark thoughts he wasn't accustomed to thinking.

The lady stared at his blank face, waiting for a reply. "Talking to you is like talking to a damned brick wall," she said, and then turned her attention toward Raymond since Tim clearly didn't give a damn. She marched over to Raymond, bent down, clasped her claws on the end of the Nutty Buddy package he was currently digging into, and attempted to rip it out of his hands. But Raymond's grasp on the package was tighter than a bodybuilder's hold on a protein bar when protecting it from fellow jealous bodybuilders at Gold's Gym.

The Nutty Buddy package was tugged back and forth, neither one of them gaining any ground.

Amber turned the corner and saw the elderly lady accosting her son.

"Let go of Little Debbie, porker-boy!" the lady screeched.

Amber shifted the items in her hands to one hand and used her free arm to shove the lady away from her son, an instinctual mother's reaction to protect her offspring.

After being pushed back, the lady placed a foot down to regain her balance but ended up stepping on a pile of fudge, chocolate, and Raymond slobber. She slipped. Her leg flew up into the air, her grimace quickly turning into shock and fear, and she fell backward and smacked her head against the floor.

Raymond continued shoving snacks in his mouth while chuckling at the unconscious lady that lay on the floor with her mouth ajar.

Amber cringed at what her push had done, but quickly regained composure. "Well, we're done here. Let's go. Did I forget anything on the list, Tim?"

"Nope, we got everything," he replied while putting the empty Little Debbie packages into the cart. "Shouldn't we check to make sure she's okay before leaving?"

"She didn't hit her head that hard. She's just temporarily knocked out. If anything, the rest will probably be good for her—ease her temper. Did you see the expression on that old hag's face as she tried to take Raymond's snacks? It was straight out of a horror movie. If she hadn't been knocked unconscious, the next thing she would've done was open her mouth wider than any human's jawbone would allow and reveal razor-sharp teeth, then release countless swarms of locusts."

With posthaste they abandoned the scene before other shoppers came into view, pushing their cart down an aisle toward the checkout stands.

Raymond lingered behind, taking the last Chocolate Cupcake out of its package and chuckling as he shoved it into the unconscious lady's open mouth. "Compliments of Little Debbie. Enjoy, sleepy-bitch-face." Then he caught up to his mom and Tim.

While the groceries were being scanned the cashier came upon the numerous empty Little Debbie packages and glanced up at Raymond. "Looks like your little one couldn't wait to indulge in Little Debbie," she politely said with a smile on her face.

In response, Raymond let out a long guttural belch in her direction.

The cashier's smile vanished and she hastily returned to scanning and bagging their groceries in silence.

After all their bagged groceries were in the cart and they were heading for the door, Raymond lifted a finger toward the small food court attached to the supermarket and uttered, "Want fries."

"Didn't you eat enough food already, buddy," Tim said.

"*Want fries*," Raymond repeated, raising his voice.

They acquiesced. Amber and Tim stared at the large TV mounted on the wall in the food court while Raymond picked at his fries.

A rerun of *What You Got, Bitch?!* was currently on the boob tube. An energetic, aggressive black guy with a very popular YouTube show had been picked up for a TV show. The charismatic host, Duhwayne, would randomly walk into stores—usually mom-and-pop stores—and shout at them, "What you got, bitch?!" and then help the shop owners market their goods by presenting them to his viewers. Duhwayne's captivating personality was the sole reason the show became a hit. Small businesses that couldn't afford commercial marketing were benefiting greatly from it. You couldn't beat free publicity in front of millions of viewers. Duhwayne instantly became famous and was admired for helping out common folks. T-shirts sporting the show's name, WHAT YOU GOT, BITCH?!, became quite fashionable.

The show was obviously a rerun because it had been cancelled a couple years ago. It had indirectly started the What You Got Bitch Movement where young teenagers started YouTubing their own shows like Duhwayne had once did, but instead of helping out the stores, they stole stuff after shouting, "What you got, bitch?!" A few lost souls had started it and the idea went viral. Soon there were countless teenagers of all nationalities uploading their own *What You Got, Bitch!?*

YouTube shows. What had started out as a benevolent idea had become nothing but basic theft.

Then the local news came on. Talking heads sat behind a large news desk, shuffling and straightening papers. "Good afternoon, Seattle. This afternoon's news is graphic in nature. Viewer discretion is advised. The Butcher has struck again, and this time in our own backyard. Thanks to a twelve-year-old boy, new information has been acquired regarding the serial killer that has eluded authorities for years. The boy witnessed the murder of his neighbor from his second-story window. Before the murder, the boy overheard dialog between his neighbor and the killer that could prove to be crucial in apprehending the long-sought-after serial killer. The boy told authorities that The Butcher knocked on his neighbor's door and pretended to sell magazine subscriptions before taking a knife out of a black briefcase and repeatedly stabbing and cutting his victim to death. He filleted the man and used his bloody organs for—"

The anchorwoman seated next to the anchorman cut off her cohost. "Ron, I don't think you need to go into those gory details for our viewers. Why don't you just get to the new information we've acquired."

Indignation arose on Ron's face. "I believe our viewers have the right to know all the important details, Veronica. If you got cut up into little pieces, Veronica, wouldn't you want me to inform our viewers about their once-beloved assistant anchor's demise in detail?"

Veronica's fake smile started showing signs of collapse. "I'm not an assistant anchor, Ron. You full well know that I'm an anchor just like you. And I don't plan on being cut into little pieces anytime soon, so …"

After an awkward pause of her staring into the camera and Ron staring at her with a frown on his face, she said, "Can you continue to the important information now … and quit staring at me?"

Ron finally focused back on the camera. "Well that was rude. Now I'll get to the important information that I would've already covered if Veronica hadn't discourteously cut me off."

He turned back to scowl at Veronica for a couple seconds before turning back to the camera to address the viewers. "The boy said The Butcher introduced himself as Ken Karver. It is not known at this time if that is The Butcher's real name, an alias that he uses often, or a one-time used alias."

Ron paused for effect while delivering a dramatically stern gaze to his viewers before continuing, "You can help authorities bring this fugitive to justice. If you see this man," a rough sketch of a man that looked grave and maniacal with a psychotic smirk appeared on the TV, "or hear an individual address themselves as Ken Karver, please call this tip hotline to relay your information to authorities working on the case. … And Seattle … be cautious of door-to-door salesmen selling magazine subscriptions."

Veronica turned to her cohost and said, "Do people even sell magazine subscriptions door-to-door nowadays, Ron? I'd assume something sketchy was afoot if someone appeared at my door trying to sell magazine subscriptions whether there was a serial killer on the loose or not."

The anchorman kept his gaze at the camera and began straightening the papers before him while answering his colleague, "So would I, Veronica. So would I." After he was done straightening his papers for no reason, he continued, "Stay tuned this evening as Brian informs us how your regular household furniture could be killing you. I'm Ron Redish, one of the many news puppets that tell you what to think and what to believe."

The anchorwoman followed quickly, "And I'm Veronica Applestone."

"Stay dry, Seattle," they said in unison.

Tim looked at Amber. "Ken Karver could be your next client."

"A serial killer with an eye witness to one of his killings. No thanks. I'll pass. Clearly a losing case."

"Would you take the case if there wasn't an eye witness?"

Amber shrugged her shoulders. "Possibly." After a pause, she added, "Speaking of losing cases. I passed on an interesting one recently pertaining to a psychotherapist psychiatrist."

Half of Tim's attention was on a commercial, so he misheard his wife. "Wow, a psycho rapist psychiatrist. Did he—or she—prescribe medication that made his clients sexually aroused so he could take advantage of them?"

"I said psychotherapist, not psycho rapist. Although, this guy might be both. Stop watching that mindless insurance commercial and listen to me. Allegedly, this shrink got bored of the typical listening and questioning protocol: 'And how did that make you feel?' and 'What makes the problem better?' and so on, and started telling his patients straight up how they were stupid and were making the same moronic mistakes over and over again. Naturally he lost most of his patients. Allegedly, he was trying to get rid of his patients on purpose so he wouldn't have to listen to them spout off their idiotic problems all day. But some of his patients stuck around, thinking his new method was groundbreaking and brilliant. So, allegedly, he started walking up to his patients as they were rattling off their problems and licked them on the side of the face, tongue fully extended and accompanied with exaggerated, gross licking sounds. I don't mean the sound that the licking itself made, but his own vocalized sound that accompanied the licking to make it more disgusting. Something like this," Amber tried to reproduce the perverted, gross sound while licking her tongue through the air, "lahhhhhhh."

Tim cringed with slight confusion and disgust. "Okay. Yeah, that's quite disturbing."

"Yeah, right," Amber agreed. "So he lost the rest of his patients except for one, a patient who thought the licking was an innovative technique her shrink had learned at a European shrink convention. So, allegedly, in order to be free of her, he completely revamped her prescriptions. He had her so doped up that she started talking to rocks and grains of dirt, swearing she was in communion with the microscopic world. She professed that numerous grains of dirt had told her that water was out to annihilate them, and if she didn't act soon, the whole world would be under water, which would bring the human species to extinction along with the dirt. She was instructed by the dirt to take up arms with their cause, so she went straight out to a small lake near her house, spat on it in disgust and rage, and then attempted to drink up the whole lake in order to abolish it. Swimmers tried stopping her, but she was hostile and bit them in retaliation. She told them she'd swallow them up too if they didn't vacate the water's dreamy seduction by the time she got to them. She died of water toxemia, drinking too much water. That shrink had her doped up on god knows what."

Tim interjected, "Allegedly."

"Yeah, allegedly. Anyway, yeah, not a winnable case, so I passed on it."

Tim noticed two kids with bulging pockets and jackets walking through the floral department. "Hey, isn't that the GMO kids?"

Amber turned in the direction Tim was looking. "Sure is. Looks like they're hiding a sizable amount of goods under those clothes."

An announcement came over the intercom, "Mr. Cash, you're needed in the floral department."

While the GMO boys walked past the floral department and headed for the front door, Nash told his brother, "That announcement is code for someone is shoplifting. Run for it, Mash."

Nash and Mash bolted for the front door while an array of goods fell from their clothes. They were forced to wait for the automatic glass door to open and then continued sprinting toward their bikes.

Eight seconds later, Tim and Amber saw the bitter elderly woman running after them while spitting chocolate cake pieces out of her mouth.

"I told you she'd be fine," Amber said.

The elderly woman ran full steam into the glass door that she hadn't allowed to open. A chocolate cake mark splatted on the area of the door where her mouth hit and made a downward trail on the glass door as she slumped to the floor.

Tim cringed. "Ouch. It's just not her day today, is it?"

Amber nodded her head in agreement. "Looks like she's got a date with the floor again."

A few bits of fries flew out of Raymond's mouth as he chuckled at the again-unconscious lady.

Nash and Mash raced to their Huffy bikes and took off out of the parking lot and then down the street.

"I told you, Mash. We're unstoppable with these Huffy bikes," Nash said while pedaling his heart out. "This city is our bitch, and we're going to use our bikes to ride her for all she's got."

Mash agreed with his brother, "Yeah, we're going to ride our bikes for all they've got."

"That's not what I—"

Something caught Nash's attention in a McDonald's they were passing: two boys wearing white dress shirts and slim black ties.

Nash applied his brakes and skidded to an abrupt stop.

His brother following suit. "What's up, Nash? Why are we stopping? Don't we need to escape?"

"We're far enough away from the supermarket clowns. We're safe. We got bigger fish to fry now," he said while walking his bike toward McDonald's, squinting through the window as he approached.

Mash followed his brother. "Hey, isn't that those morons?"

"You're goddamn right," Nash answered.

Mash hastily made for the entrance door's handle. "How dare they step onto our turf again. Let's snap their necks!"

Nash held out a stiff arm to stop his brother's forward momentum. "Wait. Take a look at them. They're downing truckloads of McNuggets. Looks like they're having an eating contest. Let's wait till they stuff themselves and bog down their fighting skills. Anyway, we can't kick their asses inside McDonald's."

Mash vigorously nodded his head in agreement. "Right. The staff would get involved and might call the pigs."

"Yeah possibly, but I meant we can't fight within the holy temple of food. It's a sacred place. We'll wait till they exit, then we'll beat the holy shit out of those morons … again. This time for good, in the name of Bobby." Nash started licking his chops with excitement in anticipation of a good beating. "Here's the plan. We'll hide around the corner. After they exit and get to their bikes, we'll race around the corner and sucker punch them in the guts. Then we'll get behind them and turn their bodies so they're facing each other. They'll most likely vomit on each other."

"A sucker punch to the gut with all those McNuggets in their stomachs will definitely make them hurl. Righteous idea, Nash."

Nash doubled over and winced.

"What's wrong, Nash?"

"A sharp pain in my side. I've been getting it every now and then. It'll go away. I also got a pretty bad headache today."

Mash said with slight anxiety, "I get headaches all the time. Is that a problem? I thought that was just a normal part of living."

Nash comforted his brother. "Don't worry, it's just aches and pains of our bodies growing up into total badasses. Your headaches will go away, just like the pain in my side will go away. It'll all go away sooner or later. And I'll tell you what's going to go away the soonest: those McNugget hording morons. It makes me mad. The longer they sit in McDonald's, the longer they defile the holy temple with their moronicness."

Nash started walking toward the Mormons' bikes. "After they've thoroughly soaked each other in chewed up McNugget pieces, we'll proceed to punch and kick the living shit out of their vomit-sprayed bodies lying in fetal positions on the ground." Nash emptied his right pocket of the food he'd stolen to get to a nail at the bottom and punctured the Mormons' tires with it. A hissing leak could be heard from both bikes. "Just as a backup plan if things don't go according to plan."

Nash and Mash went around the corner and waited, sniggering every now and then for what was to come.

Chapter 12

Elliot Brady, Tim's lead, knocked on Tim's office door and informed him that a lead software engineer position was opening up soon in one of their Bellevue buildings across the street from a Microsoft building by Bellevue City Hall, and Tim and Joe Shoup Dominion were being considered for the role. Elliot was giving both engineers a friendly heads up so they'd be sure to stay on top of their game.

Although Tim was happy to hear about the opening position, he was distraught about having to contend with someone else for it. He thought he was at the top of the heap and would easily slide into a lead engineer role when one became available. Now he'd have to pull off a scheme to ensure his advancement, which he wasn't thrilled about, but he had to play the game to win it. He had to fix the game so there would be only one outcome, the same thing a politician would do to be victorious at their party's caucuses, or even for the presidency.

He was fortunate to have the opportunity to move up to a lead role after only being a software engineer for two and a half years. Massysoft was expanding rapidly, but there was no telling when it would slow down. If things slowed down, he could possibly have to wait several years, maybe even a decade. You never knew when the economy would fluctuate, and their competition could always roll out game-changing software or some new innovative device that would steal a hefty amount of Massysoft's market share. Microsoft had done it to them before. He needed to strike and secure the lead role while the time was ripe.

Tim went over the information he knew about Joe Dominion in his head. He probably leaves his office door unlocked like most people in the office, but he also left his door open with his computer unlocked from time to time. Tim wasn't very creative and couldn't think of a scheme that didn't involve him getting onto someone's computer, but he needed to be creative enough to come up with a method other than porn.

Programmers would soon be completing code for a new system cleaner that would be bundled with the next version of MOS (Massy Operating System). It would delete unwanted files and invalid Massy registry entries, display startup programs that could be removed if the user desired, manage OS restore points, and provide a drive wiper as well as other features. Joe was tasked with reviewing the programmers' code to make sure they followed his layout instructions, and spotting any coding issues before handing the product over to Elliot for further testing.

In his spare time he could create code to initiate an aggressive drive wipe and insert it into the system cleaner's code. If a window of opportunity presented itself, he could slip into Joe's office and insert the code after Joe was done checking the software. This way, thinking it was all up to snuff, Joe would hand it over to Elliot, who would run his own tests, get his hard drive wiped by Tim's added code, and be furious at Joe.

Two weeks later, Tim had completed the vicious code and was waiting for the system cleaner software to be handed to Joe for checking.

After Joe received it, spent time thoroughly checking it over, and was heard telling a colleague that it was ready to be handed over to Elliot the next day for further testing, Tim slipped into Joe's office and inserted the code in the correct spot.

The plan went seamlessly. Tim was surprised at how smoothly it had gone. He figured his first porn scheme against

Brad could've been this easy if he hadn't been so apprehensive and fearful at the time.

The next day, Elliot received the program from Joe and installed it on his computer to run its functions to see if they were efficient and errorless.

The first thing Elliot did was run the program's basic cleaning function, analyzing data associated with Internet browsers and the operating system. After one minute and forty-six seconds, the analysis was complete. The files suggested for deletion were listed and their approximate size was displayed: 936 MB. Everything checks out so far, thought Elliot. Now let's run the cleaner. He pressed RUN CLEANER. A red pop-up box appearing and displayed a message: ⚠WARNING: ARE YOU SURE YOU WANT TO WIPE YOUR ENTIRE C: DRIVE WITH 0,1 OVERWRITING? Two buttons underneath the warning were shown: YES and NO. A ten-second timer started counting down.

Elliot was unsettled. "What the hell? This was supposed to be a basic clean. No, I don't want to wipe the drive that contains my operating system, or any drive for that matter."

Elliot moved the mouse cursor to the NO box and clicked it. When he clicked it, it flashed for a millisecond and turned to a second YES button. A pop-up box displayed: NOW OVERWRITING WITH ONE PASS. HAVE A NICE DAY. ☺

"Fuck!" shouted a bug-eyed Elliot.

A percentage started at zero and slowly started making its way to one-percent completion.

Elliot frantically tried using his keyboard and mouse to abort the wipe, but he found that they were both frozen. Every time he pressed a button on his keyboard a message popped up on the screen: YOUR KEYBOARD AND MOUSE HAVE BEEN TEMPORARILY DISABLED TO ENSURE QUALITY IMPRINTING. YOU'RE WELCOME. ☺

"Goddammit Joe! What the hell have you done?" Elliot yelled, even though he was alone in his office. "What to do, what to do? Well, nothing else to do but force a shutdown." He pressed the power button down for five seconds while holding his breath. The five seconds felt like an eternity.

His desktop finally powered down to a blank screen before the wiping process had made it to one-percent completion.

He turned his computer back on. He sat there steaming mad for a moment while his computer loaded up, and then swiftly vacated his chair and office to yell at Joe while his computer hopefully started up.

After about twenty minutes of heated back and forth dialog between Elliot and Joe, Elliot made his way back to his office to check on his computer.

He strode across the threshold of his doorway with a scowl and made his way to his computer to look at the screen, hoping the C: drive was still operating normally. Instead of a logon screen, he saw DOS, and a message on his screen: SORRY. WIPING WASN'T ABLE TO COMPLETE ON YOUR LAST LOGGED-IN SESSION. NOT TO WORRY, IT WILL CONTINUE NOW BEFORE INITIATING THE OS. HAVE A NICE DAY. A percentage counter showed the process was currently at 13% COMPLETION.

An enraged Elliot raised both arms from his sides, clawed fingers facing up in the air, and threw his head back to yell at the ceiling, "Joe! You goddamn fucktart! I'll wipe you from the fuckin' planet!"

Tim had a weird dream that night. He was with Amber and Raymond on a plane flying to a third world country for a vacation. Throughout the whole flight Tim was worried Amber would get mad at him for the seats he had preselected on the Internet when he purchased the tickets.

After the plane's touchdown, they were escorted to their transportation that would take them to their hotel. For some reason Amber and Raymond's ride was a sports car that would reach the hotel in a short amount of time and Tim's ride was an old beat-up taxi that would take much longer to get to the hotel.

Tim asked one of the staff why he had to take separate transportation when there was an extra seat in the sports car.

The taxi driver told Tim, "That's just how life is. You don't always get what you think you want, but you always get what you need to experience."

Tim didn't like that answer, but his wife had already left in the sports car so there was no use in arguing.

Tim's taxi ride was noisy and shaky.

After a while into the ride the taxi driver got a phone call. He informed Tim that his wife had gotten into a car accident. Tim asked if she was okay. The driver said he didn't know all the details, but regardless, he'd see her back home if he didn't get to see her on the vacation. In the dream, this stupid explanation seemed reasonable to Tim for some reason.

Then the taxi broke down and the driver said it might be years before they could get someone out to this spot in the middle of nowhere to repair the taxi. The driver recommended that Tim stay in the nearby valley where there was a British expat community living.

Tim told the driver that the expat community wasn't the destination that he had sought out for when entering the taxi at the airport. The driver told Tim that life was about the journey, not the destination. Tim asked if death was the destination. The man smiled at Tim but said nothing.

Tim didn't seem to have much of a choice so he went to the community. He was welcomed by the community members. A particular man, who always wore white and beige clothing, told Tim he'd teach him how to live simply and joyfully when he was ready to receive the teaching. Tim didn't know what that meant and wasn't interested in the man's offer.

Tim stayed at the community for years, missing his wife and feeling miserable. Then he finally got curious enough to ask the man about "the teaching" he was told about years ago. The man saw that Tim was ready to absorb the information, so he imparted the teachings to Tim daily. Tim opened himself up and found that the teachings transformed his whole way of life by opening his awareness to the true state of life, and life was beautiful and vibrant.

Eventually he forgot about his wife and enjoyed his life at the community, feeling better than he'd ever felt before.

Then Jeremy showed up out of the blue in the community. Jeremy said he'd been living in the community for years, but had fallen down a well where he was trapped for many years before being able to climb his way out. Tim was happy to see his friend, but was confused at how nonchalantly Jeremy had spoken about being trapped in a well for years before getting out, as if the ordeal wasn't a big deal to Jeremy anymore.

Tim woke up.

He pondered over the dream that seemed symbolic in nature, but he went back to bed after not being able to make heads or tails about its meaning. He remembered tidbits of the dream when he got up in the morning, and had completely forgotten about it before lunchtime.

In the end, after Tim's plan unfolded perfectly, Joe got fired and Tim advanced to the lead software engineer position at the Bellevue building, where he headed a newly created team. Since his house was in Woodinville, a suburb of Seattle, his commute time was shortened to a twenty-minute drive, not counting traffic. No more forty-minute commutes to the Seattle office where he had started working for Massysoft.

Chapter 13

Ken Karver strolled down the street wearing blue scrubs, white tennis shoes, and the ubiquitous white doctor's coat. He held a leather physician's bag. He wasn't wearing a stethoscope around the back of his neck because he didn't want his attire looking like a Halloween costume.

In thought, he reveled in the Masters' design while in route to his next karma-balancing act. Their genius design allowed them to rule the planet from behind the curtains.

Earthlings, full of diversity, generally weren't hostile toward each other. The Earth was like a big insect jar. Insects put into a jar together tended not to fight unless the jar was agitated enough. If the jar owners put different types of ants in the same jar without agitating their habitat enough, they might just work together to overthrow the jar owners and build a happy society where everyone was equal and free. And we can't have that. Gotta keep shakin' that jar.

The name of the game was divide and conquer. Or better yet, divide and let them kill each other. The jar owners had been using this tactic from the beginning. No matter how often they repeated this tactic, the brainless masses fell for it over and over again. Tension between races. Tension between political parties and citizens who sided with each party. Politicians used the same slogans in their speeches repeatedly, which contained hollow words like "better tomorrow" and "change." The jar owners would make a little change like putting a black man or a woman in the white house instead of the typical old white male scumbag and everyone would think it was going to be different this time. Well, the woman they tried to put in … that one hadn't worked out as planned. The yellow cube had misdirected them.

Politicians ruled over their fellow humans, so the Masters used them to implement all their agendas to ensure a continuation of separation and control. The same old record would play over and over again.

The Masters pulled the same issues out of their hats every now and then to keep everyone at each other's throats: abortion, gun control, immigration, religious ideologies, et cetera. The Masters didn't even have a side or care about these issues. The only time they took a side on one of them, behind closed doors, was if it assisted them in rolling out their agendas.

Those type of issues were only the tip of the iceberg that kept humans separated within each of their respective countries. The Masters would widen the scope by using politicians to separate countries from each other using isms (capitalism, socialism, communism, et cetera), which were all indirectly created and ruled over by the Masters; financial systems, which led to embargoes and trade wars; religions that spawned from different enlightened beings' teachings that were all comparable and collaborating in their inception, but had been radically contorted by the Masters throughout the ages; and the kindergarten method of merely labeling a whole country bad for no reason or some flimsy fabricated reason. It didn't seem to matter how flimsy any of their tactics were, the population would eat it up every time.

The name of the game was control, and the more separation that existed, the easier it was to control.

Humans that thought they were advancing around the chessboard of life as knights and bishops were actually among the multitude of pawns, advancing like fodder to their inevitable demise for the true kings and queens behind closed doors, invisible from all the pieces' perceptions on the chessboard, except for a few of the kings and queens on the chessboard that were aware they were working for the Masters.

Karver worked for the Masters in one of the numerous deep underground military bases (DUMBs) in a psychotic capacity, or at least that's how humans described his actions: psychotic. The Masters resided at the bottom floors of

DUMBs in order to direct workers on other floors, workers that didn't even know they existed on the partitioned-off, clearance-only bottom floors. Most of the Masters resided in military and agency bases above and below the earth. Militaries were just another resource they used to wield control.

Karver was periodically given a list of humans he could sacrifice in order to harvest louche loosh for his masters. Louche loosh, also known as negative loosh or just loosh, is radiated by humans experiencing intense, severe pain and suffering of their psyches. To his masters, loosh was the most exquisite food. It's like the gold standard of caviars. They had more effective ways of harvesting large amounts of loosh through ceremonial dark rituals to fill Moloch's coffers in the astral plane and fuel the Baphomet collective consciousness field, which powered up the Black Magic Grids. So Karver's loosh collecting was used as an exquisite dessert for the Masters, not the main course. His role was more to keep the human population fearful, which was one of the most effective methods used for control.

Only humans that crossed a certain moral line and didn't possess a contract with the Dark Forces made it onto the list Karver was given. They were bound by rules and couldn't touch humans that didn't cross that ethical line. In this regard, Karver considered himself to be enacting the role of karma.

Karver had the privilege to roam around dispatching any human on the list, assisting in the balancing of their karma. He reveled in his job and felt it an honor to extract loosh and cull the human population. He was given high-tech vials that had the ability to suck in all loosh in a ten-foot radius. A digital reading on the vial displayed its available capacity so he would know when to seal it and open a new one.

This type of technology may sound like science fiction to the human populace, but it wasn't considered anything special in the DUMBs—or the many other locations, in and off planet Earth, hidden from the masses—where a plethora of hidden advanced technologies resided and were used in everyday life. Every worker that took part in projects within DUMBs had to sign a non-disclosure agreement that was punishable by death if broken. The rare occurrences of leaked information of advanced technologies was almost always met with laughter and mockery because virtually every human considered the advanced technologies they'd been told about from the leaker to be ridiculous fantasies only belonging in sci-fi novels.

If you kept the Earth's population separated and at each other's throats, they tended to disbelieve leaked information from others, having not seen it with their own eyes. The design of separation was so complex that it tricked the dumbest individuals to the smartest individuals, both weren't aware of the design that controlled them and their thoughts.

The dumbest individuals were hooked on some of the simplest misdirections, like a truck-driving redneck from Georgia being hooked by racism. The smartest individuals were hooked on some of the loftiest misdirections, like doctors and scientists propagating information they had learned at universities, which they touted like a blindly followed religion. What they weren't aware of was that the information they learned was misdirection from the Masters' design. Like everything else on Earth, they indirectly controlled universities and the information that was taught within their "hallowed halls of learning."

Doctors, professors, and scientists were unknowingly assimilating incorrect or half-true information in order to regurgitate it to the populace. Because the populace held these professions in the highest regard, their disseminated information was believed as if it was coming out of the mouth of gods.

A family drove past Karver in a SUV, breaking his train of thought. Seeing Karver's white doctor's coat, the dad in the driver's seat slightly lifted one of his hands off the steering wheel to give Karver a friendly hello-and-thank-you-for-your-service motionless wave, which was closer to a *sieg heil* than a wave. The mom in the front passenger seat waved, smiled, and nodded her head to show her appreciation for his occupation.

Karver, with his omnipresent deceptive smile that ranged from a smirk to a grin at any given time, reciprocated the gesture with a grin and a slight head nod. "That's right humans, bow down to your gods," he uttered with disdain after the SUV drove past him.

Where was I? Oh yeah: Even humans who knowingly worked for the Masters, like some politicians, only understood a fraction of the controlling spider-web design.

In this way, earthlings were flies kept stuck in the great spider-web design, cocooned by constricting misinformation and misdirection while their blood and souls were continually fed upon by the Masters. As it should be, because earthlings were nothing more than flies, a pestilence for the spiders to use as worker bees and sustenance before being discarded.

Reveling in the great design always electrified Karver and made his time spent among the human masses and their fabricated societies more bearable.

Karver arrived at his destination. He sauntered up to the door and rang the doorbell. He calmly stood facing the door with a deceitful smirk, waiting for the residence's occupant to open their hatch so he could pluck the human like a clam from its shell and devour away after pocketing the pearl the clam had slaved its whole life to make. But before devouring, added spices and simmering time would enhance the feast.

Frank Panicucci opened the door and spoke to his visitor, "Hey doc. What can I do you for?"

"Well, I was at the hospital persuading a patient to do radiation therapy and chemotherapy for his cancer, along with numerous surgeries. The clown wanted to bypass all medical care and cure his cancer with a naturopathic doctor. What a fool, right?"

Frank agreed. "Yeah, doc. Natural path medicine is hocus pocus. Snake oil for chumps."

Karver's smirk widened a little. "That's right, my good man. They shouldn't even be able to call themselves doctors. Making people eat roots, tree bark, dirt and whatnot. If they stopped trying to peddle their snake oil, maybe they'd stop mysteriously dying or disappearing." Karver paused for a few seconds, grinning at Frank in silence, creating an awkward moment, and then started talking again, "So I was at the hospital doing that—as well as diagnosing countless patients with various diseases and illnesses, slapping different negative labels on people so we could recommend this medical surgery or that medical prescription—you know, easing their transition to a postmortem state or catching diseases before they get a foothold in the body. You can't be too careful, right?"

"That's right, doc." Frank nodded his big, meaty, stupid head.

"Anyway, I thought, why don't I take up the good fight and visit some houses like they used to do in the good old days. Not everyone has the time or money to visit a doctor, so I thought I'd be a Good Samaritan and make some free house calls." Karver lifted his physician's bag and stuck his free hand inside, preparing for action.

"You know what, doc. I got some pain in my stomach and chest. Been having it for weeks now and it ain't going away, so I'd be most appreciative if you came in and took a look at it." Frank backed his rotund body up and invited Karver inside his house with a swinging beefy arm.

For a moment Karver's perpetual smile fizzled out due to surprise. Then it quickly settled back on his face in the form of a grin. *Wow, they keep getting dumber every year. The great design is flawless.*

Frank led the way through his house down a hallway, passing different rooms. "Which room would be best for the free examination, doc?"

"Somewhere you can lay down on your back, elevated. Is your dining room table long and sturdy enough to hold your weight?"

"I imagine it is." Frank ambled to the dining room where remnants of a steak and veal chop sat on the big table. "Let me take the last few bites of this steak and chops before we get underway." He greedily smacked his laps as he polished off the meats and sucked on a few plump fingers afterwards. Then he removed the plate and some other items from the table so it was bare and ready for his body to lie on.

Karver placed his physician's bag on a nearby countertop, unlatched it, and opened it up. Turning his head slightly back toward Frank, he said, "Good. Now go ahead and take off your shirt and get comfortable on the table, laying on your back. Let's see if I can diagnose your abdominal and chest pains and get you all fixed up, shall we?"

"You got it, doc." Frank did as he was told and tried getting as comfortable as possible on the hard table, using his shirt for a pillow. As Karver put on medical gloves he'd produced from his physician's bag, exaggeratingly snapping the latex gloves in place for effect, Frank made some small talk to fill the silence. "Funniest thing happened last night."

"Oh yeah, what's that?"

"An owl was hooting in my backyard."

"Is that right?" Karver nonchalantly replied while staring into his physician's bag.

"The weird thing about it is I only have one small tree in my tiny backyard, nothing an owl would be interested in. Come to think of it, it was the first time I've ever heard an owl in my life."

"Must have been a great horned owl." Karver rattled off some facts, "They're at the top of the food chain for birds of prey. They're fierce predators. They hunt everything including raptors and other owls. They own the sky and woods. They can locate their prey in total darkness using sound alone. Their talons' deadly grip is used to sever the spine of large prey and is equivalent in strength to a bald eagle's."

Karver paused for a moment and stared at Frank with menacing eyes. "The bald eagle is America's national bird, but it's merely a figurehead, a puppet. The great horned owl is the true ruler. Shrouded in the darkness of the night, hidden from the common eye, it dictates all terms from its hidden throne."

"*Porco dio*, good thing I wasn't outside. Sounds like a motherfucka of an owl."

"Yes, but don't worry," Karver said, grinning down at his patient. "You're not outside. You're in here with me … and I'm a doctor."

"Well, I'm ready when you are, doc. Let's find the reason for this pain and rub it out."

"You can count on it." Karver took out a sharp ten-inch-bladed knife from his bag and hovered above his patient with the knife horizontal to his admiring grin, the light reflecting off its shiny blade.

While Karver appreciated the knife with a grin, gazing at it for a whole ten seconds, Frank stared up at his face and the knife. "You sure that's the right tool for the job, doc? That's a big knife for a doctor."

Keeping the knife at eye level, Karver tilted his grinning face down at his patient to comfort him. "Big is good. The bigger the knife, the faster the operation will be. Trust me, I'm a doctor."

"Whatever you say, doc. You're the doctor."

"That's right, I'm the doctor," Karver said, his grin widening, pleased at how easy it all was. "Now, I'm going to start with the pain in your abdominal area and work my way up to your chest pain. Use a finger to show me the area where it's hurting in your belly."

Frank lifted a meaty arm from his side and indicated a spot a little above and to the left of his bellybutton. "Right here, doc."

"Okay. Now, this is going to hurt a little."

"No pain, no gain, doc. I have a high threshold for pain, so don't worry about me."

Ignoring precision, Karver thrust the knife down to its handle into the chubby man's belly while staring into Frank's eyes the whole time instead of looking at where he was making the incision.

Frank dealt with the pain. "Shouldn't you be looking at where your cutting, doc?"

"Don't worry, I'm a doctor. I've done this thousands of times. I could do it with my eyes closed. Besides, whatever I do to you is okay because I'm a doctor. Trust me. Now, on a scale of one to ten, how painful would you say this is?"

Frank tongued a piece of veal stuck between his teeth before replying, "I'd say it's about a four, doc. Don't worry about me, just keep working your magic."

Displeased with Frank's answer, a frown crept onto Karver's face, replacing his usual smile. Then, keeping the knife up to its handle in flesh, Karver started working the knife toward the chest, slicing who knows what organs along the way, ample amounts of blood spilling down on either side of Frank's torso. "Now, a pain scale of one to ten again, Mr. Panicucci."

Frank, still tonguing meat caught in his teeth, replied, "I'd say about a five, doc. I told you I have a high pain tolerance. One time I was being tortured by a rival family, which can happen in my line of work sometimes, ya know. After taking countless punches and showing no response, the thug doing the job on me got mad and started using all kinds of various household items to bash my face and body with. The thug's grandma even started whacking me with her tea set." Frank chuckled a bit. "I must have been born with a condition or something. I got out of that jam alive because Big Tony barged into the thug's house and sat on him till he died. They didn't call him Big Tony for nothin', ya know. While the thug was dying under Big Tony, the grandma was swatting Big Tony in the head with a spatula and the whole bit. After the thug was dead, Big Tony sat on the grandma till she croaked as well. They didn't call—"

Karver interrupted him to finish the sentence, "Yeah, yeah. They didn't call him Big Tony for nothing, I know."

Karver had never experienced this absence of pain from his victims. If this dumb brute did have a unique condition in regards to pain, why had he been feeling pain in his stomach and chest lately? The brainless brute was a mystery to him. Maybe he was an incubated clone from one of the DUMBs. He looked at Frank's ears. Nope, the earlobes weren't attached to his face. He wasn't a clone.

In order to produce better results, he brought the knife up the torso even farther, making a zigzag path instead of a straight one, slicing through the liver and eventually hitting the bottom of the rib cage. He sawed at the bottom of the sternum for a bit, lifting the knife up and down.

At this point there was enough blood on the table—and dripping onto the floor—that Frank might die from loss of blood, which wasn't the terrifying death Karver was cutting for. No terror equaled no collected loosh.

Frank began to feel woozy. "I'm not feeling so hot, doc. You almost done with the operation?"

"A doctor's saying comes to mind," Karver said, not happy about how things were going but glad he'd been given the opportunity to vocalize some doctors proverbs he knew. " 'They may forget your name, but they will never forget how you made them feel.' "

"Well, let me tell ya. I'm not feelin' so great, doc."

"That may be the case now, but after I'm done, you won't feel any pain. You won't feel anything at all. That I can promise you."

"You sure ya know what you're doin', doc?"

"Shut up! Don't worry, I'm a goddamn doctor for fuck's sake."

"Okay. Sorry for questioning your authority, doc. Just wrap things up, will ya?"

Karver was pretty sure the loosh-collecting vial in his physician's bag was empty, which agitated him. It would be the first time he'd come up empty-handed after a sacrifice. "Sure, I'll wrap things up." Karver pulled the knife out of the lower chest, causing bits of blood to speckle Frank's dazed face. "I'm just going to make one more small incision to finalize the operation." Using both hands, he rammed the knife down into Frank's heart, creating a few rib-cracking noises on its swift trajectory downward. "And there we go. You should be fixed now."

Frank's empty eyes stared at the ceiling.

Karver playfully slapped Frank's pale cheek a couple times, leaving bloody handprints behind from the blood-drenched latex gloves. "See, I know what I'm doing. Now you're as good as new and feeling no pain."

Karver released his grip on the knife that was still lodged in Frank's chest and gave himself a golf clap, blood splattering off his medical gloves. "Another remarkably successful operation, doctor. How ever do you do it?" he said to himself, trying to have a little fun despite the loosh-collecting failure. He figured he'd make another sacrifice right after this one to make up for the empty vial, so there was nothing to be vexed about. Regardless of the results, it was always fun playing doctor.

Might as well get in a few more doctor's sayings while he had the chance, he thought. He cleared his throat in preparation to speak to the imaginary audience of esteemed colleagues that had gathered to witness his pioneering surgical procedure. "Gottfried Wilhelm von Leibniz said, 'A great doctor kills more people than a great general.' Or my personal favorite by Francis Bacon, the real Shakespeare, 'Cure the disease and kill the patient.' "

Chapter 14

After about three years of being a VP, Dale figured he had enough traction between his investment algorithm that he'd been continuingly augmenting as the years went by, which had been persistently profit-making, and the close friendships he'd developed with the Big Boys. This traction would hopefully allow him to slide into a newly opened senior VP position after his next scheme expelled a current senior VP.

Over a cup of Dark Java, months ago, he had thought up a diabolical scheme that he had kept under his sleeve until the timing was right to play it. Using the dark web, he'd procured a tincture of LSD that he'd use to lace a cup of Dark Java. The thought had originated when he was contemplating the legality of caffeine, which was a drug in its own right. While swimming in the caffeine's energetic effects, his mind expanded on the thought of drugs. That's when the idea popped into his head.

He'd treat the Big Boys with unlaced cups of Dark Java and lace Preston Ambrose's drink. Preston Ambrose's office was next to Andy Singer's—Andy Singer was a senior VP himself currently—and Ambrose occasionally joined some of their group office discussions, but wasn't one of the Big Boys, so he could be sacrificed, so to speak. Dale would have to buy them all Dark Javas several times before lacing Preston Ambrose's drink so that Ambrose would assume the gifted drink wasn't responsible for his altered state of mind. And since acid took a while to kick in, it would be further disassociated as the source of Ambrose's tripping. Being that the cheapest drink at Dark Java would set one back ten bucks, this scheme was going to be costly, but Dale knew it would be an advantageous investment, worth every penny in the end. Anyway, it would be a drop in the bucket with his lucrative salary.

Preston Ambrose would accept the treat. No one could turn down a free cup of Dark Java. They were being touted as the most premium coffee producer in America, and for good reason, not simply riding success by means of a branding gimmick. Dark Java owned an organic fair-trade coffee-bean farm in Kenya that produced beans for their dark roast espresso that they combined with a customers' choice of organic almond or cashew milk. Premium, delicious almond and cashew milk, not the garbage being sold at supermarkets and grocery stores across the country; no wonder many people still labeled alternative-milk options as horrible substitutes.

They roasted their beans on-sight, kept them in sealed glass containers to retain freshness, and never used beans that were more than a week past their roasting date. This, along with their slow-roasting method, assured the strongest and richest espresso possible. Premium honey could be added to any of their drinks for sweetness at the customers' request. They didn't use any type of sugar or syrup; only healthy, top-shelf ingredients were used in all their drinks.

Their signature drink was the Dark Java Premium, which possessed premium honey and organic cacao powder, making it the healthiest, most exquisite mocha in existence. But their most popular drink was their caffé latte. Its two shots of dark roast espresso were fresh enough that it tasted and felt like the equivalent of four espresso shots at a typical crappy American coffee shop, but without the edgy drawbacks. Crappy shops made up about ninety-five percent of all coffee shops in America, so it was only natural that Americans had fallen head over heels for *real* coffee when Dark Java opened their doors.

The owner of the shop was from Melbourne, Australia, where many coffee aficionados believed the best espresso-based coffee drinks were being produced in the world. Italy may still be making the best caffé (espresso shot) in the world, but Australia, where many Italians immigrated to after World War II, had been making the best caffé latte—and other coffee drinks with milk added—for years.

Dale parked his Mercedes and walked toward Dark Java in preparation to offer up the first installment of free coffee to his colleagues. He noticed an old man, who was approaching the entrance door, about to be struck by the glass door as two patrons were exiting. The leading patron was opening the door while looking back at his friend, immersed in conversation.

Dale opened his mouth to issue a verbal warning to the old man, but then closed his mouth without uttering a word when he realized that the door would take out the old-timer and lessen Dale's waiting time in the queue. There was always a queue at Dark Java due to their popularity and the fact that they hadn't gotten around to opening a second location in Seattle yet.

As anticipated, the glass door opened swiftly and collided with the geezer's head, causing him to drop to the ground like an automaton in need of repair. The two patrons apologized and kneeled down to help him. A caring lady from the end of the line came outside to assist, which lessened Dale's wait time even more. He strode past the incident like the Grim Reaper's invisible hand of death and slipped through the door while whistling in celebration.

After purchasing the coffee and returning to the office, he received thank yous from his surprised colleagues as he handed them Dark Java drinks. Then he returned to his office, ready to work and enjoy his own caffé latte. His new scheme was underway. He lifted his Dark Java to his grinning mouth.

Meanwhile, Babcock restlessly sat behind his desk. It was late September and he was flying back to New York today, not to return to Seattle till next July. He always worked himself into a horrible mood before flying. Today, he was the most ruffled and edgy he'd ever been. He decided to lighten his mood with a random firing. A good firing always buoyed his spirits. Right after that he'd depart early and spend more time at the VIP lounge at the airport instead of behind his desk. He already had his schedule moved forward and just got the notification that his chauffeur was waiting outside the building.

"Your limo has just arrived, sir," Susan's emotionless voice emitted from his speaker phone.

"Thanks, Sundae." Babcock straightened his tie, wrapped his fingers around the handle to his briefcase, and made his way to the random broker that would be leaving today with their belongings in a box. Random firings were always the best, as the poor bastards were always taken off guard, completely bewildered and deflated in one awesome moment. An awesome moment that Babcock bathed in, soaking up every drop of the dejected broker's demoralization.

He randomly chose a broker's office to barge into. After making sure the name on the door, DALE DICKERSON, didn't contain the word "senior" in the title, he shoved the ajar door open with his meaty palm. The broker about to be fired was busy at work on his computer while taking a gulp of coffee. Babcock's mouth opened to utter the words that would start his rejuvenating bath. "You're fire—"

Babcock silenced himself when he caught a gratifying sight on the broker's shelf: his finance book, *Moving Ones and Zeros Around like a Goddamn God!*

Dale swiveled his chair around and addressed Babcock, "What's that, sir?"

Babcock briskly patted Dale on the shoulder a couple times. "I just wanted to say that you're firing on all cylinders, Dickerton. Keep up the excellent work." Babcock turned around and exited the office while adding, "Marvelous work, just goddamn marvelous."

Dale shrugged his shoulders in confusion but also with much satisfaction. It appeared his hard work was finally shining through to the top of the food chain. He glowed in the wake of Babcock's praising words as he greedily downed another gulp from his Dark Java.

Babcock marched down the hall while muttering to himself like Tricky Dick, "Who's the cocksucker who's gonna get it." He passed a few senior VPs' offices and spotted one

VP's office. "Ah, here we go," he muttered. "Gonna sink this random cocksucker."

After turning the doorknob Babcock propelled the door open with enough strength to send it crashing into the wall after its full swing around, causing the VP to jump in his chair and turn around, instantly becoming fearful when he laid eyes on Babcock's meaty face.

"You're f—" Babcock stopped himself and aggressively turned his head this way and that way around the VP's office, searching. His head swiveled around like a vulture's would if it had just snorted several lines of cocaine. Nope, he didn't see his goddamn book anywhere.

As the VP silently cowered and looked up at the CEO, awaiting the meaning for the visit, Babcock finished his utterance, "You're fired!" Babcock stood there for a bit and took in a few deep breaths of delight from the dejected emotions emanating from the terminated VP. Then he exited the VP's office with newfound glee in his step.

The VP had stared up at a deep-breathing Babcock while producing equal amounts of perplexity and terror. Then the VP broke out of his trance and followed Babcock out into the hall to question him. "Why am I being fired? What did I do wrong?"

Babcock stopped in the hall and turned around. "Even if I explained the reason why, you'd still be fired. And if I had to explain the reason to you, it shows you're too incompetent to already know the reason for yourself, which is why I fired you."

The VP whined, "Okay, then tell me the reason why."

"Weren't you listening to a goddamn word I just said? See, you *are* incompetent."

"Yes, sir, I was listening. No matter what, I'm fired, so I want to know why in order to avoid doing it in the future."

"I said you're fired. You have no future here. It's like I'm talking to a goddamn eraserhead."

"Sir, I mean my future at a different firm."

"We're the only goddamn firm that matters, so it doesn't matter what you know or don't know at your next job."

"But sir, I—"

Babcock aggressively raised a firm meaty palm in front of the VP's face. "Aaah!" he interjected forcefully to silence the man. Then he turned to a different employee, who was standing in the hall after being drawn out of his office by the clamor, and pointed a stern finger at him. "You. Who are you?"

"I'm Oliver Finn. I'm his assistant VP," the broker said while pointing at the fired VP.

"Good. You tell him why he's fired or I'll fire you too. I'm off to New York now and can't be bothered with this minute detail." Babcock quickly turned and walked toward the elevator lobby, leaving the ugly scene behind him.

In Babcock's wake, the assistant VP started laying into the VP in order to retain his own job, digging deep for reasons but only coming up with nonsensical explanations. "Your ... Your bathroom breaks are too long. Your breath always smells bad. You're ... You're a communist!"

Everyone in the hallway gasped in shock.

Oliver Finn had remembered advice from an old 1930s business book he had read. If you call someone a communist, they're instantly labeled a communist in everyone's mind that heard the accusation, even if there was no evidence to support it. So when engaged in an important argument, you'd better shout out that the other person is a communist before they call you a communist. It was the modern-day equivalent of calling something a conspiracy or someone a conspiracy theorist. It didn't matter how much proof of something was put forward, after the label was applied, all proof, no matter how comprehensive or compelling, was instantly negated once the label had been applied.

Gerald van Buren exited his office to accompany Babcock for the thirty-two-floor elevator ride. Van Buren entered the elevator and pressed the first-floor button. As the elevator doors closed, van Buren said, "Thanks for clearing up some deadweight before taking off today. But you know you could've called me from New York tomorrow and had me do it."

"Not a problem at all, van Buren. I enjoy the process. But I know you would've done it with equal gusto. I know I can trust you to hold down the fort and command the helm while I'm in New York. I've grown tired of Seattle and its sprawled-out Eastside cities. The bullshit is too spread out. In New York City the bullshit is closely stacked together. I like having all the bullshit right at my fingertips. It's soothing."

"Well, at least you're not in Los Angeles, Babby."

"Damn right. Everything is so spread out in L.A. that its residents have lost their damn minds. Fuckin' La La Land out there. That's why so many of them are jumping ship. They're spreading their insanity everywhere, especially toward Seattle, like a directed-energy weapon from space. Their trees and foliage light themselves on fire every year, choosing self-immolation in protest over the city's insanity. They'd rather burn up than stay neighbors with those La La lunatics."

Gerald van Buren casually nodded his head a few times. "Yeah, they're spreading themselves around like low-quality margarine, slathering the surrounding cities under a suffocating layer of trans fat. However, pertaining to the ones that moved to Seattle, you can't blame their increased irritability for having moved away from sunny skies to dwell under a perpetual overcast dome, a geographical area where only vampires can flourish and frolic about."

The elevator doors opened on the ground floor. Van Buren stayed in the elevator, keeping his finger on the open-door button as Babcock continued the conversation with his back to van Buren, making his way through the lobby. "We got to keep them behind the lines! Where's General Patton when we need him?!"

Out the door he went, stepping into his awaiting transportation.

After Babcock touched down in New York, he had his two chauffeurs take him straight to his favorite delicatessen, Katz's Delicatessen, for takeaway.

Babcock stepped out onto the sidewalk. He took a big satisfying breath and inhaled the New York City atmosphere.

Down the street, to the left of Babcock, a waiter from an Italian restaurant exited the establishment and shouted with his Bronx accent at a running-away customer who had stiffed the bill. "Hey you! … Yeah, you! Fuck you!"

A hot dog/sausage vendor was situated on the corner to the right of Babcock, yelling out phrases with his thick Brooklyn accent, enticing passersby to purchase his meats. "Nobody beats my meat except me! Come right up, one and all, and stick my meat in your mouth! Swallow its delectable juices! Placed between two magic buns—get outta here—it's the best!"

Babcock completely soaked up the ambience of his native city. "Goddamn I love New York. All five fuckin' boroughs."

One of his assistants exited the vehicle with a notepad and pen. "What do you want today, Mr. Babcock?"

"Get me one pastrami, one Reuben, one corned beef, and one brisket."

"You got it, boss." The assistant started waiting in line while the other assistant rolled down the window and spoke to Babcock.

"There's no parking available here so I'm going to drive around a bit and have Jacob call me when it's time to return."

"Good. You do that. I'll be relaxing with a coffee in Ludlow across the street, so come get me there when it's done."

"I could just drive you home and we can send another car to get the food if you want, sir."

"No, that's all right. I want to simmer in the streets a bit, marinate in its character and undercurrent before returning to my castle. … But I'll call you if I need any hipsters in Ludlow to mysteriously disappear."

Over a period of three weeks, Dale had treated the same people every now and then to a Dark Java. Now that his gifted coffee could be ruled out as a possible variable in Preston Ambrose's mind, he moved forward with phase two of the scheme: the acid lacing. Having never done acid himself, he conducted research online to learn the correct dosage. Then he upped the dosage, going past the recreational user's dosage and moving into the area that would produce a temporary psychological breakdown, but not enough to induce a catatonic state, because keeping Ambrose mobile to interact with colleagues was necessary for the plan to work.

Preston Ambrose was reading an article about the coming economic meltdown in China when Dale handed him a Dark Java caffé latte. Ambrose thanked Dale for the Dark Java and how he'd been so generous lately. "It's more about the time spent in the queue than the coffee's price," Ambrose said. "That's why I'm so appreciative of the gesture."

"When time is money, the waiting is definitely more costly than the purchase price, for sure," Dale agreed. "But if I'm going to be waiting in line for my drink anyway, it's not a problem ordering other people some drinks as well."

Dale walked back to his office with exhilaration like a crack addict preparing his pipe. He couldn't wait to see the outcome of the acid lacing, but according to his research, he knew he'd have to wait anywhere from an hour to two hours before the acid's effects peaked. It would start affecting Ambrose in about thirty to forty minutes, but it was the peak effects that would cause him to go mental.

Preston Ambrose returned to the meltdown article after Dale left his office, partaking of his latte sporadically as he read. The writer of the article focused on the idea that China's booming growth had been made possible from its slave labor. Chinese companies made a mint by paying workers low wages to manufacture cheap products they'd sell at high gains overseas. The difference between America's boom and China's was that America had grown financially powerful through innovation. If America continued to be innovative and progressive, it could continue to stay the top-ranking superpower in the world. For a lengthier period of time, of course, as no empire lasted forever. China never slowed down after the Great Recession and continued to build ghost cities and construction projects overseas despite their falling profits. Many slave-labor factories were being set up in poor countries outside of China, taking a chunk of China's gains. China was also losing many of its wealthy individuals, which removed their wealth from being trickled back into the Chinese economy. They were desperately trying to stop their collected wealth from leaving the country, but China was failing. Wealthy individuals ran to countries that they and their accumulated wealth felt safer in. They had fled to countries that demonstrated democracy and freedom, countries like Taiwan and Hong Kong. Now that China was slowly trying to bring Hong Kong under its rule, Hongkongers were making it abundantly clear through mass demonstrations that they wanted no part of it. Embargoes and trade wars were also hurting China, halting the hawking of their cheap products and goods. Because China wasn't producing any innovative products, it was only a matter of time before their economy tanked, postulated the article's author. And he argued that it would happen much sooner than any financial forecaster foresaw.

Ambrose found the article intriguing. He finished off the last gulp of his latte and headed toward the restroom. Coffee always acted as a nice laxative, but today he felt an extra urgency. His bowel movement had worked its way through his intestines faster than usual and he found himself racing to the restroom to avoid defecating in his pants. His movement ended up being diarrhea, which had never happened to him from drinking one cup of coffee—maybe two or three, but never one.

For the next forty minutes Ambrose conducted his work in his office as usual, but he began feeling a strange bodily sensation within the last ten minutes, and the feeling was becoming more pronounced as time went by. He brushed off the feeling, thinking he must be having a heightened reaction to caffeine today. Just one of those weird energetic anomalies in the body.

He jumped into some healthcare financial news, focusing on bioengineering and biotechnology. He began reading a long article about a scientific breakthrough in China and its implications for the biotechnology companies the breakthrough research was funded by. These biotechnology companies' stocks had staggeringly risen in today's market after the announcement in China.

The lengthy first part of the article conveyed the breakthrough using ambiguous terminology. Despite its vagueness Ambrose dug into the article and read it slowly, trying to grasp every nuance the discovery would have on American biotech companies because he had invested a large amount of his clients' money in the healthcare sector of the market.

It appeared some Chinese scientists had been able to highly alter their subjects' reality using a biological compound. The article didn't state whether the "subjects" used in the experiment were insects, mice, or people. Ambrose found the nonspecific rhetoric in the article irritating.

He also started to find the body high he was experiencing to be irritating and disturbing. He had never felt this way before and the feeling seemed to be growing instead of waning. It wasn't just his body, his mind was altering from its usual state, and he found his vision getting slightly blurry. He tried to shrug it off as best as he could because his clients were counting on him to stay ahead of the curve on any major market swings and trends in the healthcare sector.

He blinked his eyes a couple times and shook his head to clear the anomalous feeling and got back to the article. The scientists had used DNA from rare worms and heavy metals in the compound mixture that they sprayed into the air for the subjects to breathe in. The subjects started feeling energetic changes to their bodily and mental functions, coupled with a radical shift in their perceptions, highly altering their reality to the scientists' specified degree.

The second part of the article dived into U.S. political matters regarding the Chinese breakthrough. The U.S. Secretary of State issued a statement condemning the development. He said it brought up major concerns not only for the American people, but for all nations, and Chinese citizens themselves. He argued that this breakthrough was associated with engineered biological warfare in the disguise of business ingenuity. It could be dumped over every major U.S. city through various means and highly alter and warp Americans' reality and cause nationwide insanity and catastrophes. The Secretary of State went on to state that they've had a close eye on China's Wuhan National Biosafety Laboratory ever since it opened in 2014, as well as its connected Wuhan Institute of Virology. Then he stated that this lab was about to release an engineered bioweapon virus in their own country to cull their population, and then release it to the rest of the world. One of their methods for distributing the virus would be to spray it from airplanes down on the world's population. It could cause a meltdown of the American mind that would far outweigh the implications of Chernobyl and all other historical disasters combined, argued the U.S. Secretary of State.

Ambrose was shocked at the seriousness the article had shifted to. He switched to the news outside of finance and found the story on the front page of many online papers.

After he unfixed his focus on the computer screen, weird things started happening that he couldn't explain: his keyboard started hovering above his desk with its buttons changing places, his mouse had morphed into a sports car and was attempting to drive off his desk, various items on his desk began swaying or dancing as if they'd come alive, geometric patterns appeared on the walls and in other various places, and the very air felt electrifying. Nothing was static, everything was moving.

His high-strung mind shifted its focus back on the article's topic. Oh my god, he thought, they'd done it. The Chinese had already dumped their mind-altering compound on Seattle and who knows what other U.S. cities. Possibly every major city in the world! He had to warn everyone in the office right now.

Ambrose launched out of his chair and zigzagged his way through his office, avoiding all the dementedly dancing items in his office, finally making it through his door and out into the hallway. He ran through the halls, swaying left and right in his motion, feeling the walls collapsing and expanding as if they were breathing. While running, he shouted, "The Chinese are coming! The Chinese are coming! Their economy is about to go belly up so they're drugging us with reality-altering spray technologies! Oh my god, my brain is melting!"

Many brokers opened their office doors and poked their heads out to see what the commotion was all about, including a delighted Dale. Dale's countenance differed from the confused and annoyed faces of his colleagues. Instead, he wore a smirk while his eyes danced in relish, taking in the spectacle as if he was rewatching the climax of his favorite action movie on the big screen.

While Ambrose was stumbling down the hallway shouting nonsense, he passed an open office door and spotted a Chinese broker he didn't recognize. The Chinese broker had earphones shoved into his ear canals, probably listening to instructions from Beijing, thought Ambrose. The Chinese mole had his back to Ambrose as he typed on his keyboard, not aware of the ruckus Ambrose had been making due to his ears being plugged up.

Ambrose swayed into the Chinese mole's office, slapped his earphones off, and began barking at the mole. "You Chinese will never get away with this! America will bomb the hell out of China!"

The broker lurched back in his chair, utterly shocked. "What are you talking about, man? I'm Chinese American.

I moved to America when I was like ... two years old. I'm just as American as you are, man."

"Yeah right, nice try. I've never seen you before. You're a Chinese mole that's clearly taken an immunity shot to the mind-altering technologies dumped on Seattle."

"I just started here last week. My name's Mark Chang. Is this some kind of initiation joke, man? It better be, otherwise you're really messed up in the head." Chang picked up chopsticks and a plate of noodles he'd been picking at for his lunch.

Ambrose immediately transfixed on the plate of noodles and became speechless. To him they were worms constantly squirming and slithering around. A piece of the article he'd read popped up in his head and was angrily narrated by the floating head of the U.S. Secretary of State: *The scientists used DNA from rare worms in the compound mixture that they sprayed into the air for the subjects to breathe in.* Then the floating head turned toward Ambrose and issued a warning: *Don't be a willing subject, Preston Ambrose. Get out of his office before he inserts a parasitic worm into your eye with the device he's holding that looks deceptively like regular chopsticks.* The floating head imploded out of existence, popping like a bubblegum bubble.

Ambrose cautiously backed out of the mole's office, keeping his eyes locked on the plate of bioengineered super-worms that were designed to devour the very fabric of the American way of life. As long as he kept them in his sights he'd be able to karate chop them away if they attempted to fly in the air and slither through his eye to get to his brain and munch on it.

Mark Chang raised his eyebrows and stared at the highly bizarre expression on Ambrose's face. "You got issues, man. You should see a shrink." Then he lost interest and swiveled his chair back toward his computer screen.

Ambrose continued to slowly back up with his eyes fixed on the Chinese mole, unintentionally moving straight through the hallway and into a different office across the way that had its door open.

Diego Martinez, a VP, didn't notice Ambrose enter his office because he was focused on work and his back was positioned toward his office door.

Brilliant blue scenery caught the corner of Ambrose's eye. He turned to his right and took in a huge poster of the Florida Keys on Martinez's wall. Palm trees swayed back and forth, a gorgeous multicolored sea of light blues and greens lapped up on bleached sand that shone brightly into Ambrose's irises. It ensnared his total attention and spellbound him for a good twenty seconds. At the very top of the poster, floating in the blue sky, displayed the text ESCAPE TO THE FLORIDA KEYS.

Ambrose realized he was in someone's office. He turned around and saw Diego Martinez typing away on his computer, still unaware of his presence. "Now I understand how you keep that nice golden-brown tan, Martinez. You're always escaping to the Florida Keys through this teleportation device. Did the Chinese develop this too?"

Martinez turned around in his chair and saw that it was Ambrose that had spoken to him. "I'm Latino. This is my natural skin color. I've never been to the Florida Keys. That poster is there to relax me." He didn't understand the Chinese comment, so he ignored it.

Ambrose winked at Martinez and said, "Right, right. Don't worry, Martinez, I can keep a secret. Just let me in on the action, will ya? We better escape to the Florida Keys right now. Every brain in Seattle is going to melt in less than a day."

Martinez tilted his head and furrowed his eyebrows in confusion and concern. "What's gotten into you, Ambrose? I'm not going anywhere, and neither are you. This part of the day is crunch time. You know that."

In his acid-induced state, Ambrose's highly charged emotions flared up at being denied an escape from melted brains. "You sonuvabitch, Martinez. You can't shut me out of your Florida Keys Chinese teleportation technologies! See you later, *sucker*." Ambrose darted toward the poster in an attempt to be whisked away to the Keys, but ended up smacking into the wall instead. After he recovered from the impact, he berated Martinez, "You turned off the device, you bastard. Let me use this technologies. I need to get outta here before my brain melts."

"No! What the hell's wrong with you today? Quit fooling around and get out of my office, Ambrose. I got research to do."

"You've sided with that wormy bastard across the hall. You're working for the Chinese too." Ambrose stumbled out of Martinez's office and started yelling down the hallway, "Hey everyone, Diego Martinez is a Chinese mole! He's got Chinese technologies! The bastard's a goddamn mole."

From the continued disturbance, brokers started walking out into the hallway to stare at Ambrose instead of merely poking their heads out of their offices.

Gerald van Buren approached Ambrose, fulfilling his duties as head of the office while Babcock was away. He tried to diffuse the situation by calmly talking to Ambrose. "You don't seem like yourself today, Ambrose. Your conduct is disconcerting."

"Of course it's disconcerting! My goddamn brain is melting! And as we speak, your brain, as well as all the goddamn brains in Seattle, are melting!"

"Are you sure about that?" Van Buren didn't know what to say, so he continued to speak calmly in an attempt to pacify Ambrose. "That's a lot of brains, Ambrose."

"You're goddamn right it is! And the Chinese super-worms are looking to impregnate them."

Mark Chang strolled out of his office with his plate of noodles and chopsticks to join the increasing number of onlookers, which included Dale.

A wave of anxiety shot through Ambrose as he noticed the Chinese mole enter the hallway only fifteen feet away from him. He pointed at the mole while shouting, "Watch out! The Chinese mole will attempt insertion of his wriggling Chinese worm technologies into your eyes."

Someone down the hall said, "It's just 'technology,' idiot, not 'technologies.' "

"They're just noodles," Chang said while walking toward Ambrose to show him.

Ambrose clamped his hands over his ears and looked at van Buren, using his terrified eyes to plead for help.

On his way to Ambrose, Chang tripped on something Ambrose had knocked over in the hall, causing the noodles to slide off the plate and fall onto Ambrose's pants. "Oh, sorry, man."

Ambrose watched them wriggling around as they tried to insert themselves into his legs. While screaming, he swatted at them and brushed them off. Once they were all knocked off, Ambrose started crying.

Gerald van Buren told everyone gathered in the hallway to go back to work so he could handle the matter alone.

After Gerald van Buren managed to calm Ambrose down, he called him a taxi and told him to go home early and sleep it off. Whatever *it* was.

Ambrose abided and holed himself up in his house till he slowly started to regain his sanity and crashed on his sofa.

The next day he woke up with an awful headache. He immediately called van Buren and expressed his apologies about yesterday. He said he didn't know what came over him and couldn't clearly remember all the events that had taken place yesterday, but felt very embarrassed about the things he did remember. Due to a splitting headache and the shame he felt, he requested the day off. Gerald van Buren readily obliged and told the senior VP that he should take two days off if necessary.

Dale wasn't too surprised when Preston Ambrose returned to work, not having been fired, because he was a senior VP. It was going to take more effort to get a senior VP fired. So he went back to treating Ambrose and the others with Dark Javas about twice a week until two weeks had passed. Then he laced Ambrose's drink again, upping the dosage from the last application.

This time, when Ambrose started tripping he locked himself in a bathroom stall, highly confused but determined not to make a fool of himself again.

After it became apparent that Ambrose wasn't leaving the restroom, Dale took a more direct approach to make sure the administered acid wouldn't go to waste. He'd call Ambrose's cellphone and coax him out of the bathroom.

After the phone was answered, he used a regal voice to announce himself as Archangel Michael and informed Ambrose that he hadn't lost his mind two weeks prior and that he was correct: the Chinese did disperse biological warfare in every major U.S. city.

Ambrose believed Dale's lie because he was tripping his ass off for only the second time in his life, didn't even know he was on drugs in the first place, and had completely lost all sense of reality after being caged in a bathroom stall for an hour. "You mean the mind-altering spray technologies?"

Dale rolled his eyes and shook his head on the other side of the phone. "Yes … those technologies. But you're special, Preston. You're immune. That's why you were able to fight off the technology at home while everyone else in the office eventually fell on the floor dead with melted brains."

"If they're dead, why are they still out there working?"

"They are not your colleagues. They're highly advanced replica clones that have been pretending to be brokers for the last two weeks. All your colleagues are dead. The Chinese were muddled when they found out about your special immunity and sent the clones to observe you, to collect data and ascertain the reason for your immunity. They couldn't come up with the reason, so they changed gears while you were in the bathroom. Right now, all your clone-replicated colleagues, as well as all the other clones in the entire building, are scouring every inch of the building to terminate you on sight. And as you probably already noticed from your symptoms, they dumped the mind-altering spray over your building again. But don't worry, you're immune and it will be easier for your system to fight it off this time."

"Oh, shit. … Okay. What do I do?"

"Follow my guidance exactly and you'll make it out alive. Along with God's help, I'll safely lead you through this. Trust me. You are far more important than you realize, Preston. You are the One."

Ambrose was breathing heavily in panic, but he was confident that he'd escape alive with Archangel Michael and the Supreme Being's help. "Okay, I'm waiting for your commands."

"Good. First, stick your head into toilet water containing urine. They have placed nanotechnology in your hair. Only urine can disable this specific type of nanotechnology."

Ambrose desperately scratched at his head as he got off the toilet and lifted the seat. Luckily he had already done his business several times while waiting it out on the toilet. Unfortunately his toilet-conducted business had gone beyond urinating, but it was no time to be squeamish, upper-echelon beings were counting on him, and he was the Chosen One.

He held his breath and dunked his head into the toilet water filled with ample amounts of his urine and diarrhea. He kept his head submerged while also dunking his hands in and scratching his head vigorously, making absolutely sure all the nanobots had been disabled. After fifteen seconds, he pulled his head out. Diarrhea and urine poured over and under his suit and made its way down to his suit pants. He had to pinch his nose to stop himself from puking. Then he collected his phone off the floor. "It's done. Now what?"

"Well done. I'll safely guide you to your office where we have remotely installed a teleportation portal for your escape. Be sure to follow my every command without question."

"Okay."

"The hall is clear. Exit the men's restroom now and go into the ladies' restroom."

"Why should I—"

"Remember! No questions. Follow my commands. There are reasons that will escape your human mind's capacity. Just have faith. Don't ask questions, don't think for yourself, just have faith and do everything we tell you to do."

"Okay. Sorry."

Ambrose exited the restroom and went into the ladies' restroom. A woman was washing her hands in the sink and turned to him with a scowl. "Hey, you can't be in here."

Dale heard the lady over the phone and gave Ambrose his next instruction. "Oh, no. She—or rather it—is one of their most deadly clones. You need to disable it before it shoots laser beams out of its eyes. Its only vulnerability is its nose. Punch it in the nose with much force."

Ambrose dashed forward toward the lady.

She started backing up. "Oh, no. Don't rape me, please."

He smashed his fist into the woman's nose. Her head whipped backward and blood started profusely streaming from her broken nose. She wiped under her nose and looked at her blood-covered hand. Then she lost function of her eyeballs as they rolled up into her head while she collapsed to the floor and passed out.

"It's done. It has been disabled."

"Excellent. Now exit the bathroom and make your way down the hallway toward your office."

Ambrose obeyed and exited the bathroom and cautiously made his way down the hall.

Dale cracked his office door an inch and peeked out at the hallway where a tall plant resided. He soon saw Ambrose appear in the hall and was surprised by the amount of diarrhea that covered his head and suit. Dale rattled off with urgency, "A clone is coming. Hide behind that plant." He watched Ambrose fight with the plant's limbs and leaves, excrement flinging from his head and clothes. He finally got behind the plant and stood still. Dale covered his mouth with his free hand to subdue laughter.

Ambrose whispered into his phone, "I'm hidden now."

After a few seconds Dale said, "Okay, it passed. The coast is clear. You can come out now."

"I didn't see anything go by."

"Of course you didn't, Preston. The clone was using invisibility technology."

Ambrose whispered with dread, "Oh my God, they have much technologies."

"Yes. Now, you have a window of opportunity to slip into your office without any clones noticing if you go now."

"Okay." Ambrose fought with the plant again as he withdrew from his hiding spot, and then he slinked to his office without being seen, dripping a trail of excrement on the floor the whole way.

"Okay. I'm in my office now. Where's the portal?"

"Oh no. The Chinese put a technology barrier around the building, blocking all outgoing and incoming teleportation portals. This has become a very serious situation. This is above my powers," Dale said in a disturbed, regal manner from the Archangel Michael character he was acting out. "I'm handing you off to God now."

Dale changed his voice to represent God. He kept a regal tone but enhanced it with a booming voice. "Preston, this is God. I have used my omnipotent abilities to temporarily hide your office with hologram technology so that I can fully explain the entire situation to you without the threat of a clone barging into your office to end your physical existence. Stay inside your office and keep the door closed until I say otherwise. And don't worry, we cern"—Dale cleared his throat—"we certainly won't allow them to portal any demons into your office."

"Yes sir, God. Thank you, God. You are a most gracious creator."

"Yes, yes, I'm the gracious One. There's no easy way to say this, so I'll just come out with it and hope your little human brain can comprehend it."

"I'll do my best, God."

"Most of your politicians and corporate leaders have been compromised. Tiny Chinese Vril drones have inserted wormlike parasites into their eyes while they slept. Now they're being controlled remotely via nanotechnology."

"What about the President, God?"

"He hasn't been compromised. He's currently working with a group to tackle the problem, but he needs your help. In fact, your very race may be eradicated without your help. So no, the President hasn't been compromised, but many politicians have been, and they're currently out to get him ... bigly. Are you prepared to fall further down the rabbit hole, Preston?"

"Yes, God, don't hesitate to dump it all on me."

"That's what I like to hear, my child. These technologies and this worldly takeover plan wasn't invented and orchestrated solely by the Chinese. The evildoers behind this plot are a parasitic race that's using China as one of their main bases. This parasitic group has systematically taken over the world without the public being the wiser. Now, as of two weeks ago, they have used China to take over the world publicly."

"The whole world?"

"Yes, it wasn't just American cities that they dropped their mind-altering, brain-melting technology on. And it wasn't Chinese scientists that developed this technology. It was given to China by the parasitic group. The parasitic group called it China Lake Spray. Besides the spray technology the parasitic group gave them, the Chinese developed, over decades, their own powerful nanotechnology that could control people. Not by force, but by the rewiring of the brain. They perfected this controlling technology only months ago, and it was dispersed into the air along with the parasite's spray technology.

"In order to further test the capabilities of their technology, and just for fun, the Chinese decided to keep millions of females around the world alive, rewiring their brains and turning them into compliant slaves for Chinese women. The programmed nanobots permanently lodged themselves in females' brains, causing them to euphorically desire a life of servitude: the uncontrollable yearning to cook meals, clean the house, and clean their Chinese females' vaginas and feet with their lips and tongue. Now that the nanobots have been implanted, there's nothing else females around the world think of other than this programming. The Chinese spared and allowed the most beautiful and famous females of the world to have the honor of serving as their slaves for the rest of their lives instead of having their brains melted like the rest of the world's population. They have taken sex trafficking and slaves to a whole new level. Now that the nanobots are embedded in their brains, sex slaves are willingly performing their roles.

"Let me tell you what's going on in ordinary life in China. Imagine Chinese females of all ages having their sweaty feet cleaned and massaged by their slave's tongue while the Chinese female is nonchalantly making out in public with her lover. Every once in a while patting her model, actress, or singer female slave on the head, saying, 'Good girl,' like they had acquired a new pet. Then, nightly, while the Chinese female is cuddling and falling asleep in bed with their lover, their slave is positioned at the end of the bed with their head lodged between their master's thighs, sucking and licking her master's vagina as she falls asleep, and continues performing cunnilingus the whole night while her master sleeps.

"In the two weeks that have passed since China took over the world, some Chinese females have even been given reality-TV shows to demonstrate and present to the Chinese population how supermodels, A-list actresses, and singers that had been known the world over for their beauty and talent are now slaves that eagerly worship their Chinese masters' bodies every second of the day when they aren't cooking or cleaning for their families. The female slaves can't fight the programming from the nanobots because their brains have been rewired.

"This is the depravity that has befallen Earth at this time. And because all non-Chinese females want nothing more than to obey their Chinese female masters, they aren't breeding. Therefore, while they're performing cunnilingus, their race is slowly dying out. The female slaves aren't thinking about the extinction of their race due to the nanobots in their brains. Soon there will be no race left on Earth but the Chinese.

"Sex slaves, and slaves in general, have always been a major problem on your planet. What has been exposed in the public's eye so far regarding this issue is only the tip of the iceberg. Now the parasitic group, working through Chinese officials, have made sex slaves legal and accepted in the public's eye as a normal everyday practice."

A wide-eyed Ambrose asked God, "At one point you said the President was still alive, but later on you insinuated that he is dead like the other males on the planet. I'm confused."

"First off, Preston, I never insinuate. God doesn't need to insinuate anything. You're confused because I only gave you a very short summary. The President and the group that is working with him used one of their many secret spacecrafts to leave the planet. They're currently regrouping on the Moon and Mars bases. They've already cleaned up all the scum on the light side of the Moon, which is actually a habitable satellite and not a natural moon. They're basically done cleaning up the dark side of the Moon, which would be seen as a sprawling city to humans if the Moon ever rotated. Now they're working on defeating the individuals from Mars and their underlings."

"We have bases on the Moon and Mars? Unbelievable! Next you'll tell me that JFK Jr. will return from the dead and eventually become the forty-sixth president."

Dale, acting as God, sighed. "Yes, it's true, and that's just the tip of the iceberg. Humans have traveled well beyond your solar system. Don't you know anything? Oh, right, you humans know nothing about what a select few of you are doing. Anyway, Preston, we don't have time for me to explain everything you don't know. If we did that, you'd surely die of thirst and hunger while locked in your office before I could even tell you half of the things you don't know. We need to focus on the task at hand, Preston."

"Okay, God. I understand."

"Getting back to every race going extinct on Earth but the Chinese. I don't want you to worry about that, Preston. I, God, have decided to directly intervene to save each race. That is where you and other Chosen Ones come into the picture. After I assist in your escape, you'll join other Chosen Ones from all different races. We'll use parthenogenesis and special incubation technology to breed each race and keep them from extinction. You're one of the candidates for the Caucasian race. So my dear child, you are important to us. And now you are adequately updated with the current events."

Ambrose had held the phone with mouth ajar and eyes bulging while listening to the whole account. "I had no idea the situation was so dire. I can't believe this is happening."

"Yes, yes, dire indeed. Now, I have a plan to get you out of the building. You'll use the glass wall near the elevator lobby to escape the building."

"How will I use the glass wall?"

"Don't get ahead of yourself. I'll give you specific instruction for every step when the time comes. Have faith. Stop thinking for yourself and listen to my orders."

"Okay, God."

"And …" Dale looked down the hall and saw Gerald van Buren waiting for an elevator to reach their thirty-third floor while he examined the trail of excrement on the floor, "exit your office now and briskly make for the elevator lobby, but don't use the elevators. I have a faster route planned for you."

Ambrose quickly exited his office, ran down the breathing hallway, and approached the elevators.

Gerald van Buren heard the sound of quickly approaching footsteps and turned around to take in Ambrose running full steam in his direction, his hair and face drenched with some type of liquid, and brown splotches were apparent on his face and clothes. When Ambrose got closer, van Buren recognized the funky smell wafting off him because it was the same smell that was coming from the trail on the floor. It smelt like … it smelt like shit.

Dale kept his head poked out of his office, looking down the hall to monitor Ambrose. "Don't worry about that van Buren clone, I have disabled his weapons systems. Now that his offense is subdued, instead of killing you, his programming will revert to playing the part of the Gerald van Buren that used to be alive two weeks ago and attempt to keep you locked in a false reality and a false sense of security. The clone will most likely attack your pride by commenting on the excrement you find yourself covered in.

Van Buren's confusion turned into anger. "Good lord, why are you prancing around covered in shit? Have you gone mental again?"

"Don't listen to him," Dale said through the phone. "It's trying to stall you till its weapons systems are operational again. Give it a powerful karate chop to the left ear. That's the Achilles' heel of that particular clone model."

Instead of answering van Buren, Ambrose followed God's orders and delivered the blow to van Buren with a loud "Hiya."

"Aaah … what the hell, Ambrose?"

"Now sucker punch him in the gut while he's attending to his ear."

Ambrose swiftly sunk his fist into van Buren's caught-off-guard stomach, knocking the wind out of him and causing him to double over and then kneel on the floor in pain.

In a few seconds, van Buren semi-recovered and got his breath back under control. "Once I noticed you'd gone swimming in your own shit, I should've known full well that you'd checked out mentally again. This time I'm not going to deal with your lunacy. I'm calling security."

"Ignore the clone," Dale said. "Now it's time for you to escape. Jump through the glass wall. Once you've broken through, I'll sprout wings on your back like an angel has and direct you where to fly."

"Those are thick double-plated glass walls. I won't be able to break through it, God."

"I have tampered with its structural integrity, allowing you to slip through it like butter. Does the Lord not provide? Have faith, my son."

"Are you sure about the wing-sprouting part? What if I fall to the pavement and get squashed like a bug?"

Dale retracted his head from the hallway and closed his office door for a second so he could yell into the phone. "Of course I'm sure! Jesus Christ, I'm goddamn God for fuck's sake! Now quit sniveling and jump through that goddamn glass wall forthwith or I'll leave you with the killer clones, revoking your Chosen One status and whatnot. Normally for that type of disobedience I'd displace your peoples, but they've already been disposed of by the Chinese."

"Sorry, God. Please accept my apology. Please be merciful to me, oh Lord."

Van Buren was back on his feet. "Who the hell are you talking to? You think you're talking to God?"

"Good," Dale said. "Now jump through the glass."

Ambrose bolted toward the glass wall, sprinting for all he was worth. When he was a few feet from the glass, he jumped into the air and used his forearms to shield the impact. *Thud!* He splatted on the glass for a millisecond and then was thrown onto the floor. He left a huge excremental imprint on the glass. The phone that was in his hand smashed against the glass, cracked, and fell onto the floor in a few pieces beside his aching body.

After hearing the loud thudding sound, Dale looked at his phone to see that the call had been disconnected. Knowing his work was done, it didn't bother him in the slightest. He slipped his phone into his pocket while grinning.

"The glass didn't crack. God … why have you forsaken me?" Ambrose cried out.

Senior VP or not, thought van Buren, this guy has thoroughly lost it for the second time in two weeks and physically assaulted me to boot. His days here are numbered. "The glass didn't crack, but your mind certainly has," he chastised the whimpering figure on the floor that used to be a senior VP he could depend on.

It dawned on Ambrose that he was now helpless in a building full of killer clones, just where God had threatened to leave him when he questioned God's abilities. He should've never questioned the sprouting-wings. Terror ran through his acid-frying brain and he started racing around the building like a chicken with its head chopped off, flinging feces on everything and everyone he came close to.

After an hour of cat and mouse games, security guards ended up cornering and subduing Ambrose on the thirteenth floor of the building, using the element of surprise while Ambrose was talking into his left shoe, desperately attempting to re-establish contact with God.

Through his connections, Dale, as he anticipated, ended up sliding into the newly opened senior VP position. At the age of thirty-two, he was the youngest senior VP in the company.

A week later someone placed a pictured plaque on the wall in the elevator lobby. The picture portrayed Ambrose running down a hall with visible brown stains all over his clothes and face. Someone had captured the memorable shot with their phone. The plaque's inscription read PRESTON AMBROSE, WORLD RECORD HOLDER FOR SPREADING THE MOST FECAL MATTER THROUGHOUT A COMMERCIAL BUILDING.

Chapter 15

Ken Karver's favorite thing to do while he walked among the surface population, besides sacrificing humans, was taking long walks. He'd always plan a long walk on his way to each sacrifice. This time it was an evening walk, the sun having set about an hour ago. During his walks he'd immerse his mind in the Masters' great spider-web design. How perfect it was. Mulling over the details of the great design never failed to titillate.

Humans used to have revolutions once a threshold of a country's population got fed up with harsh treatment and their tyrannical government. This error in the design had been fixed with a security patch. The Masters were tirelessly collecting data in order to fix any holes that appeared in their system and to anticipate growing trends that might disrupt their program.

After they fixed the revolutionary bug, it had been pretty smooth sailing. Nowadays, instead of planning to overthrow suppressive governments, humans flocked to major cities, desperately pleading to become slaves for major corporations, working countless hours of their lives to make those at the top of the pyramid wealthier. Even before humans became slaves for a corporation, they'd spend years in college, furthering their indoctrination and possibly racking up loads of school loan debt. After acquiring and working a corporate-slave job for a period of time, they'd buy an overpriced house and spend the rest of their lives paying that off. They'd drive in traffic like ants to work every day, rarely spending time at their house they were indebted to. Most of the humans' wages they slaved for ended up being taken back by the Masters in the form of countless taxes, insurances, utility bills, et cetera. All of which were unnecessary in one form or another since the Masters' hidden advanced technologies either negated or performed all these functions for free.

Anytime a scientist came up with one of the numerous ways to generate free energy, they'd be paid a visit to ensure their breakthrough was kept out of the public's hands. Either the rights to their inventions were bought, or they were killed. They couldn't have humans getting anything for free. They needed humans to spend all their time slaving away so they wouldn't have the time or energy to ponder their existence and have an epiphany about the system they lived in.

Karver's smile widened. Humans love being in debt and serving as slaves. They eagerly race toward it every day of their lives. If not known consciously, they're subconsciously aware that they're no better than sheep: utilized for their resources and culled—and perhaps eaten—when they no longer are useful to their masters. Humans are too dumb to create and operate a worldly system themselves, so the Masters are really doing them a favor.

Once kids' brains had been rewired and programmed by indoctrination, social conditioning, and brainwashing from the great design, they'd give up their dreams, aspirations, and ideals, and instead focused on acquiring as much money as they could. Another slave willing to do anything for money would roll off the assembly line. Money, an invention in which its creators decide who gets what amount of the finite pie. A person could work miracles for humankind and be given next to none of this manmade item, whereas another person could do next to nothing, or even perform major adverse actions against humankind and the planet, and be given a huge helping of it. This is because the monetary system that was initially used as a way of keeping track of goods and services rendered had been hijacked by the Masters to be used against the population.

The Masters became so confident with the monetary system and its road to servitude that they eventually took it off the gold standard, revealing their printed pieces of paper for what it was: useless paper, only good for starting fires to keep one's indebted house warm. The Masters were curious to see if this action would wake up enough humans to the charade money was, but weren't surprised when it met only minor opposition and steamrolled on without hindrance. At that point humans were so conditioned to be slaves for the Masters that most humans didn't even bat an eye when it was rolled out. It conveyed how perfect their great spider-web design was.

Further on down the road, they introduced an even more useless material to represent money: plastic. One couldn't even use it to warm their house anymore. Then when they were absolutely sure humans were completely indoctrinated into servitude, they finally revealed their monetary system for exactly what it was: nothing, mere ones and zeros on computers, an illusory idea. Humans had been so utterly conditioned to be yes-men for their masters that they actually praised the transition and spouted off the benefits for the transition instead of opposing it, and they continued spending their whole lives slaving away for this illusory item.

The Masters had successfully conditioned humans into thinking they had freedom and possessed rights—and sure, in their fabricated reality they did to an extent, but if a human got in the way of the Masters' plans, they'd find their freedom and rights evaporate in an instant. The Masters fixed the revolutionary bug in their system by making humans believe they were free and not slaves. This way they wouldn't revolt, as they'd never know they were being used as slaves, mere working cattle for the Masters. A person doesn't try to obtain freedom if they think they're already free.

A few humans have slightly broken from their programming to ask the question: "If a monetary system is used to promote slavery and control, what is a better system?" But the fact that they're asking this question instead of already knowing the answer that has been in front of their faces their whole lives, conveys that they have only marginally broken from their programming. In fact, advanced civilizations on other planets were beyond a monetary system because it's archaic and leads to greed and stagnation.

One of the examples of a moneyless system, in front of every human's face, is the family. Did your family members pay each other money to help out around the house and do chores? No, you did the work because it benefitted you and your family, you didn't need any other incentive. A brainless human might interject and say, "Well, I pay my kids a little money for doing their chores, it's called an allowance," thinking their comment was so intelligent that it negated the whole moneyless argument. Karver would tell that hypothetical human, "You pay them because you and your kids are so indoctrinated into the monetary system that your lazy, ungrateful, entitled kids wouldn't lift a finger if you didn't pay them money, which actually proves how destructive the monetary system has become for humans." Of course Karver wouldn't say this to any human because he worked with the Masters at keeping the human population ignorant and easily controlled. Instead, he'd say, "Oh, you're right. You are so smart. Don't listen to me, I'm a fool. Keep doing what you're doing."

The next moneyless system example expands beyond a family and into a scenario with more humans involved, as the world is a big place and not a family. A daughter probably wouldn't be able to fix her dad's car, so they'd have to get someone outside their moneyless family circle to fix it. Not a problem, just think of your community as an extended family. There are countless small communities living throughout the world that have lived independently from the worldly system. Most of them are using monetary systems, but it's used more as a way of keeping credits for the work one has given their community, as was the way of the worldly monetary system before the Masters took it over. These communities could transition effortlessly to a moneyless system overnight if they wanted because it doesn't control them; rather, they control and use it. And then there are all the self-sustaining communities around the world that are the most broken away from their programming and are living without money, making their own products, food, or services to trade with humans outside their communities if they need something that can't be fulfilled by one of their members. These communities share everything, so they don't turn to villainous acts of greed to gain more than others. The most enlightened of these communities don't live with the illusory concept of a finite amount of money or resources, so there is no need to try to gain more than another. They recognize that abundance is available if you tap into the flow of life, and working together makes tapping into the flow even easier.

If money was removed from Earth, humans would naturally gravitate towards occupations that they were passionate about and skilled at instead of choosing a vocation simply because it made a lot of money. This would allow the best person for the job to arise in every job category.

In order to combat this idea from taking root in the consciousness of humans, the Masters added the programmed response that this system wouldn't work because there are several meager tasks to be performed that no one would want to do. This was another reason why they kept their advanced technologies hidden from the surface population; it would make these tasks automated and not need human's toil. Also, with advanced technologies humans would have an abundance of time on their hands for hobbies, having fun, participating in more love exchanges, time to observe and contemplate how to better themselves, dive into deep thought, all of which would lead to happiness, unity, and the acknowledgement of the controlling Masters behind the veiled curtain and easily lead to the Masters being overthrown. That's why the Masters keep their advanced technologies out of human hands and program humans to spend their whole lives slaving away and not having any time to think about ideas that would lead to their freedom. If you don't give them the time to think, they'll never know the answers.

Luckily this moneyless bug in the system isn't corrupting the Masters' operating system. The idea of a finite amount of money and resources is necessary to keep humans fighting each other to possess a piece of the pie. Most humans will spew forth a variety of rebuttals as to why a civilization can't function without money and taxes because they've been conditioned and brainwashed so thoroughly that they're unknowingly offering up lies that they were programmed to speak when a divergent human expressed ideas that differed from the programming. The Masters have programmed humans to verbally, and sometimes even physically, protect all the ideas in the program, including the need for money. If a bug or virus in the system—a human thinking for themselves—expresses an idea that goes against the program, every human that hears it will lay into that person, forcibly telling them why they're wrong. A switch will go off in their brain, commanding them to protect the programming.

Programming and using humans to enforce the program—the great spider-web design—on other humans allows the Masters to sit back and control everything indirectly, never being seen by the masses. Humans have been indoctrinated from day one to believe they need to live in a monetary system and pay taxes, and everything else, because the Masters own the news corporations and the politicians and use them as talking heads to shape beliefs and opinions. However, the Masters have noticed that many humans have started to understand that the news isn't really the real news and politicians aren't what they seem; they're not looking out for the interests of the people they're governing over. The Masters have already thought up a correction to this viral bug in the system and will implement its fix soon.

Flashes of light cut through the night and caught Karver's attention, breaking him away from his thoughts. He turned to his right and widened his grin at its source: a TV shining through a large living-room window. A family sat obediently entranced in front of their big TV. With glazed eyes, body-destroying snacks in their hands, the family compliantly soaked up the ever-present Masters' programming and security patches addressed to fix the bugs in the system that arose periodically. It took Karver ten seconds to figure out what security patch was being delivered to the humans: the moneyless/government-less/revolutionary security patch. The security patch was being administered in a comedy that depicted self-sustaining communities as cultlike, dirty, and filled with crazy people. Since none of the humans watching the film had firsthand experience of a self-sustaining community, their minds were easily being shaped to detest them, which would help keep them stuck in the great spider-web design with the other human batteries instead of attempting an escape.

"Well done, humans. Obey. Let the programming flow into your system like a tantalizing drug that you can't do without. Keep soaking it up, my sheep."

The Masters have used the TV, and all other screened devices, from their inception to more effectively program and control the population. Why do you think they're called TV *programs*? They have created countless TV shows and movies to slip their agendas into the mass consciousness, completely under the radar.

In this way, humans' creative abilities were being used against themselves to create a reality for their masters. Why go through all the hassle of creating a planetary reality when you can hijack the humans' co-creative abilities and program them to create a reality that the Masters wanted? Besides, humans didn't even realize they possessed the power to create their own reality. They didn't know that the thoughts they think and the emotions they emanated had any bearing on the physical world. They thought only physical actions created reality. If they did know this fact and even a small number of them united to create the reality they wanted on Earth instead of the Masters' reality, it would create a systemic breakdown in the Masters' program. That's why it was imperative to keep them dense so they'd continue to create the very reality that they despised. The funny thing is, humans vocalize how they don't like their world, their reality, but they unknowingly continue to create the very reality they verbally or mentally attack everyday, and in doing so, they're strengthening that unwanted reality.

Stupid humans. How comical it all was when dealing with sheep. They are so easy to control.

Back in the day, earthly world explorers sailed to new lands and encountered aborigines—native peoples. After a short period of time, or instantly, the explorers came to consider the aborigines as primitive races that they had the right to control, indoctrinating them into their more civilized way of life, customs, and beliefs. They considered themselves the superior race, so they deserved to be in control. This happened on every continent and island on Earth throughout the ages. The story is the same for all aborigine peoples. Therefore, humans should understand that they deserve to be controlled by the Masters, since humans, no matter what country they live in or what race they descend from, are no different than aborigines in the eyes of the Masters. The Masters are a superior race over all earthlings and rightfully belong to be in control.

While walking, Karver looked down at the tarmac that was covering the soil. He thought, if we covered the whole world with tarmac, humans would eventually forget that the Earth even existed. They could be told that they're on a manmade satellite because the Earth became uninhabitable. It would provide easier control on Earth. They were already using this strategy on Mars for the abducted earthly slaves working in their technology production factories with great success, so why not roll out the same plan on Earth.

Karver was heading to a special sacrifice, a two-for-one special. The house he was walking toward contained two humans on his sacrificial list. Sporting a cheap suit and holding a black briefcase, he strolled up the walkway that led to the house's front door. Ready for business. He was about to double his pleasure, double his fun.

He placed his briefcase on the ground, slicked back his hair, straightened his suit and tie, and pressed a finger into the round doorbell button. *Ding-dong.* He heard a woman shouting from within, "Since you're down here, can you get that?" A muffled reply he couldn't make out answered the woman, and then the woman spoke again, "He's at the supermarket picking up some groceries."

The door opened and Karver energetically dove into his sales pitch with gusto, confidence, and a fake smile—all of the elements that embodied true salesmanship. "Ken Karver here! Karver's the name, knives are the game. There's nothing that can't be sliced, diced, chopped, or otherwise taken care of with a good set of cutlery … minus the spoons, forks, and such."

Raymond listened to Karver's sales pitch and replied with an impassive tone, but with words that showed interest. "Nice. Knives. Let's see 'em."

"Now we're talking, little man." Karver opened his briefcase to reveal a set of shiny knives.

Raymond's face enlivened a bit with eyes that slightly widened as the knives gleamed in his pupils. In his trance, he uttered one word while fixated on the knife set, "Knives."

Karver was pleased with the teenager's captivation. "Yes, knives. These knives are of the highest quality. They've been tested thoroughly and are tried and true. Not this set of course, this here's a new baby in mint condition. Look at that sheen. These are the sharpest knives in the world. They can effortlessly cut through anything. I mean anything. Care for a demonstration?"

Raymond kept his gaze on the knives while indicating yes with a nodding head.

Karver's fake smile morphed into a malevolent grin. "You're going to be shocked with this demonstration, I assure you." Karver clasped his hand around the handle of the largest knife in the set, a twelve-inch-bladed knife. He held it in front of the teenager, slowly tilting it back and forth. "Look at that. You can almost see how sharp it is by the gleaming reflection on the incline toward the blade's tip." After tilting it back and forth a few more times to present the gleaming reflection, Karver added while staring into the teenager's eyes, "Isn't that nice?"

Karver turned the knife so it was pointed at the teenager. "Now for the next part of the demon—demonstration."

Karver inched the knife very slowly into the teenager's stomach, steadily directing the knife in till flesh met the handle of the knife.

Raymond had stood stunned from the knife's first piercing to its total embedded position. His face, as well as his whole body, was locked in utter terror. Utter terror that stemmed from complete disbelief of the situation in front of his ballooned eyes.

Karver could feel it; he knew the vial in his pocket was amply being filled with loosh. "Now see how effortlessly that knife slipped into your stomach. It met no resistance. Isn't that nice? It slid in there like going into warm butter. I told you it was sharp. Isn't that impressive? As we salesmen say, 'Help the customer buy your product.' And what better way to do that than with a terrorific demonstration. Tomorrow's sales require cutting today."

Raymond didn't say a word, instead, he stood frozen in shock. This wasn't one of his videogames were he could walk away from any damage inflicted upon his body. The horror of this thought dove into his psyche.

Karver's grin turned to a partial frown and his eyes displayed a little frustration. "But I have to say, this is not a demonstration that really shows what this knife is capable of. You're way too fat, son. No muscle or gristle on your body. You do this knife test a disservice." He shook his head side to side in dismay. "See, I can move this knife all around with no resistance." Karver moved the knife in all possible directions until a section of the teenager's large intestine flopped out onto the floor.

Raymond was so absolutely filled with dread that his body stayed locked in shock, completely petrified. With his head tilted down, he had watched with wide eyes—eyes that had never bulged so substantially before in his entire life—at blood flowing out of his stomach and collecting in a large puddle on the floor, then his large intestine jumping out of his body and hitting the puddle of blood on the floor with a little splash.

While Karver continued to work the knife around, he pulled the collecting vial out of his left pocket with his free hand and saw that it was full. "Well, look at that. The younger the better." He pushed a button to seal it and turned on another vial in his pocket, which started collecting more loosh, but quickly slowed to a crawl.

Karver titled his head to the left to look past Raymond. "Is there someone else in the house that could provide a real test for my knives? Someone who's more fit. Someone who doesn't have a staggeringly high percentage of body fat."

Raymond's eyes crawled back into his sockets and he plummeted to the floor, splashing in a pool of his own blood and intestines. *Splat.* His spinal cord had been severed in the fall, which resulted in Raymond becoming two pieces of mangled, bloody flesh that glistened on the floor in front of Karver's delighted eyes.

While looking down at the messy pile that used to be Raymond, Karver said, "Are you going to invite me in or not? The nerve. Especially after the fine demonstration I gave exclusively for your benefit. Kids have no manners nowadays." He expressed his anger by kicking the bloody Raymond pile on the floor, causing Raymond's lifeless head to bob up and down twice. "That's more I like it. I can't come in unless I'm invited."

Karver closed his briefcase and picked it up with his left hand, keeping the large bloody knife in his right hand. He walked across the threshold and strolled down the hall toward the kitchen where he could hear someone putting dishes away in a cabinet. He stopped in the dark hall, around the corner from the kitchen's entrance, holding out the blood-dripping knife.

"Did you hear that owl last night, Raymond?" Amber said while putting away dishes. After no reply came she spoke again, "Who was that at the door, Raymond?" Amber shouted. She paused from putting away dishes to wait for Raymond's response, which never came.

With a plate in either hand Amber clicked her tongue in agitation and hurried around the corner to find Raymond.

When she rounded the corner for the dark hall, something stuck in her stomach. She looked down to see a hand holding a knife handle. Then she looked up and saw the man's face who was holding it.

Karver produced an exaggerated open-mouthed face, mocking pity. "Oh, woops. Looks like you walked into my big, sharp knife." Then a grin dawned on his face, expressing his true feelings about the situation.

Upon seeing his grin, Amber recognized his face. It was similar to that sketch she'd seen on TV at the food court in the supermarket. "Ken Karver?" she incredulously mumbled. Both plates dropped out of her hands and broke into several pieces upon the hardwood floor.

"As I was showing your son, who is now a mushy pile of a human over there by the front door, this knife can leisurely cut through anything." Karver gave Amber a once-over while she remained in shock, mouth ajar. She was wearing skin-tight pants and a narrow tube top—her workout clothes—that displayed most of her upper body. Karver noticed she was a little sweaty and surmised that she had recently had a workout session. "You look fit as a fiddle. Good muscle tone, laden with gristle, I'm sure. Unlike your flabby son, you'll provide a fine test for my quality knife set."

Amber blinked a few times and mumbled, "Test?" The combination of workout fatigue and shock left her standing in a hopeless state. The once mighty Amber now stood like a helpless fawn, skewered with a long knife. She looked past Karver and the dark hall to see the remains of her son illuminated by the outdoor light. His pile of bloody flesh glistened in the light. His eyes were wide and his tongue was sticking out of his mouth like a gored pig. Silent tears of sadness and fright streamed down her cheeks.

Karver saw her stare and knew she was observing the pile of flesh that was once her son. "Ah, there's nothing like a double. Provides a nice display for the runner-up. It's more effective to show rather than tell." Then Karver got back to business. "Yes, a test. And might I say that you'll be a fine-looking fish to fillet. Thank you for providing your lovely body for my knife demonstration."

Karver moved his knife around, which was met with a tad bit more resistance than when it was inside the flabby teenager's body, but the sharpness of the premium knife was still able to easily slice through Amber's abdomen.

He dropped his briefcase and plunged his left hand into her torso, fished around a bit, and ripped out a kidney. "Here we are. We won't be needing this anymore." He threw it on the floor and kicked it past Amber, watching it bounce along the kitchen floor and come to a stop as it hit a cabinet. Karver sighed. "You have no idea how many lawyers' kidneys I've kicked across the floor. I could provide a ball for every Major League Soccer match."

Karver sunk his left hand into Amber's abdomen again, this time yanking out her pancreas. "What's this?" He wrinkled his forehead. "Well, let's see what it tastes like." He bit off a piece and chewed on it a little, then spat it out in her face. "Yuck. Not my cup of tea. No offense, you just don't taste so great. I mean, don't get me wrong, you may be a sweet thing on the surface, but I just found out that's only skin deep," he said tongue-in-cheek. "Actually, I already knew that. That's why I'm here having a ball with your innards. You either cut with the knife or the knife cuts you. But I'll make you an honest salesman's deal. You give me four of your organs and I'll throw in a second knife set for free. Don't worry about the price of the first set, because I'm slashing prices."

Amber knew she was done for, bleeding out quickly and losing various organs that she probably couldn't do without. This maniac was having a party with her organs. This was one case that she wasn't going to win. She still couldn't fathom that this was happening to her. She continued to stand there like a mannequin, waiting for death to take her.

"Let's see what else we got in there, shall we." Karver rammed his left hand into her again like he was using her standing body as a punching bag. He fished around and tore out her spleen. It slipped and flopped around in his hand like a fish pulled out of the ocean. After he got a firm grip on half of it, he purposefully flopped the loose half around in his hand, back and forth. "That looks like a chew toy for a doggy. You got a doggy in the house?" He repeated the question in a high-pitched voice like he was talking to a baby while continuing to flop her spleen around in his hand. "You got a little doggy in the house, huh?"

As Amber slumped to the floor, Karver's knife sliced her open vertically on her way down. She lay on the floor in a pile similar to her son's, the kitchen light creating a glistening show from the reflection of the blood still slowly dripping from her mangled body.

Karver looked from one bloody pile of flesh to another, his customers that now lay on the cutting-room floor. "What's good for the goose is good for the gander."

Chapter 16

Nash and Mash sat in their front yard and talked about Bobby while throwing small rocks at a tree.

Nash hit the tree dead center. "I can't believe it took a little over four years for Oversized Marge to notice Bobby was missing. Like, I knew it would take a long time, but not four years."

Mash missed the tree, the rock sailed on and hit a parked car in the street. "So what are we going to do? Should we tell Jumbo-sized Marge what happened?"

"Nice shot, bro. Better than hitting the tree." Nash threw a rock at the same car and broke a passenger window. "Oh, yeah. Two points. … We can't keep it from her forever, so I guess we should just tell her. She was very angry when we didn't give her a straight answer when she asked where Bobby was. I think telling her that Bobby said he was off to the store to buy a bag of Doritos and an Oh Boy! Oberto beef jerky stick and that he never came back isn't going to cut it."

Mash threw another rock at the car and broke another window. "Damn. I could go for an Oh Boy! Oberto stick right now. Are you sure we should tell Supersized Marge?"

Nash broke another window on the car. "If we don't tell Large Marge, I'm afraid she'll roll into our bedroom and eat us while we're sleeping. She hasn't been able to afford fried chicken in a couple of days. She might turn to other types of meat on a bone: us."

Mash pegged the rearview mirror on the car. "So what exactly should we tell Massive Marge?"

Nash threw a rock where a window used to be and added another rock to the interior of the car. "We'll just tell Mammoth Marge exactly what happened: some moron killed him with a moronic book and his body just magically disappeared."

Mash added another rock to the interior of the car. "His body didn't disappear. I saw that lawyer lady—ya know, the one that got cut to pieces a month ago by that cool guy on TV … what's his name?"

"Ken Karver," said Nash. "Finish what you were saying. You saw the cut-to-pieces lady do what?"

"I saw her dragging Bobby's corpse into her car. She probably drove off and dumped him in a lake or something."

"What? Why didn't you ever tell me?"

"I didn't think it was important. Anyway, I thought it was a good thing because Meaty Marge would've seen his dead body rotting in the Linderloser's front yard eventually. If she never saw a rotting corpse, we wouldn't have to deal with it."

Nash added another rock to the inside of the car. "True, but still … you should've told me. … Anyway, I'm glad we avenged Bobby. After those two vomited on each other in the McDonald's parking lot and we beat the holy shit out of them, I felt really good. One of them will definitely need a wheelchair for the rest of his life, and I think we snuffed out the other one. Either that or he was playing dead."

"I hope he wasn't playing dead. I like the thought of him being snuffed out. I don't know, just makes me feel good thinking that. Him being dead and all."

Nash added his thirty-fourth rock to the interior of the car. "Yeah, the thought of him playing dead is dumb. That would've been lame of him. It's like, take it like a man and not a pussyhead. … After we fill that car with rocks, let's go inside and tell Mountainous Marge the lowdown on the Bobby story."

"Okay. But I don't know, though, bro. Beefy Marge might get super pissed when she finds out we've been hiding the info from her for over four years."

"Yeah, but Thickset Marge will be even madder if we wait more years. And remember, she might suck on our bones," said Nash.

"I doubt it. Hulking Marge only eats fried foods. And we don't own a deep fryer that she can use on our meat."

"Don't underestimate Fleshy Marge's need for meat, fried or not, she'll go to town on it. I saw her salivating over my leg one day when she had gone ten days without fried chicken. No joke," said Nash.

"Damn. You know it's only a matter of years, maybe months, before Overflowing-with-Fucking-Fat Marge dies on her sofa. She'll probably keel over halfway through a bucket of fried chicken."

"Hey!" shouted Nash. "You know the rules. Only one word can be used before the big-pile-of-blubber's name."

"Well, you used up all the good ones already," said Mash.

"Whatever. … I think we've gifted enough rocks to that car. Let's go tell … Global Marge the info."

Their neighbor across the street, having heard the sounds of the rocks hitting his car, opened his front door and angrily marched down his porch and driveway while shouting at the boys, "What the hell do you think you're doing?! You can't just throw rocks at someone's car for entertainment because you're bored!"

"Go back in your fucking box and shut the fuck up, Mr. Fucklestick!" yelled Nash.

"It's Finkelstein, you little cretin. I'll have your heads if you—" Finkelstein was silenced by shock when he got a good look at his car: every window broken, dents all over the body, the interior half-filled with rocks.

"What the fuck!" he yelled. "You've completely ruined my car! Is there something mentally wrong with you two? You think you live in some fantasy world where you can do whatever idiotic idea pops up in your demented heads? Huh? What the hell do you two have to say for yourselves?"

Nash and Mash looked at each other.

"Yup, let's do it," Nash said to Mash.

They both started picking up small rocks from the pile laying between them and chucked them at their neighbor.

A nonstop machinegun burst of projectiles flew toward an irate Finkelstein.

Finkelstein did his best to dodge the rocks, looking like a bad disco dancer as he swayed one way and jerked the other. "What the hell? Are you two completely deranged? You two need to be locked up in a padded room where—"

A rock found its way into his mouth during his ranting, slipping between his teeth and blasting the back of his throat. He instantly doubled over and choked on the rock that managed to lodge itself in his throat, desperately trying to work it out in a regurgitation-like manner.

"Hell yeah! Nice shot Mash. That'll silence that fucktart." They gave each other a high-five. "Let's keep it up till he drops dead or returns to his fucking box." They continued flinging rocks at the choking man, riddling his body with small rocks.

While stumbling back to his front door, Finkelstein managed to spit the lodged rock out of his mouth. After taking in a few breaths while bent down, hands on his knees, anger repossessed its hold on his emotions. His face turned crimson red. "I could have died! That's it, I'm calling the cops on you little bastards."

With rocks pelting the area around his front door, he quickly opened the door and disappeared inside while slamming the door shut.

"There, he's back in his fucking box where he belongs," Nash said. "Hopefully he'll stay in there and shut the fuck up."

"But he's gonna call the cops," Mash said with concern.

Nash shrugged his shoulders. "If he does, it's his word against ours, and there are two of us and one of him, so our word is more powerful. We'll tell the cops that Fucklestick was sucking on his dog's balls in his front yard while throwing rocks at his own head."

"I don't know. That doesn't sound too believable … and what about the car? How did a pile of rocks end up in his car?"

"We'll say he had a mental breakdown after his dog refused his advances and he started throwing rocks at his car in a fit of rage. We'll say we watched it all play out while we were drinking lemonade on our front porch and reading some kind of weighty literary book. Chomsky, we were reading Noam Chomsky."

Mash wrinkled his face in confusion. "I didn't know gnomes wrote books. How did you hear about that author?"

"While we were stealing old first-edition books at the library to sell, I heard some turtleneck-wearing bookworm say to one of his kind, 'Ah, sounds like you're ready for some Chomsky,' while handing his friend a book. For some reason that name stuck in my head."

Mash nodded his head. "Sounds like a tight plan. We're each other's alibis and we'll seem respectable by reading an important book. Fucklestick has no alibi and fornicates with his dog—they'll never believe him."

"Right. Now let's go tell Oversized Marge about dead Bobby."

Nash and Mash disappeared into their dilapidated house while a Mercedes pulled up and parked in front of Tim's house.

Jeremy and Dale exited and closed the car doors.

Jeremy looked at Dale. "Try to refrain from saying anything that might upset Tim. He's in a vulnerable state and doesn't need another reason to feel down. Actually, it's best if you say as little as possible. I'm not sure why he even told me to bring you along. Normally he has no inclination to see you outside of our café gatherings."

While rounding the car on his way to Tim's front yard, Dale noticed the battered parked car full of rocks. "I don't feel so good about parking here. Let's make sure this visit doesn't last too long, okay?"

Jeremy eyed Dale as they made their way through Tim's front yard. "Dale, did you hear me?"

"Yeah, yeah. I can't promise anything, but I'll try my best."

Jeremy rang the doorbell. After a pause, he turned to Dale. "Remember, try to be nice."

Dale responded by displaying a hideously contrived smile.

"I mean it," Jeremy said.

"Yeah, yeah. He's lucky that I even took the time out of my important life to accompany you on this little visit. If it weren't for the circumstances, I'd never have agreed."

Jeremy didn't say anything in return. He just stared down Dale, attempting to silently convey the importance of what he was asking.

The door opened and revealed a grungy-looking Tim: long stubble that was building toward a beard, unkempt hair, bags under his eyes, clothes that smelled like they'd been worn many days in a row.

"Thanks for coming, guys," Tim said while staring at the floor. "Please come in."

As they followed Tim into the house and passed the living room, Jeremy whispered to Dale, "Be nice."

Dale crinkled his nose. "Oh my god, why does it smell like vomit?"

Even though the Mormon-vomiting incident was over four years ago, Tim hadn't done a thorough job at cleaning up the mess and the living room had taken on a faint new smell that had set in permanently.

Jeremy widened his eyes at Dale and whispered, "Dale, be nice."

They followed Tim into the kitchen. Jeremy copied Tim and sat next to him on a bar stool in front of a long countertop that faced the refrigerator. Dale lingered in front of the fridge, looking at pictures and notes on the front of the fridge to quell his boredom.

Old pizza boxes and Chinese takeout containers littered the countertop. Jeremy figured Tim hadn't taken a step out of the house during the first month of his six-month sabbatical leave.

Tim looked up from the countertop and refocused his gaze forward at nothing in particular. "I asked you both to come here today to talk about the repercussions of our schemes."

Jeremy replied with an "Okay" and Dale kept looking at the things on the surface of the fridge without responding.

"I believe my wife's murder was karmic retribution for the three immoral schemes I perpetrated at work. It's too late for me, but you two still have a chance to change your ways before retribution finds you."

Dale turned around to face Tim. "I thought the colleagues you schemed against all deserved it."

"Maybe for the first two schemes, but I didn't have a valid reason for the last one. I just became greedy. Regardless, I've come to realize that any scheme, justified or not, doesn't warrant amoral action. Even if a colleague deserved what they got, my immoral actions are still weighted against me. We receive the same negative karma for any amoral act, justified or not, since it's not our place—not our right to play the role of retribution, the role of karma."

Jeremy said, "You might be right about that, but even if you are, I really don't think that's how karma works. Someone wouldn't get killed for another person's negative karma. That's not logical. If anything, the person who possesses the negative karma would be killed. But even so, none of us have done enough immoral acts to warrant being killed for them."

"I don't believe in karma," said Dale, "but if I did, I'd agree with Jeremy. Anyway, I'm only one scheme away from reaching the top of the food chain: senior executive VP. If you don't count the CEO position that is. Nothing bad has happened to me because of what I've done. It's live and let die out there." Dale extended an arm toward a window to indicate the outside world that Tim had exiled himself from for a straight month.

"I'm also only one scheme away from reaching my desired goal: becoming a senior ORA," Jeremy said. "I figure at this point I'd be damned if I stopped now or after one more scheme, being if what you say is true. But so far nothing bad has happened to me either." Then Jeremy added as politely as he could, "I think your bereavement has caused you to overanalyze the situation. And I understand that, I might've done the same thing if I was in your shoes. I was always under the impression that everything happens for a reason, but maybe some things are just random and have no correlation to a grand plan."

Dale chimed in, "Yeah, it's all chaos out there. There's no plan except for the plan you make yourself." Dale moved a magnet aside and took a coupon off the fridge. "Hey, Tim, what's this? It says good for one free rub-out and has a phone number listed on the back."

"It's something a Mafia guy gave Amber for winning his murder case," Tim replied, and quickly returned to the karma topic. "I hope you guys are right, but I have a bad feeling that karma somehow had a hand in … this."

Dale ignored Tim's second comment. "Is this coupon for real or just a joke?"

"Amber seemed to think that it was a legit coupon." After uttering his wife's name, his eyes watered up. A silent tear rolled down his cheek. "I don't know what I'm supposed to do with my life anymore. My life might as well have ended when my wife's did. I don't see any reason for me to keep on living."

Dale flicked the coupon back and forth in his hand. "Can I have this?"

While Tim's sagging head faced the countertop, Jeremy shot Dale a look. Jeremy widened his eyes at Dale and silently mouthed the words, *What the fuck?*

Fighting back tears, Tim replied to Dale without looking up, "It doesn't matter, go ahead."

Dale shrugged his shoulders at Jeremy and slipped the coupon into his suit pants. "I'm sorry for your loss, Tim. Amber was one of the great ones. Remember that time she got a client acquitted from rape charges on the grounds that the accusing female was too ugly for anyone to want to rape? She brought in an aesthetician and an orthopedist as expert witnesses to give lengthy speeches filled with medical jargon and draw technical sketches on whiteboards that proved the plaintiff's bone and skin structure was in fact way too hideously constructed to allow the possibility of any casual physical contact, let alone a rape situation."

Tim's eyes welled up even more upon hearing about his wife. He continued to fight back tears with his slumping head facing the countertop.

Jeremy gritted his teeth and moved a stiff hand across his neck a couple times to silently tell Dale to shut up.

Catching Jeremy's message, Dale fell silent and moseyed on over to a window so he could provide himself with some kind of visual entertainment while he wasted his time in Tim's depressing house.

Jeremy knew it was only a matter of time before Dale got restless and reverted back to dialog that would probably make Tim feel worse than he already felt. The man had no tact for sympathy, compassion, and walking lightly around delicate situations. Since the visit's purpose—in Jeremy's mind—was to comfort Tim, he thought it best to coax Tim out of the house for some lunch. Getting out of the house would be good for Tim, and Dale would have less chances of saying something stupid when his mouth was full of food. "I think we should go out for some lunch. It would be good for you to get out of the house for a bit, Tim."

Dale, still gazing out the window, agreed, "Yeah, a change of scenery would do you some good."

Tim took his time in replying, possibly mulling over the idea or just too saddened to reply to anything promptly. He finally nodded his head and verbally agreed.

Dale was the first one out of the house. While stepping out onto the porch, he took in an odd sight: a man running after a dog while grunting. "What the hell is that?"

When Tim exited the house and saw what Dale was talking about, he replied, "That's Bill Brady. He goes through months of withdrawal after football season is over. In order to cope with football withdrawal he'll stand in front of his window that overlooks the street, looking for pedestrians. After he spots one he'll make a beeline to his porch, pause for a bit to crouch down and yell out, 'hut hut hike,' before running full bore to tackle or sack the passerby."

"But that's a dog he's chasing, not a person," Jeremy said.

"Sometimes even a dog will do. There aren't many pedestrians in our neighborhood, and most have grown to avoid this stretch of pavement when it's the off season. We're lucky his attention is on that dog or he'd be running at us right now. He's rammed the back of my car a couple times with his body as I drove away, taking his high testosterone levels out on my car when he couldn't get to me before I got into my car."

They all continued to watch Bill Brady grunting and running down the street after the dog, and then Tim added, "I can picture him sitting in front of his large TV during football season, listening to the sportscasters repeat the same bloviating phrases and words over and over again about the players. Words like 'athleticism' and 'physicality.' I can imagine Bill listening intently to a short interview with a player or coach before, during, or after a game, thinking they were going to say something groundbreaking instead of the same stuff they say over and over again: 'We just gotta come together as a team,' and 'We gotta make them earn every point,' or 'It was really a team effort.' They should really save the players and coaches' time and ask the same questions to cardboard cutouts and play back one of their recorded answers. Brady's had to buy a new TV twice after shooting his TV when his team lost a close match. His wife divorced him years ago after getting sick and tired of being tackled throughout the house during the off season. She's got a restraining order against him."

"Great neighbor to have," Jeremy sarcastically stated. "Has he ever been sued for his antics?"

"Yeah, once. He tackled a woman's baby carriage. After the seven-month-old baby skidded across the pavement and began bawling his eyes out, Bill Brady started shouting at the toddler, 'What are you, a pussy? Walk it off! Walk it off!' After the mother shouted out her baby's age and how he wasn't able to walk yet, Bill Brady started barking in the vexed mother's face like she was a referee who had made a bad call. It was only a matter of—"

"Where did your dead wife take my dead son?!" Tim was interrupted by Oversized Marge, who had somehow managed to fit through her front doorway and waddle a few feet down her walkway. She was foaming at the mouth in rage and profusely sweating from having to use muscles that had lain dormant for years.

Tim couldn't remember the last time he'd seen her outside her house. "I have no idea what you're talking about," said Tim.

In Oversized Marge's worked-up state, Tim's answer was far from being acceptable. She began painstakingly wobbling toward Tim's fence while ranting, "I know you damn well know what went down. If you don't cough up some pleasing words, I'm going to wring your little pencil-neck like the chicken you are, you skinny piece—"

Her threat was cut short when her knees buckled under her own girth and she toppled into a blubbery mound on the ground, only ten feet from her door.

"You've got some really interesting neighbors," Dale joked while laughing. "I think that's the widest person I've ever seen in my life. She brings a whole new idea to the term 'consumerism.' "

Oversized Marge began thrashing her short, meaty arms about in order to gain a hold of the ground and attempt to push herself up, but all her floundering proved useless when her arms couldn't escape the many layers of lard that billowed from her forgotten spine. Yelling had been replaced with various grunts that looked like they were being produced to somehow assist her movements that tried to lift her off the ground. But it was obvious she wasn't getting off the ground anytime soon. She continued to thrash about on the ground, unintentionally slathering her body with sweat and saliva that dripped from her contorted mouth that kept producing grunts. Before their amused eyes, she began simmering in her own juices of sweat and drool. They figured she'd be swimming instead of simmering in those same juices pretty soon.

Their attention was called away from Oversized Marge and her juices when they heard a roar escaping Bill Brady's mouth. They turned their heads to take in Bill Brady running after a winded, desperate jogger. The jogger was giving it his all but was too tired to outrun his roaring pursuer.

At the end of Bill Brady's roar, he crashed into the jogger while wrapping his arms around the man and taking him to the pavement. Bill Brady bounced back up off the ground as he hooted and hollered with brimming enthusiasm. "Nice show of athleticism, Terry. Too bad your ass got sa-a-a-acked. Whoo, fuck yeah! That's what I'm talking about—*sports*!"

A police car rounded the corner and parked in front of Oversized Marge's house as Terry got to his feet and began hobbling down the street toward his house, away from a crazed Bill Brady who was beating his chest like King Kong.

The officers exited their police car and started barking orders at Bill Brady. "Hands in the air, sir! Get down on the ground, sir!"

Finkelstein opened his front door. He held a bloodied facecloth to his forehead. "Forget about that ape, officers. I called you about the hooligans that live in that house." He pointed across the street at the Riley's house. "They filled my car with rocks and nearly killed me with the same rocks."

Both cops quickly spun around to face Finkelstein and drew their guns and pointed them at Finkelstein. "Don't talk unless spoken to, sir! Get down on your knees, sir!"

Bill Brady used the distraction to flee toward his house, screaming to himself, "I knew they'd come to seize my weapons. I knew this day would come. Well, it's not gonna happen. From my cold dead hands!"

One of the cops shifted his aim to Brady. "Sir, stop! Sir, get down on the ground now!"

Bill Brady ignored the cop and kept running toward his front door.

The GMO kids rushed into their front yard to see what the commotion was all about.

Still hobbling down the street, Terry turned his head around to address the cops. "That football fucker has been tackling me every week. You've got to stop him and restore order to this neighborhood, officers."

Finkelstein pleaded with the policemen while kneeling on the ground with his hands in the air. "Those are the kids that attacked me, officers. They're the reason why I called you. Please arrest them." He pointed at the GMO kids.

One of the cops took a hand off his gun to speak into his radio. He requested a squad car to apprehend a suspect that was responsible for assault and rattled off Bill Brady's address as Brady entered his house and slammed the door shut. Then the officer turned to his partner and said, "I know these kids. They're hellions on wheels. Given that man is bleeding, it's safe to assume that he's telling the truth. Let's arrest the hooligans and let the coming squad car take care of the assaulter."

"What the hell is happening here?" Jeremy asked Tim.

"I don't know what this is all about, but weird things tend to happen on this street," Tim replied.

The officers holstered their weapons and made their way toward the GMO kids. The cops cautiously approached Oversized Marge, who was still squirming around on the ground in her own juices while producing grunts. She had de-evolved into a big sluglike creature akin to Jabba the Hutt. The officer in the lead asked his partner, "What do we do about this large creature?"

"I advise we stay clear of it. Given its obesity and the hunger in its eyes, it might make for one of our legs likes it's a midday snack. It also appears to be producing some type of slime that would be best to avoid contact with."

"Affirmative, stay clear of the large creature." The officer pointed his finger at Oversized Marge while giving her a wide berth. "We have no quarrel with you, large creature, stand down."

The GMO kids vocalized their complaints as the officers cuffed their hands behind their backs and hauled them to the squad car. "You can't take Mr. Fucklestick's word over ours.

There are two of us and one of him. We have alibis and he doesn't. I order you to arrest Fucklestick for sucking on his dog's balls in public and attempting to rape it. After his dog rejected his advances, he went apeshit and started throwing rocks everywhere—at his car and his own head."

"You really think we're going to believe that the man threw rocks at his own head?" one of the officers scoffed.

"Yeah, I do," said Nash. "Mr. Fucklestick has a long rap sheet of abnormal behavior that includes dog rape and dog-ball sucking. Look into his beady eyes. He's clearly thinking about the next dog he'll be manhandling. And he goes ballistic when dogs reject his sexual advances, always throwing rocks at his own head and stuff."

"Sure, sure, kid." The cops continued to usher the GMO kids to the squad car. When they reached the car the officers forced the kids' heads down as they pushed them into the back of the police car.

"Don't smoosh my head, pig," Nash growled. "I can get into a car just fine without your molesting hand. I don't need your dumbass hand to assist me. You're clearly trying to dehumanize me rather than help me. Have some respect, we read Chomsky."

"You can read all you want while you're rotting in jail, punk," said one of the cops as they got into their vehicle and headed toward the station. The cops nodded their heads through the windshield at fellow officers in an arriving police car that passed them and raced up to Bill Brady's mailbox.

The newly arrived officers exited their vehicle, marched up to Bill Brady's front door, and started pounding on it while shouting, "Open the door, sir! You are under arrest for the assault of your neighbor. Open the door now, sir!"

"I have a feeling this isn't going to end well," said Tim. "Brady doesn't take orders. He's used to dishing them out."

They could hear Bill Brady shouting out an opened second-floor window. "You ain't seizing my guns, pigs! I'll shoot every last one of you if I have to! … From my cold dead hands!"

One of the officers said to his partner, "Sounds like he's armed and just used verbal threats. We have grounds to break his door down and take him by force, dead or alive."

"That's affirmative," the other cop replied.

"Your neighborhood is more interesting than a movie theater," Dale said.

They watched the cops kick down Brady's door and rush inside with guns pointed. Soon shots from both parties were heard erupting from the house. They heard Brady yell out during a period of silence, "From my cold dead hands!" and gunfire broke out again.

When a bullet shattered a window, Jeremy said, "As interesting as this is, we should get out of here before we catch a stray bullet."

"Perhaps you're right," said Tim. "I guess I won't have to worry about Brady sacking me or ramming into my car anymore."

As the three walked toward Dale's Mercedes, Oversized Marge, still floundering in her own fat, grumbled, "Come back here and tell me where Bobby's body is. I know your dead wife sold his corpse to McDonald's. Nash told me all about it. That's my money, you hear me!" She continued to wriggle around on the ground, sloshing her blubber about, repeatedly failing to rise from the dirt and separate herself from the worms in the soil she'd worked up.

"What the hell is she talking about, Tim?" Jeremy asked.

"I have no idea."

"Does she have a husband that can help her back inside?" Jeremy asked.

"No. Her kids, who just got arrested, are all she has."

"Her predicament is her own undoing," said Dale. "But she still has food. She can roll around and eat grass if it comes to it."

"Can the human body process and use grass as food?" Jeremy asked Dale.

"Hmm, I don't know. A cow can, and she's similar in physique. Even if grass doesn't work, she has several months of stored body fat for her body to feed on. Ketosis. It would be akin to a forced keto diet. She'll emerge from the dilemma as a better person. Let's not rob that opportunity from her."

They entered the Mercedes and drove off to lunch.

Tim had a dream of the events that night. It started true to reality, but then drastically changed when Bill Brady began fleeing for his house.

"Suspect is fleeing, subdue him." The cops fired off two rounds each into Brady's back and dropped him like a bad sports habit.

"We have another suspect running away. If he's running away from us, it means he did something wrong. Neutralize him." The cops fired off three rounds each into Terry's back. The exhausted jogger was flung to the pavement. His lifeless eyes viewed a pool of his blood that kept growing in size.

Finkelstein opened his front door. "Forget about those people you shot for no reason, officers. I called you about the hooligans that live in that house." He raised an arm and pointed across the street. "They filled my car with aborted fetuses from promiscuous libertarians. Those stains will never be cleaned, they're permanent like parliament."

The cops whipped their guns around toward the new target that suddenly appeared on their nine o'clock. "Suspect has a gun in his hand. Light him up."

The cops emptied their entire magazines into Finkelstein, causing him to fly back against his door, temporarily nailing him to the wood like a martyred saint. After the cops' smoking guns produced clicks, Finkelstein's body slowly slid down to his porch, leaving a path of blood painted on his white door.

The cops released their empty mags, and before they hit the pavement, they grabbed fresh ones from their utility belts and slammed them home. Then they whipped their guns around and trained them on Oversized Marge and the GMO kids, who were drinking lemonade and reading books.

"Do we have grounds to fire?" asked one of the cops.

The other cop pulled out a pair of binoculars and focused them on the books. "Suspects are sinking their chomps into some Chomsky. Chomsky is a socialist and a threat to our nation. We are a go. I repeat, we are a go."

Bullets ripped through the air, shattering lemonade glasses, piercing the Chomsky books, and tearing holes throughout the GMO kids.

As the GMO kids' lifeless bodies fell to the ground, Oversized Marge started snapping her jaws, "You just revoked my food stamps. You've stolen my meal ticket. Tonight I dine on pigs. That's right, I'm talking about you swine."

"Suspect has threatened to eat us," said one cop.

"I don't even think that creature is from Earth," said the other.

"Light it up."

Round after round punctured Oversized Marge's blubbery membrane, producing hot air that whistled as it rushed out. When the holes were numerous and Oversized Marge started deflating, she took to the wind and whistled her way to Antarctica. Her body separated into three alien mother ships that would someday be revealed as scientists uncovered them from under the ice.

The chief of police's voice crackled over one of the policeman's two-way radio. "I've heard all about it, boys. There's nothing more American than filling someone full of bullets, but a real American hero fills everyone in their line of sight full of bullets. You boys are those American heroes. It's like the Chinese say: it doesn't matter whether it's a good or bad thing to do, we have to keep doing it because it's a tradition. Boys, there'll be a parade in your honor and we'll name a goddamn holiday after you."

The cops finally noticed Tim, Jeremy, and Dale standing on Tim's porch.

"Hold on, sir. Our work is not done here. We have three suspects that have been perpetually perpetrating schemes at their workplaces."

"Fill 'em with bullets," growled the chief. "It's our tradition. Even if they're innocent, we always stand behind our men after they kill someone. Hell, I don't need to say it, you boys know. Look at all the cops that killed innocent people and only got suspended for a few months before coming back to the force to continue fillin' folks full of holes."

"Thanks, Captain. Now that we know we have your support, we'll get back to Operation Light 'Em Up & Watch 'Em Drop."

Bullet after bullet erupted from the cops' guns and riddled the trio's bodies full of lead.

As Dale's body shifted left and right from each impacting bullet, he yelled out, "This is ridiculous! You know how much this suit cost me? You asshats. I'll have your badges for—"

Tim woke up and gasped for air as his torso shot up vertically in his bed. "Oh, man, it was just a dream. Just a dream."

Chapter 17

A major system update to Cohesive Analytics' management software was rolling out in a month. Management had decided to put aside classes for all employees to learn the features in the important update so the new software features would be utilized correctly on the day they went live, because there was no such thing as downtime when it came to business management. Each employee was to attend two classes a week for a month and take a test at the end of each week to make sure the information was being learned properly and retained. Since half of Cohesive Analytics' workforce were basic ORAs and the other half consisted of advanced ORAs and senior ORAs, it made sense to group the latter two together for the classes. The more senior employees' classes were held in the partitioned-off senior ORA wing of the building, so Jeremy got to see the fancy section of the building for the first time.

Before the second class commenced during the first week, Jeremy had noticed a senior ORA getting black coffee from the kitchen at the same time he had before the first class two days ago. Jeremy suspected that he was the only employee that used the pot of coffee in the senior ORA's kitchen. All the other senior ORAs appeared to have higher standards for their caffeine intake and purchased coffee from Caffé Vita Coffee Roasting Company, Espresso Vivace, Starbucks, or Tully's Coffee. It seemed like simple logic to deduce that this senior ORA, Guy Person, got his black coffee from the kitchen at the same time every day.

The coffee pot could be tampered with, thought Jeremy.

It had been three and a half years since Jeremy pulled off his last scheme. He had to put in enough time as an advanced ORA to even be eligible for a senior ORA position, but until now, he hadn't even conceived a scheme that would've worked regardless if he was eligible or not. He had to act now while the opportunity was in front of him; another chance might never come along. God forbid he'd have to get the promotion the old-fashioned way. He knew that his work skills made him worthy of a senior ORA position at some point, but how long would that be, and was management even competent or fair enough to notice his skills and give him the promotion eventually? He could bust his butt for years and never be assured advancement if he did it the normal way. There was no way he was going to pass up this opportunity.

For the second and third week of classes, Jeremy had crushed up sleeping pills to a fine powder and dissolved the powder in the coffee pot before the typical time Guy Person got his coffee from the kitchen. He noticed Guy finding it hard to concentrate during the second week of classes, but he wasn't drugged enough to fall asleep at the meeting table, so Jeremy had upped the dosage for the third week of classes.

For the third week of classes, Guy had nodded off for a second or two a few times, but still hadn't fallen asleep at the table, so Jeremy decided to up the dosage substantially for the last week, given he only had two more chances to get Guy to fall asleep at the meeting table and make him look like a total slacker.

Guy had already been chewed out by Sam White—the person from management that had been tasked to teach the classes—for failing the assessment tests at the end of the second and third week of classes. Since the major update was very important to Cohesive Analytics, Sam White considered Guy Person's inability to take the classes seriously as a major concern and illustrated his lack of dedication to the company.

Concurrently, Jeremy had aced the tests and did whatever it took during the classes to get the focus shining on him for management to notice: he offered up witty comments about the new features, he brown nosed, he praised the new features, and he acted super friendly and positive. If he had done all that properly—along with his proven track record—management would hopefully think of him when they sought a candidate to fill the position Guy Person would be leaving behind after having failed all the assessment tests and falling asleep for the last two classes—if things went according to plan.

It was Tuesday. Everyone except one employee was seated around the meeting table listening to the second to last tutorial Sam White would be teaching. The missing employee was Frederick Friberg, an advanced ORA. Sam had vocalized his dismay about Friberg's absence before starting the class, conveying for the nth time that these classes were of the upmost importance and shouldn't be taken lightly.

It was an hour into the class and Guy Person had dozed off several times for a couple of seconds as usual but hadn't fallen asleep yet. He appeared sleepier than usual, but Jeremy began worrying that the guy might have an abnormally high tolerance to sleeping pills and never fall asleep.

Luckily, an hour later, Jeremy's concern vanished when he saw Guy's head slowly descend to the surface of the table. He had started with both arms propping up his head, elbows on the table and hands under his chin, and steadily repositioned his arms to act as a makeshift pillow upon the table.

Many people at the table noticed, but Sam White had been facing the pull-down projector screen for the past five minutes, pointing at things and explaining a key function of one of the new features in the software update, so he hadn't noticed until he heard someone snoring.

Sam spun around with a scowl on his aged face. His spiked, closely cropped white hair seemed pointier than usual when he got mad. He started lecturing the whole room even though it was abundantly clear that Guy was the only employee not paying attention. "People, have I not repeatedly expressed how important this software update is? When this update goes live next week, you won't be able to do your jobs if you don't learn and retain this information."

After making eye contact with every serious face on a nodding head in the room, Sam pinpointed his stern verbiage toward the true offender. "This goddamn guy is trying my patience to its fullest extent. He's performed horribly on the last two weeks' assessment tests and now has the audacity to schedule his naptime during my presentation. How incompetent can a person be? Somebody wake his ass up."

The employee on either side of Guy Person eyeballed the other, trying to convey that they didn't want to touch Guy and that the other person should do it. Guy continued snoring in between the two employees.

"For Christ's sake," bellowed Sam. He picked up a marker from the whiteboard and launched it toward Guy's head. The marker struck Guy square in the ear.

Guy's head shot up and his hand babied his ear. "What the hell. What gives?"

Sam put his palms down on the table and stared Guy down. "What gives, Mr. Person, is your utter display of incompetence and apathy. Do you want to continue being employed at Cohesive?"

Realizing he had fallen asleep during Sam's presentation, Guy's expression turned from anger to shame. "Yes, of course. I'm sorry. It won't happen again."

"It sure as hell better not," Sam said, and went back to his presentation.

Twenty minutes later Guy was sleeping again. This time he wasn't snoring, so Sam didn't bother waking him up. Jeremy suspected that Sam knew there was no reason waking him up again, as he'd just fall asleep again in a matter of minutes.

Instead of waking Guy and yelling at him again, Sam paused from his presentation and wasted a minute to make a joke about Guy's name. "Let's take a minute break for a joke. Here it goes. So I called Guy's mom up to tell her that her son had fallen asleep during my presentation, and she said, 'Which Guy?' I replied, 'What do you mean which guy?' She said, 'All my sons' names are Guy.' So I took a picture of this particular Guy and messaged it to her, saying it was this Guy. She said, 'That still doesn't help me out. That Guy is one of two identical twins.' So I got irritated and yelled over the phone, 'What kind of a person are you?' She replied, 'I'm Gal Person. That's what

Person I am.' So I told her, 'Well, Gal, you're one fucked up person. Naming all your sons Guy.' She said, 'No, you're getting me confused with my horrible husband. His name is Phuk-up Person. He's Thai. Phuk means tied in Thai. He's a tied up person in our basement for naming all our sons Guy.' So I said, 'You people are fu—' She cut me off and said, 'It's you Persons, not you people.' So I said, 'Fine. You Persons are all fucked up.' She said to me before hanging up, 'What are you a moron? I just told you that only my husband's name is Phuk-up Person.' "

Everyone laughed and then the class resumed.

Everybody left the room when the class was done, leaving Guy, the sleeping Person, behind. He woke up hours later and stumbled out of the dark conference room.

After the working day was over and everyone had left Cohesive Analytics for the day, the cleaning lady heard someone snoring in a stall in the men's bathroom. She tried opening the stall but it was locked, so she loudly knocked on the stall door a few times.

Frederick Friberg, the employee that hadn't made it to the class that day, woke up and said, "Why are you knocking on my stall?"

"I'm trying to do my job," the cleaning lady said. "I need to clean your stall."

"What the hell, lady. Can't you wait till the workday has ended?"

"It has ended," she said. "Everyone has left. You must have fallen asleep while doing your business, mister. I heard you snoring before I knocked on your door."

Frederick looked at his watch: 9:28 P.M. He realized he had been sleeping for several hours as he took in another breath of his business directly below him. Not only had he been sleeping on the job for hours, but he'd been sucking up the vaporous emanations of his long ago conducted business.

"Hello, mister. Are you going to get out of there so I can do my job?"

"Yeah, yeah, lady. Just let me wipe my ass, jeez."

Jeremy got a phone call from Dale that evening. Dale told Jeremy that he'd be moving to New York in a month. He had been poached by a competing brokerage firm, Gelman & Gerwitz. Along with Stryker & Marshall, it was one of the top three brokerage firms in the nation.

Dale would be retaining the same title, senior VP, but would be given a nice raise and was promised an executive senior VP position after one of their executive senior VPs departed or in five years' time, whatever came first. The executive senior VP position was mostly an honorary title, but it came with a substantial raise and he'd be eligible to become a partner at the firm if he put the years and dedication in. Partnership at Stryker & Marshall wasn't available for any employee, there was only the CEO and the board of directors.

The main reason Dale had accepted the offer was because New York was the place to be if you wanted to be one of the biggest Big Boys, but becoming an executive senior VP sooner and a chance to become a partner one day also allured him.

They agreed to dinner the following week so they could spend some time together before Dale's departure.

Jeremy was almost certain it would be the last time he'd see Dale. First there was the growing gaps between their intermittent meetings, and now Dale would be on the other side of the country.

Jeremy had a dream about sleeping pills that night.

Many people in the world had started taking sleeping pills during the day because they claimed it made their lives better, so Jeremy, Dale, Tim, and Amber started doing it too.

Their dosage got higher and higher as time went by and their bodies' tolerance grew.

Tim stopped taking them when his wife got murdered, and told Jeremy and Dale that they should stop too.

Tim went through withdrawal symptoms and felt horrible for three and a half years before finally feeling better. At that point, he felt better than he'd ever felt in his life. So he called up Jeremy to tell him that life is immensely better when not subjected to the effects of sleeping pills. Jeremy replied by telling Tim that he knew. He had figured it out for himself several months ago when he too quit taking sleeping pills. He told Tim that he was right. Jeremy wondered why he ever thought taking sleeping pills during his waking hours would make him happier—probably because everyone else was doing it. He could now see that taking them was clearly absurd, given that he felt free and enlivened after he had stopped mindlessly popping them into his body and burying his head in the sand regarding their effects on his entire living state.

Meanwhile in New York, Dale kept upping his dosage and eventually became seriously ill.

The dream ended with Dale collapsing on the floor in his high-rise luxury apartment. He died but was resuscitated by paramedics in an ambulance that was barreling toward the closest hospital. The paramedics wore white hats. Then Dale died again and was brought back to life by the paramedics again, and this happened over and over like a broken record. Jeremy wasn't sure if Dale had died in the dream or not because Jeremy woke up before the ambulance reached the hospital.

Jeremy reached for the glass of water on his nightstand. While drinking, he thought all the sleeping pills he'd been dealing with for his current scheme had followed him into his dreams. What a weird dream, especially the ending part with Dale dying over and over again. Well, after this Thursday, the last tutorial class at work, he wouldn't be dealing with sleeping pills anymore so he'd be able to get them off his mind.

Thursday had arrived and they were situated at the meeting table in the conference room for the last class. Everyone except Henry Davies, a senior ORA, was present.

Sam set up the projector and was about to get started. "Nice to see that you could make it today, Frederick. What happened yesterday?"

Frederick stirred uneasily in his chair. "I uh … There was a family emergency."

"I hope everything's all right now."

"Yes, I believe it is. Thanks, Sam."

"Well, Henry isn't here yet, but it's already ten minutes past so we're going to get started anyway. We have a lot to cover for our last session. After today you should all be experts at our new system when it rolls out this Monday." Sam stared at Guy with a stern face for a whole two seconds before launching into where he'd left off last Tuesday.

Jeremy could've sworn he saw Sam silently mouth the word *Goddammit* as he starred at Guy, whose eyes were already half-closed.

Guy must've noticed it too because he reached for his extra-large cup of black coffee and took a huge gulp, as if to let Sam know he'd be wide awake today.

Jeremy knew Guy wouldn't be able to last an hour before beddy-bye time because of the amount of coffee he was consuming and the rate at which he was chugged it down. And as a last hurrah, Jeremy had also added a powerful laxative to the coffee pot today. It was going to be interesting to see how that turned out.

Sam briskly worked through the last educational class, making a point to eyeball Guy every now and then when his attention wasn't focused on the projector. Every time Sam looked at Guy, he saw an incompetent employee with sagging eyelids upon a periodically sagging head.

It was obvious to Jeremy that Guy was working at full capacity to avoid slipping into a slumber.

Thirty minutes into the class, Sam was finishing up an explanation for one of the new features while eyeballing Guy's closing eyelids. In the middle of Sam's sentence Guy's head fell forward and hit the table with a loud banging sound that echoed throughout the conference room. Then he instantly began snoring loudly like an elephant with a sinus infection.

Sam threw the marker in his hand at the ground to illustrate his dismay. "That goddamn guy has fallen asleep again. That's it, he's done for. Someone wake him up so I can tell him he's fired."

Su-wei, who had been promoted to a senior ORA two years ago, reached a hand over and nudged Guy's shoulder, but Guy's sleeping body paid the action no mind.

"Don't be shy, Su-wei, give him a good whack in the head," said Sam.

Su-wei used the base of her open palm to hit Guy's head with medium strength. Guy's head wobbled back and forth, his lips smacked a bit while he produced some abrupt agitated snoring sounds, and then he nestled back into his heavily snoring slumber.

"This goddamn guy is unbelievable," growled Sam. "He must have been out all night hopping and bopping at a nightclub, prowling the scene for a little teenage nooky. I bet him and all his Guy brothers burst through the nightclub entrance, poured an insane amount of alcohol into their systems, and snatched at anything with a pulse that wandered past their sloshed eyes. I bet after all the hoopla subsided, the demented Guys spilled out of the nightclub at some ungodly hour, intoxicated blood pumping, gallivanting around the city like foul beasts seeking their next series of exploitations. What a disturbing person this goddamn guy is. Him and all his goddamn Guy brothers and his whole damn Person family. Hit him harder, Su-wei. Give him a good elbow to the throat. Don't worry, I'll take full responsibility."

Su-wei shrugged her shoulders to indicate *Okay, if you say so*. She lifted her arm and aimed her elbow at the guy's throat and then lunged her arm forward, stabbing her bony elbow right in there.

Amazed by Su-wei's ultimate fighting skills, the table unanimously praised her with golf claps while Guy awakened from his deep slumber.

Not knowing what had struck him, Guy vocalized to no one in particular, "What happened? Did a bee just sting me?"

Sam laid into Guy like his mother, Gal Person, would've. "Guy Person, you've failed the last two assessment tests, and despite receiving a harsh warning last Tuesday, you've managed to fall asleep again today. You're fired! Effective immediately. Leave this room, go to your office, pack up your shit, and beat it."

Guy's mouth fell ajar. "But Sam I—"

"I don't want to hear a single excuse out of you. You're fired. Get out."

Guy sagged his head in shame, rose from his chair, almost fell over, and somehow managed to stumble his way to the door.

Sam shook his head. "Can barely make it out of the room, let alone perform his job."

Guy lowered the handle on the door and pushed the door open. Instead of the door opening completely, it banged against something halfway through its swing and bounced back a bit. Guy pushed the door back as far as he could and weaseled his way out the door and looked down at the obstruction on the floor. "Oh, man."

Everyone in the conference room watched Guy stumble to his office. When Guy reached his office and put a hand on the door handle, the sound of loud flatulence boomed from his buttocks and diarrhea began soaking his pants and soon could be seen streaming from the bottom of his pants and onto his shoes and the floor. "Ohhh," escaped Guy's mouth right before he collapsed to the floor and fell asleep on his excrement puddle. Snoring was soon heard from his passed out body.

Sam shook his head. "All night hopping and bopping I bet. Hopefully his clothes mop up most of that and ease the cleaning lady's burden. … And what the hell did the conference door hit?"

Sam walked over to the door and tried to open it fully but it hit something. Sam squeezed himself out the doorway and looked down at the floor. It was Henry Davies's head that had been obstructing the door. His passed-out body lay facedown on the floor and diarrhea permeated his pants in the buttocks region. The smell instantly attacked Sam's senses.

"What the hell is this?! Is it too much to ask for employees that aren't goddamn infants?! Sleeping and shitting their pants whenever they goddamn feel like it! Someone strap a diaper on this one," Sam said as he marched to the men's room for a quick break to clear his rage.

After a few minutes Sam returned to the conference door and looked down at Henry. Instead of a diaper, someone had covered Henry's shit-stained pants with several pieces of paper from the printer. Every piece of paper displayed one big, bold word: DIAPER.

"Good work, team," Sam said, and then purposefully yanked the door open so that it forcefully struck Henry's head again. Henry's body didn't stir, but low, rumbling flatulence was heard, and then a dark brown spot bled through one of the DIAPER papers.

Sam cringed. "I'm surrounded by oversized babies trying to pass themselves off as adults."

When the last class ended and everyone was exiting the conference room, causing Henry's head to be struck several times, Sam said, "Not you, Jeremy. Stay in your seat."

While everyone else was leaving the room, Jeremy watched Sam pace back and forth in front of the projector screen, looking at the floor with a huge frown on his face.

Jeremy gulped and wondered if the jig was up. Maybe someone had witnessed him putting the white powder in the coffee pot and had informed Sam.

When the last person exited the room, Sam walked over to the table and rested two fists upon the table at the end of his outstretched arms. His stern face stared at Jeremy for a few seconds before saying anything. Then he spoke, "I hate to do this, Jeremy. I hate firing people."

Jeremy stirred uneasily in his chair. *Oh, fuck. The jig is up. He's about to can me.*

"I fired Guy, and now I have to fire another person. And I don't mean one of Guy's goddamn family members."

Yup. I'm done for. Tim was right. Karma's coming back to bite my ass.

"I'm going to have to fire Henry too. After witnessing his shit show, I won't be able to ever look him in the face again. Besides, falling asleep on the floor and shitting yourself is definite grounds for termination. That's two senior ORAs that'll be leaving today. I've noticed your zeal throughout our classes and you've aced every assessment test. Can I count on you to move up your game to the next level, become a senior ORA? The promotion is yours if you want it."

Jeremy smiled at Sam. "I'll not only take the position, but I'll be the best senior ORA in the company."

Sam's grim expression lightened up and a half smile appeared. "That's what I like to hear, my boy. Just promise me one thing."

"What's that, sir?"

"Now that you're a senior ORA, don't pass out on the floor and shit your drawers. It seems to be trending around here among the senior ORAs."

Chapter 18

Two months after Amber's death, Tim was emotionally functional enough to tie up some loose ends from his wife's untimely departure. He didn't feel like dealing with them now, or ever, but knew that they'd have to be dealt with at some point. Some matters would be easier to reconcile the sooner they were dealt with.

The first order of business was a charge that had appeared on Amber's credit card statement a month ago. The charge was from their cable and Internet provider. Tim recalled that their cable plan had been due to expire about a month ago. He didn't watch TV except for a movie every other night, which was something a streaming service could provide for a much cheaper price. When the thought of his cable plan ending popped into his head during his intense grieving period, he figured that the plan would expire on its own if not dealt with. But judging by the charge on the credit card, it appeared it was set to automatically renew.

Tim dreaded calling the cable provider to resolve the issue because he recalled the many phone calls his wife had made to them and the aggravation she had dealt with over several asinine issues.

The first issue his wife had called about was to resolve the problem of their Internet intermittently cutting out for five to ten minutes every day or every other day. She had told the representative on the phone that her friend, who lived in a second-world country, had Internet for much cheaper and his connection never dropped unless the power went out. She wanted to know why residents in America, one of the most advanced countries in the world, had to deal with this basic connection problem. Like always, the rep rattled off some scripted reply that didn't answer her question, then tried to sell

Amber an upgrade to her Internet plan that would be faster and more stable. He recalled Amber being irate upon hearing this from the rep. She told the rep she didn't need faster Internet and that she shouldn't have to pay more to have a connection that didn't drop out, being that a stable connection was a basic role of an Internet plan.

Amber quickly realized, as did most callers after a period of time, that the rep was just another clueless person sitting in a call-center seat somewhere and didn't know anything about the workings of their company. So she had given up the questioning and agreed to schedule a technician visit to fix the connection problem. The technician failed to show up for the scheduled time period, nor did they even show up that day. So she called back and they apologized and rescheduled. The technician failed to arrive again on the second attempt. She recalled and rescheduled. The technician finally arrived on the third try. He had been rude, tinkered with some stuff and replaced some cables at their connection point, and left without saying anything.

Not only did the intermittent dropping of the Internet persist after the technician's visit, but charges had been placed on her credit card for all three of the scheduled technician's visits and for some parts and services on the third visit. All the charges amounted to a total of $382. Naturally Amber was infuriated and called them again to not only get the dropping-Internet problem fixed but to refund the charges for two technician visits that never happened and for a third visit that she was told would be free. The rep replied to all her comments with gibberish, repeatedly stating the cable company's policies. Amber told the rep that she wished she had recorded the phone call where the rep had said the visit would be free. The rep told her that that was a shame indeed, and that the cable company records all their calls for their records. Amber told her to check the recording to hear what the rep had told her, but the rep said the recordings could only be accessed by supervisors and management. So Amber asked to speak to a supervisor. The supervisor was equally unhelpful, spouting off nonsense and stating policies and procedures about how he couldn't access the company's recordings for such and such reasons. Amber was so mad that she hung up the phone during one of the supervisor's gibberish-filled responses and decided to deal with the dropping of the Internet and pay the invalid charges because it wasn't worth her precious time to get the problem fixed and the charges refunded. She had confided with Tim that that was exactly the strategy of the cable company. She had stuck to the fight for the principle alone, but came to realize that, time being money, it would've cost her much more than the fraudulent charges if she continued to pursue the fight till the end.

On top of all this aggravation, she later received a package full of gear from the cable company that was supposedly meant to help her fix the Internet issue by herself. A package she never asked for. She got an $849 bill for the package, and on the bill her name was listed down as ASSHOLE LINDEMAN. After she called the cable company and got nowhere again, she decided to take legal action against the company, but she had died before the case started.

Tim saw that none of the cable company's charges had been refunded to Amber's credit card. If Amber, the great debater and lawyer, wasn't able to make any headway, how the hell would he succeed? The answer was clear: he wouldn't be able to. So he decided to forget about it and simply call up the cable company to cancel his newly reinstated plan. He'd get a streaming service for movies and find a different provider for Internet.

Tim called the cable provider and had to wait on hold for forty minutes until he reached a representative in general customer service. Tim was annoyed before he even spoke to someone, but he figured he'd be able to easily cancel his plan now that he had someone on the line. In the worst case scenario he'd have to pay a small cancellation fee, he guessed.

The rep made her scripted-welcoming line upon receiving the call—the same line she'd say a hundred times a day until she wanted to blow her brains out—and asked how she could help him today.

"I'd like to cancel my cable and Internet plan," Tim said in a friendly manner despite being peeved for having been on hold for so long.

The rep replied in a lifeless tone that was supposed to pass for something like sympathy. "Oh, I'm sorry to hear that. May I ask why you'd like to cancel, sir?"

Amber and Raymond had been the members of the family that utilized the plan, but Tim didn't want to talk about their deaths. "I won't be using the service anymore."

"You mean you won't be using both cable and Internet anymore?"

"Yes, that's correct."

"I might be able to understand not using cable, but no one can live nowadays without an Internet connection, sir."

"Don't worry about me. I'll be just fine. I just want to cancel everything with your company."

"Can you tell me why you don't enjoy our service enough to go without Internet?"

"Having to talk to you about what I want in life is one big reason why I don't like your company's service."

"But I'm trying to help you, sir."

"Okay. You can help me by cancelling my cable and Internet plans."

"But would that really help you? I don't think it would. Please explain to me how having no cable or Internet would help you?"

"Because that's what I want. I'm going to get rid of my TV and live like a monk in an empty room, spending my time reciting mantras and praying to help out dysfunctional people like yourself in our dystopian world."

"I'm sorry that's how you feel, sir. Let me bring up your account details. … I see here that your cable plan got renewed a month ago."

"That sounds accurate. I thought the plan was going to end and not be automatically reinstated, so I didn't call you guys up."

"Well, the problem is that it's been a month since it renewed. If you had cancelled within the first two weeks of it being renewed, we would've been able to do something for you, but now it's past its cancellation point."

"I haven't even turned on my TV in a month. I haven't used it at all."

"Whether you use it or not, it's your plan that you've agreed to pay."

"Can I pay some kind of cancellation fee and get it cancelled?"

"I'm afraid that the cancellation fee would cost more than the yearly plan that you have already been renewed for, so you might as well keep enjoying all those great shows that you've been watching and don't worry about it."

"I said I haven't been watching any TV for a month. I don't watch TV."

"Come on, everyone watches TV. No one can live without watching the hit shows: *Cruel Kings You Like*, *Humanizing Cops*, *Detective I'm-Gonna-Getcha*, *Fake History*, *Listen to People Sing*, *Renovating Houses for No Reason*—all great shows."

"I haven't heard of most of those. I don't watch TV. My wife and step-son used to watch the TV."

"Well don't you think they're going to be mad at you if you cut off their TV?"

Tim realized he had to go where he didn't want to. "They're dead, okay. The police suspect they got murdered by that serial killer that's still at large: Ken Karver. So I'd say they won't be mad about missing out on TV."

The rep paused for an awkward amount of time before replying. "Oh, I'm sorry, sir. I don't have a script response for a murdered family member, so I'm not sure what to say."

"That's fine, you can just cancel my cable and Internet plans."

"… I'm going to transfer you to the billing department. Hopefully they can assist you better."

"Okay. Thank you."

Tim waited on hold for thirty minutes before a rep in the billing department answered. "You've reached billing. This is Adam, how can I help you?"

"I'd like to cancel my cable and Internet plans, please."

"Let me bring up your account details and see what we're working with. … Looks like your cable plan renewed a month ago and is past the cancellation date, sir."

"I know, that's what I already spoke to a representative in the customer service department about. After I told her that all my family members that used that cable plan got murdered, she transferred me to your department so you could assist me in cancelling my plans."

"You're saying that your wife is dead, sir?"

"Yes, that's correct."

"The account is under the name Amber Lindeman, so only Amber Lindeman can cancel the account."

"Are you deaf? I just told you she's dead. How can she cancel the plan if she's dead?"

"Look, sir. We get all kinds of excuses around here, so I can't take your word for it. You have to give our company some proof. I suggest that you dig up your wife's corpse and take a picture of it so you can send it to us. Make sure you include your face in your selfie with your dead wife so we know it's your dead wife and not just any dead wife. Once we receive the photo of your smiling face with your wife's corpse, we can proceed."

"Are you serious? Why would I be smiling in that picture?"

"That's none of my business, sir. You don't need to smile. Your face being in the selfie will be adequate, smiling or not. So purchase a shovel if you don't have one and get to digging up your wife."

"I'm not going to dig up my wife's body for any reason, especially not for some fucking cable provider."

"Please refrain from swearing, sir. I'm only trying to help you."

"Like hell you're trying to help—telling me to dig up my wife's corpse. I simply want to cancel my plans. That's all I want to do—cancel my plans with your company."

"I'm sorry to hear that, sir. The reason they're called plans is because it's something that has been thought about and decided upon. Once a plan is in effect, you simply can't stop what you've already planned to do. You have to see your plans through like a responsible adult."

"Is this really the billing department, because it sounds like the bonehead department? A responsible person doesn't sit around all day on a couch watching TV, nor do they dig up their wife's corpse for a selfie."

"Our policy states that only the person who the account is under can cancel any plans that have been set into motion with our company."

"Eat a bowl of dicks!" Tim hung up the phone.

He was sweating and shaking. It took him thirty minutes to calm down.

He figured he had talked to two incompetent reps and would call tomorrow and surely reach someone who could do something for him, or someone who would at least not advise him to dig up his wife's corpse for a smiling selfie.

Tim called the cable provider the next day and waited on the line, listening to Muzak that was periodically interrupted by a recorded message that told him to please continue to hold and that his call was important to them. *Yeah, right. My call is so important. If it's so important, why do I need to wait an hour before reaching some underpaid, clueless clown that will do nothing for me but validate my fears that I waited on hold for an hour for no reason.*

A rep in general customer service finally answered Tim's call after fifty minutes and lifelessly rattled off their scripted opening line.

Tim took the phone off speaker mode and responded amicably, hoping it would persuade the vulture on the other end of the phone to not pick his bones clean. "Hello, Matt. I hope you're doing well today. I am calling to cancel my cable and Internet plans with your fine company."

"I'm sorry to hear that. May I ask why you want to do that, sir?"

Tim really didn't want to relive the same cancellation foreplay that he had to endure yesterday. He felt a surge of emotions that tempted him to throw his phone down and shatter it into a million pieces on his hardwood floor. He suppressed the temptation and replied, "My wife and step-son were the ones that utilized it, and sadly, they died two months ago."

"I'm so sorry to hear that, sir. Let me bring up your account information. … I see that both plans are under the name Amber Lindeman. Is … was that your wife?"

"Yes, that's correct."

"Well … unfortunately, sir, only the person who opened the plan can cancel the plan."

Tim threw his head back, thinking here we go again, but he kept his composure and didn't start shouting, rather, he countered with a facetious reply. "Please give me the phone number to a medium that can summon my wife's spirit, or the phone number of a necromancer that can raise my wife's deceased body from her grave so that we may proceed with this matter."

"I don't have such phone numbers, sir." Then after a pause, and maybe realizing that Tim was being sarcastic, he continued. "Perhaps the technical support department can assist you better. I'll go ahead and transfer you right now, sir."

"If you think they can assist me better, okay," Tim said, noticing that the rep had transferred him before he had completed his sentence.

Tim put his phone back on speaker mode, not knowing how long he'd be on hold for this time. It could be ten seconds. It could be three hours.

How can technical support assist me better? Is raising my dead wife's body a technical issue that they could solve? Tim imagined the cable provider technicians driving their white van into the cemetery and rolling up to his wife's grave like it was a typical service trip. They'd dig her up and attach various cables to different parts of her body and resuscitate her corpse with electroshock therapy. Then they'd hand her a $1,913 bill for equipment fees and installation assistance before driving away to their next target.

After Amber's corpse managed to make it back home, she'd call up the cable company to cancel her plans and they'd tell her something like, "I'm sorry, ma'am, if you've been dead for more than two weeks before rising from your grave, our company considers you a different person than the person who died, the person that the account is under, and only that person can cancel your cable and Internet plans. But I tell you what… we can upgrade your package to a premium service where you can access the informative channel that will help you construct a time machine so that you may go back in time to before your death and cancel your cable." After Amber agreed, watched the informative channel and constructed a time machine, went back in time and called the cable provider from the past, they'd reply, "I'm sorry, ma'am. One of our technicians used our company's time portal to go back in time to add a note on your account, stating that an invalid Amber Lindeman will be time traveling in order to cancel her cable plan." After Amber's walking-dead, time-traveling corpse shouted that she was told by a rep that she could cancel her cable plan if she went back in time, they'd say, "Do you have a recording of the conversation with the rep you spoke to?" Amber would tell them yes, but the recording is still in the future. So they'd say, "I'm sorry, ma'am. We can't confirm what the rep said without a recording."

Then Amber's walking corpse would take them to court, but she'd lose her first case when her jawbone fell to the floor during her opening speech and wasn't able to be reattached, denying her further speech. The shock of losing her first case would cause Amber's corpse to fall to the floor, returning to its nonliving state, or dead-again-undead state, or whatever those geeks who were fascinated by zombies and vampires called it, Tim thought.

A technical support rep answered after a ten-minute wait. "This is Mike in technical support. How can I assist you?"

"I was transferred here from customer service because a rep there said your department might better assist me in cancelling the cable plan that is under the name of my dead wife."

"That definitely doesn't sound like a matter for our department. There's nothing that technical support can help you with for that issue. Let me transfer—"

"Wait. Why was I transferred to your department if you can't do anything to solve this problem?"

"Well, sir, I'll tell you what ... I can assist you in upgrading your plan to a platinum service so you won't miss out on all the great shows on the myriad of platforms currently available for your TV: *Rich Entitled Kids Doing Various Drugs*, *Your Money or Your Life*, *Look at This Instead of That*, *Eat Till You Drop*, *Moderna Design Presents the Latest in Kitchen Luxury Appliances*—"

"Please stop. The technical support department shouldn't be trying to sell anything; it's not the sales department."

"Well, sir, our company doesn't have an actual sales department because every department is a sales department. Hell, I don't even know how to do anything technical. My paycheck comes from sales. I'll be honest with you. When I have to drive out to service a technical problem, I tinker around and make it look like I'm doing something and drive away before the customer can check to see if the problem is fixed or ask me any technical questions. I only get paid if I make sales, so please don't let my paycheck be a big fat zero again next week."

"But you're a technician, how did you get your job?"

"I went to a technical college and was trained to handle some technical matters, but after four years of working hard to produce sales in the technical support department, I forgot all my technical training."

"That's ridiculous … but I thank you for your candor. Please transfer me to a department that can assist me. And please inform them about the call so I don't need to talk to another stranger on the phone about my dead wife."

"Will do, sir. I have noted your account and am transferring you to the billing department now."

Tim waited on hold for thirty-five minutes before a rep in the billing department answered. "This is Amy in billing. How can I assist you today?"

"Can you check the note on my account? A rep in technical support said he'd tell you what my call was regarding so I didn't have to repeat myself."

"Sure, let me take a look. … Sir?"

"Yes."

"I see two notes added to your account today. I'm not sure which one you're talking about, so I'll read them both to you and you can tell me which one I should use to help you."

"Uh … okay."

"First note: Customer wanted necromancer's phone number so he could raise his wife's corpse from the grave. He's tired of having sex with her decaying, immobile body and wishes for her to have movement and some sort of flexibility. Apparently his current dead wife isn't sexy enough to get him off. Offered upgrade, but got denied. Transferred to tech support. Second note: Gave customer much technical advice on his unit and how to use it properly. Advised that he should keep his unit away from his wife's corpse. Offered upgrade, was denied. Transferred to billing."

"Those assholes. What kind of customer ser—by the way, the first rep didn't offer me an upgrade like he noted."

The rep gasped over the phone. "He didn't? Failing to offer an upgrade is a severe violation of our company's procedures. He'll be fired for sure, I can assure you that, sir. You can feel at ease knowing that he'll be terminated today."

"The second rep—the technician—told me that he drives out to people's houses and pretends to fix things and drives away."

"But did he actually offer an upgrade like his note says?"

"Yes, he did, but—"

"Okay, he's fine then. Thanks for relaying that info, Mr. Lindeman. Now, Mr. Lindeman, I was wondering if I could entice you to upgrade your current package to a more premium package so that our company can better service your needs."

"You're kidding, right?"

"No, sir, our premium packages are pretty stellar. Customers are always raving about how their lives changed after the upgrade."

Tim seethed. "I've made it clear that I don't want an upgrade. I want to cancel my account with your satanic company and return to my life."

"I'm sorry to hear that, sir. Unfortunately my department deals with billing matters and can't cancel accounts. I'll transfer you to the general customer service department for that matter."

Tim's eyes bulged in anger. "No! Don't transfer me! I've already talked to that department. Please—" He stopped talking when the hold Muzak starting playing, notifying him that he had already been transferred.

"Sonuvafuckingbitch! Goddammit!"

Tim almost threw his phone on the ground but restrained himself for the second time. He put the phone on speaker mode and went back to reading a book after pacing back and forth in his kitchen in anger for several minutes.

A rep picked up the phone after Tim had been on hold for two hours and thirteen minutes. "Thank you for calling Comca—"

"Stop. No scripted lines, please. Just please help me cancel my account with your company so that I can start living again."

"Uh … I'll do whatever I can to help, sir. Let me pull up your account. … Oh, wow."

"Forget about the notes on my account. They're garbage. Just please help me cancel my account that's in my dead wife's name. And please don't tell me that only the person whose name is on the account can cancel the account because that person—my wife—is dead. She was murdered."

"Oh, I'm sorry to hear that, sir."

"Yeah, she was killed two months ago. The cops think it was that serial killer."

"No, I meant I'm sorry you want to cancel business with our company."

Tim lowered the phone and wiped his forehead in agitation. He took a deep breath and returned to the phone call. "So how can I cancel my account?"

"Well, sir, since we get customers claiming many outrageous things—wives getting murdered by serial killers—we can only proceed when some kind of proof is given."

"Okay, so how can I prove to you that my wife got murdered by a serial killer?"

"It doesn't matter the cause; her being dead would be good enough—I mean her being dead would be grounds for you to cancel her account being that you're her husband. You can mail her death certificate to our headquarters so that we can be sure that she's in fact dead and then we can cancel your account—with a cancellation fee of course. By the way, the cancellation fee would cost more than the year of service that you've already paid for. So I suggest not cancelling and keep enjoying those great shows on TV: *Remodeling Houses While the Homeless Die on the Streets*, *Fake History*, *All Aliens are Evil*, *Doctors Talking About Their Lives While Killing Patients, Pouring Green Slime on Random Children*—"

"Stop! Stop! I don't watch any of those shows. I don't watch TV. And if you try to upgrade me, I swear to God, I'll ..."

"I'm sorry, sir. If I don't try to sell something, I'll get fired." Then he quickly rattled off, "Would you like to upgrade to a more premium package?"

"You little shit. You already know my answer to that."

"I'm sorry to hear that, sir. Perhaps I can transfer you to the billing department so you may be serviced better."

"Don't you dare transfer me again. I've already been transferred to every department and have been put on hold for hours."

"… I'm fairly new here, sir. But I think I know what you're going through. I've heard other employees here talking about it. Sounds like you're caught in what employees here are calling The Circle Jerk."

"The Circle Jerk?"

"Yes, until you accept that you'll never get your problem fixed—whatever it is—you'll be endlessly transferred from department to department until our call center closes. Sometimes you'll be left on hold even after everyone at the call center has left for the day. Until you get exhausted with our run-around service and give up all hope, you'll be stuck in The Circle Jerk. Right now, this very minute, you're in The Circle Jerk, sir. Do you wish to continue circling or are you going to hang up your phone and go watch TV?"

Before Tim could respond, the phone call was taken over by somebody else. "This is supervisor Tom. I want to let you know that there is no such thing as The Circle Jerk, Mr. Lindeman, and the rep that you were just talking to has just been fired for lying to you. You can sleep peacefully knowing that he's terminated and that there is no such thing as The Circle Jerk at our company."

"I uh …" Tim actually felt bad for the terminated rep.

"Now, Mr. Lindeman, I've been reading your notes and I'm so sorry what you've been put through. I have a solution for you."

"Oh, thank God. I thought I had wasted my whole day listening to incompetent workers and waiting on hold."

"Get ready to count your lucky stars, Mr. Lindeman. I can't cancel your account, but I can do something better. I can upgrade you to our premium package at no additional cost. Our premium package includes a channel that is dedicated to grieving spouses with dead partners. Not just any dead partners, but those that have died specifically by the hand of serial killers. Our company is here to help you get through this rough period in your life. I know exactly what you're going through; my wife was also butchered by a serial killer. She got diced up into little pieces and the whole nine yards. The cops had to make a trip to the store to buy extra Ziploc bags just to get all her little pieces collected and accounted for. Oh yeah, it was awful, you bet. But a show called *So Your Loved One has been Dissected by a Serial Killer?* will help you through this period like it helped me."

Instead of saying anything, Tim hung up the phone. He had given up all hope and wanted to escape The Circle Jerk, so he took the advice of the terminated rep and ended the call. He accepted that he wouldn't get what he wanted and just wished to not deal with the policies and rules being thrown in his face. It was way too tiresome and wasn't getting him anywhere.

Tim couldn't help thinking that his experience with the cable company was an exaggerated comparison to how the general system of the whole world was setup. Or maybe the comparison wasn't even exaggerated at all. Everything in the world that dealt with money, which was basically everything, was intentionally bogged down with pages upon pages of detailed confusing rules and policies so that no one outside the current powerful circle could get a foothold in their controlling system. Everyone in the powerful circle did whatever they wanted and ignored the rules they created because they were either comprised of the very people in power that would look the other way when they broke the rules, or they simply threw money at the people outside the circle to look the other way or do their bidding.

Everybody outside the powerful circle would get exhausted and become hopeless when trying to deal with the detailed policies and procedures and end up giving up. The few motivated people that pushed forward, regardless of the difficulties, found themselves facing legal prosecution or something of the sort that would make sure they became aware of their place in the world. Their place was not in The Circle. The world was full of two different types of people: a few powerful people that ran everything, and a lot of dejected, exhausted, hopeless people that did whatever the powerful people wanted so they could be thrown some of the leftover scraps periodically.

The powerful people were like the fish-tank owners. They'd periodically throw bits of food in the tank and watch the fish fight over it. When the fish weren't fighting for food thrown to them, they'd take bites out of each other and even kill each other because they didn't like certain types of fish that were different from them—different species and colored scales; or because the fish had simply wandered into their territory of the tank—like imaginary lines on the Earth separating countries; or the fish was the same type of fish as its opposition and it was just in its nature to be the most powerful fish in the tank.

The hand that would periodically feed the fish, provide the tank with items, add fish to the tank, remove the dead fish, clean the tank, et cetera, was akin to a nation with a big government, or even a worldwide Deep State that had its tentacles in every nations' pies. When the big hand didn't provide, anarchy soon took over the dependent fish in the tank.

Now, if the fish hadn't been stuck in the tank, they'd be happily providing for themselves in oceans or lakes. The fish would be under a few natural laws of the oceans and lakes, sure, but they'd be able to go wherever they wanted and do whatever they wanted as independent fish with freedom. After the cable company phone call, Tim felt like he was one of the fish in the tank.

Tim shook his head and couldn't believe the dark analogy he had mentally entertained. He figured he was really down in the dumps to think such dystopian thoughts. He told himself that it wasn't true and these thoughts were simply arising because he was very depressed at the moment.

After sulking on the couch for a few minutes, he realized that he had to cancel his wife's credit cards. He'd have to bite the bullet for the reinstated cable plan instead of getting a refund, but after he cancelled the credit card that was on file at the cable provider, they couldn't bill him for anymore plans, equipment fees, installation help, or whatever bullshit charges they tacked onto his bill. They could keep sending Tim bills in the mail, which he'd ignore, but they wouldn't be able to automatically deduct money from a credit card anymore.

He called up the credit card company. After he gave them three pieces of information—told them Amber was dead, gave them Amber's social security number, and gave them her mother's maiden name—they cancelled the card.

Tim may not have gotten a refund from the cable company, nor had he been able to cancel his cable and Internet plans after hours of holding and conversing with robotic halfwits, but the cable company wouldn't be able to charge him anything else now that the credit card on file was cancelled, which took him less than three minutes to do. Problem solved.

He hoped one of NASA's defunct satellites would enter a decaying orbit, somehow not burn up in the atmosphere, and crash into the call center that had just kept him prisoner on the phone for several hours. He imagined all those lunatics at the call center spouting off scripted phrases and empty-headed impromptu dialog right before being incinerated in an exploding fiery ball.

If Hitler had indeed escaped to South America after WWII instead of committing suicide in a bunker (and he had), he surely must have been the true architect behind the umbrella conglomerate that secretly owned every cable provider in America. It was Hitler's way at getting back at America. It was his top priority before kicking the bucket; that and making deals to get his daughter on the throne in Germany when she came of age. Hitler may have lost WWII, but he had won in the long run. *You are a genius Hitler. You are a genius. You sonuvabitch.*

Chapter 19

Ken Karver casually walked away from the police car that contained a fresh cop's corpse. The policeman's throat had been slit and blood had flowed downward—and was still trickling down—soaking the officer's uniform and car seat. He sat lifeless in his vehicle, blank eyes directed toward his windshield, the occasional crackling sounds of dispatch being heard over the two-way radio.

The occupation of those that "protect and serve" made up the highest amount of people on Karver's karma-balancing list. There were some other occupations that topped the list, but cops held the number one spot. They were the grunts that did the bidding of those higher in power. Most of those higher-powered people had blood contracts with the Masters, so they never appeared on Karver's list no matter what karma they accrued.

Karver hadn't even intended on sacrificing Officer Vasquez today; it was merely a nice coincidence that Karver ran into him on his way to his next intended target. More loosh for the vials. Unfortunately cops tended to produce the least amount of loosh. The experiences their job imparted on them generated apathy toward mortality and nurtured violence, so their psyche typically wasn't considerably traumatized when the same type of experiences had been turned around and directed on them. Somewhere deep in their subconscious they knew they had it coming and weren't surprised when retribution arrived.

No one in the quiet suburb Karver was walking through had noticed him dispatch the cop. Almost every house he'd passed had the sign of a security company staked in their front yard, silently conveying to every passerby to stay the fuck off their property.

The sight of the signs satisfied Karver, kindling his smirk and stimulating a wider grin. Humans in America had been so successfully separated and turned against each other in the name of divide and control that they willingly locked themselves in their indebted houses or apartments in fear of their neighbors. A far cry from the days of old when families helped their neighbors and cherished the camaraderie of their communities. Nowadays, if you visited your neighbor for a cup of sugar—not that humans did that anymore—you might be welcomed by a gun and a verbal warning telling you to get off their land.

Not that they actually owned the land they resided on; the government owned all the land. A person couldn't really own land, but they could happily pay property tax to the State their entire life and tell other people they owned it. Did the State come out and manage your land—mow the lawn, clear fallen trees, etc.—for receiving property tax? No. The State would never set foot on your land. The State wouldn't even know it existed if it wasn't listed on some computer along with an amount of money that they perpetually received for it.

Karver wondered if humans now understand why the Native Americans were baffled by the idea of ownership of land. How can you own something that's in fact a part of another living being? Gaia, the spirit of Earth, would laugh if you told her that the State owned her. The situation would be akin to a group of people coming along one day and deciding they would divvy up your body into parts. They'd tell you not to worry; you could perpetually pay them so you could continue to use your own arms, legs, mouth, and such. What thoughtful people. How nice of them.

Humans should gladly pay their property taxes for the land their indebted houses sit upon so they can rest assured it won't be confiscated while they spent most of their lives away from it, slaving away in some office, store, or factory for their masters.

That's right, humans should take pride in knowing they're free. They should continue paying property taxes and all the other countless taxes. Taxes that have funded the creation of underground bases, underwater bases, space bases, fleets of spacecrafts, advanced technology—all of which humans had no idea existed and were never meant to use. The role of a human was to continue to slave away in their fabricated reality, unknowingly creating a better world for the Masters. Taxes also paid for countless projects that kept humans enslaved. Meaning, humans slaved away all day for wages so they could lose their money to taxes that paid for projects that were aimed at keeping humans even more enslaved than they currently were. Humans were paying their masters to enslave them.

Even when money wasn't being forced from humans in the way of taxes, they were still freely giving their extra money to the Masters by way of charities, because virtually all charity endeavors were fake fronts for money to be added to a slush fund for dark projects.

If a rare freethinking human attempted to convince a hypnotized human that they didn't need to pay taxes for the world to function, the brainwashed human would readily prattle off all the empty rebuttals they were conditioned to counter with to silence the freethinking human speaking to them. The brainwashed humans were the code that kept the Masters' program running smoothly and the freethinking humans were the viruses in the program that needed to be removed, quarantined, and deleted.

Ruling over humans was all too easy. *Keep it up, humans. Keep paying your taxes and being good slaves,* Karver thought as he meandered through the suburb, viewing the controlled surface population from behind his ever-present smile.

Humans weren't dumb enough to not be aware that the system they lived in was broken. They just had no idea that it was intentionally created broken for a reason: control. Humans constantly tried to fix their broken system by approaching each compartmentalized section separately, not knowing that each section was weaved together in a matrix that kept the others stable, in a checks and balances type of way, but much more efficient. A human could take initiative and argue about an issue their whole life, barking in people's faces till their face turned blue, thinking they were making a difference in the world. None of the issues could be fixed by tackling each one separately, because it was only a matter of time before the great design's checks and balances would revert the solved issue back to its intended broken state, erasing the person's lifelong hard work overnight.

None of the pieces of the puzzle were really important by themselves—money, different forms of money, taxes, debt, slavery, news, media, conditioning, brainwashing, politicians, secret societies, political parties, political issues, religions, programming, all the isms, et cetera. They were only important collectively to uphold one single thing: control.

Karver passed a stenciled mailbox that read GRANDMA BAKER. "You're not trying to hide at all, are you, Grandma Baker? No, your goal is to lure them in like a grandma version of a Venus flytrap."

Karver strolled up to the front door and rapped on it. He waited on the porch, sporting a cheap suit and holding a black briefcase. He lifted his free hand to slick back his hair and press down his black tie against his white oxford shirt.

The door opened and left a screen door between Grandma Baker and Karver. Mrs. Baker cheerily greeted her guest, "Well, hello there. To whom do I owe the pleasure?"

Karver's name had made the rounds on the media, so he used a new alias. "Bushy Clinton, ma'am. And may I say I'm pleased to stand before you on this fine day. I noticed your mailbox on my way to your door—Grandma Baker is it?"

"In the flesh. What can I do for you today, Mr. Clinton?"

"Please, call me Bushy. I'm an insurance agent. I specialize in life insurance but I'll insure anything. If you've got a hip replacement, I can insure it. Facial hair, fingers, nose—I can insure it. I can even insure against damages caused by an alien abduction."

Mrs. Baker opened her screen door. "My my, I guess you can insure anything nowadays."

"Sure can, ma'am. If you've got the money, you can insure anything. Just give us the cash and hope you never get it back—I mean, hope that your worst fears don't come to fruition. Instead of letting your fears control you, throw money our way and we'll protect you … if it falls under our guidelines of course."

Grandma Baker smiled at Karver's remark. "Well, it's not every day that I get to spend time with a well-dressed man like yourself. Please come on in and we'll converse over some tea."

She stepped aside so Karver could enter her cozy house. She showed him to the living room, which had been converted into a tea room, Karver noticed. No walls separated the tea room from her small kitchen, and the tea room had a view of the backyard where a collection of plants and flowers thrived, giving a lush green backdrop to the tea room and kitchen.

Karver sat down in one of the wooden chairs at a thin wooden table that supported a few knickknacks. Also on the table sat knitting needles within a half-finished scarf. "Looks like you have a knitting hobby."

While preparing the tea—boiling water, selecting tea bags from her collection—Grandma Baker replied to Karver without turning around. "It's not just a hobby, I've made a career out of it. I've published numerous books on how to knit your own clothing, a whole series called *Knitting with Grandma Baker*. But I haven't written a book in a while because I've moved on to a new hobby."

"Oh yeah, and what's the new hobby?"

Upon hearing the question, the inside of Grandma Baker's head became a theater where a movie reel started producing images against her skull that displayed stories for the audience. The first being when she discovered her new hobby. She was knitting a sweater and enjoying the calm atmosphere of her living room when her chubby, beer-drinking, sports-watching husband woke from a nap on the couch screaming, "Touchdown!" At the moment her serenity had been broken, she unconsciously reacted by swinging around and plunging a knitting needle into her husband's throat. While blood squirted from his throat and his shocked face produced gurgling sounds, she lifted from her chair and drove the other knitting needle into his ballooned stomach over and over again. Blood and beer gushed out of his belly like a punctured fish tank. As her husband gurgled and deflated, she stared down at him with a beaming smile. She had found her new hobby: annihilating assholes. She had cut up her husband into nice little pieces and used him as fertilizer for her backyard garden. Never again did her cozy house get raped by blaring sounds of sports emanating from a television set. The TV went into the garbage and the living room was converted into a tea room. The movie reel came to an end and flapped a couple times before a fresh reel was fixed onto the projector and a new story came to life:

Weeks later a tree service man showed up at her door and asked if she wanted her trees removed for a fair price. She invited him in for some tea. While he was explaining how he'd remove her trees if she employed him, she raised two clenched hands and plunged her knitting needles into both of his eyes simultaneously. Into nice little pieces he went and provided excellent fertilizer for her trees. She could sense her trees smiling down on her while she fed their roots with fertilizer. Fertilizer that once had the intention of killing those same trees.

Since then she'd happily welcomed in any snake-oil-peddling vermin that slithered to her doorstep. And there had been quite a few, as snakes prayed on the elderly and their senility.

The projector was turned off and darkness covered the theater in Grandma Baker's head as her focus switched over to the next snake-oil peddler in her tea room: Bushy Clinton.

"My new hobby is gardening. I'm always in need of fresh fertilizer for my lovelies in the backyard. Have a look for yourself," she said while tilting her head toward the backyard and pouring hot water into two mugs. "Aren't they lovely?"

Karver gazed out the large window at the greenery. "They sure are. Would you like to insure your garden?"

"I didn't know you could do that."

"Oh, sure. Anything is insurable. All you need to do is give us an ongoing good chunk of your income and hope that you never need to bring a claim forward, which allows us to keep your money forever. Of course, if you do try to bring a claim forward, we'll fight you tooth and nail to make sure it's a legit claim. If we didn't do that, people would take advantage of us poor little insurance companies. I'm sure you understand. Anyway, yeah, you can insure anything these days. That horrible tacky shirt you're wearing—insurable. All the ridiculous grandma knickknacks you got scattered about your house—insurable. Your decrepit, sagging face—insurable. Well, at your age it would cost a pretty penny, but it's still doable. Yup, we'll allow you to give us your money for any reason nowadays, and you can rest assured you'll never get it back, which is a good thing because getting it back would mean that you've put a claim forward because something you cherished got damaged, destroyed, or whatever."

Grandma Baker approached the table wearing a frown and holding two tea mugs. After placing the mugs on the table and taking a seat opposite Karver, she glanced outside at her garden and turned back to Karver with a smile on her face. "Well, I don't appreciate some of those remarks, Bushy, but I'm going to overlook your crudeness because I'm keen on purchasing some insurance for my garden. I'm sure your services will ensure my garden's safety, and even help it grow. But I'm interested on what some of the clauses would be in the fine print: insurance claim void if soil in garden is walked on too often, or acts of Mother Nature are not covered."

Karver stared down at the mug of tea placed before him, wondering if it contained cyanide or rat poisoning. He looked at Mrs. Baker and winked. "You're already covering your bases. I've got to hand it to you, you're still spry at your age."

Mrs. Baker took a sip of her tea and stared at Karver's tea mug instead of keeping the conversation going.

Karver's polite smile melted from his face and morphed into a dreadful scowl. "Now tell me, Grandma Bullshit, what did you put in my tea?"

Grandma Baker's fake smile also melted from her face and she lunged across the table for her knitting needles while saying, "Don't look a gift horse in the mouth." She snatched up the needles and clutched them tightly in her hands as she started lifting off her chair to get closer to Karver.

But before she made it off her chair, something became intimately acquainted with her face. After Karver quickly dumped the tea aside onto the floor, he flung the empty mug toward her shriveled head. The mug forcefully collided with her forehead and knocked her out cold. The knitting needles fell from her hands and clinked on the tiled floor as she slumped in her chair.

Grandma Baker screamed when she came to and saw her knitting needles pounded through her hands and hammered into the table, effectively stapling her hands to the table. She tried wiggling in her chair but barely moved an inch due to the rope that tied her torso and legs to the chair. She looked up at Karver, who was going through her pantry in the kitchen and shaking his head.

Karver noticed she had awoken. "I can see by looking at your food and drinks that you think you're eating and drinking healthily." Karver laughed. "Good thing I visited your house today, because you probably would've dropped dead tomorrow from shoveling all this poison in your body for who knows how many decades. You definitely are a fighter, that's for sure. I would've had you pegged for cancer years ago."

Grandma Baker snarled at Karver, "Get stuffed with hay! My food is healthy. Drinks too, except for the cyanide tea you didn't drink. A civilized guest would've politely drunk it and done the customary convulsing spasms on the floor before biting the dust."

Karver chuckled. "The funny thing is, there was poison in your tea too. There has been two different kinds of poison in every single one of your mugs of tea throughout the years. They won't kill you outright like cyanide would, but in a way they'll do something worse: they'll torture you for years instead of killing you. They'll strip you of your power—power I'm sure you never knew you had thanks to our programming. They'll allow you to live so you can be a slave for your masters. Let's start with the first poison: fluoride."

Again, Grandma Baker attempted to shake herself free of the rope tied around her but got nowhere. She came to the conclusion that she wasn't going anywhere till this lunatic untied her or killed her. "Get your facts straight, you lunatic. Fluoride is added to our drinking water because it fights cavities. It occurs naturally in nature."

Karver laughed and clapped his hands mockingly. "Good response. That's exactly what we tell you to think. But I'm going to let you in on a little secret, grandma. Fluoride doesn't do a thing to protect your teeth. Sure, fluoride can be found in nature, but so can toxic mushrooms that will kill you. We didn't even need to show people like you the falsified research that claims fluoride fights cavities. You just took your government's word for it because your government is looking out for you and your teeth."

Karver laughed. "Fluoride is a highly toxic substance. Even our controlled FDA requires companies to include a warning label on products that contain fluoride, like toothpaste. We put the warning on your toothpaste, and other products, to let you know you're putting poison in or on your body and you ignore it. Why do you think fluoride is used in pesticides and rodenticides to kill insects and rats? Workers at public water systems have to use hazmat suits when handling fluoride and dumping it into the water supply. A whole list of health problems are associated with fluoride: cancer, arthritis, thyroid disease, diabetes, fertility issues, cardiovascular disease, kidney disease, calcification of the pineal gland, bone diseases, lowering of IQ, and the list goes on and on because it's very toxic. Countless things can go wrong in one's body when they continue to ingest small amounts of poison every day. It doesn't take a genius to come to that conclusion.

"We even gave cities the right to vote whether they wanted their water supply poisoned with fluoride or not, and most cities voted to be poisoned based on one little lie we gave them: fluoride fights cavities." Karver laughed. "We weren't surprised, though, humans are stupid. That's not my opinion, it's a fact. Just look around you. They want everything spoon fed to them, so why not spoon feed them poison to keep them dumbed down and living like good slaves. You know where we first started using fluoride in drinking water: the concentration camps during WWII. Fluoride kept them weak and pacified. Every city that has fluoride in their water is like a concentration camp. There are many concentration camps in America."

Mrs. Baker didn't believe a word he was saying. She just kept scowling at him while he ranted. "That's a bunch of baloney. And you keep saying 'we.' Who is 'we?' Is there a warehouse somewhere full of lunatics like you, spreading peanut butter all over their bodies and bouncing off the walls?"

"I can't tell you who 'we' are, but you can use the word 'Masters.' As in your masters."

"I don't have any masters—I'm not a slave. I'm my own master."

Karver grinned. "Of course you are."

Grandma Baker looked over at a bottle of water on the table. "Can you pause your ranting and pour some of that water in my mouth? I'm parched."

"Sure, gladly. It contains fluoride too."

Mrs. Baker frowned. "I don't believe fluoride is bad."

"Whether it contains fluoride or not, it's still unhealthy because it's bottled in plastic that is leaching poison into the water."

"What? I'm sure the company uses BPA free plastic after that study was conducted."

"Correct, they use BPA free plastic, but BPA alternatives have been proven by scientists—not scientists that are working for the Masters, but viruses in the program—to be just as bad or even worse. It's all part of the great design. Humans find out one thing is bad for them—BPA plastic—so the Masters replace it with alternatives that are equally as bad or worse and present them to the public as safe with nice little stickers that read BPA FREE, and the ignorant humans believe it and continue to drink up the poison." Karver laughed.

"Yeah, right. Not that I believe your ranting, but you said I was drinking two poisons in my tea. What's the second one, Mr. Know-it-all?"

"Your tea itself. Every single brand you have in your tea drawer, both bagged and loose tea, is swimming with toxins, pesticides, GMOs, and artificial ingredients. You think they're healthy, but you're poisoning yourself every day when you sit down to drink it with a foolish smile on your face."

Mrs. Baker shook her head. "GMOs are safe and their aim is to tackle starvation throughout the planet by providing a cheaper method to produce food."

Karver's sardonic smile widened. "Thank you for validating how effective our brainwashing methods are. And please keep assuring the starving kids in third-world countries around the world that they'll be saved by the expansion of GMO production." Karver clapped his hands a few times. "Marvelous, just marvelous. But I hate to break it to you, grandma, GMOs' rap sheet is similar to fluoride's."

"Well, anyway, my bread is non-GMO. So there."

"Yes, I saw that, but it's not organic, which means you're still eating weaponized wheat and other glyphosate-soaked grains. Non-GMO is one gold star, but it takes at least two gold stars to make food not poisonous nowadays. Notice how I said not poisonous instead of healthy? When a few knowledgeable humans—we call them viruses in the program—find out they're being poisoned, they lobby and get gold stars for products. Most of these viruses think they're being poisoned by careless companies trying to make an extra buck and bypassing quality laws instead of finding out they're being deliberately poisoned. We fight the passing of these gold-star bills they bring forward, but sometimes they pass anyway. So we're always thinking of new ways to keep poisoning the population. Oh, high-fructose corn syrup has been outed? No problem. Hello GMOs. GMOs have been outed? No problem. Hello glyphosate and other harmful pesticides. Humans have been eating grains for years, but now all of a sudden some of them are becoming 'gluten intolerant.' Humans who are 'gluten intolerant' are actually just more sensitive to the glyphosate that's poisoning their grains. Everyone is 'glyphosate intolerant,' just like everyone is 'cyanide intolerant.' It's just that some people feel worse after eating glyphosate because they're healthy and more in touch with their bodies—they're not 'gluten intolerant.' Jesus, Buddha, Krishna, and the other enlightened beings that incarnated on Earth were in touch with their bodies and you never heard them complaining about being gluten intolerant. They didn't give any speeches to their followers about being gluten intolerant. Not a single Greek or Roman complained about being gluten intolerant." Karver scratched his chin. "Hmm, I wonder why that is?"

"If you peanut-butter-lathering lunatics are so powerful, why don't you just force laws on the public so you don't have to deal with the people who try to fight you into labeling food, poisoning water, or whatever crimes against humanity you're supposedly doing?"

"That's the first intelligent thing you've asked, or said. I'll tell you why. The great design that's in effect in America is different from our great designs in the past. America is running the latest program, the best program. It's a program that takes into account all the past data collected from Earth's history to make a program that controls the population in the best possible way. It took a lot more effort to create the great design's matrix for America, but once it was created, we found it much easier to maintain. A person doesn't try to obtain freedom if they think they're already free. Americans believe they're free, so they don't try to overthrow their masters. This latest design was so effective that we rolled it out to every country in the world we could, which was virtually all of them. Almost every country on Earth fell into line rather quickly and was absorbed into the updated matrix, the Masters' great design. Not only do people in this matrix think they're free, but they're programmed to verbally and physically attack anyone who speaks out against the matrix, which allowed the system to be self-controlling while the Masters dwelled behind the veil, out of sight and out of mind of the controlled-sheep population.

"However, data collected is showing an increased amount of people figuring the program out—viruses in the system are growing in numbers. We found that this solar system is moving into an area in the universe that is highly charged, and that's why more and more humans are waking up from the matrix. In order to combat this cosmic evolution, we're reverting to a hardline approach. One that is more tyrannical than any of our past designs. Soon we'll be ruling with an iron fist that will make China's rule look compassionate. We'll initiate WWIII with a false flag event or unleash a bioweapon virus global killer, then we'll impose martial law and execute those that our collected data shows are untrainable—too enlightened to be brainwashed—and program the small-remaining population to be our slaves. We let you know this by posting it on the Georgia Guidestones. Then our program will be so secure that very few viruses will emerge, and when they do, they'll easily be taken care of before they spread. It's unfortunate that our latest great design that worked so well needs to be scrapped, but we're used to changing plans and tactics to stay in control of new paradigms. When we are successful—and we will be—our New World Order will rule over the Earth and be impervious to viruses in the system."

Mrs. Baker's stomach grumbled. "I'm getting a little hungry. I could go for a couple toasted glyphosate-soaked pieces of bread. You mind popping two slices in the toaster and using a butter knife to spread butter on them? If you're going to force me to listen to your crazy rhetoric, you can at least have the decency to feed me while I sit here."

Hearing the words 'butter knife' and 'glyphosate bread' made Karver remember one of his sacrifices. "One time I killed a guy with a butter knife and his own bread. I fed him toasted glyphosate-soaked bread with butter and waited till his body processed it. Then I used the same butter knife to cut a pathway to his large intestine to gather the bread paste his body processed and spread it over some more glyphosate-soaked toast to force feed him with. I did this till the vicious cycle ended his life. By the way, we're working on a bill that'll make glyphosate mandatory for all grain production. We figure that it worked for cow's milk, so why not grains."

Grandma Baker shook her head. "More lies. What's wrong with milk? Milk is healthy and great for your bones."

"Yes, raw cow's milk is very healthy. It's been drunk for centuries the world over because of its health benefits. That's exactly why we had to poison it. Like the idiotic fluoride lie about cavities, we informed the public that raw milk contains harmful bacteria and needs to be pasteurized and homogenized to ensure people's health. After milk is pasteurized and homogenized, it's not only not healthy anymore, it's very unhealthy and has the same rap sheet as the other culprits we've talked about."

Mrs. Baker shook her head again. "Again with the lies. There's evidence that shows that unpasteurized milk contains bacteria and pathogens that could kill people. That's why it's pasteurized."

"You're not wrong there, just misinformed on how to correctly fix the problem. Milk being unpasteurized wasn't the problem—like I said, people safely drank raw milk for centuries—livestock being subjected to unsanitary and poor hygiene practices in the modern age was the reason milk started containing bacteria and pathogens. To correct this, you fix the livestock issue, the source of the problem. You don't put milk through a process that eliminates possible pathogens within the milk from killing you quickly to pasteurized and homogenized milk that slowly kills you over time instead. That's obviously not an intelligent move." Karver laughed.

"But again, thank you for illustrating how effective the great design is at keeping humans weak and brainwashed. The only reason I'm telling you all this is because I'm going to kill you anyway. I'm merely letting you know how stupid you and your species are before I do you in.

"In fact, there is absolutely nothing healthy in your house. And you thought you were eating healthily this whole time. Every food and drink item in your pantry and refrigerator is slowly killing you. General supermarkets aren't much different: over ninety-five percent of the food and drinks neatly stacked on shelves are slowly killing humans. Just like your water supply we've poisoned, we've made sure the places you go to purchase food are overflowing with poison for you to freely ingest. But we don't force you to eat poisonous food, you choose to eat it yourselves. Most of the poisons are shown right on the food or drinks' ingredient list for you to peruse through."

"Yeah, right. Like I can understand half of the words on those ingredient lists."

Karver laughed while filling a pot full of fluoride tap water and putting it on a burner to boil. He hadn't laughed so much in his life. He thought how fun it would be to inform every human how dumb they were before he sacrificed them. "It's pretty simple. If you don't understand what an ingredient is, you shouldn't be putting it in your body. Natural flavors …" Karver laughed. "We are always joking about how dumb you sheep are. It's easy to control the herd when the sheep mind is controlled. Whatever we program them to do, they do it."

"I don't like how you keep saying 'we' and 'our.' If you're going to kill me anyway, why don't you tell me who 'we' are?"

"Even though you're going to die soon, I can't tell you who the Masters are because it's a rule. I can only tell you that you're a slave and that a group, whom I'm calling the 'Masters,' owns you, whether you know it or not. I can't tell you who they are because in the unlikely scenario—but still probable scenario—you visit a hypnotherapist that practices past life regression in your next incarnation and brings forth our present conversation. Not that humans would believe you, but the Masters are clear on the rule to never say who they are because you can't revolt against your masters when you don't know who your masters are, and you won't think of revolting if you don't know you're a slave in the first place."

On Karver's sacrificial list, Grandma Baker was down as a possible worker for the Masters in her next incarnation. She had worked for the Masters in some of her past incarnations. It was standard procedure to inform these sacrifices about parts of the great design's matrix before sacrificing them because it had a great effect on their psyche. In the same regard, it was also procedure to sacrifice them in a very painful manner to strengthen their path to the Masters in their next incarnation, because people who were loved tended to love other people, but hurt people hurt people.

Karver grabbed the boiling fluoride water in the pot and walked toward Grandma Baker. "Now, I'm going to keep your head on the boil."

Mrs. Baker's eyes bulged with intense fright. "No, please. Don't do this."

He dumped the scalding liquid on top of her head and watched it run down her face while she screamed.

"Ahhhh! You evil bastard!"

"Oh, go boil your head," Karver said as he prepared another boiling pot and listened to Grandma Baker's pleas for ten minutes till the next boiling batch of fluoride water was ready. After it was ready, he poured it on her head in the same way and listened to her wail again.

"You evil lunatic! You won't get away with this."

Karver grinned. "Sounds like you're boiling with rage."

Karver kept up the routine, letting her agonize over her burning head and face for ten minutes till the next batch was ready to pour. After countless batches, Grandma Baker was officially boiled and her tormented spirit left her boiled body behind.

Karver collected a good amount of loosh on that one. He enjoyed his job as the main generator of fear in the program and was fortunate. His many colleagues had to make their sacrifices and killings look like suicides, accidents, or natural causes. They never got the credit in the news for their part. They killed celebrities, inventors, naturopath doctors, revolutionists, and freethinkers. They helped keep the great design free from influential viruses in the operating system and helped spread sadness when the killed person was famous. Untimely celebrity deaths were the most effective for brewing up negative emotions from the populace. People would share their sadness on social media and it would go viral as a potent negative program within the matrix.

If George Orwell hadn't naturally died of tuberculosis seven months after publishing his masterpiece, *1984*, we would've killed him for sure before he had a chance to write another groundbreaking novel that would've assisted in waking up the population from their programmed state of hypnosis. *1984* conveys too much of our plans for Earth. Luckily our matrix has done its job in dumbing down the masses and has kept humans away from perusing intellectual books like *1984*. It has been almost as effective as erasing the book from history. Let it sit on shelves collecting dust, far from being a threat to the Masters' great design. Most humans stay away from meaningful novels because they've been programmed to gravitate toward popcorn genre fiction, which isn't much more thought-provoking than low-quality TV shows. The matrix has turned most human's attention spans into that of a fish's, so most humans can't even focus long enough to read any type of novel whether it's literary or even lies within a meaningless genre.

Karver took his briefcase full of knives and whistled on his way to the door. On his way out he turned to Grandma Baker's boiled corpse and said, "It's been fun, but I got bigger fish to boil." Then he headed toward his next sacrifice.

Chapter 20

Dale had been working and living in Manhattan, New York City, for three years. He had taken up residence in a luxury condominium on the 66th floor of the 432 Park Avenue residential skyscraper, which was the tallest residential building in the world upon its completion in 2015. The skyscraper was situated on Billionaires' Row and afforded a grand view of Central Park and Manhattan. While some stood in awe of the tall geometric building, others mocked it: *New York Magazine* stated that the building's units were "fancy prisons for billionaires."

In 2021 Dale was planning on moving into a condo unit in Central Park Tower, which was set to be the newest tallest residential building in the world when it opened in late 2020, if its projected completion date didn't get postponed. His plan to move was only one example of how Dale was always striving for higher status as his money and power rapidly accumulated. Most of his wealth came from his personal investment portfolio, but still, he hadn't abandoned the want to become a partner at his firm because it provided a certain sense of status of its own.

Not too long ago he had to spend countless hours refining and improving his lucrative investment algorithm to keep money flowing into his accounts, but nowadays he was swimming in earnings received by way of inside information from numerous connections he'd acquired on his rise in the financial and business scene. He was reeling in windfall profits that he'd never seen before. His connections afforded him with gains that most people couldn't dream of acquiring in their wildest dreams, and the best part was he didn't need to use an ounce of his brainpower or intellect to make it happen. He'd reached that upper echelon tier where wealth was casually doled out to those that were on the list, on the take. It was akin to having one's own money-printing machine sitting in their den. A privately owned banking system that printed money out of thin air and accumulated debt from anyone who laid hands on it—no different than the FED.

Even though Dale had surpassed his aspirations of success, he was never satisfied with his current level of wealth or power. He always figured the next victory would provide him with an overall sense of accomplishment where he could relax in complacency and soak up his attainment. But every triumph was shortly celebrated as the next pinnacle stared down at him from above. Like the loss of enthusiasm shortly after a product was purchased, he casted aside his sense of accomplishment and hungered for the next greater and better conquest. He knew he would be fulfilled when his true aspiration had been procured. It would come soon, he could feel it. It was just around the corner.

Dale had been warned by a colleague years back that his hunger would never cease no matter how much money he accumulated, power he gained, or lofty status he obtained. He was told that the greedy train ride he'd boarded would never reach a suitable destination he'd want to disembark at. The next stop would always be imagined as grander and better. This advice had come from a colleague that ended up getting let go because he couldn't pull his weight in the numbers-accumulating game. This had proven to Dale that the colleague was a failure, and therefore his advice was bogus. It had simply been vocalized jealously. Dale knew his train ride would soon come to the destination that he desired.

Dale sat in the back of a taxicab while the driver, GATHII OBAMA, read the taxi driver certificate, fell asleep behind the wheel while they were stopped at a red traffic light. The light turned green and impatient drivers started laying down on their horns and shouting curses out their rolled-down windows. Dale reached through the opening in the plexiglass partition to shake the cabbie awake.

Upon waking and seeing the light had turned green, the cabbie blinked his eyes a couple times and stomped on the gas pedal. "Sorry, sir. I covered another driver's shift. I have not slept for a long time," Gathii said while blinking his eyes and clenching the steering wheel as he barreled down the street, trying to make up for lost time.

Dale extended his left forearm to look down at his watch before replying to the driver. "What country are you from?"

"I'm from Kenya."

Dale checked his phone for messages while saying, "You could just say you're from America. Hell, you could say your wife used to be a man. I wouldn't know. New York City is the mixing pot of the world, the harbor of the American Dream."

"Yes, American Dream," the driver repeated. "I came here for American Dream. I get job driving taxi, I find wife—also from Africa—everything like dream for a time. Then my wife and I get depressed from working long hours for little pay. We start feeling bad because no one in America cares about our wellbeing."

Dale thought a little conversation to keep his driver awake at the wheel would be mutually beneficial. Dale was pulling off the biggest scheme of his life tonight, and the last thing he needed was for his plans to go askew if the cabbie fell asleep and got into a car accident before Dale reached his destination. After he reached his destination and left the taxi, the cabbie could feel free to fall asleep and splash into the East River, drive smack dab into a semi truck, or whatever. "If you don't like America, you can always go back to Kenya."

"Oh no, can't go back. It's worse in Kenya. Wife and I might get killed in Kenya. But … sometimes while driving through filthy city streets day after day for little pay, I feel death might be better than this life."

Dale wrinkled his forehead. "You're a real positive thinker, aren't you, Gathii? Let me guess, you don't think Americans care about you because you're from Africa?"

Gathii shook his head while focusing on the road before him. "It's not that. It's not about being Kenyan or American.

It's the system of the whole world. Nobody cares about anyone else. They're all trying to get the money and the power. The world has been poisoned. I tried focusing on the little things that make me happy and ignore the big problems—my wife's advice—but the big problems keep shitting on me and my happy little things. My little things are covered in shit. They are dripping in it, sir. I try to help people and make the world a better place, but big people keep shitting on me. You'd think when people get the money and the power they seek, they'd be happy and turn around to give back to the small people and help the world, but it's the opposite: they use the money and the power to make the world an even bigger big shit. It's like a disease, like a spreading virus. That is when I know American Dream is dead—dreams anywhere in the world are dead. Life is pointless when nobody cares for other people and everyone continues adding their personal shit to the shit pile. But it can only pile so high before big-shit tower falls. That's what I'm wishing and waiting for now, the tower to collapse. Hopefully in my lifetime the big-shit tower falls. After it falls … then we'll see if dreams can take shower and wash off their shit clothes and start shining brightly again."

Dale subtly shook his head and nonchalantly replied, "That's quite the shit theory you got, Gathii. Interesting stuff. I'll have to tell my mom about it."

Gathii eagerly nodded his head in support. "Yes, tell your mom. Tell everyone the big-shit tower is going to fall. After the collapse, the biggest shitters will be hanged in the streets like the dogs they are."

"Hmm … right … sure," Dale dismissively said while looking at his phone. He knew the cabbie had it all wrong; he had it backwards. There was no such thing as a towering shit pile that was growing in size; therefore, nothing would be collapsing except for Gathii's hopes. Smart people—like himself—that had acquired money and power weren't nice because they had learned that caring about and helping others made them exposed and vulnerable, which led to failure. One *had* to look out for number one to get "the money" and "the power" the cabbie spoke of. Because the cabbie had never obtained money or power, he didn't know how finite it was. It was a limited resource you couldn't simply spread around the world for everyone to enjoy. Crafty, competitive people knew this and fought hard to get their share of it. People like the cabbie were naive enough to think everyone would be happy sharing an equal amount of the pie. They lived in a fantasy world that socialism and communism touted. If the pie had been equally divided to everyone in the world, each person would hold a tiny sliver after the distribution was complete. Then everyone would be miserable and all those naive people that had fought to make it happen would finally learn what they already knew: life was miserable with only a sliver of the pie.

Of course the cabbie had suicidal thoughts and dreamed about shit towers piling high up into the sky; he was one of the caring people that had tried so hard to become another tile on the floor under the feet of cunning people—like himself—who were moving toward success by walking upon the altruistic pathway naive people had constructed out of themselves. And that was more than fine with Dale. The greater number of people that thought like the cabbie the better. It made it easier for people like Dale to snatch up a bigger piece of the pie.

Luckily the cabbie was really close to his destination, so Dale would soon be leaving the bitter, naive, sleepy man. Maldekmars Club, the private club he was headed to, was normally a three-minute walk from his condo, but Dale was coming from Downtown so he'd taken a taxicab on this particular occasion.

"No, no, no," Dale mumbled under his breath as the taxi got caught in heavy traffic and stopped behind a truck. Maldekmars Club was only about a two-minute walk away, so Dale decided to pay the driver and hoof it the rest of the way to avoid being late to his date. He glanced at the meter and shelled the money out of his wallet. When the driver didn't take the cash in his extended hand, Dale looked into the rearview mirror and saw that the driver had fallen asleep again. Dale prodded the driver's shoulder with his money-holding hand.

Gathii was jostled from his slumber and haphazardly slammed his foot on the gas pedal before even looking at the view in front of him, thinking he had fallen asleep behind another red light that was now green. When he noticed he was caught in traffic instead of stopped behind a green light, it was too late, he had smacked into the bumper of the truck in front of him.

The sudden stopping of momentum had caused Dale to bang into the plexiglass, his hand still outstretched with the money. "Goddammit! Are you trying to kill me before I can get out of this shitbox? Here, take the money. I'll walk the rest of the way. And don't even think that I'm sticking around to give a statement for the accident." He shook the hand that held the money, urging Gathii to take the money before dealing with the accident.

Gathii took the money, noticed the vehicles stuck in traffic around him weren't going anywhere for a while, and exited his cab to check the damages and talk to the truck's owner.

While Dale made his way between cars to reach the sidewalk, he noticed a shotgun hanging in the truck's rear windshield. Then he saw the truck driver exiting his vehicle. He was a stalky man wearing a dirty plaid shirt, a scruffy old cap, and a massive scowl plastered on a red face. After Dale reached the sidewalk, he took one last glance back at the front of the truck's license plate: GEORGIA. "Oh, shit. Good luck with that, Gathii," Dale mumbled to himself as he turned his head and headed toward Maldekmars Club.

The truck driver stared at Gathii, who was examining the damage on his bumper and wondering what he was going to tell his boss. The truck driver's beady eyes took in the taxi driver's figure: black as midnight and short in height. "Hoowee!" he yelled as he took off his dirty cap and slapped it against his thigh. "Looks like we got ourselves a nigger. You ain't even a full-sized nigger, so I gonna call you a niglet. Looks like you done knocked my bumper real good. What you got to say for yourself, boy?" he said before spitting some chewing tobacco onto the road while approaching Gathii.

A nearby driver, who heard the truck driver's racist remark, chastised him. "Hey! You can't say that word."

The truck-driving hick turned toward the driver. "I can say any word I please. What are you, a nigger-lover?"

The driver indignantly replied, "What are you, from the 1800s?"

The hick spit some chewing tobacco in the man's direction instead of replying to his comment, and then he focused his attention back on the taxi driver that had rear-ended his truck.

Gathii clasped his hands together in pleading fashion. "I'm so sorry. I will pay for the damages. There's no need to report this." Gathii noticed the shotgun hanging in the truck driver's rear windshield. "Again, I'm so sorry, sir."

The truck driver sauntered closer to Gathii, pausing for a few seconds and directing an ear to a car in an adjacent lane that had its window down and a football game blaring from its radio. "Yeah, you better be sorry, niglet. You making me miss the game over this hoopla," he said before turning around and eying the shotgun in his truck. "Perhaps I need to introduce you to Betsy. She's as pretty as a peach and turns people into strawberry jam."

The next two things that Gathii took in might have saved his life: the Georgia license plate he saw in the gap between their vehicles, and the sportscaster's voice blaring out of the nearby car mentioning the Atlanta Falcons. Gathii had learned every state's capital because he thought it would be on the U.S. Citizenship Test. He ended up only being tested for the nation's capital and the capital of his state, New York, but now he thanked God he had memorized all of them and was able to place Atlanta in Georgia. "I'm also sorry that I'm missing the game. Go Falcons!" he yelled as he awkwardly lifted one arm in the air, feigning fandom.

The hick blinked his eyes a couple times in surprise and stared at Gathii as if he was staring at an entirely different person than he had a moment ago. "Well I'll be. You a Falcon's fan?"

"Yes, sir. Tried and true since I entered this great country. Their symbol of a noble bird brings tears to my eyes."

The hick slapped his cap against his thigh again. "Hoowee! Well then, your skin color can be overlooked. Just like there's no black or white among police officers—they're only blue—there's no black or white with sports either. Black and white sports players and fans all become one color: sports color. Tell you what"—he spat more tobacco on the street—"this old bumper of mine don't mind another dent in it. You keep your money. Fellow Falcons fans don't niggle over bumpers. They're called bumpers because they're meant to bump into things."

Gathii's terrified expression morphed into a smile. He couldn't believe this twist of fate. Sports was a very powerful thing in America, he surmised.

"Touchdown Jets," blared the sportscaster's voice from the same nearby idling car still stuck in traffic. The driver of the car, a Jets fan, celebrated by moving his arms around and vocalizing jubilation.

Upon hearing the sports news and viewing the joy of the Jets fan, the hick reacted by working up a gob of chewing tobacco and spitting it on the hood of the driver's car. Then, to the Jets fan's lament, he began pounding his fists down on the car to express his anger about his team's losing performance. While doing so he turned to Gathii for Falcon assistance. "Don't be shy fellow Falcon, you can lay into this Jets fan's car with me. Everything's fair in sports and war."

Gathii felt like a fly caught in a spider web. He felt like the hick could turn on him at any moment if he didn't do the right thing, causing their newfound fellowship to evaporate in an instant. So Gathii started kicking a tire and pounding a fist on the car while yelling, "May noble Falcons shit upon your car."

The Jets fan voiced his resentment, "Quit hitting my car, Falcon fuckers. Your team sucking doesn't give you the right to beat on my car. I'll call the cops if you don't back the hell up."

The hick's beefy arms and paws reached into the car and grabbed the Jets fan by the collar and jerked him around like a rag doll. "Them's fightin' words. You done asked for it. I'm gettin' Betsy."

The Jets fan tried to pull himself free from the giant hick's clutches, but hopelessly failed as he continued to get tossed around the interior of his car, his head bouncing off the steering wheel, seat, roof, and his halfway rolled-down window.

The hick unhanded the man, spat tobacco in his face, and trooped over to his truck to snatch Betsy, his double-barreled shotgun.

The Jets fan indignantly yelled, "I'm calling the cops. You're gonna be sorry you messed with me, you backwater bastard!"

The hick incoherently rambled to himself along the way to his truck, "Goddammit, I'll show you … Jets joker." He entered his truck and reached into the back to collect his stopping-power weapon and a case of shells. He continued muttering to himself, "Betsy's got the power to stop him from rootin' against the Falcons. She won't just stop his mouth from rootin' for the Jets, she'll stop all his bodily functions real quick like. Gonna strawberry jam that sonuvabitch."

He exited his truck with the shotgun, forcefully making contact with the pavement with his booted feet far apart for balance like he'd just jumped to the ground from a massive tank. He opened the shotgun's twin barrels to make sure unspent shells resided inside.

The Jets fan stared at the hick and his shotgun like a deer caught in headlights, disbelieving the image his eyes were sending to his brain.

The hick approvingly nodded at the fresh slugs he saw in the chamber and slammed the double barrels back into place, locked and loaded. "Sports!" he yelled as he marched toward the Jets fan with a tight grip on the double-barreled shotgun.

Chapter 21

After the doorman in front of the Maldekmars Club checked Dale's identification and allowed him admission, Dale was informed by the staff where his meeting with Ms. Rottenschild would be located. Dale nodded his head and headed off to the specified location.

Aryana Rottenschild had been the one to contact Dale for the date. Their meeting was made possible because they were both members of an exclusive dating app, Elite Shakers & Breakers, where applicants were rigorously vetted by their possessed wealth and moral disposition. A psychological test had to be taken to ensure the applicant didn't advocate the moral dispositions of the general populace. Any applicant that was shown to be too caring, emotionally triggered by certain phrases, or lacked conviction in gaining money or power was rejected with a false reason. To ensure an applicant possessed enough capital, bank holdings had to be verified. The repeating short clip that made up the logo for the app was a suited man holding another man upside down while he shook all the coins loose from his pockets. After the coins stopped falling to the ground, the suited man brought the coinless man down on his knee, breaking his spine. The short clip summed up the Elite Shakers & Breakers members quite flawlessly.

Dale passed the tests and had become a member of the app a year ago. He had had some fun flings with other movers and shakers who were equal or greater to his caliber, but this was the first time someone very high on the ladder had contacted him. Aryana Rottenschild was an heir to the wealthiest banking family in Europe—actually, in the whole world, as people in the know knew to be true. The Rottenschilds were old money. Their family tree had been holding the reins of civilization for centuries. So naturally Dale was champing at the bit when

Aryana had requested a meeting with him. It was his chance to work himself into the main vein of power where ultra-wealthy individuals resided, the ones that were conveniently omitted from the annual wealth rankings made public by magazine publications and online lists. When a family held a certain amount of wealth and power for a long enough period of time, they slipped behind the curtain and out of the population's spotlight. While behind the curtain, they pulled the strings attached to leaders of governments and companies.

Dale walked through several rooms in the extravagant Maldekmars Club as he made his way to the room where he was told Aryana was waiting. Pervasive amber-gold décor and low lighting gave the ambiance of the club a secretive and regal air. Upon the high ceilings, where majestic chandeliers hung, were either expansive murals or detailed patterns carved into mahogany ceiling tiles. Two other colors accompanied the golden glow: thick crimson curtains covered the windows and white marble decked the floors and sometimes walls, depending on the character and nature of each room. Unlike the opulent facade of a Las Vegas casino, the Maldekmars Club possessed the finest and most expensive materials down to every nook and cranny throughout the building.

Dale recognized Aryana's blond hair and porcelain face and seated himself at their table for two.

Aryana ran a hand through her hair, eloquently brushing it away to reveal more of her finely sculpted face. "I'm glad you could make it, Dale."

Dale reciprocated her smile. "Of course I made it. Only a fool would pass up the opportunity to meet someone as ravishing and powerful such as yourself."

After they had placed their orders with their waiter, received their food, and covered enough verbal foreplay, Aryana directed the conversation toward more meaningful business. "There's always a person placed before significant power structures. We call them gatekeepers. My handler—I mean, my mentor is my father. Without his guidance and tutelage, I wouldn't be where I am today. I wouldn't possess the fortitude and skills I now have if it weren't for his leadership."

Dale slowly nodded his head. "Yes, he's quite an accomplished man. A titan worthy of admiration, for sure."

Aryana carefully dabbed the corner of her mouth with a quilted cotton napkin after eating a small piece of her beef striploin, which she had ordered rare. It was practically swimming in blood on her plate. She placed the napkin on the table, making sure the spots of blood on it faced down on the table, hidden from possible scrutinizing eyes that weren't minding their own business. "You know, Dale, with my connections I can assign you with an equally prestigious mentor."

"Oh yeah? Who would be illustrious enough to mentor someone as prominent as myself?" Dale smiled, conveying that he couldn't bring to mind anyone who was high enough above the ladder from himself that could possibly bestow tactics or a means that he didn't already have access to.

Aryana leaned forward across the table and whispered a name into Dale's ear.

Dale's eyes instantly bulged. As Aryana returned to her upright posture, Dale gingerly nodded his head, indicating that he would not only be interested, but he would be honored. His fork load of salmon dipped in spinach soubise and mint oil that had been ready to be elevated toward his mouth now lay stationary on his plate.

Aryana seductively smiled. "I thought that might change your tune. With this opportunity there's no limit to how high you can fly, how powerful you could become."

Dale awoke from his temporary trance. "I'll say," he said before finally lifting the piece of salmon to his lips.

Before Aryana took another bite of her blood-soaked steak, she again leaned forward and whispered to Dale, "Your initiation will be held in the secret underground chambers of this club."

Dale's eyes went wide again. "I didn't know there were underground chambers under the Maldekmars Club."

Aryana displayed a devilish smile. "Well of course you didn't know about it. It wouldn't be a secret if just anyone knew about it. And that's nothing compared to what will be revealed to you once you've shown your dedication and worth."

Dale smiled, and while lifting his snifter to take a sip of cognac, he said, "If the sky is the limit, count me in."

At a table near them, two old gentlemen were watching breaking news about a shotgun-toting hick that had blown away thirteen people stuck in traffic just around the corner from the club. The newscaster stated that witnesses said a man from Georgia had gone from vehicle to vehicle asking if the occupants were Jets fans. Any occupant that had answered with a "Yes" got their face blown off. Police arrived on the scene and quickly gunned down the trigger-happy hick.

The old gentlemen put their phones down and one asked the other, "Was that one of our orchestrated shootings to promote fear and general negative energy? I don't recall that one being in the works. It doesn't paint a good picture for sports and is counterproductive to our agenda in the entertainment area that keeps people focused on shallow matters instead of intellectual concepts. However, the number of deaths reported looks like our numerology code."

The other gentleman replied, "No, that wasn't one that we planned. I would know about it. It just goes to show how well our negative energy programming is working: now incidents like these are naturally occurring without us having to orchestrate them. The population has been exposed to fear and general negative energy for so long that most of them would continue to simmer in their programming even if we switched off its continual bombardment. A toast to the great spider-web design and its self-replicating capabilities."

They lifted their whiskey tumblers and joyously clanked them together before taking greedy swigs of the golden brown liquid.

At another table close by, two prominent men from the pharmaceutical, virology, and chemistry fields talked about their latest engineered-virus outbreak.

"We continue to create different coronavirus strains that hopefully won't lose their effectiveness and will spread farther than their predecessors. We're trying to make them more tenacious than the original coronavirus strains, which were supposed to infect the world's population and create an endgame scenario while we hid underground till it blew over, but it didn't work out as we anticipated. Hopefully the next batch of COVID-19 strains will get the job done. We've had the patent for the coronavirus for a while and of course have produced the antidotes for us and the toxic cocktail vaccine for the sheep, just like we have for our past bioengineered viruses: H5N1, SIV, HIV, Ebola, Marburg, MERS, SARS, Zika—the list is so long. You know, standard procedure."

The other man replied, "Some factions are pleased, but many factions are voicing their complaints about how the virus isn't as effective as it was supposed to be. The Good Club wanted it to cull a much larger percentage of the population. The original virus' strain was specifically engineered to target the Asian respiratory system. Releasing the coronavirus in Wuhan, a test city for 5G, a central transit hub, and during Chinese New Year, was a brilliant strategy. Then we tailored different strains that would target other ethnic groups in other countries. We released these different strains in South Korea, Italy, and Iran. They started out well, but then for some reason lost their effectiveness and didn't work out like our China strain. Also, we've been having a pushback to making our vaccine cocktail mandatory in many countries. Soon we'll be releasing a different strain in America and will utilize the CDC and the WHO to make our vaccine cocktail mandatory in the US, which will help push it to be mandatory in other UN and non-UN countries."

His colleague replied, "I hope so. We're seeing significant dropping numbers for people purchasing flu shots and a greater stance against general vaccinations is spreading like wildfire. We need to correct this problem. I guess the sheep aren't as dumb as we thought they were. It's gotten so bad that we've had to offer flu vaccinations for free, hoping that we'll get more people to willingly poison themselves. It isn't as easy these days to poison the general population in first-world countries with vaccinations like it still is in third-world countries with our 'altruistic vaccinating programs.' "

The other man adjusted his glasses. "Right. Hopefully our upcoming coronavirus strains will trigger the endgame scenario we were hoping for. Then we can pull our tried and true method of creating the problem, controlling the narrative, and offering the solution. The 'solution' will be our mandatory vaccine which will be filled with our special poisonous cocktail. Even those that know what's in it will have to submit to injections or be arrested when it becomes mandatory. But if the next strains are effective, it won't matter if the population doesn't willingly line up to poison themselves with our vaccination cocktails; we'll simply deliver the cocktail in the form of a virus right to their door."

The other scientist jested, "We'll offer a free product with free delivery. It will be a deal the public won't be able to pass up."

Both men busted up laughing at the joke.

At another nearby table, two scientists were consumed in an equally malevolent conversation.

"The current levels of solar and cosmic radiation is combatting our EMF, scalar, and energy programs. We've had to roll out 5G sooner than expected to keep the population simmering in a soupy field of agitation. We've also had to ramp up our directed scalar technology directed at specific cities."

The other scientist replied, "Yes, it's a concern. We're always on the lookout for the next Nikola Tesla so we can steal their ideas and technology and nefariously augment them to serve our needs. Genius like Tesla's doesn't sprout every day, especially within the dumbed-down population we've cultivated."

"That's true, but there's a growing trend of inventors selling positive scalar field devices on the Internet. Most notably is Ken Rohla at freshandalive.com. This goes beyond the little orgonite necklace trinket fad. These positive scalar devices have the ability to shield and nullify our negative bombarding frequencies to whole houses. This goes beyond necklaces that effectively do nothing. We're going to have to release more scientific misinformation and direct it at these devices and scientists to quash this growing trend. More social conditioning in this area is a must, lest we lose one of our greatest technological weapons. Its importance lies not only in its powerfulness, but in the fact that it's something people can't opt-out of. If people learn about flu shots, poisoned food and water, etc., they can opt-out of putting it in their bodies. But they can't opt-out of our negative scalar fields. They can vocalize their opting-out all they want, but they'll still get zapped." They chuckled. "But if they purchase these positive scalar field devices, they'll actually be able to opt-out, effectively. We can't allow that. How dare they not allow us to own their existence. The audacity of these Neanderthals."

"Agree. All the many compartments in the great design are effective in keeping our agendas thriving, but this area is the most important: when a person lives their whole life in a disharmonious frequency field, they remain weak; stressed; highly conducive to programming; depressed; more conducive to contracting viruses from a lowered immune system; emotionally, mentally, and physically drained—you name it, the effects go on and on. And the best part is that they think their deplorable state is the norm and that's what it feels like to be alive. It's like sticking a person in an operating microwave when they don't know the microwave even exists." The scientists laughed.

"Speaking of microwaves, they're still using them to heat their food and liquid today, zapping every last ounce of nutrition out of the lifeless food we're already giving them." Both scientists busted up with laughter.

At another nearby table, two men in dark suits conversed.

"So what's the next major planned event?" one of the men asked the other.

"We can't talk about it at this time because it's still in the stages of planning, but hopefully the coronavirus will provide an endgame and we'll not need to deploy any new plans."

"Well, I'm sure it's something grandiose. The past events worked perfectly with only a minor amount of people talking about them online, but our 'conspiracy theory and theorist' labeling method and programming has worked well: the general population have been dismissing truthers' information before even listening to it and have labeled them wackos. If those wackos were able to present all their evidence in a court of law, they'd win without a doubt. A court of law where we didn't have the judge in our pocket, that is. But since we get the population to label them wackos and ignore their information, it completely negates all their evidence. We'll keep up the payments to our many online shills to discredit the top influential truthers on the Web, which in turn will program online trolls to unknowingly work for us for free in debasing these viruses in our system. I love those useful idiots. We've embedded shills in every truther community. Some act like sleeper cells; we activate them when it's time to create infighting in their community. These shills are good at taking over their social media groups, and sometimes even whole movements and projects. We've directed extra funds to destroy three truthers in particular because they've become way too influential. These particular truthers have received insider information from traitors. We have gone the extra mile with them and have gone beyond online activities to attack their physical meetings, wrap them up in legal disputes, and drain all their funding so they can't afford to spread the truth anymore."

The other man asked, "Who are these three individuals? The truther area isn't my department, so I'm not familiar with their names."

"They are David Wilcock, Corey Goode, and Cobra. And other prominent truthers are emerging that we need to start attacking as well. Characters like Ben & Rob from the Edge of Wonder. If we don't stop this truther movement, wearing a tinfoil hat is going to become popular among the sleeping masses. If that happens, we're done for. We'll have to dump a huge fresh batch of slimy shills on them forthwith, and hopefully the trolls and useful idiots will get a whiff of the magic and also spew their texted goo onto the scene. Yeah, we'll have our countless troll farms notified and have shills attack them everywhere online. We'll also have our companies mess with them every step they take. Being that we control virtually every company—Google, Amazon, IngramSpark, Facebook, PayPal, Twitter, Barnes & Noble, Mailchimp, PublishDrive, YouTube—we know everything they're doing, even their messages and e-mails that they think are private. Wherever they try to get important information out in an attempt to awaken the sleeping masses, we'll shadow-ban it or outright ban it. We've found that the former works better. If they self-publish a book, we'll have shills bash it with fake reviews everywhere online. The average person lives under a rock and will believe whatever we want them to believe. … Anyway, 9/11 in America and 3/11 in Japan proved that our plans can be orchestrated with most people believing our narrative. Our New World Order can't be stopped."

"Actually, things have changed. The Alliance has grown in strength. They stopped our nuclear missile from hitting Hawaii on January 13th of 2018. We were going to blame it on North Korea and Russia and finally get World War III started, but they thwarted our plans when they shot down the missile over the ocean. In damage control we had to state that it was a false missile alert. That wasn't the only time the Alliance stopped our plans. Before the missile incident, our Las Vegas shooting didn't go exactly as planned. It was effective in spreading mass fear, but it was also supposed to take out a main individual in the opposition. You know who I'm talking about. But one of our major plans will either start WWIII or wipe out the population with a bioengineered virus. As we always tell our scientists to say to the public, 'It's not a matter of if, but when.' "

Dale felt his phone vibrating in his suit pants. It broke his concentration from Aryana's dialog. He leaned a bit to the right in his chair to produce the vibrating phone from his pocket and checked the caller ID. The results made him cringe.

Aryana offered up a preemptive answer to his yet to be uttered question. "I don't mind at all. If it's important, especially if it's business, you should take the call."

"It's important and business. Thanks for understanding, Aryana."

Aryana smiled and chewed on another piece of her blood-soaked steak.

Dale swiveled in his chair and brought the phone up to his ear farthest away from his dining partner and aggressively muttered in the phone, "You were only supposed to call if there was an emergency."

The voice on the other end of the line said, "It is an emergency. He's locked himself in the laundry room. I can't get to him."

Dale's irritation grew. "Does he have a phone? And are there any windows he can escape from in that room?"

The voice replied, "No and no."

Dale had perfectly planned out this evening, but this fool was ruining it. "Stay there and guard the door. I'll get there as fast as I can. Goddammit. The whole point was for me to be elsewhere when it went down."

"Yeah, sorry about that."

Dale ended the phone call and turned to Aryana. "I really hate to do this, but I have some very important business that needs to be attended to right now. Believe me, if it wasn't—"

She cut him off. "It's okay, Dale, business is business. I understand. Your dedication to business is the very reason why I invited you below." She tilted her head to indicate the basement floors below them. "We were almost finished eating anyway. Go attend to your affairs and I'll contact you when I've set up a meeting with your mentor."

Dale lifted from his chair. "Thank you for understanding, Aryana. It really is important—"

She cut him off again by raising a palm and displaying an expression that reiterated what she had already stated: *It's okay, business is business. It comes before anything else in life.*

Dale took two steps away, halted, and rushed back to Aryana. "If anyone happens to ask, can you say we spent another three hours at the bar before we left?" In his haste, Dale couldn't believe he'd just asked such a question to someone he'd just met. And what would she think of him for having said it?

She casually smiled. "Not a problem, Dale. I'll be the firmest alibi that you've ever had. Don't worry about it." Her smile grew wider as she looked at Dale's bewildered expression that dawned upon hearing her reply.

Did she just say alibi? She's just joking … right? "Right … thanks, Aryana. I look forward to your call."

While smiling she raised her glass of red wine to toast his departure before taking a sip. She watched him rush out of the dining room from above the rim of the wine glass. Then she stabbed the last big piece of her beef striploin and used it to mop up as much blood on the plate as possible before fiercely feasting upon it.

As she used a napkin to dab a trickle of blood running down her mouth, she produced her phone with her other hand and initiated a call. When the line was answered, she said, "He's agreed to have a handler. After having him poached from Stryker & Marshall, I didn't think it would take him three years to move forward, but he's doing so tonight."

She listened to the other person on the line say something.

Aryana replied, "Yes, it appears he ran into some complications because he had to leave early to deal with it himself, but I have no doubt that he'll get the job finished, given his track record."

She listened to the voice on the phone.

"Don't worry," Aryana replied. "It's a minor detail that will be worked out. He'll be a great asset once he's acquired. Trust me. His profile clearly shows that he's a dead ringer to our modus operandi."

Chapter 22

Dale was fortunate that Aryana had chosen the Maldekmars Club for their meeting spot because it was right by his condo. He very well couldn't have his destination recorded by a taxicab company. He ran to his building to collect his Ferrari Roma, which he had to buy in Italy because it hadn't been released in America yet. Ah, the pleasures that wealth and power provided.

He revved the engine and bolted out of the parking garage, nearly driving over a pedestrian within the garage's concrete maze in the process. The Roma flew out of the garage and into the street. Dale avoided traffic areas shown on the Roma's digital display and gunned the sleek automobile toward uptown, on route to the senior execute VP's house, where the executive would've been lying like a large butchered piece of meat on the floor if the hired killer had done his job correctly. *If you want something done correctly, you have to do it yourself.*

As the years passed at Gelman & Gerwitz, Dale became increasingly impatient to step into the role of a senior executive VP. All the senior execs seemed permanently parked in their positions. Eventually he had given into the temptation to use the GOOD FOR ONE FREE RUB-OUT coupon that was originally bequeathed to Amber for her judicial services to the Mafia.

It was a mix of having the coupon and a growing detachment from morality that prompted the action. The longer Dale had lived in the upper echelon of society where a buffer separated his existence from the everyday man, the less he found himself caring about morals and ethics; not that he ever cared about them that much anyway, but now he was in a whole new ballpark. Those words—morals and ethics—didn't exist in the high world of finance and business. Say either one of them to a one-percenter and they'd look at you like you just invented a word out of thin air and were dumber for having said it. Then you'd be blacklisted in their book.

Instead of stopping at a yellow light that was turning red, Dale laid down his horn and shot through the intersection. It was his way of letting everyone at the intersection know that he was above mere traffic rules, and the long honk he produced was an aggressive warning that stated: *You're in a world of hurt if you hit my luxury car while I'm ignoring this red light.*

"You can't stay locked up in the laundry room forever, pal!" Tony, the coupon killer, yelled through the thick laundry door.

Tony heard a TV turn on in the laundry room and then the exec replying, "Are you sure about that? I got hundreds of channels to surf. Oh, and *Eat Till You Drop* is on, nice. Good thing I wasn't able to disconnect my cable over those fraudulent charges two months ago."

Tony seethed. Goddamn rich people have a TV in every room of the house, even the laundry room. "Sooner or later you're going to get hungry."

A crinkling sound was heard through the door. "Nope. I got a stash of Doritos and soda I keep in here, safe from my health-food nut wife's stubborn hands." The crunching sound of chips being masticated trailed through the door while the exec surfed channels. "Oh nice, *Rich Entitled Kids Doing Various Drugs* is also on. My favorite. Yeah, this is like a little vacation in here." More chip crunching sounds were heard.

"Goddammit," Tony mumbled. Then he shouted through the door, "What about when you need to use the bathroom, buddy?"

"I got that covered too. I can urinate and defecate in the washer dryer unit."

Tony played with his knife. "It'll start to smell in there."

"Nope. I'll simply wash a load of my excrement. It's a top of the line unit that can handle any shit you throw in it. That's exactly what the salesman said when he sold it to me." *Crunch,*

crunch, munch. "Say, I got a proposition for you. I'll pay you double whatever the guy paid you to kill me to kill him instead." After a few seconds of no reply. "I'll triple the money. What say you?"

Dollar signs popped up in Tony's mind. He wasn't getting paid to do the job, but this Dorito-eating sonuvabitch didn't know that. He could say any figure he wanted.

He shook his head. He couldn't do it. He needed this kill to get inside The Family. Once he killed this Wall Street scumbag, he'll have proved himself to The Family. Then he was in, and he would eventually make more than whatever this Dorito-eater would give him. Besides, he knew he could trust the Mafia more than any wealthy exec. Wealthy execs were dirtier than any gang member. Wealthy execs took ganglike syndicates to a whole new level.

There was no way he could trust this guy. After getting handsomely paid to leave, he'd be sprawled out on his couch with the exec's payout money strewn across his living room table, happily watching *Remodeling Houses While the Homeless Die on the Streets* while eating a can of chili con carne when the pigs would bust down his door and bark at him while filling his body full of good old American-hero bullets. Then they'd plant some drugs and a gun in his hand to make it look real nice in their paperwork. "I don't think so, pal. You can't buy your way out of everything in life. This ain't about money, this is about you being dead."

Crunch, munch. "Well, we'll see how long you can wait out there. At some point my wife will get home. Feel free to kill her if you want. It would save me millions to bypass our inevitable divorce settlement."

Tony noticed a remote control on a cabinet a few feet away and thought it might be for the TV in the laundry room. He grabbed it and put it by the inch gap under the laundry room door and keyed in a random channel. The TV changed channels to a heated discussion where a few political pundits were interrupting each other and shouting like children.

"Shit, not these assholes," cursed the exec. "How'd you do that? You got the remote out there?"

"That's right. Come on out or keep listening to those idiots shout at each other." Tony flipped his knife in the air and caught the handle on its way down. He was champing at the bit to sink the knife into that damn Dorito-munching exec.

The exec used the touchscreen menu on the TV to change the channel back to *Rich Entitled Kids Doing Various Drugs*.

Tony changed the channel back to the shouting political pundits.

"No. Stop it! ... How can these clowns shout all day long without blowing out their throats? They must've received a master's in shouting at university." He turned the channel back to his favorite show.

Tony tried to change the channel again but nothing happened.

The exec saw the tip of the remote under the door. "Ha! I disabled the remote on the touchscreen menu. You can't force yelling political pundits on me anymore. The kids on drugs reality show is secured." *Crunch, munch.* ... "Oh, nice. Bobby is going to eat that cupcake that he doesn't know is laced with ecstasy and meth. Ha! This is going to be good. What's he going to do at the wedding while high out of his mind? I love this show."

Tony gritted his teeth in hatred. As long as he was waiting for this prick to exit the laundry room or for the guy who hired him to arrive at the house, he was going to indulge a little and down a beer. He quietly left his post, hoping the prick would think he was still guarding the door. He went to the kitchen and found beer in the fridge to guzzle down.

After one bottle of beer was done, he thought that it couldn't hurt if he had just one more. Just one more and he'd feel even better and go back to guarding that munching prick.

In between bouts of laughter while watching Bobby licking and grinding on random girls in the wedding hall, the exec turned his head and glanced at the gap at the bottom of the door and noticed that the killer's shadow was gone. He turned the TV's volume down a little, clasped his hand around the handle of a wooden bat that happened to be in the laundry room. The Louisville Slugger was a relic he'd kept from his youth. Now the stashed-away relic in the laundry room had become useful again. This time it would slug a head instead of a baseball.

While tightly gripping the bat with one hand he cautiously turned the doorknob and eased the door open enough to take a peek before assessing that the coast was clear. Now out of the laundry room, he quietly closed the door behind him and tiptoed toward some sounds he heard coming from the kitchen.

He could've made a detour to the den and collected a pistol that would've easily corrected this situation, but his wife had talked him out of buying a gun. She said guns were for cops alone to carry and protect citizens from deranged people and gangs. He had replied by telling her that most of the time cops followed orders from above and were no different than gang members. She thought that was ridiculous. He wondered how quickly her stance on owing a gun would've changed if she found herself in the situation he was now in. Luckily his current intruder was only wielding a knife, which was the only reason he'd left the laundry room. If the intruder had brought a gun, he would've been able to shoot the lock on the laundry room door to weaken its stability and kick in the door. But this guy was clearly an amateur, bringing a knife instead of a gun to a killing job.

The exec peeked around the corner and looked into the kitchen. The killer had his back to him and was drinking a beer. He knew that the spacious kitchen would allow him to make a full, powerful swing at the man's head, so he inched forward while clutching the wooden bat with both hands. As he closed the distance between them, he wrung the handle of the bat like a baseball player itching to hit a homerun.

Once he got close enough, he swung the bat with all his might and clobbered the unaware man solidly in the temple. After the loud thudding noise, the man collapsed and hit the floor right after his dropped beer bottle had, breaking into numerous pieces and scattering around the kitchen.

Even though the killer looked like he was done for, the exec wasted no time in laying down three more powerful bat blows to his head, making absolutely certain that the skull was cracked and the brain fatally compromised. "Can't be too careful. I've seen enough movies to know they always come back. You definitely aren't coming back," he spoke down at the cracked skull.

The exec watched the blood pooling on the kitchen floor under the cracked head for a while. Then he dropped the blood-splattered bat, left the kitchen, walked through the living room, and went up the stairs to fetch his phone to call the cops.

He was hopped up on adrenaline. "I feel great," he said as he ascended the stairs. "Damn, I really feel like buying some stocks now. I got that stock fever ... but I should probably call the police first."

While the exec was upstairs making the call, Dale walked through the front door that entered into the living room. He saw dark pieces of something scattered around the part of the kitchen floor that was visible from the living room, and shuffled over to check it out.

He entered the kitchen and saw a man with his head cracked open. The instrument that had done him in, a bloody wooden bat, lay beside him. The dead man wasn't Joel Amoral, so it must be the coupon killer, Dale assessed. A knife that clearly didn't fit the style of the other cutlery in the kitchen was lying on a countertop near the body. *What an amateur. He brought a knife instead of a gun. I'll never hire a coupon killer again.* Dale shook his head in disgust. *If you want something done right ...*

He slid the biggest knife out of a stainless steel knife set on the countertop, choosing not to handle the killer's knife, as if it was tainted with failure. He slinked back into the living room and kept his ears perked like a cat's, hoping to hear something that would indicate where Amoral was, but he heard nothing. He pondered going up the flight of stairs to the second floor or checking out the other rooms on the ground floor.

Joel Amoral rounded a corner upstairs and got a quarter down the stairs before he froze when noticing Dale Dickerson at the bottom of the banister with a large knife in hand. His dumbfounded face wondered why Dickerson was in his house, but the knife in Dickerson's hand alerted his common sense to quickly deduce the reason, just not the why.

Dale took advantage of Amoral's delay and managed to get a quarter up the stairs before Amoral backtracked up the stairs and fled for a room.

Amoral cursed himself when he realized that he'd fled to a room without a lock. But it was too late, Dickerson was too close for him to exit and choose a different room. So instead he climbed a ladder and picked up a bucket of black paint that lay on the ladder's shelf near the top. The high vaulted ceilings in the room had been put off by the hired painters till tomorrow.

He saw Dickerson rush into the room and pause in confusion once he spotted the ladder. Amoral felt just as ridiculous as he looked, holding paint at the top of a ladder, but it was the first defense strategy that had come to his mind.

While he clutched the paint bucket, he issued a stern warning down at his pursuer. "I called the cops. They'll be here any second. If you don't leave now, they'll catch you for sure."

Dale smiled while looking up at Amoral. "You just called them. Their sluggish response time will allow me to finish things up here." Dale slowly approached the ladder. "You couldn't just retire early, could you? You gave me no choice, Amoral. Next year I won't be the youngest broker in the company to reach a senior exec position. I don't settle for ties."

Amoral was confounded by Dickerson's words. "You'd kill me over something as stupid as that? You're deranged."

Dale reached the foot of the ladder. "When I set a goal, Amoral, I always see it through. Nothing stops me from moving forward. *Nothing.* In your mind it may seem extreme to kill you, but in my mind you're just a bug that's in the way. What does anyone do when a bug is in the way? Squash it of course."

"Even if you don't end up rotting in a jail cell after killing me, you'll still go to hell when you die," Amoral threatened Dickerson.

Dale shook his head. "Hell doesn't exist. Right and wrong don't exist. Succeeding is the only thing that matters. You can only get to the top if you realize this and have the balls to squash bugs like you when they get in the way."

Dickerson's words petrified Amoral. His arms grew weak in holding the heavy paint bucket. "I knew there was always something off about you."

Dale set the knife on the floor and used both hands to shake the ladder. "Be a good bug and come on down."

The movement caught Amoral off guard and caused him to drop the paint bucket in order to grab ahold of the ladder to avoid falling. The paint bucket hit a step on the ladder on its way down and flipped over, causing the black viscous liquid to leap out of the bucket and completely cover Dale's head and arms.

Immersed in darkness, Dale backed away from the ladder. He used his fingers to attempt scraping paint away from his eyelids, but his paint-soaked fingers didn't help so he had to keep his eyes shut.

Amoral looked down and saw Dickerson thrashing about in paint. His eyes targeted the knife lying on the floor. He made haste down the ladder to get it while Dickerson was blind and discombobulated.

Dale, still unable to see, heard Amoral rushing down the ladder and knew that he needed to get the knife first. He fell to his hands and knees and frantically padded the floor with his palms to locate the knife. His left hand hit a leg of the ladder and his right hand discovered the knife. Carefully fingering it till he found the handle, he snatched it up. He could tell from the approaching noise on the ladder that Amoral would be on him in a second, so, with one hand on the ladder, he blindly lunged the knife in his other hand up to sink into the descending exec.

Amoral went wide-eyed as he saw the knife thrust into his thigh. The pain seared through his body and messed up his footwork, causing him to topple off the ladder and smack onto the floor, landing sideways and whiplashing his head down to whack against the floor right after his body had.

Wasting no time, Dale felt for Amoral's body with his left hand, and once he found him, he repeatedly brought the knife down into Amoral's body. Oozing black paint flung everywhere as the knife was repeatedly brought up and down.

As Amoral screamed and felt the blade of the knife penetrate his body over and over again, his final thoughts were not about Dickerson, but how his soon to be bitchy ex-wife had indirectly killed him by not allowing him to purchase a handgun for protection in the house. Actually, she'd soon be a widow and inherit his entire estate instead of being his ex-wife. If he'd had a handgun, he would've easily stopped both the intruders that had entered his house. Then he thought, maybe she planned it from the beginning: denied him a gun and then hired someone to kill him. The first intruder must've been hired by his wife, and Dickerson had showed up afterward not by some astronomical coincidence, but because God was an asshole: when He decided it was your time, there was no argument about it, you were a goner.

When it came time for his wife to identify his corpse, that bitch would be smiling in the back of her mind behind her fake saddened face, licking her imaginary chops at all the wealth that would soon inundate her. That cun—.

Dale plunged the sharp instrument until the screams from Amoral's mouth eventually ceased.

Dale stood up and brought the bottom of his suit jacket up to his eyes to clear the paint from his eyelids. He opened his eyes and took in the sight of Amoral's body. It was covered in red and black, eyes staring blankly at the high ceiling. Then he thrust the knife one last time into Amoral. This time in the neck, making sure the paramedics would find him dead on arrival and not be able to resuscitate him.

Dale unbuttoned his suit jacket and removed it. He sighed. Paint was still dripping from it. "Goddammit." He indignantly looked down at Amoral's lifeless body. "You know how much this suit cost? What a waste of a fine garment. Thanks a lot, asshat." He shook his head in disdain.

He inverted the suit jacket and wrapped the bloody knife inside it. Then he rushed down to the kitchen and put the suit and knife inside a paper grocery bag. Using a hand towel, he quickly wiped the black paint from his hands before exiting the house.

Police sirens could be heard, but they were safely in the distance. He rushed to his Ferrari Roma, threw the paper bag on the passenger's side floorboard, and drove off in a calm manner in order to not alert any neighbor's attention. He imagined all the dipshits in the movies gunning their cars and peeling out from the scene of the crime, needlessly drawing attention to themselves.

Dale had driven for about a minute before seeing red and blue flashing through the night. Two police cars headed down the road toward him. He kept to the speed limit and stayed calm. The siren-blaring cop cars rushed passed him, one after the other, heading toward Amoral's house.

Dale watched them in his rearview mirror. They didn't stop or turn around. They just kept on going till they were out of sight.

Dale smirked and condescendingly said, "That's right."

Chapter 23

On his way home on a long dark road, Dale noticed a car behind him getting a little too close for comfort. He squinted his eyes and peered into the rearview mirror. *Wait … is that—*

Red and blue lights illuminated behind him and a couple bleeps from a siren were heard.

Fuck. Dale slowed down his car and edged over to the side of the road. He turned off his engine and wondered why he'd been pulled over. He wasn't speeding. He didn't go through any red lights. He had been obeying all the laws as he drove home like a model citizen … after having killed some guy. Is that why he'd been pulled over? Were they on to him? Maybe a neighbor had spotted his car leaving the scene of the crime despite his cautionary measures.

Dale looked over at the paper bag on the passenger floorboard. The inside-out suit jacket with some black paint and blood on it was visible in the bag, so he leaned over and used a hand to reposition the suit so no blood was showing. But if the car got searched, the bloody knife would quickly be found and he'd be screwed.

Dale looked into the rearview mirror and watched the cop exit his patrol car. *This asshat is taking his sweet time. He may be fine wasting time because his life is pointless, but my time is important. I've got stocks to buy and sell in international markets. This dipshit cop surely doesn't own any stocks. He probably owns stonks.* Dale noticed the cop looking at his face via his rearview mirror's reflection as he approached Dale's car. The cop squinted his eyes at Dale and then abruptly stopped and took on a defensive stance while drawing his firearm. *Oh shit, they are on to me.*

Officer Samuel Green spoke into his two-way radio, "Non-moving violation of expired tags has escalated to shots fired. Need backup. Suspect is African American and driving a stolen black Ferrari."

Officer Green took his hand off the radio and started shooting bullets through Dale's rear windshield and barked, "Stop resisting arrest and exit the stolen vehicle!" With no response from the suspect, he continued his approach and kept firing. While moving forward on the dark road and concentrating on his aim, he didn't notice the large rock in front of him and tripped. While stumbling to the ground he dropped his gun, which hit the ground and fired a bullet into his gut as he was falling down.

Officer Green grabbed his two-way radio. "Officer down. Send backup. Suspect is armed, dangerous, and black. Approach with extreme caution. … Oh God, he shot me. Get this guy!" He let go of his radio and leaned forward on the ground to retrieve his gun.

Dale lifted from his bent-over position and slowly poked his head out of his broken side window. "Are you okay, officer?" Then Dale lunged back down over the seat divider as he saw the cop bring his gun up in the air in his direction.

Officer Green shot two more rounds toward Dale. Then he said, "Stop trying to talk like a white person. You can't fool me. You're as black as a Nigerian, you sonuvabitch!"

Dale realized that the cop thought he was black because his head and neck were covered in black paint. The racist cop had starting shooting because he saw Dale's black face in the rearview mirror. As far as he knew the police still hadn't connected him to the murder, they had only connected him to being black. *Fuck! They're going to kill me. Apparently being black is a bigger crime than being a white murderer.*

Dale pressed the button on the steering wheel to turn on his Ferrari Roma, causing all the dark digital screens and displays to light up in sequence until the cockpit was magically aglow. He floored the gas, shooting up pebbles at the grounded officer behind him and peeling out onto the road. The Ferrari Roma's turbocharged 3.9L V8 engine ripped down the dark road and reached 62 miles per hour in 3.4 seconds, leaving the racist pig in the dust. Well, I guess "racist pig" is a redundant term, thought Dale.

After Officer Green got out of the fetal position that had protected him from the barrage of peddles spat at him, he grabbed the radio. "Suspect has fled the scene. He's driving a stolen black Ferrari. Suspect is black, armed, and dangerous. I repeat, suspect is *black*!"

Unfortunately for Dale it didn't matter how fast he was driving away from the downed pig, because he was driving toward cop cars that were responding to the call for backup.

He met two cop cars heading straight toward him at a four-way intersection. He turned right. The cop cars pursued him in single file.

Dale couldn't make out the cop car second in line behind him, but the cop car directly behind him looked like an old Ford Crown Victoria. He mockingly laughed and shook his head, knowing it had no chance in pursuing his Roma.

The vacant road they were on was straight for a while and looked like it curved to the left a quarter mile down the road. Dale checked the Roma's digital display to see how sharp the turn ahead was and figured he could round it doing about sixty-five miles per hour. The Crown Vic would definitely have to round the bend much slower.

In the meantime he'd put some distance between them on the straightaway. He floored the gas and shot forward. The Ferrari Roma's vortex generators efficiently generated downforce on the front axle with a negligible increase in drag. The Roma's spoiler was flush with the rear for aerodynamics and automatically deployed when Dale hit sixty-two miles per hour. The spoiler provided downforce to the rear of the car.

When Dale reached the bend, the Crown Vic had already lost quite a bit of ground. Dale braked enough to prepare for the turn. In high performance handling or braking situations the Roma's spoiler moved to its highest position, generating a maximum downforce of about ninety-five kilograms, making the car aerodynamically balanced.

Dale eased into the turn. In order to improve handling and road grip, the Roma's incorporated Side Slip Control 6.0 included an algorithm that provided an exact estimate of sideslip to the on-board control systems, and Ferrari Dynamic Enhancer's lateral dynamic control system gently adjusted the brake pressure on one or more wheels depending on the driving situation. All this allowed the Roma to sail through and out of the turn without a hitch. So much so that Dale had to take his foot off the gas to see how the Crown Vic would handle the corner.

Dale eagerly watched the turn behind him from his rearview mirror. The results were comical. The Roma must have made the turn look less sharp because the overzealous cop in the Crown Vic apparently thought he could match the Roma's abilities and ended up losing his center of gravity in the turn and flipped over and off the road.

Dale guffawed, but his laughter was cut short when the second cop car rounded the turn, not as efficiently as he had, but still quite skillfully. After the turn, the remaining cop car started approaching faster than Dale anticipated. It was then that he caught a good look at the cop car and realized how it had taken the turn fairly well and was now closing in on him: it was one of those souped-up Dodge Chargers made specifically for police. Depending on how it was augmented, it possessed a V6 or a V8 engine under its hood and held a top speed anywhere from 155–200 mph. 200 mph was his Roma's top speed.

Shit! No more playtime. Dale put the pedal to the metal. He now had a worthy adversary. As he zoomed down the road with the Charger in tow, he wondered how many everyday, hardworking citizens had received exuberant traffic fines for harmless minor infractions to pay for each one of those bad-boy Chargers. The police force wasn't too different than the Mafia or any well-organized gang, he thought.

Dale shook his head as he glided around a corner. Every turn taken garnered extra distance between his Roma and the pig's Charger, but this strategy alone wouldn't be enough to get him in the clear. He had to lose this Charger before more cop cars got on his tail. Eventually backup would arrive since the pig was periodically radioing their position. Dale had seen enough movies to know this about car chases involving the cops.

He swerved into a warehouse complex that held a maze of pathways between several storehouses. As he was rounding the corner of a warehouse building, he noticed a few heavy-duty concrete cylinder posts a little up ahead, so he slowed down to let the Charger get close behind him.

He could see that the pig was itching to hit the back of his luxury car. This was good because his attention would be elsewhere instead of on this. Dale jerked the Roma to the right and didn't give the Charger enough time to notice and avoid the concrete posts. Dale imagined that the pig's eyes must've been bugging out at that precise moment as the concrete posts burst into view and rushed toward him.

The Charger attempted to avoid the posts at the last moment but failed. Dale watched in dismay as the Charger barreled through the concrete posts instead of being stopped in its tracks. *What a beast.* But it still affected the Charger, and along with its quickly changed direction in an attempt to avoid the posts, the Charger was sent skidding toward a white van that was parked by a concrete corner of a building. The Charger swerved and missed the parked van by an inch, but it hit headfirst into the building's concrete wall and came to a screeching halt. After the loud impact echoed throughout the warehouse complex, the Charger lay in ruins with its front end completely crumpled and steaming.

Dale removed his right arm from the steering wheel and pumped it in victory. "Yes. Eat concrete, asshat."

He sped out of the warehouse and took the long way back to his condo to avoid responding cop cars. His Ferrari Roma, still in pristine condition without having incurred a single scratch or dent throughout the whole ordeal, purred all the way home.

The white van that now lay pinned between a concrete wall and the totaled Charger held two cable provider technicians. They had parked at the empty warehouse after a late-evening service call to rack up another hour's worth of pay before heading back. There were two of them instead of the usual one because the one in the passenger seat was being trained.

The technicians gawked at the totaled Charger right before them. It was clear the cop hadn't been wearing his seatbelt because his head was smashed into the windshield, which had broken upon impact. The cop's head was embedded into the broken windshield and was bleeding onto the dashboard and the deployed airbag, which obviously hadn't stopped the seatbelt-less cop from smacking into the windshield.

Jerome, the young black man in the passenger seat that was being trained, said, "Damn, did that just happen? I'm not hallucinating am I?"

Liam, the thirty-nine-year-old white dude in the driver's seat, said, "Nope, I'm seeing it too. He must have been chasing that black sports car that was zipping around. Looks like we're going to be here till his backup and a tow truck arrives because we're completely pinned in."

"We can still get out of the van, though," Jerome said. "Should we help him out? Get that glass out of his head and call an ambulance or something?"

"We're going to sit in this van and not do a goddamn thing about it," Liam uttered with palpable anger in his voice. "Let me tell you why. When I was twenty-three years old, some friends and I were exiting an all-night rave. I'm not sure if my Latino friend scowled at the cop that was lingering outside or if the cop was just in a mood, but he walked up to my friend with hatred on his face and asked if my friend had any drugs on his person. None of my friends or myself had drugs on us. We were on acid and healthily benefitting from a good dose of psilocybin. We were connected to the all-encompassing love vibration of the cosmos, one with everything and feeling great until the pig walked over to us like some demon. My Latino friend isn't one to suck up to anyone, even the law. So instead of answering the cop's question, he said, 'Emilio isn't here right now, so if you could leave your name and number, I'll be sure to never call you back.' The cop didn't like that answer and immediately handcuffed him. While he was handcuffing him I stepped toward the cop and put out a hand in a calming way and told the officer that none of us had any drugs in our possession. The cop must have felt threatened by how close my hand had gotten to him, because he started handcuffing me right afterward. While he was attempting to handcuff me, I was squirming my arms around, trying to break free from his grasp. This aggravated the cop, so he said he was going to write me up for resisting arrest.

"He took us to the police station. We were released an hour later, but the cop did indeed charge me with resisting arrest. I didn't know what that would do to my life at the time, but I soon found out that the charge was a misdemeanor and would be on my record for the rest of my life. That didn't mean much to me until I found out that I was unemployable wherever I went due to it popping up on my record whenever employers ran their mandatory background checks. The bachelor's degree that I worked my ass off for became irrelevant. I couldn't get a job anywhere. I couldn't even get a job at McDonald's. I couldn't keep a girlfriend because they'd always leave me when they found out I couldn't get a real job and had a record. It didn't matter how I explained it, they automatically considered me a criminal, as if the misdemeanor charge had been stamped on my forehead by God himself. Basically, I was blacklisted from having a life. My life was over just because that cop pinned that misdemeanor on me. I stewed in hatred for years until I came to terms with it and realized I couldn't do anything about it. So yeah … fuck that pig. He can bleed to death for all I care."

Jerome was surprised by the story. "Damn, you got blacked."

Liam nodded. "I guess that's one way of saying it. I always thought that kind of thing couldn't happen to me because I was white. I was dead wrong. Now I understand what it feels like to be a black man in America."

Jerome looked him up and down. "Yeah, you white, but you might as well be black on the inside after they got their hooks in you. … How did you get this job then?"

"My brother is in management. I had to beg him for a week to convince him to use his authority to get me this job. I'll never be able to use my degree to fulfill my passion in life, but at least I can live a somewhat normal life with this job."

Jerome nodded his head. "Yup. You definitely know what it feels like to be black. But you're still lucky you didn't end up in the prison business."

"Prison business? What do you mean?"

"My friends and I call the slammer the prison business because that's what they've made it, a business, a company that works for profit. The establishment may repeat its lie to citizens that prisons have to spend such-and-such amount of money to keep each prisoner incarcerated, but in actuality, the taxpayer pays that whole bill. The prisons then make a profit for each inmate on their sheet. That's why America has a staggeringly high amount of people in prison compared to any other country in the world. It's a business, and they're always looking for more employees. And once you work for them once, your criminal record makes you unemployable so that crime is the only way you can survive, making it highly probable that you'll soon end up in the slammer as one of their employees again. It's a vicious cycle that they cooked up on purpose; it wasn't just a flaw that happened to arise in the system."

Liam said, "I didn't know anything about that, but I have an open mind and see how that could be true."

Jerome nodded once. "Oh yeah, it's true, but the truth doesn't need me to defend it, so I won't try to argue the facts. You can scour the Internet for information if you feel inclined."

A silence rested inside the van for a few seconds as they watched the unconscious cop bleeding to death in the totaled Charger. They had front row seats to a drawn-out execution.

Then Liam continued his training. "You know how there is no black and white when you're a cop, they're only blue because of their uniform. No matter what color their skin is, they're despised by all ethnicities when they dawn that dark blue uniform that brightly shines its totalitarian authority."

"Yeah, I know what you're saying."

"Well, we're similar as cable providers. You may be a man of whatever color you were born, but the moment you put on your cable provider uniform, you become something else. You're not black or white, you're cable-provider color."

Thinking it was a joke, Jerome laughed.

Liam shook his head. "No, I'm not joking. When you wear this uniform," he tapped a hand to his cable provider uniform, "you're seen in a whole different light. The color of your skin doesn't apply anymore. People will look down on you, frown at you as you walk by, spit in your general direction ..."

Jerome suppressed laughter at Liam's comical speech.

Liam pointed to the slogan on the totaled Dodge Charger before them. "See that? 'To Protect & Serve.' We cable providers have our own slogan. Did you see it on the van?"

"No, I didn't. What is it?"

" 'To Connect & Provide.' We keep the population connected to the Internet and provide them with countless channels that provide a lifetime worth of entertainment. Unlike the cops' false motto, we stand by our slogan."

Liam's statement made Jerome recall his older brother's experience with a cable provider—not just any cable provider, but the one he now worked for. His brother, Eric, had had a self-employed job that relied on a stable Internet connection. After a couple months of his Internet being hooked up, it started dropping out for five to ten minutes regularly. Eric was losing business because of this and knew he'd soon be out of a job if he didn't get it fixed. But even after countless calls to the cable provider and many service visits by technicians, which he was billed for every time, the problem persisted. So Eric went online to find a solution to the problem. His online research ended up uncovering no solutions, only a cache of similar horror stories from customers like himself that had been screwed by the cable company. Without the problem being corrected, Eric soon lost all his online business and had to get a job way under his skill level to pay the bills: stocking shelves at a grocery store. He ended up slipping on a can of GMO peas in the backroom and his head had become an ornament on a forklift. Dead.

Then there was the matter of cable TV. Jerome watched movies and was an avid reader. He didn't watch TV shows. He was an intellectual, a smart guy just like his brother had been before the canned-pea incident, but he didn't have the funds to get into college in order to collect that piece of paper that would allow him to get a decent job. He found it absurdly comical that even without years of education at a university, he could do a better job in a "proper career" than most that had degrees. He figured it was the elites' way of keeping the caste system in play.

He didn't watch TV and considered the plethora of channels as a means of pacifying, conditioning, and dumbing down the general population instead of bestowing real entertainment. Anytime Jerome wandered past a TV and heard canned laughter from some horrific sitcom emanating from its screen, he got slightly nauseous. A laugh track was a show's way of telling its audience that they weren't smart enough to know when to organically laugh for themselves. And without fake laughter after every deplorable one-liner, the viewer might realize how unfunny the show actually was. They might realize that they're wasting their life, turn off the TV, and do something else—anything else. Even staring at trees is more meaningful.

As far as Jerome was concerned, his company's slogan was just as false as the police's. He'd only applied for the job because it paid better than other jobs he was able to get without a degree.

He wondered if the cop bleeding to death in front of them was one of the police officers that actually followed the police's motto. There was no way for him to know for sure. There were so many cops that had lost their way that it tended to seem like they were all corrupt, but he knew that some officers were actually doing their jobs to help people. They had the best intentions, despite some of the sticky situations they sometimes found themselves in.

Similarly, he recognized that many people became politicians to help their country, but after being a politician for a period of time, they soon became aware that the political system was completely broken and in the hands of ruthless individuals that thwarted all progress and kept the status quo in place. JFK must've been trying to help the population immensely, because they assassinated him. Every president that actually tried to do their job either got assassinated or had assassination attempts. But Jerome had a sixth-sense feeling that the main man behind the JFK assassination plot had recently been fried in the electric chair after being found guilty in a secret but legal military tribunal. Read my lips, fried chicken has been served for justice.

While Jerome had been thinking all this, Liam had been going on about the cable job like they were saviors liberating the world, "… so we give them connectivity and a wealth of entertainment to make their dull lives worth living, and in return they spit in our faces instead of honoring our heroic deeds. It's akin to the soldiers that returned from the Vietnam War."

Again, Jerome suppressed laughter upon listening to his trainer's ranting. He felt for the guy and was sympathetic about his life being ruined by the cops, but it was apparent that his hatred and frustration throughout the years had somewhat twisted his mind and outlook on the world. He could've dropped his victim mentality and made the problem of not being able to get a job in the system the best thing that ever happened to him: it could've forced him to live outside the system at a self-sustaining community, be self-employed, or something where he'd be far happier than willingly breaking his back working a forty-hour workweek for the Man with nothing to show for his labor after his rent, bills, and taxes sucked up his entire paycheck.

If he lived and worked at a self-sustaining community, he'd see firsthand the fruits of his labor, how it benefited others and himself. Then he'd actually be able to feel pride in the act of working instead of work being an action that only drained his soul till cancer came along to finish him off. Jerome thought of this because he had considered joining a self-sustaining community himself, and maybe he would one day.

Liam ended his speech and pulled out a large tablet. "Anyway, while we're stuck here until a tow truck arrives, let's dip into our own supply and watch some television. What do you want to watch, *Fake History* or *All Aliens are Evil*?"

Jerome subtly sighed before replying, "*All Aliens are Evil*."

Dale cruised his Ferrari Roma into 432 Park Avenue and parked it in the garage. After exiting it and closing the door, he paused to appreciate the remarkable car. Not only was its interior and exterior design breathtaking, but so was its performance. He gently ran a finger down its hood like he was caressing a lover in bed.

The cops must've recorded his license plate, but they also thought a black man was driving the car, and since he was immediately shot at, they must have thought his car had been stolen. He'd call the police and report his car stolen and then a couple days later call again and say he just happened to find it abandoned on the curb somewhere. Or something in that nature. He'd think more about it tomorrow. It wouldn't be a problem and he wasn't worried about it. What was important is that he wasn't connected to the two dead bodies in Joel Amoral's house. He was confident it wouldn't be pinned on him, but if it became a problem, he was positive Aryana Rottenschild would provide a solid alibi.

He jumped into the shower and scrubbed his body clean of the black paint. By the time he was done and toweling himself off, he felt his raw and tender face stinging. He looked in the mirror. The image looked like a different person, a different being. The collected steam in the bathroom from the long shower whisked around the red image in the mirror.

He continued to stare at his reflection and think about what he'd done today. It was the first time he had taken a human life, but he didn't feel the least bit bad about it. It didn't seem to matter whether Amoral was dead or not. If he felt anything, it was a sense of pride for having successfully fulfilled his biggest scheme yet. According to his work contract, for all intents and purposes, he was already a senior executive VP. At some point in the future he'd be eligible to be a partner at his brokerage, but that didn't seem to matter to him that much anymore. He now had a loftier trajectory in mind after Aryana had told him who his mentor would be. The sky was the limit.

Dale leaped into bed and quickly fell into a deep slumber. He slept like a baby. He dreamed he was on a train with Jeremy and Tim. Jeremy sat across from him on the other side of the train. Tim was seated in a nearby booth and was conversing with a calm British gentlemen dressed in beige clothing. Dale kept tripping the passengers that walked by, never losing his enjoyment from watching each tripped person fall and face-plant on the floor. For some reason the people never figured out that it was Dale who had tripped them. They'd grimace and look all around before continuing on down the train.

He looked over to the booth Tim and the British man had occupied, but it was now empty, like they had simply teleported off the train. To this he felt indifferent; he didn't care about Tim and he had no business being in his dream anyway.

As the train curved to the left, Dale saw the intended destination in the far background behind Jeremy: a fast-paced, dirty city filled with skyscrapers and crime. Then the track straightened out and the view behind Jeremy changed to a scenic meadow where a brook babbled its way to a peaceful oceanfront in the distance.

Jeremy, who Dale thought had intended to stay on the ride till the city, stood up and said it was his stop. Jeremy fearlessly jumped off the train while it was still in motion instead of waiting for the next official stop. Dale thought Jeremy would've been a goner for having leapt from the speeding train, but he immediately saw an unharmed Jeremy calmly walking in the meadow, headed toward the oceanfront where the waves lapped gently against the shore, receded, and continued the rhythmic sequence, which seemed to convey a blissful eternity. Seagulls flew overhead in the distance and the message in "Get Free" on *Lust for Life* by Lana Del Rey ethereally sailed across the sun-drenched, golden meadow. Jeremy had walked out of the black train ride and into the blue ocean and sky.

Dale didn't see any sharks in the water, so he wasn't impressed with the beach. There would be plenty of sharks in the city, he knew that for sure.

Aioli suddenly appeared in front of him in the seat where Jeremy had once sat, and she was eyeing him intently. She brought up a hand and tapped a finger a few times on the text written on her shirt: KARMA PATROL. "Watch out," she cautioned Dale while doing the tapping. Then her figure slowly dissolved until her apparition had entirely departed, leaving behind only flecks of dust illuminated by rays of sunlight streaming through the window.

Dale turned his head and noticed a large executive booth filled with card sharks. Their booth was filled with smoke from the cigars they were puffing away on while downing whiskey and playing poker. Dale walked over to them and asked them if he could be dealt in on the next round. All the card sharks turned their heads and looked deep into Dale's eyes. Dale stared back into their eyes, which were completely black.

After the card sharks had analyzed him by peering deep through his eyes and into his soul, they approved him, and one of them said, "Sure, sit down dear boy and have a cigar. If you do, I'm sure you'll go far. Hell, you'll fly high and you'll never die."

Another shark said, "By the way, we're not playing poker. Did we tell you the name of the game, boy?"

"No," Dale replied.

The shark said, "We call it riding the gravy train."

Pink Floyd's "Have a Cigar" started playing over the train's speaker system as if the card sharks had selected it on a jukebox.

Dale sat, puffed on a cigar he was given, drank several whiskey tumblers, played riding the gravy train with the sharks, and became delightfully intoxicated.

They rode that gravy train all the way into the city. As drunk as lords they belted out guffaws and verses from songs the whole ride. The train reached the city and the end of the rail at the last station, but instead of stopping, the train ran full steam off the tracks and chewed up the pavement as it barreled through the city, running over countless people before stopping at a hidden station.

One of the sharks said, "In order to get to the heart of the city, you must ride over many people. It is the gravy train, after all."

They threw the remains of their cigars in their unfinished whiskey tumblers and stood to button up their suit jackets while laughing and patting each other on the back.

One of the sharks lifted a handheld mirror in front of Dale's face. Dale saw that his eyes were now completely black like theirs. The shark lowered the mirror and said, "You're one of us now. Come on, follow us. We'll get our gear, get you all sorted out, and get down to business."

The sharks alighted from the train and strolled down the platform that had direct access to the heart of the city. Dale saw people rushing around in all directions. It looked like he'd entered a loony bin. The people were either hypnotized, tearing their hair out in fear and anxiety, counting money, stealing money, or killing other people. Others were spending their time enjoying life: playing music, performing in theatrical plays, inventing devices, writing novels, and delving into the arts.

The sharks focused on the people creating negative energy. Dale saw the sharks' mouths frothing and salivating and delightfully smelling up the palpable negative energy that was akin to the cigar smoke that had filled their luxurious train booth minutes ago. Dale followed suit and breathed in the same energy. It felt orgasmic and made him strong and powerful.

A knives salesman approached them and asked Dale if he was interested in purchasing his wares. One of the sharks told the salesman that Dale was with them now and didn't need to purchase anything. Normally the salesman would've been pleased with the remark, but he seemed annoyed in this particular case due to the timing of it all and walked away in dismay while eying his wristwatch.

Then the sharks pulled out human-sized cages and tranquilizer guns. They provided Dale with the same gear.

A shark told Dale, "Now we're going to play the second part of The Gravy Train. This part is called The Middleman. See all the people running around?" With a regal flare he swooped an arm around, gesturing to the people. "You tranquilize them and put them in cages. Once they're in your cage, they work for you. It doesn't matter if they're the people giving off negative or positive energy, it's all the same. Remember, you tranquilize them, don't kill them. If you want someone killed, or a whole town for that matter, you must cage the correct people so they'll do your bidding. Murderers will silence an adversary or your competition. Mercenaries are the best for large-scale killings. This way you don't have to get your own hands dirty. Not unless you want to that is. If you want a bill passed or rejected, cage a politician. If you want to fulfill your sexual desires, cage any woman, girl, boy—whatever's your fancy. If you want to make a lot of money, cage musicians, inventors, writers—creative types. As a Middleman, you'll reap almost all the benefits from their creativity. They'll even thank you for it as they walk away with their miniscule percentage of the royalties. Musicians, writers, and actors can't bring their art to the populace unless they're in your cage, so they're the easiest to cage, as they'll walk right into your cage without being tranquilized. In fact, they'll beg you to allow them to crawl into your cage."

Dale said, "Couldn't you just make more money by caging a banker?"

The shark smiled. "No, you can't cage a banker. They have vicious teeth and will chew their way out of your cage in no time. No cage can hold a tenacious banker. Besides, bankers will help you quadruple your earnings. It's better to work with bankers after you've made money from your caged workers. Bankers are your allies, don't cage them." He pointed to a group of bankers devouring a family. Their long, sharp teeth were dripping with blood and kept ripping into flesh. The shark grinned at the sight. "Look at those snappers. What beautiful creatures."

After eyeballing and enjoying the bankers feasting for a bit, the shark gave his attention back to Dale. "The point is, people are just numbers to be used in your math equations. They're not important. It doesn't matter if they live or die, or how they live and die. Their worth is only a collective effort in the equation—they're like batteries—and if you've placed them in the right spots in your equations, they'll always equal whatever you want them to equal and your agendas will be fulfilled. They're simply automatons to be used for your bidding, or even solely for your entertainment."

Dale woke up and used a hand to straighten his pillowcase while still half asleep. He mumbled to himself as he turned over and went back to bed, "Put them in cages … automatons … fulfill agendas. Got it. Hmm, how splendid."

When the press got wind of last night's car chase, they sent reporters to the hospital to get a statement from the cop that had been shot in the gut. The injured cop's superior, Captain Roper, allowed the reporters to gather around the injured hero in his hospital bed so that he could deliver the narrative to them. A narrative that Captain Roper had supplied him with.

"Officer Green," began a reporter, "ballistics show that you were shot with your own gun. Can you comment on that?"

Captain Roper became agitated. "How did you get that information? That information hasn't been released."

Officer Green answered anyway, not adhering to the story that he was told to stick to. "While the suspect was resisting arrest he managed to get a hand on my holstered gun. I tried to wrestle it free from him but took a bullet in the gut in the process."

The same reporter asked another question. "You only speak of one shot being fired, but investigators at the scene of the crime said there were numerous spent bullet casings near your patrol car. Can you comment on that, officer?"

The agitated captain was now irate and stepped in between the injured hero and the reporter. "That information can't be released to the public at this time because it's part of an ongoing investigation."

Again, Green answered the reporter's question despite his superior's agitation. "Uhh … After I exited my patrol car, I saw through the suspect's rear windshield that he was aiming a gun at me, so I protected myself by laying down fire."

The reporter shot back, "If the suspect already had a gun, why did he attempt to take yours?"

Captain Roper was now raging mad. He glared at Officer Green and then turned to bark at the reporter. "What's with these questions? Are you internal affairs or something? Are you anti-American?"

Green attempted to answer the reporter's question, spouting out the first thing that came into his head. "Umm … After the suspect emptied his gun on me—luckily I wasn't hit—he exited his vehicle and ran into the dark, escaping the area my patrol car's headlights lit up. The suspect was so black that he blended into the dark along that pitch-black road. For all I know he could've been doing jumping jacks out there in the dark while sticking his tongue out at me—I couldn't see a damn thing. He effectively used his blackness against me like a weapon. When we catch him, we'll use this against him in court. Just like a martial artist's hands and feet should be registered as lethal weapons with the State, very black people need to register their skin color as a deadly weapon or shouldn't be allowed to walk around at night. The suspect's blackness will be classified as a weapon in court."

Captain Roper swung around toward Green. "What the hell are you talking about?! Don't say another word, you blockhead!" Then he turned to the reporters. "Okay, that's enough questions for the hero. Officer Green needs his rest. Please exit the room now."

After the room had been cleared of reporters and the door closed, Captain Roper growled at Green. "You were supposed to stick to the story I gave you! Not only was your story idiotic, but it clearly would label the police force as racist! We don't say stuff like that to the public, especially not the press. 'Very black people need to register their skin color as deadly weapons for nighttime.' What kind of a blockhead statement is that?!"

Green tried to explain himself. "But he was blacker than midnight, sir. Once he stepped out into the night, he might as well of evaporated into thin air like a ghost."

"Shut the hell up, Green!"

Green lowered his head in shame. "I'm sorry, sir."

"You better be sorry. You're lucky I got connections with gentlemen that own the press companies. I'll get the story erased. Your little idiotic rant won't be seen in the papers tomorrow. … By the way, a martial artist only needs to register their limbs as deadly weapons in the U.S. territory of Guam, blockhead."

The superior told the injured hero to keep his trap shut and not speak a single word to anyone about the incident. Then he left the room to make some calls to take care of the press problem.

Not a single word ended up in the papers. The ambitious reporter, who had asked the questions, worked for an "independent press" outfit and soon realized that her company was just as unconcerned and indifferent to the truth as the major elite-controlled presses were. She found out later that the press company she worked for was indirectly owned by one of the major presses. After she did some snooping around, it turned out that virtually all independent press companies weren't actually independent at all.

After some press bigwigs caught wind of her nosing around, they offered her a nice-paying gig at one of their prominent press companies. They had her report on the front lines of the latest war where she'd be sure to catch a stray bullet or two and cease to be a problem.

Chapter 24

Three years as a senior ORA for Cohesive Analytics had shaped an outlook that Jeremy hadn't foreseen throughout all the years he was striving to be successful. He could see more clearly after having resided at the top, no longer needing to focus on acquiring promotions.

The path he had been traveling on for so long had materialized his goals: a hefty annual salary, a top position at the company, a large house, and an ample sum of money in the bank. His large house wasn't needed, as he was still happily single, but it seemed like the appropriate thing to acquire once he had the financial means, and everyone had said it was a good real estate investment, regardless of his marital status.

The money and prestige he'd procured did have its comforts, but the joy he thought he'd also procure once reaching the top was absent. The feeling was unmistakable. More than enough time had passed for him to recognize that it wasn't merely a mood or something that would pass with time. In fact, the more time that went by, the worse he felt.

When it became clear that his feelings on the matter weren't temporary, he began to closely observe his inner state, his role within the company, and the actions of the large companies he helped manage.

With power comes responsibility, and his responsibilities seemed to be eating up all the time in his life. He didn't have enough free time to enjoy his hobbies: reading, hiking in nature, taking meandering strolls, quiet moments of contemplation, relaxing at a café, etc. These activities had been a type of medicine and meditation that kept his wellbeing and contentment alive. This he realized after he hadn't been partaking of them due to his miniscule amount of free time.

Even when he had managed to fit them into his schedule, his all-consuming thoughts and obligations revolving around his job poisoned his mind and didn't allow him to appreciate his hobbies any longer. When he engaged in hobbies it felt like he was solely going through the motions, his lifeless actions bore no fruit and failed to soothe his soul. It felt like his soul was slowly drying up. He was on his way to becoming a shell of a man, if he wasn't one already.

He had enjoyed the analytical aspects of his job that allowed him to flex his brain, think outside the box, and figure out puzzles placed before him, but he grew tired of sitting in front of a computer for the better part of his days. But the biggest tragedy of his predicament began to unravel when he witnessed how his brainpower and ideas had been used by the conglomerates he assisted. Whenever he got wind of the twisted outcomes enacted by the companies that used his ideas and algorithms in real life, he'd feel disgusted. They'd perverted his genius into something horrible: clearing large portions of a rainforest, displacing or decimating small villages, poisoning the water supply of towns with mining or improperly discarded chemicals, etc. He now could relate to the scientist's plight of having their inventions used against humanity instead of for the betterment of the world. Not to say that his ideas were as genius or important as the inventions of the greatest scientific minds in the world, but he could now relate and sympathize with their anguish.

If there was one thing that Jeremy learned from dealing with powerful companies, it was that the world revolved around money and power and intelligence would always take a backseat to greed, which bred a society of fools. No wonder most companies weren't implementing smart business models and revolutionary devices weren't being invented or making their way into the public anymore. The leaps forward his civilization had seen in the past decades seemed to be more like backward steps once a magnifying glass and scrutiny were applied. Almost every modern revolutionary idea, system, or invention seemed to be acquired by powerful people and used to fuel their greed and ability to stay in power rather than advance humanity.

These powerful people used their huge companies as facades to hide their actions and Trojan horses to deceptively implement their nefarious agendas. When an enormous company did something that could've been construed by the public as sinister, a company could always chalk up the reason for any of their actions to a means to make a financial gain instead of its actual villainous purpose. They'd pay a fine that seemed large to the common man but was a drop in the bucket for their huge companies. Jeremy wouldn't have been surprised if he learned that the companies were even being given back the fined money in some way behind closed doors.

The worker bees for these companies actually believed that financial gain was the only factor in their companies' actions. And even when some saw through a company's facade, it was a lot harder to point the finger at the few powerful individuals in charge of these malicious actions when they hid behind their conglomerates, camouflaged in a sea of their oblivious employees.

If an invention couldn't be used to collect money from the population, or even worse, if it nullified existing money-making businesses, it was bought and put on a basement shelf to rust. Jeremy could recall how long it took the electric car to make it to the public. He recalled reading how U.S. car and oil companies purchased transit systems in American cities between the 30s and 60s so they could scrap them and put diesel buses in their places. New York, Chicago, Boston, and Philadelphia were lucky their transit systems didn't get purchased and abandoned before being completed. The horrible traffic in Los Angeles in particular prompted him to think about how the planned subway system in L.A. was purchased and halted so that money could keep filling up the coffers of certain powerful individuals. Not to mention how L.A.'s efficient streetcars were bought and yanked out of circulation in the 60s.

He wondered how many irate L.A. drivers stuck in hellish traffic for hours on a daily basis would react if they had all the facts in their hands about their scrapped subway system. It alone would fuel horrendous rage when they realized that literally years of their lives had been—or will be—unnecessarily spent in bumper to bumper traffic before retirement. Once given the facts, he was sure that a good amount of L.A. drivers would completely snap, make their way to the homes of the powerful individuals responsible, march through their grand marble foyers, barge through countless mahogany doors, and fill those greedy cocksuckers full of American-hero bullets.

It was no wonder that the foreseen future depicted in sci-fi movies and literature where people were commuting in automatic flying vehicles and possessed a wealth of devices that would dispense with common day chores never became realized in our present world. Those advances had been and are still being halted in the name of money and power. Here we were still relying on dirty fossil fuels for energy more than a century after vehicles were invented, and archaic batteries for giving power to devices—just two examples Jeremy could think of off the top of his head.

Greed and power kept humanity from advancing. Jeremy wasn't a conspiracy theorist and didn't spend time researching numerous topics on the Internet, so if he was aware of enough of these facts without having given the effort and time, he figured he'd be overwhelmed by a plethora of ugly truths if he did have the time in his life to go digging. His long work hours had made him unable to go hunting for such information, and the rest of humanity was in the same boat, working long workweeks. He wondered if that was by design so that people wouldn't have enough free time to realize what was really going on in the world. He had come across ideas like these in some of the books he'd read back when he had more time for hobbies. Books like *Atlas Shrugged*, *1984*, and *Brave New World*. Jeremy used to think the people who talked about these types of things were paranoid—possibly crazy—and had too much time on their hands, but after years of working with conglomerates, he'd been exposed to the ugly truth firsthand instead of by way of the Internet.

After it had become abundantly clear to Jeremy that his road to success had actually been a road to misery, he took the steps that he thought were necessary to get back in alignment with the harmony of life and retain his contentment. Most of these steps were simply cutting off the fat and simplifying his life. He quit his job and sold his big house. He bought a cozy house in a quiet part of town. In his younger years before the lust for money and advancement had dominated his thoughts, he had a romantic idea of owning a bookstore due to his love for literature, so he finally followed through on it. He purchased a store in an area where the commercial rent wasn't too high and converted it into an independent bookstore that sold new and used books. He should've realized the error in his ways and rerouted his path a lot sooner, but better late than never.

After all the details of his life transition had played out, he found himself slowly returning to contentment, feeling alive like he had in his youth. It didn't come immediately. He had to recondition his mind by living joyously and strengthening positive synaptic pathways in his brain. One could say that he had to rewire his brain. But with the right mindset—or rather, not letting his mind get in the way—the rewiring wasn't too difficult. He began to enjoy his hobbies again: reading, being in nature, taking leisurely walks in the park and through the city streets, and spending moments in quiet contemplation or stillness.

He'd often cozy on up in a nook of his bookstore and enjoy reading for the better part of a day. Other days were spent in the great outdoors taking in everything that nature had to offer. Even short visits to a local coffee shop with a book became things that he looked forward to. It was all a matter of outlook. It was like Abraham Lincoln had said: "Folks are usually about as happy as they make their minds up to be." It wasn't what you did, but how you did it that made you happy.

A quote by Thomas Merton also came to Jeremy's mind: "We cannot be happy if we expect to live all the time at the highest peak of intensity. Happiness is not a matter of intensity but of balance and order and rhythm and harmony."

His analytical job had his brain working overtime so he hadn't been able to enjoy whatever he was doing. His mind had been perpetually thinking about what he needed to do or simply what he was going to do next. He realized that with such a mindset a person would never fully enjoy anything they did because they weren't focused on what they were doing in the moment. Since life is only lived in each moment—not in the past or the future—life would never be enjoyed unless you lived in and enjoyed the present moment.

His old job had also kept him from spending enough time with his few close friends. His biweekly lunches with Tim had turned into biyearly lunches. Now he was able to see Tim and his other friends more often.

Tim had also eventually gotten his life back on track after working through the loss of his wife. Jeremy thought it was nice to see Tim dating again, but it was even nicer to see that he was comfortable by himself and wasn't relying on another person to make himself happy anymore.

Tim had expressed his thanks to Jeremy for giving him that powerful book: *The Power of Now* by Eckhart Tolle. It had sat on his bookshelf for years, untouched, until he finally gravitated towards it about two years after his wife's death. After consuming the book, he purchased and read its sequel: *A New Earth*, and found it just as rewarding. He had told Jeremy that the two books had completely reshaped not just his outlook on the world, but how he interacted with the world, and most importantly, with himself.

Jeremy had felt the same way after he'd read the two books many years ago in his early twenties, but realized the weight of the world and his loss of sight for what was important had pulled him away from that enlightenment. It had taken him about fifteen years to regain that enlightenment.

After wondering for a while why he had allowed himself to depart from a life of liberation, the reason formed in his mind during one of his contemplations: when one is living in a society that holds entirely different views about what is important in life and how one should think and interact within life, it can be easy to lose one's newfound enlightenment and return to the faulty mindset held by the society the person is immersed in. It can happen slowly or quickly. He had forgotten what was important and allowed himself to get swept up into what society deemed was important and made one happy.

Despite his ability to think outside the box and be a freethinker, he'd fallen into the trap of social conditioning. He didn't get down on himself once he realized this because he knew that it wasn't easy to hold divergent thoughts and ideas when being immersed in a society that constantly pushed its point of view in every facet of life.

Looking back on the years and what he experienced in life, despite his acquired "success," it was obvious that society's way to happiness couldn't be more wrong. In fact, it was running headlong in the completely opposite direction of where contentment could be found. He made a mental note to keep this lesson in mind so that he wouldn't get swept up in the raging energy that society created, and one day society, one way or another, would be made aware of its error and transform itself.

He couldn't save the world outright, but he could aid it by living a life of integrity and contentment. If enough people did the same, the hundredth monkey effect would reshape the world, and in this way, he *would* be saving the world within a collective effort. Till then, he'd dive deeper and deeper into the calming depths of the sea, safe from the storms on the surface. And when he found himself coming up for air to interact with a distressed or frazzled person, it would be his wealth of knowledge instead of his wealth of coin that would allow him to act like a cruise liner upon the surface of the sea, too immense for waves to agitate.

While at the surface, he'd view small boats being viciously aggravated by waves and seed them with the blueprints for their own cruise ships if the timing seemed right or if they asked for it. But the boat captains had the right to own vessels that were the size of their liking. It was their free will to do so and he wasn't going to force a blueprint upon anyone who hadn't asked for it.

Free will not only decides the size of a vessel, but it dictates that each spirit is in charge of how they operate their vessel and how pure they keep their vessel.

Chapter 25

It was a lazy Sunday afternoon. Jeremy was nestled in his favorite nook of his bookstore near a window that afforded a view of greenery outside. He was rereading *The Little Book* by Selden Edwards when he overheard two twenty-something females talking as they meandered through the aisles of books. One was recommending a book to her friend.

"Sally, come here. You have to read this book," she said with excitement.

With a book already in her hand, Sally strolled over to her friend. "What book?"

Amy proudly presented the book to her friend. "*The Eye of the Moon*. It's the second book in the 'Bourbon Kid' series. Remember *The Book With No Name* that we both loved? This is its sequel."

Sally's eyes lit up. "No way! I'm definitely buying it."

Amy looked down at the book in Sally's hand. "Oh, nice, you're getting the last novel in Valerio Massimo Manfredi's 'Alexander' trilogy. Those books are stellar. No one writes about ancient Greece better than Manfredi."

Having heard their excitement over literature, Jeremy's heart blissfully swelled. They had good taste in literature too. Their love for literature especially made Jeremy glad because they were of the young generation, a generation whose attention spans had dramatically declined from being exposed to fast-paced digital technology since birth. A generation that the horrible pharmaceutical company was recklessly forcing Ritalin and Adderall on like they were vitamins or candy. He cringed when he thought of how their bodies and minds were being poisoned and warped before even reaching adulthood.

As the two females scampered away, Jeremy recognized a familiar face browsing through the bookshelves: Shinjiro

Watanabe, a client he worked with when he first moved into the role of an advanced ORA at Cohesive Analytics several years ago. Working with Shinjiro had been one of the few highlights at Cohesive because they had similar minds and would sometimes hold philosophical and meaningful conversations during luncheons after business matters had been taken care of.

He placed his bookmarker in the book and called out, "Nice to see you in my bookstore, Shinjiro."

Shinjiro turned toward the voice. "Jeremy, what a surprise. *Your* bookstore? You don't work at Cohesive Analytics anymore?"

They conversed for a bit between the bookshelves and got each other up to speed on their current affairs. After which, Jeremy motioned toward the bookshelves with an outstretched arm. "Were you looking for anything in particular or just browsing?"

Shinjiro straightened his glasses with a delicate hand and replied, "I'm looking for an epic apocalyptic novel. The subject is a guilty pleasure of mine."

Jeremy extended an index finger upward. "I know just the book for you." He led Shinjiro through the bookshelves and procured a book from a shelf a few aisles away. "I believe *Swan Song* by Robert McCammon would suit you well." He placed it in Shinjiro's hands so he could read the synopsis.

They talked a bit more and, having missed their luncheon conversations, Shinjiro invited Jeremy to lunch at his favorite tonkatsu restaurant after he purchased the book Jeremy recommended. Jeremy accepted and left his bookstore in the capable hands of his bookworm staff.

After sitting down at the restaurant and ordering their pork cutlets, Jeremy asked what Shinjiro missed most about Japan. Shinjiro had moved to Seattle for work at the age of thirty-one and had never moved back to Japan, but he visited his family members once a year. He was now fifty-five years old.

After testing the temperature and taking a sip of his miso soup, Shinjiro answered without hesitation. "That's easy. Zen."

"Zen, eh? It's a way of life and not a religion, right?"

"That's right. Zen is a present state of mind where one honors the task they are partaking of, even if that task is sitting still and doing nothing. Zen is engrained in the Japanese way of life. You can see it everywhere: when a sushi chef delicately slices a piece of raw fish, when a retired man watches an autumn leaf fall from a tree in the park, when a mother prepares and places a cup of tea before her child. When actions and thoughts are done with mindfulness, being fully present in the moment, the person performing the action or thought gives honor to the food, an idea, a task, a person, etc. Even if one doesn't practice Zen, Shinto, or Buddhism, Zen is expressed in their daily life because it has been engrained in Japanese culture. But I'm afraid the younger generation is being tested; the fast-paced electronic world has its advantages and can be embraced correctly, but too many youth are losing their Zen presence by it and not honoring the moment. Instead, they're multitasking and not fully enjoying—or not enjoying at all—the tasks they're doing, which makes their actions heavily degraded. … That's what I miss most, Zen. That act of the moment being honored."

Jeremy gingerly nodded his head as he recalled vacationing in Japan. "Yeah, I understand what you're saying. There was a type of calmness that I felt in Japan. Even when walking through crowded streets in Tokyo, I didn't feel anxiety in the atmosphere like I would at a crowded mall in America. People aren't aware that their thoughts and emotions emanate from their bodies. When a person is frazzled, or not centered in some way, they're not aware that they're not only polluting their own body, mind, and spirit, but also the people around them."

Shinjiro smiled. "That's a fine observation." He reached his chopsticks toward his shredded cabbage salad. "I have missed our conversations. There are not too many people that share the same wavelength as we do." After a broad smile and a slight nod from Jeremy that showed his reciprocation for the statement, Shinjiro said, "Adding to your fine observation, it goes further than even to the people around you. Since we're all One, even a single person's thoughts and emotions can have an impact on the global consciousness, the soup that we all reside in. Every single person has the power to affect the world with their thoughts and emotions alone, and when there are enough people holding beneficial temperaments, the world will transform in the blink of an eye. What one does can be important, but what one thinks and feels—the conscious state they hold—is infinitely more important."

Shinjiro took a sip of green tea and returned the cup to the table with mindful precision as if he was at a tea ceremony. "Returning to your original question, there are things that I don't miss about Japan as well: the strenuous work ethic, the quickness in which a person judges another, the nonacceptance of uniqueness ... Every country has its pros and cons. Obviously I enjoy America enough to have stayed here for many years. I've had work offers from back home throughout the years, but I chose to stay here because I could feel that it was the right place for me at the present time."

After partaking of some salad, Shinjiro said, "I'm curious as to what you liked most about Japan."

"I'd have to say the calmness I felt while in the country and the food. ... Oh, and the fact that there's no tipping."

Shinjiro nodded his head. "Yes, I dislike tipping in America too. It reduces one's entire interaction with someone else down to the end result: money given or received. One's interaction between the staff is poisoned even before the interaction starts because the customer is just a means for a staff member to get as much money from the customer as possible. Everything the staff does is fake and empty when it is done solely for money they wish to receive in the future. Instead of honoring one's patronage, the customer is treated like a walking wallet. For me, it is a complete dishonor to not only customer service but to the art of food and food preparation. In Japan, customers are not reduced to walking wallets; a restaurant is honored that a customer has chosen to eat their food. Food is nourishment for the body and the process of its preparation and digestion should be honored."

"I've never thought of it like that, but it makes sense," said Jeremy, "and the worst thing is that tipping has spread everywhere in America. Places that don't even offer service have tip jars and do their best to make you feel like dirt if you don't give them money for nothing. I don't know how this came to be acceptable. I've stopped going to many places because of this. It makes me feel so uncomfortable that I just don't want to deal with it."

A Japanese waitress politely and quietly put down their pork cutlets and walked away.

Jeremy took note of this and remembered more details about his dining experiences in Japan. "Another thing that I loved about dining in Japan was that the staff typically didn't interrupt conversations between diners at the table. They'd politely put the food down and leave. They understood that you came to the restaurant to share time with who you were accompanied with, not them. Even if you were alone, your solitude was honored and not interrupted."

"Yes," agreed Shinjiro. "I like how observant you are. An observing mind is a caring mind." Having been consumed in conversation, Shinjiro realized that he had forgotten to grind his sesame seeds for his tonkatsu sauce and went to work on it before his cutlet lost its warmth. While grinding the seeds with circular motions, he said, "By the way, you can rest assured that there's no tipping here. This is an authentic Japanese restaurant, so tipping is not allowed. The staff's wages are paid for by the owners and the price of the food, as it should be."

Jeremy observed Shinjiro and followed suit in grinding sesame seeds before pouring tonkatsu sauce on them. "Great. I feel more at ease to know the staff isn't obsessively worrying about how much money they can pry out of my wallet and I can actually enjoy my food. ... But if someone asked you if you believed in tipping or not and you answered 'No,' they'd look at you like you were the scum of the earth because they don't consider all the factors involved. Even if you try to explain the bigger picture, they typically are unwilling to even attempt to open their minds to a different viewpoint."

"Yes," said Shinjiro. "A wise man doesn't answer a multifaceted question with a 'Yes' or 'No' response alone. A one-word reply for an issue is a kindergarten response that has no value or meaning. Two people could basically feel the same way about an issue but still argue about it and possibly even come to hate each other because they settled on different one-word answers. Take Global Warming for example—or Climate Change I believe they're calling it now. If one doesn't believe in Global Warming because they believe it's a cyclical trend that's breaking hot and cold records around the world, not a result of man's mishandling with the world, the person who believes in Global Warming will most likely despise the other person because of their one-word reply before even hearing that they both have the exact same stance on polluting the planet: they're not for it, of course. Both people want to stop pollution of the earth, water, and sky and keep the planet green, yet they'll argue to death over some useless label that means nothing since both people care and feel the same way about protecting the planet, their home. In the end, it doesn't matter what useless label you choose to support, so why support either one, just help the planet like both parties want. This is only one example of the myriad of cases where people who want the same thing end up fighting each other because of meaningless labels and phrases."

"Yes, isn't that absurd," said Jeremy. "If a person who believes in the label 'Global Warming' hears someone else say that they don't believe in Global Warming, they automatically think the person is for polluting the planet. What a childish mindset. It's only powerful individuals that are for polluting the planet because they can save a lot of money when dumping their waste in nature instead of disposing of it properly, or by using dirty fossil fuels for energy instead of cleaner options.

And the funny thing is, all those powerful individuals sternly agree that Global Warming is a problem when addressing the public, but behind closed doors as they count the money they've collected from imposing Global Warming taxes on their competitor companies, they could care less. The biggest companies in the world that are pushing this agenda continue to pollute the planet and aren't paying any taxes themselves, or if they are on paper, it's secretly going right back into their pockets along with the other taxes they've collected. They're using Global Warming as a front to tax their competitors and put them out of business. I've learned this after working with these major conglomerates. It's everyday people that aren't polluting the planet that argue with each other about the issue even though they *all* want to keep the planet clean. It's comically absurd."

Shinjiro chuckled. "Yes, I guess it is funny. Sad, but funny." After finishing a piece of his tonkatsu, Shinjiro said, "Common citizens pretty much all want the same thing and generally agree with what's considered right and wrong. Instead of agreeing with each other and working together to make the world a better place, they argue over made-up labels. They argue with each other instead of addressing and dealing with the powerful individuals that are dumping and dispersing their waste into nature, or the many other actions that are being done that are creating disharmony."

"Right," Jeremy agreed. "We should be finding out who's making these meaningless labels that the common man argues over. Could it be the powerful individuals that are making them in order to confuse the common man and keep them focused on arguing with each other so they won't interfere with the powerful individuals' agendas?"

Shinjiro shrugged a little, but he did so with a little smile on his face that implied *Yes*. "Perhaps, perhaps. I think you're on to something there. … Almost all arguments are needless because the two ideas being fought over are both broken ideas that stem from a faulty system that's poisoned by money and power. If you take away money from the equation, people would find that most of the broken ideas and labels they argue over would instantly evaporate. It would behoove humanity to focus on addressing the root issue to solve the myriad of problems stemming from it, and many a root's problem is money. Money is the main problem that's holding us back from advancing as a civilization. Well, if you want to be exact, the main problem is the mindset of those who govern, regulate, and influence this planet, which is mostly done with money. So humanity's mindset is the main problem, and I say 'humanity's mindset' instead of the elite's mindset because those that govern and regulate the world disseminate their skewed mindset to the common man like an infection, so it also becomes the common man's mindset. But money is the main problematic tool that those with the skewed mindset who govern and regulate the world utilize to fulfill their agendas."

Shinjiro interrupted himself. "Please forgive me. I tend to be very articulate and detailed when talking about important, multifaceted concepts. I don't mean to dominate the conversation and go on a rant."

"Not at all. Don't worry about it," Jeremy said. "I always enjoy listening to your ideas and am a detail-oriented person myself, so I can relate. I wholeheartedly agree with what you're saying about money. I'm surprised most people seem to feel that money is too sacrosanct to live without. I've heard all kinds of baseless reasons why we need to have a monetary system. For example, money breeds competition and competition brings advances in technology and products. Well, I've found that it does the exact opposite. Now that we're on the cusp of a new technological paradigm, most major inventions—if they were able to see the light of day—would offer a radical change to our planet and help humanity move forward in leaps and bounds. But those inventions are being stopped or hidden because they would completely decimate whole businesses that are making billions of dollars a year on the archaic methods of the past. Free energy is the biggest one that comes to mind. After working for major conglomerates at Cohesive Analytics, I've seen firsthand how big businesses operate. Revenue is their top priority and what's best for humanity doesn't matter to them. By putting two and two together, and not jumping out on a far-fetched idea, it's completely logical—not only logical, but intelligent—to deduce by looking into public records available that big businesses—managed by powerful individuals—have hindered and altogether stopped benevolent inventions and systems so they could continue to make windfall profits. So why would it be outrageous to postulate that many modern-day inventions or systems that would've greatly benefitted humanity got scrapped because they had no lucrative value for these powerful individuals? And not just that they had no lucrative value, but would take away trillions of dollars of revenue, which would equate to loss of power from these individuals. Even if you don't believe that Nikola Tesla invented free energy a hundred years ago, wouldn't it be irrational and narrow-minded to dismiss all the modern-day accounts of inventors getting killed or their inventions getting bought and hidden away? If we're talking about trillions of dollars at stake, wouldn't powerful individuals who owned these big businesses stop at nothing to keep their revenue and power? We've already seen countless examples of the outlandish things big businesses—or rather the powerful individuals that own them—have done just for a million dollars, so it's fair to say that there's nothing they wouldn't do when billions or trillions of dollars were at stake."

"Beautifully stated," expressed Shinjiro. "Now, perhaps you'd like to eat some of your tonkatsu before it gets cold," he said with a smirk.

Jeremy laughed. "Right. Like you, sometimes I'm incapable of making a short statement about an issue."

As Jeremy used chopsticks to collect pieces of his pork cutlet and dip them into tonkatsu sauce before savoring them, Shinjiro continued the conversation about money. "One of the rebuttals I hear often after putting forward the idea of a moneyless civilization is: 'What about the jobs no one wants to do like garbage collection and such?' To this I reply: once the bottleneck of money is removed from the pipe, our present-day technology—suppressed or not—can automate almost all uncherished tasks, including garbage collection now that we have self-driving vehicles. But let's say garbage collection was still a job we had to do, just for an example. Let's say you live in a community with only 365 people and garbage is collected once a week. There are 52 weeks in a year, so 52 people would have to collect the garbage once in the first year. It would take 7 years for all 365 residents to have collected the garbage. Do you think a person is going to wake up every seven years and say, 'Goddammit, I have to collect the garbage again? This is ridiculous! Let's go back to a monetary system and have some guy who drew the short stick collect it all the time so I don't have to collect it once every seven years.' "

While eating a piece of tonkatsu, Jeremy laughed at the hypothetical scenario.

Shinjiro continued, "I don't think anyone would say that. No one would want a person like that living in their community. After giving this example, which can be used for any unwanted task, the person that posed the question about who would do the undesired jobs quickly realizes how unintelligent their question was."

Shinjiro took a break from talking to finish his last piece of tonkatsu and drink some green tea. Since Jeremy was still working on his meal, Shinjiro thought he'd continue the conversation. "Without a monetary system and with our modern-day capabilities, we could easily give every single person on the planet not only the necessities of life, but the best things that can be produced today. In fact, our current throwaway society uses more resources than we would use if we had a moneyless society and provided everyone with quality products that lasted a long time, if not a lifetime. So the argument that we don't have enough resources to give everyone in the world the best things is unfounded. Our current monetary system is the reason why our planet is swimming in cheap, low-quality products, because businesses want to spend the least amount of money to create a product, which makes it low-quality, and businesses also make products that don't last on purpose so they can make more money when the customer has to buy the same product again, and sometimes rebought an absurd amount of times. If money was taken out of the equation, only the people whose passion to make certain products would be making them, and they'd be the people who'd make the best products since it would be done out of passion instead of the want for money. People have more than one passion, so if there were already too many of the best people working in a particular field, a person could gravitate toward one of their other passions in order to benefit humanity. It would be the opposite of what we have today: almost everyone hating or being indifferent to their careers. We wouldn't need a bunch of companies in every single product category. Instead we could have one or a few that enjoy making the very best for everyone, and their products would either last a lifetime or close to it. They wouldn't need money to do their jobs because they would love their jobs since it's their passion, and they wouldn't have to worry about acquiring things they need to live because other people with their passions would happily provide it. No one would be arguing whether someone should be giving money to feed the starving children in Africa instead of buying a luxury sports car because everyone would have food and a luxury sports car. Of course, that's just an example, as we wouldn't even need cars if our current technology were to be unsuppressed, as you mentioned. With our current technology being utilized in the world instead of being suppressed for money reasons, and the deletion of jobs that only revolve around money and have no value, people would only have to work about twenty hours a week or less to get more accomplished than our current forty-plus workweek we have now. For the products that couldn't be provided to every single person in the world because of a lack of space on earth, they could be shared. Like yachts because there's only so much space at harbors. A person could use one every few months. How often do rich people use their yachts anyway? They'd most likely still be using it the same amount as they did before the change."

"I've imagined similar ideas when contemplating a moneyless society," Jeremy said, "but you just covered some of the pitfalls that I stumbled on. You are a wise man, Shinjiro. We need people like you in positions of power."

"Thank you, but I think you know that being wise and benevolent is a sure way to be held back from acquiring a position of power in our current world."

"Right," Jeremy agreed after drinking some green tea, "and if you did manage to secure a platform to address that speech to the world, someone would negate your entire intelligent speech by simply calling you a socialist or a communist, and a large amount of people—a scary amount—would side with the one-word-label utterer over you and your wise ideas."

Shinjiro chuckled. "Yes, which would perfectly illustrate just how badly our current flawed world has contaminated the mindset of the common man; that a meaningless one-word label or phrase could refute what should be known by everyone as common sense. What would be even sillier about being silenced by that one-word label in particular is that capitalism, socialism, communism—all of them—are ideas that convey who has the right to money and things in the world, and as I explained in my speech, we don't need to argue about that because everyone can have the things and services they need, and money is just useless paper no one needs. With our current technology a utopia is actually quite easy to construct, and you could call it any meaningless label you want—capitalism, socialism, label-less-ism—whatever—it wouldn't matter. All the governments on our planet are failing because they're run by people who don't have the best intentions in mind for the population, not because they're capitalistic, socialistic, etc. At some point people will realize that these labels stand for nothing, and it will be like waking up from a dream. A bad dream where label-maker devices are running after people like monsters."

"Ha, right," Jeremy said. "Defeated by one word that your whole resplendent speech articulately decimated beforehand, conveying that the utterer and his supporters were too dense to comprehend the dialog that would've saved them from a life of slavery and unhappiness. Of course, if there hadn't been any one-word utterers, the powerful individuals that wanted to stay in power would make sure a number of false remarks as to why your ideas wouldn't work would find their way into the media to be disseminated to the common man and subdue any thoughts they had of living in a utopia."

Both men took a sip of their green tea.

"But on a brighter note," began Jeremy, "if there's one thing the six-volume series of *The Decline and Fall of the Roman Empire*, and history as a whole, has taught me, it's that the rule of empires is temporary. They never last forever. Today's globally flawed mindset based on greed and control will soon eat itself and—"

"Will eat itself like pop music?" jestingly interrupted Shinjiro.

Jeremy chuckled, "Yes, it will eat itself like pop music, and crumble like the once great Roman Empire did. All the indicators that popped up during the Roman Empire's fall are being seen in our world today: a heavy reliance on slave labor, massive corruption from the elite, infighting by these same elites attempting to stay in power, and a rising of discontent and opposition among powerful or influential individuals and groups who have become utterly tired of the status quo and tyrannical rule. Like it did in the Roman Empire, this dissent will lead to a revolution of some sort. It's happened repeatedly throughout our history. … However, history has also shown us that the gap in power will be usurped or filled by another suppressive regime, dictator, or oligarchy. Out with the old king and in with the new."

"Your brighter note has just turned into a sour note," Shinjiro said. "Albert Einstein explained that dilemma with his quote: 'No problem can be solved from the same level of consciousness that created it.' Meaning that we won't see this pattern broken until a sufficient raising of the global consciousness has been reached. Unfortunately, when the common man becomes aware of his suppression, he thinks he is powerless to do anything about it. When in actuality, the common man's power to create and sustain the current worldly system is by far the most influential because they hold the greatest numbers on the planet, whereas the main suppressors are few. The common man is in the majority, so the common man holds the most power, but unfortunately they give their power away to the few that tell them to do so. If a certain threshold of people believed in their hearts that a transition to a moneyless civilization would be best, it would manifest itself in the physical world. The common man already possesses the power they wished they had, they just don't know it, and the powerful few do their best to keep that knowledge from them."

Jeremy pondered that statement while slowly nodding his head.

Shinjiro offered up an idea. "Perhaps we can end our lunch on a more positive note with a Zen-like story, if you don't mind."

"Sure. That would be nice. I'm always grateful to soak up the wisdom you've acquired from your years."

"Good." Shinjiro smiled. "But don't let age fool you; I know many an old ignorant man."

"Yes, of course," agreed Jeremy. "Age is just as likely to make one bitter as wise, especially in the current world we live in."

"Indeed, my brilliant pupil," Shinjiro jested at their age difference with a smile. Then he began, "There is a Zen saying that states: everything is okay as it is. This realization can only be understood from the broadest viewpoint possible, as one would naturally look at the state of the world right in front of their eyes and not believe anything to be okay at all. We are all fragments of the Source that have chosen to have an experience outside of Source and play different roles in a theatrical play of sorts. Some will play heroes and some will play villains; without all the characters, there wouldn't be a play to enjoy. No play lasts forever, as that would cease to be entertaining and become boring. When the play is over, the curtain will fall. When the curtain rises, all of the players will be holding hands and congratulating each other on their well-played characters. Then they will depart the stage and go backstage to reconnect with Source. However, some method actors get stuck in their characters after the play is over and need a cleansing Source bath to remember who they are. So seen from the highest possible big-picture scenario, everything is okay as it is."

"Okay." Jeremy squinted his eyes in thought. "But are you saying that it's okay to be a villain and that the heroes, or general cast for that matter, shouldn't try to stop them since everything is okay as it is?"

Shinjiro smiled lightly. "What I'm saying is that from the highest possible big-picture scenario, it is okay to play the role of a villain to fulfill the part in the play, but that doesn't mean that the heroes—or the general cast—should stop playing their roles; the play can't end until they succeed in playing their roles too. And you'll be pleased to know that the Source is all-loving and everything is part of the Source, even the villains, so there's no possible way that a play could end without love prevailing, since everything and everyone is comprised of love when the anomaly has been stripped away."

After Jeremy and Shinjiro's reacquaintance, they continued to enjoy thought-provoking conversations over lunch periodically. They were men with a big-picture mindset, free from the confines of division; they had risen above small-minded thinking and didn't consider themselves citizens of a particular country or brethren of a particular religion. Instead, Shinjiro knew himself to be a spirit of the cosmos, and Jeremy considered himself a man of the world, and years later, after Jeremy's continued spiritual growth, he'd come to also know himself to be a spirit of the cosmos, part of the Source, the alpha and the omega. They grew from each other's insights and honored each other's company and ideas.

Chapter 26

The sound of the door buzzer jolted Dale awake, ripping his consciousness out of a nightmare where someone he didn't know was trying to kill him. What a bizarre dream, Dale thought as he lifted himself off the sofa, where he must have dozed off for a bit because he hadn't gotten a good night's sleep. He must have slept for about twenty minutes because he had ordered a pepperoni pizza before lying on the sofa, and now it had arrived.

Dale hadn't left his condo for a week due to the coronavirus situation in New York City. The only exception being the arranged meeting that Aryana had set up in the underground chambers of Maldekmars Club yesterday evening. He wouldn't have missed that meeting for the world.

As he groggily made his way to the door, he recalled hearing an owl hooting last night. Perhaps that's why he hadn't been able to sleep well. But that didn't make any sense because there weren't any owls in Manhattan, let alone outside the windows of his 432 Park Avenue condo on the sixty-sixth floor, so the owl must have been an annoying dream. He was having a lot of meddlesome dreams lately.

Despite having restless sleep last night, he was feeling elated because the meeting Aryana had arranged with his mentor—his handler—yesterday evening had gone perfectly. He'd signed a contract of sorts and would soon be reaping all the benefits from his newfound powerful connections. The sky is the limit, he told himself as he approached the door and opened it up to collect his gourmet Pizza Gate pizza.

A man who looked too old to be a pizza delivery guy stood in his doorway holding a boxed pizza. A creepy fake smile was plastered on his face. The type of smile that was conveyed by the mouth alone and didn't make its way up to the eyes, which seemed to portray an entirely different agenda.

Karver lifted a hand to adjust his pizza hat while saying, "Ken Karver here delivering your gourmet pizza. I'm not sure if you're one of our loyal customers or a first-timer, but you'll be delighted to know that we've implemented a new service: we don't cut your pizza till we put it in your house in order to retain its freshness. We've also found that our affluent customers enjoy viewing their pizza get cut up and fragmented before their very eyes. So if you don't mind ..." Karver made a facial gesture that asked for permission to enter the house so he could perform the cutting.

Dale eyed the pizza box. "Sure, but let me see if you got my preferred toppings correct before you slice it up."

"Of course." As he opened the box he said, "But I'll have you know that Pizza Gate has never once delivered a topping that wasn't specifically requested, because we know that devouring the right toppings on a pizza gives the eater a pure, childlike satisfaction."

Dale furrowed his forehead as he stared at the pepperoni on the pizza. "We're just talking about pizza, right? Because I actually just want pizza tonight, nothing else."

"Sure, whatever suits you, Mr. Dickerson. May I apply the knife now?"

Dale stepped back and fully opened the door for the pizza guy to enter. He gestured with an arm toward the direction of the kitchen. "Go to the far window and turn left and you'll see the kitchen."

Karver followed the specified path past a long table full of irregular modern sculptures and slowed his steps for a moment by the large window to stare down toward the streets far below before rounding the corner to the kitchen. As he slid a knife out of the knife set on Dale's countertop, he said, "That's a nice view you got there, Mr. Dickerson."

Dale strolled over to the window, crossed his arms, and looked down at the specks of people going about their lives far below. "This view is my favorite thing about this condo. It reminds me how small and insignificant the general population is. I could drop a gold bar at this height and watch it flatten one of those bugs below. The surrounding bugs would strain their necks up into the sky and wonder what god decided to intervene in their little day. Once the surrounding bugs discovered it was gold that had fallen from the sky, they'd instantly forget about the dead bug and start fighting each other tooth and nail over who would possess the gold. Wouldn't even matter if the bar was fake gold, it would happen all the same."

Dale's words were like a symphony in Karver's ears. He rarely heard statements like those from humans. As he cut the pizza he picked up where Dale left off. "I couldn't have said it better myself, Mr. Dickerson. All those ants scurrying about like rats in a maze, going back and forth to the same few locations day after day, thinking the cheese they're sniffing for will somehow magically appear on the routes they cover over and over again. They're born into the programmed maze, so they can't even conceive of a different way of life. Not only can't they believe in a different way of life, but they're programmed to scoff and ridicule the few that do. After the ridiculing, they go back to pushing the buttons and pulling the levers that they're programmed to. Ah, the good old rat race that never ends till cancer comes a knockin'."

Surprised, Dale turned his head in the direction of the kitchen. He was pleased that one of the ants knew their place in the world. The man had spoken as if he wasn't one of the bugs, but if he was a pizza delivery guy for a living, he was clearly one of the bugs.

Karver felt a notification coming through on his advanced-technology screen. He fished it out of his pocket, unfolded it, and viewed a change that had been made to his sacrificial list: Dale Dickerson had been removed from the list.

"What the ...?" Karver mumbled under his breath. The man must have recently signed a blood contract and administration had just updated the list. He'd never had a sacrifice he was in route to be removed from the list. Forget about in route to, he was standing in the man's house with a knife in his hand. If he had dispensed with the foreplay, he could've had the job done before the update came through. Hey, who's to say he didn't perform the sacrifice before the list was updated. This doesn't need to be a wasted trip after all. At this point it would be a tease not to go all the way, especially after getting thrilled from viewing the pizza sauce on the knife.

Karver left the pizza in the kitchen and walked toward Dale with the sauce still dripping from the knife.

Dale chastised him when he saw pizza sauce being dripped onto his floor. "Hey, you're getting sauce on the floor, dipshit." But when Dale saw the sinister expression on the pizza guy's face, his anger turned to fear as the man kept approaching him with the knife. Being unarmed, Dale followed his instincts and fled his condo through the door that had been left open. With the sinister pizza guy chasing him, he chose the stairwell instead of waiting for an elevator.

As Dale descended the stairs in his immaculate suit, he remembered his handler saying he'd be throwing a test at Dale to see if he was resilient enough to weather a storm. He never imagined that the storm would be in the form of a maniacal, knife-wielding pizza guy.

Dale didn't bother screaming for help as he raced down the stairwell because 432 Park Avenue was a ghost tower. Like the other towering residential skyscrapers on Billionaires' Row, a staggering percentage of the condo units were empty due to being owned by seasonal occupants, or having yet to be sold. Over half of the luxury condos on Billionaires' Row were owned by foreign nationals that bought them as trophies or diversified investments and rarely stepped foot in their luxurious New York City condos. Dale was only one of seventeen people in 432 Park Avenue that was registered to vote. He figured that 432 was anywhere from over seventy to eighty percent empty at any given point during the year.

How had this situation come to pass? He was a master of the universe fleeing down a stairwell from a deranged delivery pizza guy in an empty building that towered high into the New York City skyline.

He exited the stairwell to a floor where he recalled a Russian tenant he'd shared the elevator with had gotten off a week ago. It wasn't hard to remember because it was one of the few times he'd not been alone in one of the building's elevators.

He pounded on all three of the doors on the floor. There wasn't much room to avoid a swinging knife so he hoped that the pizza guy didn't know what floor he'd exited onto. He kept pounding on the doors.

The Russian man opened his door and stepped out into the hallway and stared at Dale, who was currently pounding on another door. He called down the hall to Dale with a thick accent, "What are you doing? You make noise I don't like. Ah, you are elevator guy."

Panting, Dale approached the man to explain, but then noticed the pizza guy dashing down the hall with a Luciferian grin, knife held ready to stab.

Karver dashed forward and lunged the knife toward Dale's neck, but Dale ducked out of the way just in time to avoid the advancing knife. Instead, the knife ended up plunging into the Russian's neck. The Russian's eyes went wide and he tried to vocalize his terror but only gurgling sounds and blood came out.

Dale darted into the Russian's condo to find a weapon, and took the opportunity to compare the unit to his own while he did so.

Karver pulled the knife out and watched blood pump out of the tear in the man's throat. Karver looked into the man's eyes and shrugged his shoulders. "Well, you just happened to be on my list too." Then he followed Dale into the Russian's condo.

Karver found Dale standing behind the Russian's teenage son, the only other person in the unit it seemed. Dale was gripping the boy's arms from behind and appeared to be using him as a human shield. The boy was trying to break free from the hold and paused in fright when he saw Karver enter the living room with a blood-dripping knife.

"Вот дерьмо, it's a demented pizza guy," said the Russian teenager.

Dale warned Karver. "I wouldn't come any closer if I were you."

This amused Karver, who continued to approach. "Oh yeah, what are you going to do? It's not like the boy is a grenade."

When Karver got close enough, Dale pushed the boy forward, impaling him onto the knife, which gave Dale time to sidestep and make his way past Karver without having to worry about the knife cutting him since a Russian-teenager safety barrier had been applied to it.

"You weren't on my list," Karver said as he pushed the boy off the knife like a discarded inanimate object. The boy thumped on the floor. As Karver turned to give chase to Dale, he recognized that he hadn't broken any rules because it was Dale that had pushed the boy into the knife. "That one's on you, my man, and may I say what a fine job you did," he called out to Dale before giving chase.

Dale couldn't believe his luck when he exited the Russian's condo—which wasn't as grand as his own condo, thank Satan—because a Chinese man on the same floor had exited his unit and could provide him with another human shield and diversion. Two overseas tenants just happening to be in 432 at the same time on the same floor—how rare and fortunate.

The Chinese man was pointing at the Russian lying on the floor in a pool of blood. With a terrified countenance, the Chinese man repeated something in Mandarin to Dale, "他死了吗? 他死了吗?"

Dale didn't understand Mandarin, but it was obvious to him that the Chinese man was scared that a dead person was outside his luxury condo. A luxury condo that was supposed to provide a buffer from the common riffraff. Rushing over to the man, Dale offered some soothing words, "Don't worry about him, he's just fine. I think it's typical Russian culture to lounge around in pools of blood for a hobby's sake."

Their conversation—if you could call it that, since they didn't understand each other's language—was quickly interrupted when Karver appeared, jumping over the culture-practicing Russian.

Dale positioned himself behind his new human shield as the Chinese man's eyes went wide by the sight of a man approaching him with a bloody knife. The Chinese man frantically waved both of his arms in the air in Karver's direction as if he was conjuring magical energy that would protect him. While waving his arms around, he spat Mandarin at the knife-wielding man, "滚开，老外! 滚开，外国魔鬼!"

When Karver got close enough to strike, Dale gripped the Chinese man's arms from behind and started using him as a marionette to intercept and block each slash of the knife from Karver.

The Chinese man was on Karver's list, so he had no issue in slicing up the man as he worked his way to Dale. In fact, Karver mentally applauded Dale's marionette performance. While slashing away, he spoke through the marionette as if he didn't exist and addressed Dale, "It's bold of you to directly use a person as a puppet. Normally it's only done indirectly. I admire your style, Dale. And luckily this man is on my list as well."

As Dale continued to move the Chinese man's arms around, he thought he might have passed the test when he heard Karver's words, but he wasn't going to leave himself unprotected until he was sure. After all, Karver was still thrusting his knife toward him. "Is this list of yours like a grocery list or something?"

While Karver continued to thrust and slice away, he calmly replied, "Grocery list, I like that. Yes, you could call it my grocery list. When I venture out onto the surface of the planet, humans are like food products that are neatly stacked on shelves, ready for me to pluck and consume them when they're ripe or have been placed on sale by management. I cross out items on my list as I leisurely stroll through the aisles, whistling to the fabricated pop music being played over the speakers."

"So how does one get off your grocery list?" Dale questioned as he maintained the movements of the Chinese man, who was beginning to resemble a pincushion.

Karver wasn't going to tell Dale that he had in fact already been removed from his list. Instead, he offered up, "The only way for an item to be removed from my list is for it to expire."

Upon hearing the chosen diction, Dale knew that his only way off the list was to kill the possessor of the list. This was the only way he'd pass the test that had been placed before him by his handler. He needed to move from a stance of defense to a stance of offense, and his human shield would soon be dropping dead anyway, so he made his next move. When the next knife thrust sunk deep into the Chinese man's torso, Dale heaved the human shield into Karver, dashed around the temporarily linked men, and darted to the stairwell.

Once he reached the stairwell, he paused for a second to decide which direction to go: up or down. If he went down to the lobby to seek help like a normal pathetic person, Karver might get arrested, but he'd probably fail the test his handler had tasked him with. The only way to pass the test was the same way as getting off the grocery list: killing Karver. He'd have to go up the stairwell and return to his condo so he could get his hands on a weapon that would allow him to take offensive measures.

He galloped up the stairs with Karver trailing behind him. He didn't have a gun in his condo because he never needed one. His money could be used to hire a man, or men, with guns to do what he desired, so he had never bothered to purchase a gun.

Then the solution hit Dale: a piece of art hanging on his wall. The artwork was a prominent Japanese-American artist's re-envisioning of the Edo Period. The art piece was a crafted samurai sword. When he purchased it he recalled the artist stating, "The blade was masterfully sharpened in the same manner that a katana would've been forged in feudal Japan so that the piece's core essence could act as a portal to inspirit the way of the ancient honorable samurai in our modern age."

At the time he had been leaning toward acquiring the artist's rendition of samurai armor, but now thanked his lucky stars for having chosen the katana art piece instead.

After Dale reached the sixty-sixth floor, he sprinted back into his condo and pulled the katana art piece off the wall. He unsheathed it to make sure the blade was in fact as sharp as the artist had stated. The temper line of the katana unmistakable narrowed down to the edge, visually ensuring that indeed the edge was as sharp as a razor.

Karver entered the condo to find a cocksure Dale gripping a katana. Karver paused his forward momentum for a moment and said, "Now that's the stuff. Now we've got ourselves a real duel." Even though he was outmatched by length, he charged toward Dale like they were knights in a jousting match.

Dale kept his composure and waited till the timing was right. When Karver was almost upon him, he swiftly brought the katana down on Karver's outstretched arm that held the knife. It may not have been as clean a cut as the movies would've depicted, but the katana did slice through its mark with surprising ease.

Karver's arm, along with the knife it held, dropped to the floor. He almost kept up his momentum enough to hit Dale with his new bloody stump, but he stopped short and turned to the line of irregularly pointy sculptures on display next to them. He used his one arm left to toss the sculptures one at a time at Dale as he backed away from him and his katana.

Dale tried his best to deflect each spiny sculpture, but had gotten slightly punctured a few times in the process and was highly annoyed at the damage his premium suit had taken. His rival had moved down to the last sculpture but wasn't attempting to throw it because it was too irregular to get a firm hand on, so Dale charged at him with the katana raised, aspiring to decapitate Karver.

Dale was already imagining himself stomping around his condo like a warrior: bloody katana in one hand and Karver's head held by its hair in the other. He pictured Karver in Valhalla looking down at him in admiration, thinking, *Well, I'll be. That guy's got the right stuff.*

But in the final moment, Karver tilted the last unusual sculpture so that the long spire on it pierced right through Dale's heart, having been assisted by Dale's own forward momentum.

The katana dropped out of Dale's hands and clattered on the floor. He looked down at the artwork's spire that had torn through his suit and lodged itself in his body, and was perhaps sticking out his back, he felt. In the last five seconds before losing consciousness—and eventually dying six minutes later—a major scowl appeared on Dale's face, and he uttered in contempt, "Do you know how much this suit cost?!" Then his head slumped down.

Karver let go of the sculpture and watched it and Dale hit the floor. "Death by high-end art; that's a new one even for me." He stared down at the mess on the floor. "You provided no loosh my friend, but you made me feel more alive than ever. Much obliged," he said while taking his pizza hat off his head. "Don't worry about my arm. We have the technology to replace it with a new biological one. But I'm enraged that you didn't tip me for the pizza delivery," Karver theatrically feigned anger as he threw his pizza hat down on Dale's body. He chuckled to himself while rummaging through Dale's condo to find items for a tourniquet to stop the stump's bleeding.

Once he got the tourniquet all sorted out, he started whistling and headed toward the open door. If he didn't live in a DUMB, he thought he'd surely make his lair in a New York City skyscraper penthouse residing on Billionaires' Row so he could look down on humanity every day while also being far enough away to remain disconnected from the bugs below and their fabricated reality.

Before Karver had a chance to exit the unit, two men sporting crew cuts and tactical gear stormed into the condo and pointed SilencerCo Maxim 9 integrally suppressed handguns at Karver.

Karver ceased whistling and said, "You guys arrived early this time."

Without speaking a word the two men began to riddle Karver with American-hero bullets. Round after round of ammunition discharged silently and throttled Karver's body so that it wildly jerked with each impact. If an onlooker hadn't known he was getting shot, they'd have thought he was enacting a jerky Haitian voodoo dance.

After his dance, Karver collapsed on the floor. His body lay motionless in an expanding pool of blood as his open eyes fixated on the high ceiling. An unmistakable smirk was permanently etched on his cold face.

Miller, the younger of the two men, crept up to Karver's body with his gun still trained on his target. "Look at that, the bastard's still got a smile on his face." Then he holstered his gun while shaking his head.

Buzz, a Special Operations Command veteran, also holstered his gun and put his hands on his hips while exhaling deeply after another job well done. "The Alliance has been trying to kill this guy for a long time, and now we've finally done it. The reign of fear he supplied for the Dark Forces has at last come to an end."

Miller scratched his head. "That was much easier than I had expected, sir, but I'm getting a weird déjà vu feeling about this."

Buzz sauntered over to the window to take in the majestic view of Central Park and the rest of New York City. "You probably had a wet dream about exterminating that psychopath last night due to being all amped up in anticipation." Then he knitted his eyebrows while looking out over New York. "You know … I'm getting the feeling that I've seen this view before. It's not easy to forget a view as grand as—"

The door buzzer jolted Dale awake. *That was a crazy dream. Who the hell is the Alliance? I must have dozed off for twenty minutes on the sofa. Well, my pizza is here. Did I order pepperoni, a meat-lovers, or … man, I can't remember what I ordered. How odd. Well, I'll see what I ordered soon enough.*

He groggily made his way toward the door, shaking his head to clear the cobwebs. As he approached the door a smile crept up on his face. He had recalled the success of the meeting with his new handler last night. He'd signed a blood contract and the world was now his oyster.

Dale opened the door to reveal a sinister-looking pizza guy that looked too old for the job. His uniformed pizza hat looked like it belonged on a six-year-old kid. The man was sporting a grisly grin.

"Ken Karver here with your gourmet blah blah blah. What's it going to be this time: death by way of high-end art, drowning in the pool, beaten to death in the lobby while a Chinese man yells at you, having your head beaten into numerous steps on the stairwell, getting stabbed with scissors while a Russian guy is yelling at his son …? I'll tell you this, you're not going to kill me with that katana again this time. Nope, this time we'll do it nice and quick."

Dale had displayed a quizzical grumpy countenance during the odd speech. "Just give me my pizza, dipshit. Save your babbling for the loony bin. And you can forget about getting a tip after delivering that crazy rant."

Karver dropped the pizza on the floor, unveiling a knife he had been holding under the pizza box. He swiftly plunged it deep into Dale's throat and retracted it.

With wild eyes, Dale clenched his neck with both hands and tried to stop the bleeding. His last thoughts were: *I know the lust for tipping has gotten out of hand in this country, but this is ridiculous. How could a master of the universe be snuffed out by a peasant who'd been stiffed a tip? Especially one wearing such a silly hat.* He looked down at the escaping blood that had saturated his suit jacket and became irate. He attempted to yell at the peasant, *Goddammit, do you know how much this suit cost?* But the only thing that came out of his mouth was unintelligible gurgling sounds before he collapsed like a big tower of shit to the floor.

Karver heard the elevator door ping. He dropped the bloody knife, pulled a Beretta out, and aimed it at the elevator till the door slid open and exposed two crew cut men.

A double report from the Beretta echoed through the hall. *Bang, bang.* The marines, now with nine-millimeter holes in their heads, flopped to the floor of the elevator.

"Headshot! Double kill!" vocalized Karver, mimicking a first-person shooter game.

Then Karver heard the sound of boots stomping up the stairwell and repositioned himself so that he'd have a clean shot at the first approaching marine. When a head appeared, *bang*!

Karver heard the headshotted man fall down the stairs and the other marines cease their stomping as they ducked for cover. For amusement's sake Karver shouted in their direction with a videogame announcer's voice, "Killing spree!"

Crouched on the stairs, Buzz turned to Miller and vocalized his dismay. "Christ, it's merely a videogame to him. Goddammit, I told those lazy bastards not to take the elevator. Miller, hand me the Sonic."

Miller unholstered the handheld sonic weapon, which was one of many advanced technological devices that the public thought was only science fiction, and handed it to Buzz.

Buzz pointed it in the direction of Karver and activated it.

Karver let out a scream and fell to the floor with his hands covering his ears.

"Go team!" Buzz yelled.

The remaining four-marine team rushed up the stairs and stomped over to where Karver was flopping around on the floor like an electrocuted fish out of water. They trained their guns low and rained down enough American-hero bullets to make Charlton Heston smile in his grave and give a big thumbs up.

"How many times do we have to kill this guy?" grumbled Buzz. "Goddamn temporal warfare. They're trying to tweak the timeline to their liking." He pointed to the two dead marines in the elevator before going into Dale's condo. "The relatives of those two lazy bastards are going to experience the Mandela Effect over their deaths."

Buzz's team followed him to the grand view in Dale's unit. Buzz looked through the window and out over the city. "But I tell you, I never get tired of this view."

After they silently appreciated the view for a moment, Buzz's mind returned to the dilemma and he began to rant. "They know they're done for, so why don't they just surrender? We've used Project Looking Glass technology and know that there's no possible outcome—no possible timeline where the Dark Forces win. Hell, they had the same technology, so they must also know they can't win."

Miller gave his opinion. "Sir, I believe they know it but would rather take as many people down with them as possible before they go out. They'd rather blow up the whole planet instead of surrendering. They're past the point of rehabilitation, so they know they'll be sent back to Source to be cleansed whatever the outcome is."

"Yeah, I guess you're right," replied Buzz. "They're so used to getting their way after being in control of Earth for so long. Their spider-web design was so effective that they've grown cocky, and perhaps, despite the view of losing in all the possible timelines, they think there's some kind of tear in the fabric of the universe they can exploit to stay in power. Well, that's not the case; the

Dark Forces are done for. We've already taken control or destroyed most of their DUMBs and have amassed an unbelievable stockpile of damning evidence against them for court trials when the many sealed indictments get unsealed."

Miller interjected, "I thought the Alliance was going to continue processing those indictments in secret military tribunals?"

"The situation has changed," Buzz said. "The military tribunals that started in the beginning of 2019 were our only option at the time because they had too many corrupt judges in the judicial system. You can't prosecute criminals in a system that's run by the same criminals. But we've removed those corrupt judges and are putting legitimate judiciaries in their places so we can finally start unsealing the indictments in public courts for the whole world to witness, as well as continue the military tribunals. The Dark Forces are playing their typical political games to stop us from instating the new judiciaries, but the only thing they're doing is delaying the inevitable. There's a staggering amount of sealed indictments, the most ever in history. It'll be a show to see; the public's going to love it. A treasure trove of powerful criminals are soon to be held accountable. When Jeffrey Epstein's sealed indictment was unsealed people were shocked, so just think how overwhelming the next over 150,000 sealed indictments will be. Wyoming's got the least amount of sealed indictments. The cowboys must've already taken care of 'em. Yeah, it's only a matter of time. The sleeping masses are going to have an awakening when the truth is thrown at them." Still looking out at New York, Buzz added, "Goddamn, look at that view, men."

Miller addressed Buzz while looking out over the city. "Humanity will be shocked to their core when the truth comes out and they become aware that they've been slaves in a diabolical, intricate system, but they need to be aware and freed as soon as possible."

Buzz widened the stance of his boots a bit and gripped the top of his bulletproof vest with both hands while inhaling and exhaling deeply. "The Alliance has been fighting for decades to get this done."

"Really? Decades, sir?"

"That's right. Long before you were born. The Alliance tried to work with JFK in dissolving the controlled system, but we weren't as powerful back then. It's different now that the scales have tipped in our favor. Once the Alliance reached that pivotal point on the scales of power about three years ago, we made massive advances against the Dark Forces. Too bad the general public is still unaware of our advances because it hasn't reached their daily lives yet, and the Dark Forces made sure the public was kept in the dark about it with their continued media censoring and programming while they tried turning back the tide in their favor, but that never happened. So many people have flipped from the Dark side to the Alliance, and now we hold more power than the Dark Forces. But even after they've been completely removed from the reins of power, it's going to take the Alliance—backed by the newly awakened populace—some time to tear down and restructure the intricate system the Dark built. A utopia isn't going to sprout up overnight. It'll take a transitional period to properly implement all the suppressed technologies and rehabilitate humanity from the harsh conditions they were exposed to for so long in the matrix. A time of rehabilitation is necessary to allow a higher percentage of humanity to be ready for the Solar Flash."

"Solar Flash?" inquired Miller. "What are you talking about, sir?"

"The Great Solar Flash is akin to an unprecedented coronal mass ejection from our sun. It will provide spiritual advancement for people who are ready to receive the energetic download."

"I think I've heard of that," replied Miller. "Wasn't that supposed to happen at the end of 2012, the end of the Mayan calendar?"

"Originally, yes, but our space relatives worked with Ra—the spirit of our sun—to postpone it. You see, the last time the Dark Forces thwarted the Alliance's plans to take back the planet was in 2001. The Dark Forces became aware of the Alliance's plans and demolished the buildings that held the evidence that would've taken them down. Then they blamed it on terrorists and used the 9/11 ruse to further their agenda. Without humanity being freed in 2001 and having about ten years of rehabilitation, the 2012 Solar Flash was delayed for the benefit of humanity. But there are cosmic plans in place that will allow the Solar Flash to be delayed for only so long. If I remember correctly, the end of the Great Solar Flash window is around 2035. At that point it will happen whether humanity is ready or not. That's why it's important to free the world from the Dark Force's matrix and give them enough time to rehabilitate before the Great Solar Flash. Otherwise there'll be a huge percentage of chaff and little wheat to harvest, which will have nullified the efforts of the millions of incarnated Starseeds—or whatever you want to call them—who incarnated on Earth to raise the global consciousness and allow more people to spiritually evolve."

Miller blinked his eyes after taking in Buzz's information. He'd never heard of this intelligence before. "Excuse me for asking, sir, but how does a military man know so much about spiritual matters?"

"I don't understand most of it. I'm just regurgitating intel I came across. Intel that my rank has provided me a look into."

Then Buzz continued after a short pause. "As I was saying ... the coming utopia—if that's what you want to call it—will be made possible on Earth when we implement everything that's been hidden from the population: we'll roll out a new financial system that isn't debt based—we've been working on it for a while—to work for us till we transition to a moneyless civilization, which would erase the word 'job' because people will be happily working for themselves and humanity, and everything will be done in less than half the amount of hours we currently work; we'll release the suppressed advanced technologies that will completely reshape our world: they'll clean the Earth so it's pristine again, they'll advance medical care to a level no one could imagine, they'll make transportation to anywhere in the world fast and easy, they'll erase all those pesky daily chores, and so on; then we'll introduce our highly advanced spacecraft fleet that has been in operation for many decades, and eventually the general public will be allowed to use it to travel to other planets not just in our solar system or galaxy but in the universe—something that the SSP (Secret Space

Program) has already been doing for decades; and eventually humanity will be introduced to its space relatives in mass contact instead of the selective contact that's been going on for a long time.

"Our space relatives have immeasurably helped out the Earth Alliance to defeat the Dark Forces. You have no idea, boys. They deserve our profoundest gratitude. Our evolution and their evolution is intertwined; only by working together can our species evolve. I've personally worked with, fought alongside, and seen many different species of our space relatives die in battle for the cause, so when anyone tells me they don't exist, I punch them in the goddamn face forthwith. I can just picture some eraserhead saying he doesn't believe in aliens right before he sits down in front of the boob tube to eat his goddamn microwave TV dinner; meanwhile, those same aliens he doesn't believe in are fighting to save Earth and are the only reason he's still alive and able to shovel shit he calls food into his pie hole every goddamn day of his pathetic life."

"I know what you mean, sir," said Miller. "I fear humanity might be past the point of rehabilitation."

"How do you get people to lose faith in humanity?" Buzz asked before continuing on to answer his own question. "You shape public opinion. It can be done in many places: the news, movies, shows, music, Internet ... The Internet is heavily controlled by the Dark Forces with algorithms and fake accounts because that's where most people have been going to get their news or to do research for themselves. Most people are persuaded by what the majority's opinion is, so the Dark Forces have created a fake majority online. There are way more fake accounts than real accounts online today. It's staggering. The Dark Forces have created countless troll farms to relentlessly spam the Internet with their agenda. Billions of fake accounts are used to create disinformation, bully people that are putting out information that the Dark Forces don't like, get people arguing with each other, create a fake majority opinion about topics, and create an illusion that a good portion of humanity is vicious and cruel. That's how you make people lose faith in humanity. People go online and are met with fake accounts everywhere, operated by paid trolls that sit behind a computer all day. Despicable minions that have sold their souls for thirty pieces of silver. The big tech companies thought they could get away with anything, overseeing everything online and manipulating everything. But the NSA, one of the first agencies the Alliance took back, has collected a plethora of incriminating evidence against all these evil tech companies, and they're still collecting data to this day; not that more evidence is needed to prosecute their executives and completely overhaul their platforms so that they work for the people instead of against the people. Big tech thought they were the all-seeing eye, but there's an all-seeing eye watching *their* every nefarious move. They'll be dealt with and restructured at some point. We can't do everything all at once."

Buzz paused and shifted his stance before changing subjects. "Setting up a utopia isn't my department, which is probably obvious given my temperament and language. My role is to dig my boots in the ground with my men and remove the Dark Forces from positions of power and influence, and if that results in their death, then so be it. Nothing can stop what is coming. One way or the other they'll be removed. After that, others who are more equipped will work together to build the utopia on Earth.

"We could have transitioned a lot quicker if the public had done their part by using their purchasing power intelligently and effectively. When people buy poisoned food and products made by the Dark Force's companies, people aren't only slowly killing themselves, they're also funding their controllers, which keeps them in power. When a person buys something, they're ultimately funding a way of life, and the problem is most people are funding a way of life that happens to be enslaving and killing themselves. Unfortunately people didn't see it that way. If they had, we could've gotten our planet back much quicker."

They continued to stare out at New York City from their lofty altitude.

"Regardless of that failure, we're moving forward," said Buzz, "because we'll be arresting all the major players before the end of spring and herding them into Gitmo. Then they'll get fair trials in secret military tribunals, which certain civilians can be legally tried in since that bill went into effect on January 1, 2019. They would continue to wreak havoc on the world and try to take back control before being sentenced if we waited for the slow wheels of justice in the public courts. We couldn't allow that.

"Yup, when the summer solstice arrives, we will have already won, but the people won't know it or see it. Even with the top players removed, their minions and companies will still be causing problems till we get to them, which we will in due time; we can't do everything at once. But they'll be held accountable; there will be no free passes.

"Most of the top players will be handed the death penalty for their crimes against humanity. This will all be done without the public's awareness because they won't be able to handle it at this time since so many of them are completely unaware of the scope of deception and evil the Dark Forces perpetrated on a daily basis. Instead of rejoicing in the removal of their evil overlords, they might think we're being fascists, and the Dark's controlled news outlets would spin that narrative for sure. The fake news would try to use the people's love for their famous and so-called prestigious icons to try to make these monstrous individuals look like the victims, when in fact, they are completely diabolical, or compromised at the least.

"As with the removal of worldwide evil shadow overlords, titans, leaders, and politicians, there's going to be a gaping hole left in the movie and music business in America after the cancer has been removed. Real talent will be able to fill the void after these connection-based bad actors are removed and exposed.

"But the court cases rolling out in public trials will gradually awaken the public and prepare them for the worst information, which includes the satanic acts perpetrated against countless children. At some point in the future, some of the information that was used to process the major players in military tribunals will come through in public trials. Then these players will be sentenced to death or hard time before the public's eyes. After humanity has become aware of only a quarter of what these satanic individuals have done, they'll believe execution to be too light of a sentence."

"Won't people notice the absence of these major players in the world?" Miller asked. "And how could we execute someone that's already been executed months prior?"

Buzz gritted his teeth. "This is where it gets weird, Miller. We'll use CGI, body doubles, and clones when these people need to show up for major events. After being found guilty in public trials, the criminals at Gitmo will then be transferred to regular prisons and fake executions will be made for those that have already been executed."

Miller's eyes went wide. "What? Clones? Are you playing with me, sir?"

"Absolutely not," Buzz responded with a stone cold straight face. "Cloning has been around since the 1940s. The quality has improved throughout the decades. The Dark Forces have used cloning activities for their sadistic pleasure in DUMBs nightly, as well as for other purposes. The use of clones has been prevalent, just ask Donald Marshall."

Miller stood silently with his mind reeling, needing a moment to process the astounding information.

While still gazing at the city below, Buzz continued, "They thought their coronavirus bioweapon would usher in their New World Order, but with Project Looking Glass we were able to foresee events and quash its widespread effects and piggyback on it with our Defender-Europe 20 drill, which was never actually just a drill. The Dark has been using fake drills for years for their massacres and shootings, and now we've stolen their playbook and used it against them. I'm looking forward to the green-light orders that'll send us rolling into Europe and assisting the Alliance across the pond. I'm particularly looking forward to seizing the Vatican. We've got to make sure all the literature and information they've stolen throughout the centuries gets safeguarded so it can be returned to the people."

"Won't the Draco be in the underground area of the Vatican, sir?" asked Miller. "I'm not looking forward to facing off with them."

"Yeah, they'll be there, but just as the Dark Forces have their malevolent space family working with them, our benevolent space family, which is far more powerful, will be assisting us to remove them. Nothing will stop us this time. Where we go—"

An important notification came through and interrupted Buzz: 4.10.20 SAYS RIG FOR RED COMPLETE. GREEN LIGHT INITIATED. PREPARE FOR RED ON RED.

Buzz put his hands on his hips. "Pack up your gear gentlemen, and let's remove these bodies. It's time for us to pay a visit to Europe and do our thing. The storm has officially begun. And you'll be happy to know that we're not coming back to do this Karver thing again."

Miller looked concerned. "But they'll use temporal technology to send Karver back again, sir? We've got to stop him."

Buzz shook his head. "It's come to our attention that Karver is the Dark Force's main fear program. The fear program, like their media program and money program, can't be stopped until we fix the root problem by taking them out at the source. Once we stop the top players, we'll be able to turn off all their programs as easily as turning on a light switch."

One of the marines responded, "Don't you mean turning *off* a light switch, sir?"

"Nope. We'll be turning on the light, and this time when all the cockroaches and rats try to scurry to their holes, they'll find that we've sealed them up, just like their fates are sealed in indictments. There's nowhere for them to hide anymore."

"Oorah!" Buzz's men shouted enthusiastically.

"Let's get going, boys. Europe, here we come. Don't start the party without us. This is what we've been training fo—"

The door buzzer jolted Dale awake and ripped him out of his dream. *I guess I dozed off. What a crazy dream.* He looked down at his suit and gave a sigh of relief. *Good, no blood, still immaculate. Time for some pizza. … I'm tired of this coronavirus bullshit.*

He got off the sofa and padded over to the door as he tried to recall what pizza toppings he'd ordered. He swung the door open.

"Ken Karver here … again."

Author's Note to Readers:

You've just read a treasure trove of information. Use your discernment to decide what's truth or fiction. Petitioning you to think for yourself is one of the major messages in this book. You shouldn't believe something just because I said it was true, nor should you believe something just because you've been socially conditioned to. You've been given free will on planet Earth, so use it and be empowered by it.

"A person doesn't try to obtain freedom if they think they're already free."
– Jasun Ether

About the Author:

Jasun Ether was born and raised in the Seattle area. He has spent over a decade traveling and living internationally, which has been more instrumental for his education and personal growth than his university education in psychology. He's taught English abroad for seven years. He currently lives wherever the wind has taken him in the world. His only interest as an author is to produce entertaining novels that are filled with truth, meaning, and empowering ideas, and which help humanity raise its consciousness, one reader at a time.

Website: www.jasunetherbooks.com

Made in the USA
Monee, IL
05 January 2021

56536568R00267